Nick McCarty has been a professional writer for more than 40 years. FOX is his first novel.

He has worked mostly for television on series like Bergerac, The Onedin Line, Z-Cars, Dangerfield, Spearhead and The Regiment. He wrote the Anne Boleyn segment of The Six Wives of Henry VIII with Dorothy Tutin in the title rôle and Keith Michell as Henry.

He is an award-winning writer for radio. His original plays and adaptations include A Confidential Agent, A Tale of Two Cities, Hard Times, Zorba the Greek, Far from the Madding Crowd and many others.

He is currently working on a musical for the theatre and plotting the next in the FOX series of novels.

By the same author

The Iliad Retold - with illustrations by Victor Ambrus (Kingfisher Books)
Troy, the story of its discovery by Heinrich Schliemann (Carlton Books)
Rome - a brief illustrated history (Carlton Books)
Alexander the Great (Carlton Books)

For Susan, with thanks

First published 2007

ISBN 978-0-9554771-0-2

Text prepared for digital printing by John Didlock
Cover art by Nick McCarty

FOX

Cromwell's Spy

by

Nick McCarty

KENELM
London
2007

Prelude

Fox lay in the shadow at the edge of the conifer forest and looked down the steep slope to the river and up the gentle slope to the trees beyond. In the trees behind him the birds began their morning chorus while beside him Shea breathed deeply as he slept.

The horses had been afraid when they'd come to the ruined farmhouse, tucked under a dark ridge, back along the valley. The horses smelt the carnage before Fox and Shea reached the outer wall. It'd been dusk then and they'd been moving carefully, keeping cover for four hours. Hard and delicate going as they edged into enemy territory.

Their horses baulked at the same moment and had to be forced into the farmyard. Shea slid off his horse and, crouching, ran for the cover offered by the wall of the simple farmhouse. Sword in hand, he edged towards the door. He looked back at the man who still sat his horse. Fox nodded, Shea kicked open the door and moving fast, went into the silent farmhouse.

The boom of big blue flies filled the room.

Shea kicked aside one of the three smashed chairs that lay close to a rough plank table. In the wide hearth, cold grey ashes were piled.

In the corner of the room was a bed half recessed into the wall and the curtains that would have been drawn at night were torn from the pole that had held them. On the wall opposite, the bed hung a crucifix.

Broken bottles, smashed plates and mugs lay scattered against the chimney breast where they'd been thrown. A man lay in the corner of the room with his body covering that of a naked woman. Shea didn't go closer. They were certainly dead and were already beginning to stink. A girl lying on the table was staring at the roof beams through sightless eyes, her long dark hair falling almost to the floor.

Fox stood in the doorway and blocked the light for a moment. The flies boomed again. He walked across and looked down at the girl. He noticed how her ears were pale and pink where the sun had never touched. Like Alison, his wife, when she was a girl . . . or Rebecca, his daughter.

This naked girl lying splayed on the table was no more than fifteen and the flies clamoured about her neck where some soldier more merciful than the others who had used her, had slaughtered her.

Fox looked for a moment more at the girl then he jerked his head at Shea. They had work to do but first they would hide their horses inside the nearest outhouse.

Fox stepped out and breathed deeply to get rid of the stink of death. For all his years in the army he'd never become used to what he'd just seen. He knew men would laugh at him if he said as much, but they'd never laugh to his face.

Fox walked to the trough by the wall and, looking down into the water, saw a dirty, sunburned, brown-eyed face staring up at him. His thick hair was shorn against lice and dirt and sweat streaked his face. He dipped his head into the cold water.

Shea came out of the farmhouse a moment after him and looked across at Fox, then turned back to the open doorway, crossed himself and pulled the warped wooden door and latched it against the booming noise of flies.

Shea walked to the water trough and washed his hands clean of the girl's blood. Fox shook his head at his old friend.

"I laid her out and covered her," Shea said. "'Twas the least I could do for her. Wasn't she the age of my sister when I left home?"

Fox shrugged, took the reins of his horse and led her away from the farmhouse to the long stable built onto the back of the farmhouse. Light filtered into the dim room from two holes left in the stone wall and showed a wooden stall to hold feed built into the white stones at the end of the stable. There had been a cow here until recently but she'd gone with the soldiers, no doubt.

There was still some feed in a rack. Fox took a handful of the oats he always had in the saddle scabbard for the gun he never carried with him. He hated the unreliable weapon and relied on sword and knife to do his work.

"If you need more you're finished as a scout. Your cover is gone, your use over. The knife is silent and the sword too if well used . . ."

The two men left their horses and began the walk up beyond the ridge into the dark forest as the sun began to fall behind the hills.

Fox and Shea had been a team since they began to work as scouts and intelligence gatherers for Colonel Fairfax and the army of Gustavus Adolphus. Both loved the freedom of being between armies and alone in country they hardly knew.

Not to be forced into lines on the dusty barrack square, learning advance and retreat and forming squares under the battering sun or the pouring rain. Not for them the red-faced screaming drill sergeants and the routine of army life. All shining, polishing, stamping and running in aimless formations; not for Sergeant Fox or Pat Shea.

They'd come to the edge of the forest in the night and slept under the shadow of a huge holly bush. They took watch turn and turn about and now, as the dawn light began to flicker across the valley, Fox was awake and watching. It seemed unnaturally quiet. He expected the night sounds of birds hunting, a dog fox crying for a vixen or a kill. There had been nothing. The night had been silent and now even the dawn chorus was still.

The spring dawn light spilled along the valley spreading shadows under the lip of the wood on the far side. Below Fox, to his right, a narrow, old stone bridge and by the river was the still smouldering ruin of a mill house. The marks of enemy cavalry could be seen in the muddy track that led from the bridge, curving away to the narrow pass between the hills.

Fox shivered, not because of the danger that they lived with all the time they were in the field but the chill of the morning. He pulled his old cavalry cloak closer as he stared down over the still river valley and knew he'd found the perfect place for an ambush.

A whole division of the army of Gustavus Adolphus could be lost here on this river valley. It was a perfect killing ground.

If Fox was right, and even at 22 he had the experience to be, this high valley would see slaughter if his colonel advanced, as he planned, onto the flank of the enemy. Fox lay and waited and watched for the signs that would confirm his suspicions.

Sergeant John Fox had been a mercenary for five years. Not for him the deadly existence in the Shropshire village where he'd been born.

Once his parents had died and his sister with them, nothing could keep him in that dull valley under the purple hills.

He had no wish to follow his father as a cooper or to farm his family's smallholding. Other, older men advised him to stay and make his life in the village. He'd laughed in their faces and he had few regrets. He had only one regret, in fact, and there had been nothing he could do to change that at the time.

He'd travelled through Europe with the Swedish mercenaries fighting wherever and whoever he was asked to fight.

He had many English comrades in his troop and even his colonel was a Yorkshire gentleman. Black Tom Fairfax had made his reputation by taking risks and refusing to count odds. Some said he was reckless. Others, that he never listened.

Fairfax had the unnerving habit of letting other people offer advice, letting others talk and then allowing the discussion to lapse into silence. He would then do what he had already decided.

Fox knew that much of Fairfax's apparent recklessness was based on sound knowledge. He knew because he provided so much of it. Fox was a natural point soldier, scout . . . a spy.

Born and raised in the country, he could read the land as easily as a gentleman might read a book, which made his knowledge invaluable.

Over the years he had 'carried his lance', Fox had discovered a natural skill in languages. He'd lived and fought in France, in Germany, the Netherlands and Italy and the languages had stayed with him. Importantly, he had come to accept and relish the fact that he was a loner which made him the perfect eyes for a reckless commander like Fairfax.

John Fox was known to Fairfax personally. He was heartily disliked by the young officers who surrounded Black Tom. They saw nothing worthy of notice in this quiet, almost taciturn young countryman.

Until two weeks ago Fox had been a sergeant. He had found a friend being battered senseless by two troopers from another regiment.

The cause of the argument was of no concern to him but he took on the fight, wounded one man near to death and left the other senseless.

The cause of the fight had been an insult passed about the fighting abilities of the English. No-one mentioned that when Fox was stripped to the ranks and sentenced with the man he'd rescued to the triangle and fifty lashes.

Fox had said nothing as they lashed his wrists to a cart wheel. He'd said nothing as the drum beat began that timed the lashes and said nothing as the farrier laid the rope's end across his naked back.

Lieutenant Harwood, one of the bright young officers who presided at the drum head court had, it seemed, enjoyed the flogging and the humiliation of the sergeant spread-eagled on the wheel.

When he was cut down, Fox turned to the young lieutenant and merely said, "One day . . . So mind your back in the dark, Lieutenant . . ."

Fox walked away from the pale-faced officer, through the ranks of watching men, to his bivouac where Shea, his friend, poured salt on his bloody wounds.

Across the valley the sunlight reached the edge of the pine trees. Fox nudged his sleeping companion. Pat Shea, a rat-faced Irishman from the slums of Dublin, was awake on the instant. Fox grinned at the young man he'd trust with his life.

Filthy, darting, quick and dangerous, the little Irishman had lived alone in Dublin since his parents died on their patch of Connemara land. He'd been ten, he believed, when it happened. The army had become his family and Fox an older brother. They were the perfect team in the field. Both of them able to work alone but tuned to the same pitch when they worked together.

Shea woke to see Fox with his finger to his lips.

The Irishman yawned, inched back into the shadows and took a canteen of water from the leather bag he carried.

Opening it, he offered it to Fox, who shook his head and went on looking for signs across the stream and into the tree line beyond.

Shea shrugged, took a small sip, closed the bottle and inched back alongside Fox. He looked slowly from left to right and back again and then leaned closer to whisper.

"It's a bad place."

Fox nodded once.

"There's marsh the other side of the stream . . . all down the valley. Soft ground. No use for cavalry at all."

"Tell me something I don't know, trooper, or shut up," Fox murmured. The Irishman's eyes glittered with anger for a moment and he then slid back into the shadows. Fox was always short-fused in the morning, Shea knew, but where Fox went, his shadow was always the ratty Irishman.

The muddy track led up into the forest and for much of its winding way it was buried deep in a ditch between dense hedges.

It reminded Fox of the countryside around his Shropshire home. The valleys, sloping down from hard, high ground, dipping into deep mysterious ditches which could so easily hide anything. An ox cart, a rider, a troop of horses, even field artillery pieces being moved into position. From that track, four well-placed guns could cover the line of advance of any army coming from the south along the valley.

Six men with two artillery pieces could hold the bridge near the mill house against conventional sword and pike and charging horsemen and cause untold damage. Protected, as they would be, by the marshy land on their left flank and by the stream on their right. The only speedy route for Fairfax to bring his cavalry would put them into the perfect killing field. He would lead his men into a massacre.

Fox understood Fairfax's need to move fast. The Colonel was determined to break the right flank of the enemy and to destroy an artillery squadron in the process. But to do it meant leaving the body of Gustavus Adolphus's army exposed on one flank.

It was a delicate manoeuvre even if done at a measured pace but to advance at speed, to commit so many men and horses to this gamble, needed the very best of information.

One error, an ambush well laid, a momentary delay, a build up of troops to get behind his advance and Fairfax and the army would be destroyed.

Once he had committed his force to the advance there could be no going back.

Fox grinned at Shea. He sniffed the morning air, looked out over the soft mist shredding and rising across the valley, the dew glinting still in the bright yellow light and thought again of Shropshire.

He'd been thinking more and more of his village and of the only reason he had had for staying there.

Alison was sixteen when he first left. He'd been refused permission by her sickly father to court her. She had not begged him to stay. She had not wept at their last hurried meeting near the crooked hawthorn copse on the track to the standing stones. She knew he must choose what he wanted to do with his life.

Fox believed it was her uncle, who wanted her for his son or for himself, who had made the decision not to allow the son of a barrel maker near Alison. She was an only child and with her would come the farm and the land her uncle coveted for his son. What did it matter if Alison loathed him? What did it matter that even his father had no wish for his son to join him in his trade out of Bristol into France? He was wise in that, as Fox admitted, for the son was a fool.

The land was good land, the farmhouse was substantial and no son of a village cooper was going to take the land out of the family. Alison was forbidden to see Fox again.

Alison promised Fox she would never have her cousin to her bed and would wait. When he left he didn't know that she was with child for she didn't tell him that either.

Fox could not believe she would wait when he angrily brushed off the dust of an England bedevilled by a king, Charles, who was hag-ridden by a beautiful French wife and a fool called Buckingham. Already in

England the signs were that change must come as his father had predicted when he and John Fox had talked in the evenings before the old man died. His father was a thinker and could even read tolerably well. Fox had never forgotten his father's stoic dying nor the simplicity of his burial which had left John Fox alone in the world, an angry boy.

For Fox, whose life since then had been the camps and the billets of common soldiers, all that hardly mattered now. But lately he'd been seeing in dreams the sweet and gentle face of the only person in the world who could tame his temper.

Fox smiled at the thought of Alison as a clatter of rooks into the lightening sky called him back to the work in hand.

Across the valley and to the right of the bridge, way back near the skyline, the ragged black rooks wheeled and turned like so many Calvinist preachers, Fox thought. He hardly gave the birds a second look as he began a careful search of the shadows along the edge of the woods. He found nothing at first and then, as he'd expected, a tiny sudden glint of sunshine on metal.

He saw another and another as the soldiers hidden in the undergrowth at the edge of the valley woke and, for a moment, were not as careful as they should've been. Men, in numbers, were concealed across the valley.

It meant two things to Fox. First, the enemy knew what Fairfax was planning which meant that they had an informer in the English camp. Second, that he had little time, for Fairfax needed to how many men lay in the hills, from which regiments and who was in command.

Fox knew that Fairfax would move as soon as his baggage train was in place and the men re-supplied with ammunition and food. Fox had forty eight hours at the most to discover what he needed to take back to his Colonel.

After the first flurry of movement Fox could see no more signs across the valley. There was still the absence of bird song which was explained by the presence of the men lying in the hills over the road through the valley.

Fox lay on his back and looked into the canopy of trees as he considered his next move. He needed to take a man from the enemy lines for questioning. He reached back and Shea put a canteen into his hand. He drank some of the brackish water and passed the canteen back to Shea.

An army can march, lie and fight on an empty stomach but cannot survive without water. Those men had been hidden more than two days, had had a long march over the head of the valley to get where they were and would need to drink.

They would wait probably another two hot days before Fairfax and his troopers began their fast advance along the river which they hoped was an easy route to the flank of the enemy army. Water was the key.

Fox began to quarter the valley looking for the place where the officers would let the men re-supply their water bottles.

To the right there was a great open space between the trees, the valley floor and the river. To the left, where the valley rose amongst a jumble of rocks and boulders, was a point at which the trees from both ridges of the valley joined and the river fell into dark shadows between the trees and rocks. If Fox had wanted water and wanted to remain hidden while getting it, it would be there he'd send the parties to replenish water bottles and flasks. It was there he'd expect to find an enemy soldier to question.

Patrick Shea crawled alongside Fox. As he came closer, Fox smelt him. That feral smell of a man unwashed for weeks, in the same clothes for weeks. Fox knew he, too, stank of the reek of sweat and bad teeth, powder and dirt.

Fox showed the Irishman what he had seen and Pat looked across the line of the woods and nodded. Then dipped his head and looked more keenly and then pointed to a large copse towards the head of the valley away from the watering place. It commanded the length of the route Fairfax would take.

Pat leaned close and whispered to Fox.

"Will you watch them trees, Foxy. See them bushes below. Somethin' wrong with them, that's sure."

Shea waited with the patience of the born poacher. He waited while Fox stared at the clump of bushes amongst the copse of trees until Fox saw what he had seen.

Fox cursed himself for not having noticed that the bushes at the foot of the trees in the copse had been cut and were already dying. They were being used as camouflage for sure but what lay behind them?

"Guns, Foxy. Artillery pieces looking down the line of march. Grape shot and cannon balls and such from them and gunfire from them up the hill and Black Tom Fairfax is butcher's meat."

Fox said nothing as he began to make out the outline of the forward artillery piece. The cut bushes concealed the wheels of its carriage and the long heavy barrel.

Fox put a hand on Pat's greasy sleeve and indicated they should move into the trees behind them.

"We'll move along the ridge, down to the stream where it meets the other trees and find us a soldier," Fox said.

Shea whispered, "Ask him a few questions? Go back to Fairfax and give him the news. You'll get your chevron back, Foxy."

"And what do we do with the soldier we talk to so pally?" Fox shrugged. It was all the same to him. This was war and he a soldier and a survivor. It was no was time to get soft about such things.

"That girl in the farmhouse, Pat, could've been your sister."

Pat looked at him then and shook his head to clear away what he remembered.

"God help the man we take then. For sure, I won't, except to send him to hell."

He grinned suddenly and showed the broken, black stumps of his teeth.

They took bread from their leather satchel and ate quickly. Then checked their short cavalry swords. Pat took a long bladed throwing knife from the scabbard across his back and felt the keenness of the edge.

A jay screamed its barking call across the valley while high in the steel sky a buzzard mewed, wheeled and turned easily in the first warm air of the morning. He might have carrion enough soon.

The two men eased their way up through the trees making no sound beyond the occasional scuff of leaf mould or the tug of a briar on a serge jacket.

They were in their element as they moved in easy stages, one moving, the other still, passing and re-passing each other, checking and constantly alert.

Not for the first time Fox wondered at the skills of his partner. Here was a town-bred man with the innate skills of a hunter. It was easy for Fox to blend with the land, to read the signs, to understand what they told him, as he'd been born to it. Pat often showed an almost uncanny foreknowledge of what they would find.

For two years and more these two had worked as scouts for Black Tom Fairfax and he trusted them. The Yorkshire gentleman was proud as any peacock that strutted the lawns in his Yorkshire home. Fairfax knew that what Fox and his partner reported was never based on guesses.

Fairfax was no respecter of breeding or blood, his only judgement of a man was by what he did. The covey of young, well-placed officers who formed his small staff could see no merit in the stinking, dirty men who'd come in after days in the no-man's land between armies with tales to tell.

But Fairfax listened and from time to time, acted on what Fox or Pat Shea brought in. Fox liked the man and even trusted him - as much as he trusted any man.

The sun rose higher. The day was set fair to become one of those unseasonably hot days. The soldiers lying in hiding along the edges of the forest would suffer in the heat. Dressed in heavy uniforms, belted and strapped about, leather stocks to force up their chins, boots wrapped round with cloth and trousers of heavy canvas, they would sweat like Swabian pigs.

They'd be plagued by flies and mosquitoes from the marsh beyond the stream. As the sun began to warm up, its heat would grow intolerable and inevitably they'd need fresh water in their canteens.

Their officers knew that Fairfax planned to march this way to surprise the flank of their army. The enemy officers knew he'd fall into their trap because he was ambitious and hot-headed. They knew because they had been told. Someone was betraying the army Fox marched with.

And while Fox worked his way through the trees, the problem of which officer it might be nagged at him. The officers knew the colonel's plans and Fox and Shea knew because they had to be told what to look for. But mostly men were kept ignorant and merely obeyed orders.

By the middle of the afternoon Fox and Shea were amongst the rocks at the head of the valley. They could hear the tantalising sound of the water as it cascaded over pale grey rocks. It was a strong force, fed with the run off from the mountain snows further to the east.

Fox lay in the shadow under a vast boulder perched against a pine. Pat, he knew, was waiting for him to move. He lay very still and felt, for a moment, a terrible chill.

"Fancy," he muttered and moved into the jumble and clutter of rocks from the edge of which he would have an uninterrupted view down onto the stretch of river from which he was sure the enemy was taking water for their ambush party.

He wondered what Pat was doing. He'd usually call, a chattering jay, an owl, a dog fox. Two calls meant go on. One meant danger. Maybe he hadn't heard it over the roar of the water as it fell swirling down the rocks and debouched onto a small beach of pebbles where men could easily fill canteens.

Even as Fox watched, a small party of men carrying many canteens stepped out of the trees and began to fill them from the pale green waters. From his vantage point he kept a tally of the number of canteens being filled and carried away.

The sun moved through the afternoon and the ground became even hotter. The last of the watering parties left as silently as it had come.

Over a thousand canteens of water, over a thousand men lay hidden along the valley waiting for Fairfax to arrive. Fox lay and closed his eyes for a moment and saw the regiment in line of march.

Outriders to the left and right and well forward would be allowed to pass along the track. The first and second companies of soldiers would pass below the waiting enemy, hidden above them.

The last company moved into place behind the colour party with the battle standards carried by the halbardier sergeants, guarded by axemen. As they glittered and swayed along the floor of the valley, they'd pass the narrow bridge in good order. Unconcerned, unknowing.

As soon as that colour party passed the bridge, the controlled, concentrated gunfire from the forest would decimate the lines of men.

On the right flank, from the large stand of trees the field, pieces would fire on maximum depression and sweep men and horses aside in a charnel house of blood and bone and screaming horror.

Fox opened his eyes as he heard the single yelp of a dog fox, cut short, from his right where Pat had been covering his back.

High over him a buzzard swung lazily against the bright sky, banked, turned and swept the ground. Its cold shadow speeding over rock and over the killing field beyond.

Fox knew Pat was already dead . . . The single yelp cut short said it. A soldier's desire to revenge a dying comrade swept over him. He moved now, soft and easy across the rock shelf and into the narrow declivity he'd climbed an hour, two hours before.

He had to reach the top of the climb before anyone discovered him.

Pat would have said nothing. They might believe Pat was alone and go back to report what they had found unless they were utterly cocksure. Then they might wait and see.

Fox eased himself over the rocks and inched into the shadow of the first of the pines then crawled under an overhanging rock shelf, his short sword in his hand to stop it clattering on the rock.

He turned into the natural amphitheatre where he'd left his friend and found himself staring into Pat Shea's eyes.

Pat was propped against the roots of a fallen pine with his short sword holding him in place through his upper chest. Fox could only hear the roar of the water and the blood in his head. Instinct took him as he moved very fast to the right and turned with his back to the cold rock.

Standing, grinning, opposite him was a giant of a man, a sergeant of the Austrian army. He held his sabre out and the blade was bloody. The sergeant made a feint to the right, then to the left and lunged.

Fox parried the thrust of the longer sword with his short one and shifted his weight to take himself further to the left and closer to Pat who had slumped forward onto the short blade that held him pinned amongst the tree roots.

Fox had a moment to see his comrade's eyes dim entirely and then he turned and slashed at the sabre arm of the dragoon as he came in fast for the kill.

The huge Austrian stepped onto the rock, wet with the blood that had stopped pulsing from Pat's throat. He hacked at Fox with a ferocity that snatched the cavalry sword from Fox's hand.

The dragoon, panting, stood back for a moment to savour what he would do to the man he had at his mercy.

Fox felt the earth from the toppled tree under his fingers and gouged a handful from the roots. As the Dragoon moved he threw the earth and pebbles and blinded the soldier for a moment. Long enough for Fox to reach over Pat's shoulder and to take the long bladed dagger from the scabbard on the dead man's back.

The dragoon had already recovered and moved fast across the rock, blade lifted for an easy kill. His leather boots slipped across the bloody rock and his own impetus dropped him at Fox's feet and he screamed as he fell.

Fox stamped on the man's hand. The sword fell from the broken fingers and the dragoon's leg, trapped between two boulders, was clearly broken. Fox kicked the leg and the man screamed again. Then Fox knelt close to the man's agonised face. The dragoon waited, staring, afraid now.

Fox took the man's broken hand and softly ran the blade of Pat's skinning knife across the wrist. A line of blood sprang from the razor sharp cut. Fox knew he had very little time before the rest of the enemy forward patrol came to their comrade's scream.

"I want to know how many, I want to know who is in command, I want to know which regiments apart from yours, and I want to know how long they have known. Who betrayed us? And I have no time to waste," he whispered in German.

He laid the blade of the knife close to the groin of the dragoon and waited. The huge man tried to move away from the blade but was trapped by the foot twisted between the rocks. He began to sweat in fear and turned his head from side to side.

Fox jerked the blade through the canvas trousers and cut into the man's thigh . . . Then eased the blade closer to the sergeant's balls.

High over the boulders at the head of the stream, a buzzard began to circle. It was joined by another and then another. They mewed like cats.

Fox moved with the steady lope of a man used to wilderness. This was his natural habitat which usually he would have delighted in. But now he carried the death of a comrade and he knew from the chill he'd felt at the start of the morning that he had little time.

"Never ignore the small signs, never abandon instinct . . . know yourself and know that there are skills men have lost, senses men have forgotten. But if you listen, if you will hear, sometimes a small sign will come. Heed it and you may survive another hour, another day . . ."

His mother knew things. She was feared in the village and yet heeded when it came to medicine or births or easy dying.

Fox moved very fast over the ridge and down into the next valley; down through the forest towards the sun and Fairfax's regiment. He had with him the regimental badge of the man he'd killed and papers he carried . . and knowledge he'd taken from the man before he died.

As he ran, the knowledge that they had been betrayed thudded through his head . . . no name, no rank, nothing more than the dragoon admitting that the enemy knew Black Tom Fairfax's plans for an advance.

Fox came cautiously towards the ruin of the farmhouse where they'd concealed their two horses. Instinct saved him.

He stopped in the lee of a stone wall and watched the ruins. He inched Pat's knife from the scabbard he'd taken from his old comrade and waited.

A curlew called across the meadow. Nothing moved.

But something had changed. Something ticked in the corner of his mind.

He reached back, trying to picture the ruins as they were when he and Pat had left the horses. Two jays clattered across what had been the farmyard and swooped, in a flash of blue and black, into the trees on the far side of the farm.

Fox, with all the patience of a man used to relying on it, checked and checked again. To the right and behind the house, the byre inside which the horses waited. Outside the door a hay rake lay broken against the wall as it had been when they left.

Closer to the house, the head of a well, which contained he knew, a dead dog and a child's body. Past that to the small and mean rick of straw hoarded as feed against the next harvest . . . A clamp of moulding potatoes kicked open by Pat, who'd taken some for later.

Pat, what had Pat said . . . what had Pat done?

Fox lay still in the ditch and watched the farm buildings through a broken section of tumbled stones. It was a poor place to try to scrape a living - a place like that he knew only too well in the border lands near Wenlock Edge and the Long Mynd. The land of peat and stone, curlews and bitterns, and grinding poverty.

Fox wiped his smeared and filthy face and looked at the farm house again.

The shutters hung, smashed by whoever had come before. The roof was half burned off as if they'd wanted to hide the evidence of what they had done.

A horsefly from the muddy yard stabbed his hand like a red hot needle and Fox made no move, no sound. He knew if only he could remember what Pat had done. Instinct told him. If only he could remember before he moved to take the horses.

Pat had come out of the room in which the slaughtered family lay. He'd looked round at Fox.

Fox lay in the shadow of the wall and tried to remember. Pat was at the open door gasping for breath. The flies were back again, thunderously buzzing about their work. Pat had turned to the open door, waited a moment, crossed himself, then carefully closed the door and latched it. He had latched it.

Fox crawled along the ditch below the wall and away from the ruins towards a deeply etched streambed. He dropped down into the water and began to move fast as the sun beat even more strongly. He had only a few hours to stop Fairfax marching into a terrible ambush.

Instinct, his mother had said. Let instinct guide you . . .

He'd seen Pat take a deep breath of fresh air, seen him cross himself and seen him close and latch the door into the inner room. He remembered the booming of the flies which began as soon as the living man had gone.

But the flies were silent now and, more important, the door was unlatched.

Open. Someone was there. Waiting.

Fox could not go to earth for he had a message to deliver. He could not risk taking the horses. He'd have to run for all their lives.

Above, still circling the other valley, the buzzards, mewing, mewing. Even at that height, they could smell blood. They began that cautious swirling circle, lower and lower . . . and suddenly down . . .

And they could see, in another valley, tiny from such a height, a man running.

1

Two men met in the room over a watchmaker's shop near the Thames. Rain ran down the small windowpanes and a grey sky made the room darker than would have been usual in the afternoon. The younger of the men sat at a wide table that served as a desk and behind him was a bulky cabinet of dark oak carved with fantastical motifs. His name was John Thurloe and he was beginning to plot treason from this small room.

The older man was tall and had the air of one who disliked being cooped up inside even on days as wet as this one. His boots were muddy and his leather jerkin had seen much use. The knife in his belt was ornamented and gilded and certainly the work of an Arabian craftsman. He fingered the handle of the knife absently as a man might finger prayer beads. Fairfax was a soldier and one-time mercenary and he was bored with life in the Yorkshire countryside. His wife's estates were not enough to satisfy a man like Black Tom Fairfax and the younger man knew it.

He stood looking out of the window and only turned back into the room when the man behind the desk spoke.

"Dammit, I need reliable men."

Thurloe looked up from the desk at the tall figure opposite him. Fairfax smiled as the young man pushed his long black hair away from his pale face. Fairfax turned away from the desk and looked out of the window again, across the rooftops beyond. He was often impatient of younger, less efficient men.

Thurloe was drumming with a barely concealed energy on the sand box beside his hand.

It was this energy in the young man that made him so attractive to women. That and the slanting eyebrows and the dark eyes beneath them. John Thurloe sighed, sat back from the table, and ran a tired hand over his face in a gesture of resignation.

"I'm sorry," he said. "I anger too easily. Anxious more than angry."

His eyes settled on the pale face watching him. They stilled and Fairfax was chilled as he saw the ruthlessness mirrored in those pale eyes. Thurloe might be something of a popinjay in appearance but he was not a man to take lightly.

The square-fronted collar over his dark jacket, the puffed sleeves and severe buttons to the neck hinted, by their very simplicity, at a dandy underneath. Born into the church, an Essex man from Abbots Roding, a lawyer and a man in a hurry, John Thurloe did not conceal his impatience to get on. Women might be attracted to him but he had little time for them. Cool, legalistic and with a vision, he had no time for anything except to make his vision a reality.

Fairfax remembered the first time they'd talked of it. It'd been near Hampton Court. Thurloe had suggested that a walk away from eager ears and prying eyes might be a good idea. They'd walked beside the Thames, the young lawyer and the older soldier.

Thurloe was twenty-two and already a coming man at court. He had friends and connections who had already helped him to a position. But it would never satisfy this thrusting young man. Fairfax had seen his like on battlefields across Europe. Young men with dangerous ambitions became dangerous friends.

"What is the one thing on the battlefield you value above all else?" Thurloe had asked the soldier.

They walked on past the Palace and turned into the deer park where no-one was to be seen. The young man spoke quietly and seemed almost detached. Fairfax was at once repelled and attracted by him as he knew others were. He wondered if this boy had already pulled others into his world by his naked enthusiasm.

"Well sir . . . what do you value most?" he insisted. He stopped as he spoke and pulled Fairfax's arm so he too stopped and faced him. Fairfax stiffened as the young man realised his error and took his hand from the older man's arm.

"I'm sorry Colonel. I don't wish to be over-familiar but I need to know the answer."

2

"You already know the answer Mr Thurloe, I suspect, but I will tell you anyway. Intelligence, Mr Thurloe, good intelligence of the other side. With good intelligence you may win anything."

A herd of roe deer stood under the trees and watched them as they walked by.

Thurloe stopped again and nodded and then asked quietly, "And intelligence of your own side? Isn't that important too?"

Fairfax stood by an old oak and the young man stood staring up at him eagerly waiting for the Colonel's reply.

"That information is often harder to find than how the land lies with one's enemy. We need a means to tap that information."

"Exactly, Colonel Fairfax. A system for gathering intelligence. That is my vision. Spread throughout the country, throughout Europe . . . wherever we have interests we need intelligence, for we will have enemies also. My vision is to create a web to catch intelligence from everywhere, even about those we believe to be our friends."

His face broke into a smile that would flutter hearts. Then, later, walking along the Thames towards Kingston, Thurloe talked. How he talked! And Fairfax learned that he was the first to hear this young man's dream.

Swans glided on the water and martins dipped in flight to tip the water with their beaks as he talked. A barge moved slowly up the river towards the heart of London as the two men walked and talked together. It was the beginning of a friendship; the start of real trust between them.

Sitting in this panelled room at the top of a London house on Philpot Lane the young man planned, cajoled, plotted, persuaded and dabbled in the affairs of state. Yet few men knew him for what he was or what he might be. None, save those Thurloe admitted to his secret, knew the house. On the street below was clock maker's shop and behind it, through a door only known to a few, a flight of narrow stairs which emerged on a small landing lit by a skylight. The main door led into the room where Thurloe spun his web . . .

He worked hardly a stone's throw from the stink and life of Billingsgate into which came fish and oranges and onions, wheat and rye, food for the service of the City. John Thurloe often came across the river, to the Watergate, which served as a harbour.

From time to time, he'd walk across the twenty arches of squared stone that made up London Bridge. Beneath his feet, vaults and cellars and, to each side, houses. The bridge was a busy continuation of the street.

Direct, hard and uncompromising, Black Tom had a Yorkshireman's stubborn determination to get what he wanted. Tempered only by the rigorous faith of his wife, he too had begun to dabble in those affairs of state that so occupied John Thurloe.

"Tom," the young man said quietly, "I need trustworthy men as we both need trustworthy men. Men of courage, men able to act alone, men willing to act alone . . . men . . ."

"I know what we need, John."

Thurloe sighed as he turned back to the endless papers.

"From what I've already garnered from papers, reports, hints, rumours, I know we need a better system, Tom. A means to gather more and yet more. Know your enemy because what you said was true, intelligence means you win. And if we lose, Tom, we lose our heads perhaps. The King must be curbed and that damn fool Buckingham must be gelded."

Tom Fairfax looked anxiously at the door of the small room. To speak of the King and his favourite like this was treason indeed.

"It's all right Tom," the young man said. "No-one will hear us."

Tom walked to the window and looked across the narrow street. The sky was steel grey and the rain went on like Noah's flood. Fairfax looked down Roode Lane past the Church of St Margaret Pattens to St Mary-at-Hill church. He looked on through the roofs around the wharves and jetties clustered on the edge of the water and giving harbour to the small wherries, barges, small trading boats and fishermen who sold in Billingsgate.

Beyond the rooftops below him and the myriad slopes of tile and timber clad houses, the towers of churches sharp against the grey sky, he could see the glint of the river. Out of his sight it curved away to his left under the bridge, towards the sea and, to the right, to the reaches beyond Richmond and on into the countryside away from London to Oxford, the King's town.

Black Tom remembered the bright skies over the bridge into Florence. It too was built up on either side with shops. He remembered the arcades and red-bricked buildings, the squares and yards filled with flowers and music and beautiful whores.

He remembered also the sharp green countryside of Austria and of the German plains. He heard in his mind the rattle of horses and the roar of men in battle. For a moment he forgot the miserable affairs of state he and this twenty two year old man were engaged in and even forgot that what they talked might be treason.

In the narrow street below, men hurried, dodging and jumping the puddles and the middens outside each house. A young woman hurried past, a shawl over her head. He watched her as she turned into a dark

4

alleyway and wondered for a moment how such a woman lived in such a squalid, dank place. A figure moved in a doorway up the hill.

Two dogs fought over some offal they'd found in the street. Black Tom shuddered and turned back into the room.

"There's a woman standing in a doorway half hidden by the overhang of the house opposite. She's been there since I came into the watchmaker's shop."

Thurloe nodded. "She has a green shawl and red hair. I know," he said. "She's been there two days now. Screwing up her courage to come to see me, I think."

"And you say no-one knows you have a place here?"

"No-one who'd object to what we're doing knows."

"The girl . . ?"

"Will make her mind up no doubt. I was told about her by a connection. She'll make up her mind one way or another and the rain may bring her to the point sooner rather than later. I am told the young lady is willing but possibly dangerous. We will see. I'll wait."

Tom Fairfax stared at the young man and marvelled at him. He was no longer in a hurry. Fairfax wondered what intelligence he had about him in a file or locked in the massive cupboard behind him. He already knew more than enough about so many people.

"You know my boy, sometimes you frighten me," he said.

"No sir, not you." He laughed, but the eyes didn't smile. "No sir! There's no need. I know where your sympathies lie, sir."

"You know too much then. What I think might be said to be treason. I admit it. But I think it only. I write nothing and say less to the world."

John Thurloe nodded and plucked a paper from a pile on the desk

"Tom Fairfax," he read "One time Colonel in the armies of Gustavus Adolphus, good soldier, admired by his men, disliked by many of his officers for the reckless way he seemed to have. Yet he won skirmish after skirmish, battle after battle."

"How? Why? Don't tell me the answer. I know the answer. Intelligence. Married to a good woman, Alice . . . estates in Yorkshire to farm. He loves to ride, hunt, to live the life of a country squire? I choose to think that's not enough for Black Tom Fairfax."

He put aside the paper and looked at Fairfax who was irritated at the supreme confidence of the young man.

"Maybe I'll be content with it," he said.

Thurloe looked slyly at the older man.

"Why then come to London and mire yourself in politics?" He laughed and jumped to his feet; excited to be able to prove the older man wrong.

5

"You, who are a man of action, turn into a clerk. Which is why you're here with a man who hates action and lives to be a clerk. Yes?"

Tom Fairfax said nothing for a moment and saw the rolling moors and the heather on the hills, the wide expanses of his land. His children and his dear wife.

He had risked it all, to come and mire himself, as the young man said. Why indeed?

"You were ever at the front when battle began. It's in the records. You drank little, kept your own counsel and never moved without consideration. Like me. And now we move, my friend, towards treason. Oh yes, admitted. I go further and men already speak of it secretly. I know. I know what they say. It's all here, writ down."

The young man pointed at the papers on the desk.

"The King and his party go too far and demand too much. So who will stand against him and his law?"

The voice was quiet, cold, calm. Like the man.

The soldier shrugged and the younger man went on.

"There's something rotten in the House of Stuart. His name is Buckingham."

"Treason, my friend," said Fairfax, "Those words alone could hang you, quarter you, disembowel you and spike your head on Tower Bridge."

The rain roared on the roof tiles and splashed over the edge of the roof into the street below.

The girl was still there. She looked up at the window and for a moment Fairfax, looking down, saw the pale face and the hint of auburn hair under the shawl. Then she turned and retreated into the stinking alleyway.

"Knowledge is power, and power could mean safety. I don't mean simple knowledge, I mean deep, intimate knowledge."

The young man began to pace the room as he spoke in short sharp bursts. He had concealed his energy and now allowed it to show as he spoke.

"I mean real knowledge. Useful background, family ties, marriages, debts, wealth, health, connections, here and abroad. Habits, vices, friends, secrets. I mean such things. I mean levers to turn a man or a woman to our use."

"You have such knowledge of me?"

The sardonic smile on the mouth of this pale-faced man chilled the soldier again. Here was a ruthless man. Hidden already in the wainscoting of power, waiting for the moment to offer what he garnered to the right man.

Sitting in this room like a spider in a corner, pulling in secrets.

6

Directly below them in the watchmaker's shop one Samuel Phelps plied his innocent trade. Behind, and up the stairs, in this office was a man whose mind was thick with secrets

. . .

"You won your battles, Colonel, because you refused to move until you knew all there was to know about your enemy. Who, where, how many, who they trusted, who you could turn to. Intelligence in the field is worth a regiment of men. Intelligence in parliament will be worth a country, a kingdom, even."

Fairfax sat now at the table. He knew he'd been right to come to be infected by this terrible ruthlessness, this determination and this quiet man, deadly in his intentions.

"I need a special man. Someone to trust, someone who can act alone, someone who can travel abroad and vanish into the very stones. I need that man. A man who, if necessary will kill. I need him urgently."

He paused, and then went on softly.

"There is a man in place in France who claims to be a willing agent for me and yet . . . I am not sure he can be trusted. I need to know. I've lost one man already so it's a dangerous hunt to send a man on. You know such a man?"

Fairfax looked into the pale face, the sardonic mouth, the large nose and the thin moustache beneath it. The thick, almost heavy, lower lip . . . the hair receding slightly that presaged early baldness and the ice cold eyes . . .

"I have the man," he said quietly, "Oh yes! I have the very man."

Outside, in the rain sodden street, the girl in the green shawl stood in the shadows and watched and waited . . .

2

John Fox was angry. He tried hard to disguise it from Alison. He'd promised her he would try to control his anger as a good Christian should, but he'd not learned yet how to do it. He took no insults from any man and while Alison and her sectarian Christians urged him to turn his cheek at any provocation, he still boiled with rage inside and from time to time it erupted.

Alison had not cured him of that since he'd come home from the wars, nor had the elders of the chapel where each Sunday he tried to make his peace with a God he found hard to believe in.

Since he came back to the village and married the mother of his daughter, he'd been a target for the young men. For six years they sought to make a reputation by provoking a fight with this wild man from the wars. Fox had a reputation for fighting, earned not only in the wars but also in the surrounding countryside when he was a boy.

None of these youngsters had ever made him lose control, yet. But Alison knew it was only a matter of time and if he did lose it with one of these village men, she was afraid of what would happen.

Alison's Uncle Michael had only to open his mouth and John felt the bile rise. He had to impose on himself the rigid control he had practised for all the years of his dealings with the elders in the chapel.

If Alison saw the anger rising in him she'd take his hand and hold it to her cheek. She'd bend to kiss it, hold him still, gentle him as she'd gentle an angry dog. But, however much she gentled him, his anger still burned as it burned today.

He strode away from the warehouse near the mill where he'd met Michael briefly. Alison's uncle was a fool but he was a rich fool and was the only man who could give a soldier work. As usual Fox came away from the meeting blazing with rage at the fat, self-satisfied man.

Fox walked up through the straggle of houses that limped down the side of the valley. Hurried past the small inn and the church and the leet hall that served as the meeting place for village business, on past the tiny whitewashed Meeting House on the edge of the village.

He marched on up the donkey track made by the silver miners in ancient times high up on the Tops and the windswept moorland. He hurried past the hawthorn hedges and the stone walls that tippled over into ancient fields, past sheep and the first insistent lambs. The sheep hurried into the shelter of the stone walls and hawthorn hedges as a mewing sounded high overhead.

In the arch of the sky soared a buzzard. Its wings swept upwards and forwards as it soared on the first warm air off the spring land. Fox stopped and watched as the bird slipped sideways and then soared higher in a spiralling circle as it looked for prey.

A lamb with a crooked leg was slower than the rest and as it tried to make the safety of the hedge the mewing bird was suddenly silent as it dropped like a stone onto the struggling lamb.

Fox moved on and left the bird to beat the life from the lamb with its cruel beak. Fox pushed himself to a sweat as the track ran into boulders and rocks. The hedges lay below him now and the land grew steeper.

He stepped over the rim of the high hill and looked across the vast purple expanse of the Tops towards the ridged outcrop known as the Stiperstones. Dark rocks rose from the heather and the poor soil that supported only sheep and conies, pheasants and grouse . . .

A clatter of wings startled him. Two grouse shot across his path, low, fast and afraid of this lone intruder. Far away, across the dark heathers, lay the furthest edge of the Tops and Wales beyond.

Fox pushed on to the Stiperstones and climbed the vast, sharp-edged outcrop. He sat on the edge of the formation known as the Devil's Armchair and watched the thin clouds racing across the pale sky. Alone in wild country. God, how he missed being alone.

But he'd made a promise to Alison who'd waited for him carrying Rebecca his daughter and born her and her own shame until he came home to them. He alone knew how that had pained her and her dying father who'd hated him.

Hated Fox so much he'd not left him a share in the family farm or the land he'd owned. All of it left to his daughter who he had loved and grieved for.

Fox lay back and closed his eyes and went over the conversation he had earlier with her uncle down at his mill house by the stream. He tried to fathom the reason for her uncle sending him to France so early in the year.

"Why should I go to Bordeaux now?" he'd asked her uncle, and the fat man sneered at him.

"Because I need you to and because you agreed when you came to work for me you'd learn the trade. You don't know it all yet by a long chalk"

Outside the mill house where the two men faced each other, Fox could hear the water pouring smoothly through the run-off beside the wheel in a steady powerful glassy flow. Soon he knew the miller would engage the wheel and the water would begin to turn it and through the system of belts and pulleys the stone grinding wheels would also begin to turn and make the fat wheezing man beside him more money. For he owned the mill as he owned the yard. Indeed as he owned much of the village and a tithe of the wool from every sheep on the Tops and in the fields below. He even took a tenth of the barrels Fox's father made.

Michael had a fine home and warehouses in Bridgnorth which held bundles of fleeces and the barrels of wine brought from Bordeaux up the river from Bristol. Michael was rich and, like most rich men, begrudged anyone a penny piece that was not tithed to him too. Some said he'd driven his wife to an early death. In fact she had died giving birth to Saul who was as mean as his father.

John Fox hated being beholden to Alison's uncle.

"You're no farmer," the older man had said when Fox came back from the wars and married Alison. "I've no time for you but you made her an honest woman so that's something to be glad about. At least the family can hold up its head again. Apart from her saft notions she's a good enough girl. But you'll never settle to a farm."

Alison had wanted him to take over the land. To sow and harrow, to store and scarify, to harvest and rejoice in the immutable seasons that are farming. Fox had tried for a year and nearly suffocated from it. Then her uncle came and offered him a place.

"You have languages, you're used to travel. You can work for me and learn something of the trade. Maybe you'll learn as much as me one day." Fox took the work.

10

Michael knew little except how to use those about him who'd serve him well. The miller owed him money until he foreclosed on the mill itself. He'd let the man stay out of charity and because he was the best miller for miles about and needed work.

The fleeces he bought at keen prices in the market because men knew if they sold to him at least they'd be paid. What he made from them was his risk and his business . . .

Michael owned a share in three Severn barges that plied from Bridgnorth south towards Bristol and the port. He knew nothing about barges or the river but enough about money and cargoes to ruin the previous owner and to keep on his best barge master.

Michael was feared about the valleys. Wherever men traded in wine or wool his name was a synonym for greed and cold blooded dealing. And Fox, whose French was fluent, was his representative in the vineyards of the Loire and Bordeaux.

Three times a year Fox would leave the valleys for a month or more and travel to taste, buy and arrange to ship the flinty wines of the lower Loire and the thin red wine from Bordeaux and occasionally the fuller red from Gascony.

Alison hated the times he was away but it was the price she paid for marrying a restless man. She could not keep him on a short curb all the time.

This afternoon he'd left the mill house fuming as Michael had laughed in his face. That cruel cunning face screwed up with a cheerless mirth.

"I have letters for Marcel in Langon and another for Pierre in Bordeaux."

He went on, "I'm unhappy with the price of the wine and more unhappy with the cost of the freighting from the port. You will take the letters and bring their replies . . ."

"I'm not a damned messenger boy . . ."

"What else d'you think you are, John Fox?" the fat man had asked. Behind him, Saul, his son smirked, thinking himself unseen.

"Send him. Your grinning son. Send him," said Fox, and headed for the door and the sunlight. "It's what he's fit for."

"I'm sending you, Fox," said the older man quietly. "I should tell you I've bought up your debt to the seed merchant in Shrewsbury and to the thatcher in the village. I've your promissory note to the timber yard in Bridgnorth. If I foreclose . . . you understand? My dear niece is the only thing keeps you from penury."

He even produced the papers for Fox to see. Everyone worked on promises and money rarely changed hands in the country so that a man like Michael who had it and to spare could pressure anyone he cared to.

"You will go to France and take the letters and you'll bring back replies. That's what you do. Orders, you see."

John had walked out then, past the grinning fool of a son who he knew had lusted for Alison as his father had . . . Saul was a young man quite willing to take what he wanted, knowing his father would threaten or bluster or buy him out of any troublesome consequences.

A lark rose on a pillar of song higher and higher into the sky and another and another. Fox allowed his temper to cool.

Alison would be sorry to see him go away for another six weeks. It was a hard time on the land and though he was no farmer, he was a pair of hands and useful to her.

She'd farmed for her father when he first fell sick and since then had run the land and the beasts with help only from two village men and a boy and occasionally from her husband.

The farm was on good land and the house itself was the envy of many and was lusted after by Uncle Michael.

"I know I shouldn't be so prideful, John, but every time I walk out into the yard, every time I see the horses ploughing the lower fields, or the sheep at lambing or the bees in their skeps . . . I feel so proud not to have let it go to another man."

"You've a right to be proud," he'd say as he held her to him in their ancient bed. "It's a stiff backed religion that won't let you be so."

And she'd kiss him and smooth his long hair from his face and kiss him again more urgently. Even here, in the Devil's Armchair he felt that surge of desire, of need, of warmth, as he thought of her.

How could he tell her that Michael had their debts to hold over them like a sword?

Fox got up from the cold stone and walked back down into the valley. Past Mother Baugh's hovel, built into an abandoned Roman silver drift mine. The old, miserable hag who was feared and hated by the villagers, was nowhere to be seen. Alison would come to see her from time to time and bring her food. Virgins would come, it was rumoured, and so remain virgins.

Mother Baugh lived with the shades of Roman legions and ancient miners who had dug into the hills here. She lived alone without fear and some whispered "Witch!" if the ragged old hag crossed their path and they'd ward her off with the sign against the evil eye. She'd laugh at their fears.

12

A few chickens pecked at the earth and a cat lay in the spring sunshine on a stone near the doorway. It didn't move as Fox's shadow passed over it.

Fox walked on down to the lane where he gathered some pimpernel and wild orchids from a ditch, then cut across two fields and under the wooden arch into the yard of the farmhouse.

The long stone barn on the right of the yard and the slated roof told something of the wealth of the farm called Windover.

There were many people housed worse than the plough horses in Windover. Tucked as it was between two folds of the hills, the farmhouse itself was stone, brick and timber built.

Begun a hundred and fifty years before and continually added to, it had housed Alison's ancestors. An imposing door had been added with a date, 1552, but that was just the date of the door and the two steps up into the house.

Fox stopped at the corner of the barn and watched as Alison came out to scatter corn for the hens that scuttered across the yard to gather round her feet.

Her long hair was pushed demurely up into a white cap, her quiet clothes without a hint of frippery or ribbon as was right and proper for a Christian. She turned Fox's heart over every time he saw her.

"We have no need of folderols John," she'd say when he offered to bring back lace from Brittany. "We are as God made us."

And he thanked God for that mercy at least. That she was as she was.

Rebecca called from a window high under the eaves.

"Father . . . father . . ! Mother . . . see. He's back."

The two women he loved most in the world smiled to see him. Alison walked to him after putting aside the basket she had emptied for the hens. She took his hand and smiled up at him. He bent to kiss her.

Alison and Rebecca were about to be disappointed and he hated to do that to them. He handed the flowers to Alison and she took them and bent her face to them in a movement that nudged his heart.

The curving line of her brown neck and the swell of her breasts showed under the grey smock. She turned her face up to him then and looked so gravely at him. She knew.

"You're going away, John?" she asked quietly.

He nodded and put his arm round her. They walked into the house as Rebecca ran down the stairs and hugged him. Fifteen and beautiful, she looked at their serious faces and shook her head.

"It's not fair. I hate Uncle Michael."

Rebecca took the flowers from her mother and stamped into the back of the house where she began to arrange them in an earthenware jug.

Alison walked after her daughter and Fox stood in the doorway of the cool kitchen. A fire glowed in the huge hearth, an ancient hunting dog lay across the stone flags before it. The evening sun sparkled on the uneven glass in the window.

Alison came back and sat quietly at the head of the table in the ancient armchair John's grandfather had made. She looked up at him and smiled a little. "She'll calm down soon," she said.

"I'm sorry," he said, "I argued with him. I'm sorry Alison. But he makes me angry. I'm not a man to take orders from such as him and there's no good reason I should be a damned messenger boy for him. I told him to send that slug of a son of his . . ."

Alison motioned to him to come and sit down. He stepped into the room stooping a little to go through the door. The house had been built for men who were Border men. Short, stocky, hard men, more Celt than Anglo-Saxon. John Fox was bigger than her people. He stood near enough six foot and was deceptively broad with it.

"I'm to go to France with messages from him for a wine grower and a friend in Bordeaux. I told him there was little point. I could deliver them when I went in summer. He insisted . . ."

He leaned closer to her. Rebecca put the flowers onto the long table close to them both.

"I hate him," she said. "He makes you two so sad. I hate that."

Alison shut her eyes and leaned back in the chair.

"You must learn not to hate him Rebecca. Learn to love him."

"Do you?" her daughter asked, and Alison opened her eyes and began to laugh.

"You trapped me, Rebecca. I do try to love him," she said.

"He's always wanted this house. Always," Rebecca went on. "Cousin Saul said he was going to get it one day and he'd live here and you'd all be thrown out . . . he told me."

"No," said her mother. "You mustn't say such things, Rebecca. He's a sad boy."

The girl went on, "Cousin Saul says his father comes to the village from time to time to remind himself of what he lost when you refused him. So I do hate him. God will probably forgive me."

The girl hugged the two of them and then turned and left the room slamming the door as she went. Alison watched her go and shook her head in exasperation. John took her hand.

14

"He won't have it, Alison. Not while I live and breathe he won't have this place."

Alison nodded and pulled the jug of flowers closer to her and looked at them fondly.

"I'm so lucky," she said. "When d'you go?"

"Two days. He wants me to ride over to Bridgnorth and collect the letters there. I'll go down the river on a Bristol bound boat. He's arranged it already without even asking. That makes me so angry."

Alison put her hand on his mouth and shook her head.

"No anger John. No anger please. No more arguments with him either. Please. Promise me."

Fox looked away from her anxious face, stood up and paced to the window and back. The dog by the fire whined, lifted his head and lay back again. Fox whirled about to confront his wife.

"There's something . . . something he's not telling me. Something squint about this. I don't trust him, Alison and I don't like being threatened. I'm not some yokel boy, I'm a soldier and a man and I won't be threatened by such as him."

Alison stood then and took her man and held him and tried to calm him as she'd tried to calm him since he'd come back to stay for ever, as he'd promised her. He'd even tried to join the quiet witness in their meeting house. He'd promised to try to be as forgiving as she was.

His anger subsided as he leaned down to kiss Alison and her hands were behind his head, holding him close. Holding him . . .

3

The countryside around the village is as mysterious and changeable as clouds. Looming over it, the moors that lead to the Long Mynd and beyond are high, windswept, desolate and grim.

The Stiperstones and the Devil's Armchair stand razor sharp against the sky . . . At its foot sheep-cropped heather, hiding grouse clattering under foot amongst the sedge grasses around peat brown pools.

Fox knew the land here.

Then, as a terrified child staring up at the moon, he had walked alone across the stones as clouds raced in a storm-filled night. He crouched in the mouth of an old drift mine where men had scrabbled and clawed for a thin vein of silver ore in the centuries before. He'd been afraid then and yet drawn to the loneliness of it.

There were tales told in the village of Roman legions marching and vanishing into the ancient mine workings. Stories of witches flying ragged under a moon on stormy nights, frightened the village children with a fear of shadows.

Fox had felt that fear as a child and never since. He knew the Mynd as a summer place of drowsing bees and the occasional distant bark of a dog fox. He loved the Mynd on a bright winter's day. The tinny clatter of the bellwether ewes in the rocks and craggy places and the thud of a hare's feet sounding danger.

16

As he rode away down the valley he looked back to see the mysterious land he was leaving.

In such a place Merlin might still wait or King Arthur lie sleeping.

Alison had told him she'd pray for him to come home safe and she begged him to leave behind the old short sword he'd cleaned.

"No fighting, John, promise me you won't fight?"

He'd tried to explain that a man needs something to defend himself on such a journey.

"Just have faith, John, and you'll have no need of such things . . You promised me you'd put war behind you, John."

And he'd put the sword aside for her sake. As he hugged Rebecca to him to say goodbye she whispered that he was to look in his saddle bag but only when he was on the road to Bridgnorth.

"I've put a present there, father," his daughter said and hugged him again.

When he looked round at the end of the track they were standing arm in arm waving from the steps of the house. He raised his hat to them and rode on. Still he felt the itch that warned of something out of kilter.

Fox rode down the steep sided valleys where the spring streams fell among birch trees into clattering rock pools. In the lower hedges, old man's beard was bright green promise, the buds of the blackthorn rose tinted and tight still and winding amongst them the hint of the coming pale pink dog roses . . .

He rode away from Alison and Rebecca and felt that terrible instinct. For once in his life he ignored it and rode on.

Below, tucked hard against the sheltering banks, small villages, ancient churches, old drovers' tracks. Nestling amongst clumps of elm, more ancient habitations built on older habitations and yet older . . . Ancient stone walls made from stones brought from up the valley penned in more sheep.

Lambs frisked beside their mothers and in the fresh grass dew still sparkled on nets of cobweb spread and shimmering in the early sunshine.

Fox rode easily on the road to Bridgnorth, to the river Severn and Alison's uncle's house.

Fox would go the river route to Bristol along the valley floor, past tree lined banks and beech trees that would soon be showing sprigs of pale yellow as the leaves began to spear out and live. By the time he passed this way again the countryside would be lush with early summer.

He looked about him, breathed deeply and felt that eager surge he always felt when he rode out alone to make a long journey. Pat Shea had been right when he told him he'd never be as happy in the company of

17

other men as when he was alone, moving across the land with a secret purpose. But then Pat Shea claimed to have second sight like every Irishman Fox had ever known.

He rode at a steady pace along the grass track away from the wife and daughter whom he loved. Something was arsy varsy and gnawed at his mind and yet he rode on because he'd been tamed by his wife. It seemed that she'd succeeded in turning her man from the wild, dangerous, angry, calculating man he'd been into a merchant and a farmer.

Fox stopped at the side of the road, led his horse to the stream that ran clear nearby, took off his hat and leaned over a rock pool up stream of his horse. He drank.

He looked into the pool and saw dark eyes, the soft sun burned face of a man without purpose. He saw the hard line of his mouth slackening. He shook his head after he'd drunk, and drops of water scattered diamonds into his moustache and across the pool.

Standing, he remembered the present Rebecca had promised him. He unbuckled the saddle bag, reached inside and found, wrapped in a shirt, the long knife that had been Pat Shea's and under the shirt, he found the scabbard. Quickly he slung the blade across his back as Pat had carried it. Fox smiled. He'd not go naked into the world after all. He blessed Rebecca, his rebellious daughter, for her gift.

He sat then and thought for a moment about that past when he'd ached to be away into the dangerous land . . . the killing fields. To taste the danger, to feel the tingle of the blood as it raced through his hands and arms and body as he waited, waited and watched.

It was not what he learned as much as the terrible excitement of being so close to danger that had made him feel alive. A feeling he never felt in the village, or with Alison in their bed, or on the moorland which he'd so loved as a child.

He watched a humble bee amble across the grass and then make the effort to lift itself out of the stalks of grass to fly. Fox felt himself as encumbered by the weight of his family and the routine of his life, as that humble bee by its own weight.

He was not free and knew he never would be for he loved Alison more than life and his daughter even more fiercely.

He took up the reins of the horse, turned away from the stream and rode on ignoring the voice of instinct that said 'this leads to a killing field'.

****

18

On the road to Worcester, Michael's fat son Saul, pushed his horse to its limit. He rode as if the devil were chasing him along the sunken tracks between hawthorn hedges and earthen banks, urged the horse on and laid on the whip. He had urgent business with a particular man who was reported to be in Worcester.

He slashed the horse unmercifully, galloped through villages and past hovels at the trackside. Rode and never spared the horse. Now Cousin John had left the village it was time to move. His father told him so.

He'd been afraid to move before for fear of what his cousin might do if he discovered the plans his father had for the future. But now John Fox was out of the way and only cousin Alison stayed stubbornly in it. And she would go soon enough when he'd passed on the message his father sent.

A whisper in the ear of the man he was riding so hard to meet, and the wrath of God will come down on the village and the land about, his father had said. "The sooner whispered the sooner the rumours will begin and the sooner you'll have the house and the land, and Rebecca will be put firmly in her place."

Saul sawed at the bit of the horse, slewed her around a bend in the road and looked then across the river to the distant spire and the soft stones of Worcester where King Charles' witchfinder, Matthew Hopkins, or another of his like, was searching out witches and bringing with him the wrath of God.

Saul eased the horse to a walk, smiled to himself at the very idea of taking the house, and savoured the idea of curbing Rebecca, his overbearing cousin. He'd look forward to breaking her in at the same time that he took the house that rightly should have been left to him and his father. Rebecca was pretty enough and a virgin no doubt. It would be amusing.

Whoever thought of leaving such a place and such lands to the hands of a woman? Saul rode on, smiling at what he was about to unleash.

4

Fox came to Bridgnorth in the early evening. The five-arched bridge that joined the two halves of the prosperous river port was built of ancient stone. On one of the buttressed arches stood a two storey house. Its windows looked up and down the river and its pitched roof and chimneys told of a certain affluence. On the left bank of the river, the church spire pushed its way over the gabled slate roofs.

Along the quayside barges, waited to load cargoes for Bristol and the lower reaches of the river, behind them timbered warehouses, white and pale pink, washed by the late afternoon sun. Over each high window a gibbet hung on which goods were winched up to safe storage against river flooding, rats and theft. Below, the offices of merchants and traders and, behind them, the houses of the better off curved up to the ridge over the town.

Fox walked his tired horse over the bridge where, to his right, he smelt baulks of timber waiting to be squared off in the sawyer's yard.

Steps led from this quayside up to the road and onto the bridge. Beyond them a tall kiln chimney and stacks of raw red bricks.

Across the river the timber frame houses and three-storey mansions with five large windows on each floor were elegant indeed . . . They stood close along the quayside and narrow alleys between the houses led into the body of the town; up into the secluded courts and yards of the houses built hugger mugger up towards the church. Uncle Michael's house was there in a small square close to the church.

Fox rode past round stone bollards where barges were moored and on towards the warehouse on the end of the quay. Freshly painted, it smelt of new sawn wood, where a large extension had been built alongside the main stone building. Evidence that Alison's uncle Michael grew richer by the day.

Fox dismounted and led his horse behind the barrels and timbers watched by two men lounging in the doorway of the warehouse.

A boy came to him, smiling, as Fox took his leather bag from the saddle.

"Take your horse, Master Fox?" asked the boy, and Fox nodded.

"Water, good feed and rub him down, Peter," he said. "And ride him back home for us in a day or so, please."

He gave the boy a coin and turned to the two men who still watched him from the shadow of the doorway. He didn't know them. The first man chewed on a straw and looked Fox over and saw a quiet-eyed man, tall and easy in the way he walked, easy in the way he held himself. The man shrugged and looked away. The second man just stared at him, dead-eyed.

"Is the Master here?" Fox asked.

"You Fox are you?" the second man asked.

Fox put the leather bag onto a pile of sawn timber and threw his riding cloak across it. The leather scabbard of the long knife stayed across his back. He nodded and waited.

"We got a message for you from the old man. He said he'd see you at sunset at the house. He said you'd take passage on our wherry to Bristol. We'll be here, Fox. You'll take Llewellyn's boat to Caen. It's arranged."

And the man spat the straw from his mouth. Fox felt the blood stir but merely nodded. The man who'd spoken looked across at the other who still leaned on the wall and there was contempt in his eyes.

"They do say you were a soldier boy," he said, "And they say that now you took religion in some way? Singing songs for the Lord, is that it?" He grinned across at his companion who sniggered.

Fox looked from one to the other.

The first man spat into the dust at Fox's feet. Fox studied the man for a moment . . . What he didn't understand was why the man was as pushing as he was.

Fox looked along the quayside and saw the boy leading his horse away.

The second man sniggered again. He seemed simple. Half witted.

"No soldier boy this one, too soft. Too frit from the look of him."

The boy with the horse looked back and seemed anxious. He lifted a hand and Fox raised his.

"Be careful not to cut yourself on that knife. That's for big boys . . ."

Fox turned slowly then and looked at his tormenter and the man saw the darkness in those eyes for a moment. Fox picked up his cloak and his bag and walked away from them.

He stepped quietly along the quayside past sailing barges loaded with timbers, bales of Welsh wool, barrels of wine, bricks, clay, sawn planks . . Below them the water swirled fast under the arches of the bridge . . . .

It was curious. Uncle Michael had always waited for him down here. Never wanted him to come to the house up the hill, near the centre of town. Never asked him to stay, never offered the least hospitality nor extended a hand of friendship. Why was he bidden to the house tonight? Michael could so easily have been waiting with the letters he wanted delivered . . .

Fox walked away from the two men. Sunset, the man had said. He'd be there.

In the mouth of the alley opposite the large stone-fronted house that looked over the tiny square in front of the church, Fox waited. Ten, twenty minutes he waited and watched. Habit. No-one had followed him. No-one was watching the square. Fox moved out of the shadow of the neighbouring houses and fast across the cobbled square.

Before he'd finished knocking, the door of the house opened and Michael stood in the ill-lit hall. Fox entered without a word and Michael closed the door quickly.

"I can't offer you much. A glass of wine, some cheese . . ."

Fox nodded and, leaving his leather satchel near the door, he walked quickly after the older man into the back of the house into a small, ledger-lined room.

"Why are you sending me on a fool's errand?" he asked as Michael poured a glass of wine from the decanter on the table beside his desk.

There was bread and cheese on a wooden plate beside the wine. He pushed it to Fox.

Michael put two letters on the desk in front of Fox. "No concern of yours. Just deliver them and be done with it."

"Why not send your son? Even a fool could deliver a letter. Time he tried his hand in France isn't it?"

The older man stopped blustering as he stared into the dark dead eyes opposite him. He tried to smile.

"You know Saul, I doubt he could get to Worcester without a nursemaid. He disappoints me. Alison has more spirit than my son. So, eat and have more wine and go your way. I've arranged your passage down the river to Bristol."

"I saw the boatmen. I don't like their looks. I'll go my own way."

"No," the older man spoke sharply and then fussed about pouring more wine. "It's all paid for. You go with the two men, they're Llewellyn's men and he will take you across to Caen from Bristol . . . It's all arranged."

Fox ate some of the cheese on the plate and the bread. He drank a little of the bright red wine and stared by the light of the fire at the older man who touched the first of the envelopes.

"They're important and you'd better deliver them safely."

Fox looked across the table at the pale, fleshy face of the man he knew hated him. The fat man was sweating along his hairline. He puffed out his mouth as he breathed, fatly. Fox noticed that his left hand shook a little as if he had a fever.

What was making this man so nervous? Fox looked about the overheated room at the piles of papers, the cabinets that held yet more ledgers and shuddered. This could be his fate in time. To squat behind an oak desk and shuffle papers about and never to breathe fresh air or to feel wind on his face. Never to be free of the dull routine. To become as flabby in mind and body as Alison's uncle.

Michael stood hurriedly, anxious to end the interview and knocked the wine glass off the desk. It shattered at Fox's feet. Fox ignored it, took the letters, stood up and walked out of the study past the wheezing man. He walked quickly down the hall, took up his bag, and stepped out into the square in front of the church. Distantly a clock chimed behind some darkened blinds.

"You'll find a bed at the Rising Sun," wheezed Alison's uncle from the door, "On the quayside."

"I know where it is," said John. "I thank you for your hospitality," he added, ironically. Turning he slung his saddlebag across one shoulder and stepped down into the alley that led to the river. Behind him the door slammed shut and he heard bolts slot into place as he moved carefully down in the dark shadows of the alley.

****

A girl screamed and then close by came the sudden rush of running feet and from a corner ahead of him, a girl ran as if in fear of her life. He had no time to stand out of her way as she flew straight into him.

He held her and she struggled and slashed at his face with her nails, panting and clearly terrified . . .

"Here now! Hold still now," he said and caught her arms and pinned them so she could not scratch his eyes out.

"Easy now, easy now. What is it? What is it, girl? I'm not going to hurt you. Easy now. Go easy. Easy."

He talked as he would to a frightened animal. Her sobbing breath slowed and she stared, terrified into Fox's face. She was dark haired, short and would have been pretty if she'd not been so frightened.

"Who're you running from, girl?"

She shook her head and tried to speak.

"'Tis my mother. I think she . . . There's blood and . . . Help me . . . Please . . . help me. I'm afraid whoever did it is still . . . still . . . Please help me."

Fox let the quivering girl go and motioned her to be silent. He listened hard. All he could hear, apart from her panting breath, was the beat of his own heart. He cursed leaving his sword behind.

"Please master. I'm afraid."

The girl clutched at his hand and he nodded.

"Show me the way . . ." he said and followed her down the slippery alley.

Suddenly she ducked into a narrower alleyway between poor houses whose roofs almost touched . . . There was little light ever came into this alleyway. The stink of the water running down the channel in the centre of the cobbles was worse here than in other parts of the town . . .

Fox slipped on some vile piece of offal as the girl stopped and pointed to the dark doorway of a house.

"She's in there," she said and waited for him to pass her.

Fox walked quickly past her, slammed the door wide open, hard and fast, and was into the room at speed. He'd skirmished in enough enemy villages to know that speed and noise are the only ways to move in such a place.

He stepped a long way into the room to give himself space if he needed it. As soon as he was in the room, which gave directly onto the street, the door slammed shut behind him.

He turned fast. His back against the wattle and plaster wall. Facing him in the dim light, was the silent man from the Quayside and to his right the boatman who was supposed to take him down to Bristol. The silent man had a huge cudgel of knotted wood while the other was armed with a seaman's boarding sword, heavy bladed and good for close combat work. For chopping and slashing.

24

Between them a small but heavy table. As the door shut, Fox ran at the table and slammed it hard into the groin of the silent man by the door. He screamed. Fox plucked the long-bladed knife from the scabbard across his back.

He didn't stop moving for a moment and came directly at the boatman with the sword. He worked the long silver blade in a terrifying pattern of light in front him. The boatman slashed at his face with the short sword as Fox swept his broad hat from his head and spun it into the face of the boatman.

At the same time he followed inside the man's sword arm and sank the knife deep into the boatman's neck. Even as the blade entered the man's neck, Fox pulled it out and cutting backhanded across the man's face, opened a stream of blood where the eyes had been.

He stepped back from the man who clawed at his blinded eyes. The wound in his neck suddenly spurted blood. He fell across the table and twitched once as Fox shoved him aside and leaned into the silent man who was clutching his shattered groin.

"Who sent you?" he asked. The silent man shook his head and Fox moved the knife in a fine arc and took the man's ear neatly from his head.

"Who sent you?" he asked again. The silent man shook his head spraying blood onto the wall and across the table. He moaned more in fear than pain.

"He knew," he pointed at the dead man in horror, "He said 'Fox. Fox. Easy', he said, and 'He'll be carrying plenty of money'. We were supposed to be on the river, kill you and pitch you over and be done with it. He told me I had to help do it now. I was afraid of him."

Fox leaned forward a little and the man screamed once.

"Don't!"

Fox wiped the bloody blade on the man's jerkin and walked quietly out into the alley. There was no sign of the girl.

5

Three days later, at five in the morning with the sun coming up over the city of Bristol, Fox left the barge he taken from Bridgnorth. The bargee was known to him and had agreed to leave in the early morning before light when Fox made it worth his while.

"I'm going down the centre of the dock, Master," he was assured by the elderly bargemaster but Fox shook his head. He took up his small bundle, a leather bag with money and papers and Pat Shea's blade. He jumped from the slowly moving barge onto the path and stepped quickly away into the early morning shadows and mists.

Before the red-roofed houses of the affluent and the hovels strung along the river, away from the Downs, is land suitable for sheep. On the other side is land that drains down to the Somerset Levels, lowering skies and the magic mount of Glastonbury Tor.

Far away a bittern boomed in the undrained marshes that led away to the wetlands beyond the city.

Fox had known the Levels as a place for eeling and fishing when he was a boy. It was a land of withies and osiers, of heron and snipe, of web-footed men and women and a place where outlaws traditionally hid. A low lying land under a vast pale dome of sky.

Hereward the Wake passed here and King Arthur lay not far away near Cadbury Hill with his fabled sword. For John Fox, as a boy and as a young man, it had been a place to go to ground should he need to. He

26

remembered it as a place for taking small flat bottomed boats out netting birds with his wilder friends. Then selling what they took in Bristol market and coming back up the river, four days by foot, to the Shropshire bleaklands by the Devil's Armchair and the valley near home.

He even remembered fondly the beating from his father who never knew of the silver coin he'd made from selling the netted birds that he had hidden in his own place high on the moorlands.

The Levels was where he learned that women did not have webbed feet.

Fox smiled as he walked towards the dark mass of the city lying below the gorge through which the old river carved its way. So he came unseen and alone as the city woke to the new day.

Through Peter's Gate down to the jetties and quaysides he welcomed the smells of sea and spices and timber, of exotic fruits and rum. The noises of forges and wood yards and the sight of men beginning to emerge from ale houses, flop houses, small rooming warrens. Here were the whores and porters and ale house keepers, the flotsam and jetsam that always lie along quaysides in a busy port.

Slops were thrown into the gutter from overhead or from alleys and doorways. A door opened and for a moment the screaming argument of a whore for her shilling which stopped, as soon as it began, by the door banging shut.

Two sailors leaning on each side of the doorway of a penny gaff sniffing the air. Their ditty bags at their feet, they'd outspent and were ready for passage and it hardly mattered where.

The stink of tar and molasses, the salt smell of curing barrels, the tang of exotic fruits and tobacco leaf, the jumble of ropes and lanterns, marlin spikes and chains, wet weather gear and boxes cluttered in the chandler's corridors and windows. Fox walked through it all. As he strode on he looked about the waking streets and wondered idly if the men who'd tried to rob him had been told of his coming and if so, by whom.

Fox made for the office of the merchant as he'd been instructed by Alison's Uncle Michael.

He'd walked such streets from Leghorn to Brest, from La Rochelle to Bilbao and he loved them all. And trusted none. And yet only three nights ago he'd fallen for the oldest trick in the crimper's trade . . . a pair of pretty eyes with tears in them . . . Only his fighting skills had saved his life.

So Fox's eyes flickered endlessly to all points of the compass and, from time to time he'd turn without hesitation and walk back on his track and then dive into an alley to re-emerge a quarter of a mile further on or on another quay entirely.

The movement, the promise of change and venturing surged through his blood again and he felt that freedom he missed so very much at home. He was almost grateful to Michael for sending him again on this journey to Bordeaux, despite Alison's sadness.

He stepped out of the hustle of the quayside and into the office of Matthew and Son. The smell of spices from the Indies and Arabia that forever steeped the wooden panels of the building wafted down the corridor.

He thought again for a moment of the attack. It still seemed curious that he'd been the target of such an old ploy. He shook his head and stepping round a vast sack of nutmegs, walked through the door into the clerk's room.

A dusty land of ledgers, ink, quills, books and papers and all those things Fox feared could entrap him. He stepped quietly into the inner office and watched the crabbed white hands of Matthews, the old man who was their connection to Bordeaux. From him he'd receive instructions and letters of introduction.

The soft hands slammed shut the ledger their master had been conning. The white face looked up, pale eyes glittering. Matthews reminded Fox of nothing so much as a grub in an old apple. Dun coloured and soft fleshed.

Fox took the letters of introduction, passed the time of day and learned the name of the ship he was to take passage on. He took his leave for the moment and stepped into a street already filling with the barrows of market traders looking for produce from the ships moored alongside.

The men of affairs were standing in small groups discussing the latest arrivals and partings while hard eyed crimper's men were watching for likely crews to kidnap.

He turned and saw in the dark entry to an alley one of the two sailors who'd been waiting with their ditty bags earlier, further down the quayside. He was in view for a moment, then gone.

Fox walked quickly across the cobbles away from the rotting debris and the smell of the docks into the yard of a large inn. Pot boys turned and ran inside when they saw him, calling his name. By the time he'd reached the door an enormous fat man stood there in apron and shirt sleeves beaming in welcome.

"Sergeant, come in, come in and welcome. I expected you last night. Your bed ready, and food and drink . . . a good bottle of wine. I'd a taste for the craic last night and you spoiled it for me."

28

The Irish innkeeper, brother to Pat who'd died so cruelly and an old soldier himself, stepped inside after Fox.

Steven Shea kicked shut the door of the inner snug bar after a growl to a pot boy to bring ale, a bottle of best Bordeaux and a plate of meats to break their fasts.

The two men faced each other across a dark oak table stained with the rings of a thousand glasses and pots.

Fox walked to the window and looked out guardedly.

"God's bones, but you're a suspicious sod," said the old soldier, "Ever on the watch."

"Aye - and I'm a living sod," said Fox looking about the room before he turned and sat with his back against the wooden panels alongside the window which let him see whoever approached the front of the inn. He was himself in dead ground and would be behind the door if it opened.

"It's a strange time of year to be going to France, John," said the Irishman as he sat down with him and took out an old pipe and began to fill it,. "And you're like a cat on hot bricks. Why, friend?"

"I don't know . . . instinct . . . something not quite as it should be. I'd trouble with a cutpurse on my way here. I've orders to go to Bordeaux to see a man who I know has no interest in doing business with my wife's uncle. Yet her uncle insists I go. There's a passage arranged."

"What boat?"

"The Rose of England. Master is . . ."

" . . . Llewellyn's the master and he's never the sort of a man to mix with. Something of a chancer to tell the truth. My advice is not to go with him at all. I can see to that for you."

Fox nodded his thanks. The pot boy brought the drink and glasses and plates of meat and bread.

"Why go?" Shea asked, "If there's nothing to go for."

"He's conjured something from the air," said Fox and suddenly he grinned, "I'm not unhappy to be free of the farm that's the truth. Sweet Jesus, a man would die of suffocation . . . counting sheep, or bales of wool, or bottles of wine or . . . selling and buying from dull men and duller women and you have no idea of the boredom of farming, Patrick. So I'm glad to be running free . . . like a boy let loose from the apron strings."

Fox smiled at his old friend.

"And you feel guilty, no doubt, for the wife doesn't understand." The Irishman sniffed with all the disdain a man who never married feels for a wife.

"I do," said Fox, "For Alison doesn't understand. True."

"What else?" asked the perceptive Irishman, raising his tankard, "Your continuing health," he said.

"Two men were waiting near the warehouse where I made a meeting with Merchant Matthews."

'Two men?"

"Sailors, from the look of them, who were watching but not watching. Waiting on my coming out and then were gone again. It may be nothing, my friend, but instinct makes me itch."

The huge Irish trooper looked into his ale then got up, opened the door and looked outside to be sure the passage was empty. Then he came back in, latched the door, sat at the table and leaned close to Fox.

"There are things . . . I hear things. There is trouble brewing in London. People pass through here. Military people know me. Trust me from time to time with confidences. The King is . . ."

The vast man hesitated for a moment.

"'Tis between us, Sergeant Fox?" the big man waited until he had a nod.

"There's rumour and trouble coming that's for sure. They say the King is hag-ridden by his froggie wife and by that harlot Buckingham, his painted favourite. That's what is said."

Fox shrugged and sipped the wine. It was good. Indeed it was some he had himself arranged for shipment when he first began to work for Alison's uncle.

"Does it matter to me? What do I care for the King? I sit at home like an old man, I have a daughter, Rebecca, whom I love, and a wife I love as well. We live our quiet lives, go to the meeting house of a Sunday . . . work . . . read a little . . ."

The big Irishman burst out laughing and shook his fat head slowly.

"They'd never believe it in the Regiment, John. Sit at home and read and go to the meeting house? And pray no doubt!" He laughed at the very idea of it.

Fox wasn't laughing.

"My wife prays for both of us as I don't have her faith . . . yet. It's a strange sect she belongs to that talks about peace and good works. I am not a member but am allowed in the services for Alison's sake. You may laugh but you have no idea how hard it is for an old sweat like me to sit on a wood bench and stay silent when all I want to do it raise hell and Cain together, like we used to do."

The two men raised their drinks in fond memory of past times.

The Innkeeper, still smiling, murmured a name and Fox had him by the throat across the table.

"What did you call me?" he asked. "What was it?"

"Fox . . . . Fox . . ." The big man clawed at Fox's hand squeezing his throat. "We used to call you 'the preacher' when we talked about you after you left Colonel Fairfax's employment . . . after my brother died. We heard you'd gone soft. All for a girl. Let me go, Jesus, I thought it was all peace and light with you and your religious friends," the big man croaked.

Fox let him go and shook his head.

"My wife tries to teach me to keep my temper guarded but it's a hard thing to hold onto. I've not learned yet."

"There are those, John, who want to see you. There are those about them who want to see who they want to see. If that's not too Irish for you. They have work for you. Black Tom . . ."

Fox held up his hand in refusal.

"Not even for him. No more of that. I'm a merchant who deals in wine and wool to and from Bordeaux. I'm going to France and then home to my wife."

"There are rumours that Parliament will confront the King and will take his power from him. That we shall no longer be subjects to King Charles and his wife."

Fox stared at him.

"Are you telling me . . ." he began and then shook his head, "I've been too long in the country, my friend. None of that is my business. So why tell me?"

"Your friend Black Tom thinks a meeting might be to your advantage."

"No . . . he was my colonel once but not my friend. I promised my wife there'd be no more fighting. It's all finished and behind me and Colonel Tom is from another life, another time. I'm a merchant from the Borders."

"You're Sergeant Fox. A man who speaks French like a frog, German like those bullet-headed guardsmen we hated and even Spanish when necessary. You're Fox who'd take any man in single combat, knife or sword or singlestaff. My brother would not have let you walk away when the colonel asked to see you."

Steven Shea was angry and shook with it and Fox looked away from him.

"You're not some bloody milk sop woman's man. Despite they called you Preacher Fox, it was never to your face. Black Tom is in Bristol and wants to see you. I said I'd fetch you to him."

"Then tell him you failed." Fox got up from the table and walked to the door. "All I want's a quiet life, peace and quiet. God above, didn't I get your brother killed? Isn't that enough?" he asked bitterly. "Now I'm going to my room and will wait for the early morning tide."

"What . . . reading the good book is it?" mocked the Irish soldier, "You were with my brother when he died, sure you were. You never had him killed. That was his fate. Soldiers get killed which is what they're paid for. It's how it is. I'll tell the Colonel you've no wish to see him because of your wife? Will I tell him that?"

Fox hesitated for a moment

"He's at the Sign of the Horse and Grapes. Ask for Mister Rosemount and you'll find him. He said . . . well, ask him."

Fox nodded once. Reluctantly.

"Change my passage, Steven. Tonight . . . the tide's at 2. I'll go then."

Fox walked out of the room. The Innkeeper smiled and supped the last of the ale, dug a podgy hand into the plate of cold meats on the table and ate. The thing was baited and Black Tom would be grateful for they both knew their man.

6

Fox knew he was being watched though it was expertly done. Indeed only once had he seen the watcher. He had turned a corner near a stall selling apples, stopped and come back to the stall as an auburn haired girl with bold eyes and simple but well kept clothes turned the corner. She clearly expected him to have moved on.

The girl turned the corner and came straight on. It was very well done and if Fox hadn't been expecting her, he'd never have known that for a second she was thrown by the fact that her quarry had stopped so abruptly.

She walked on past him and he watched her go. That easy rolling walk he'd last seen on a dancer in Bilbao before he'd gone home to Alison and the village. He took an apple from a barrel and flipped the stall holder a smile and a farthing.

"Wouldn't mind a bite of her apple, mister," grinned the stall holder, nodding after the girl. He laughed, showing bad teeth and exhaling worse breath. Fox walked on.

The Sign of the Horse and Grapes lay in a corner between two quays where it commanded a view across the larger ships and over to the tall masts of the ocean-going traders berthed on the other side of the wharf alongside the warehouses.

Behind the inn lay a rabbit warren of lanes and alleys which led back up into the main body of the city. No-one could pass in front of the inn and across the small square without being observed. Beyond the square, playing a penny whistle, a sea-going man played for anyone who'd listen.

The player was one of the sailors from the seaman's gaff Fox had seen earlier in the morning. Fox stood in a doorway watching the square, hidden in the darkness of the alley. He moved back into the shadows and began to work his way through the stinking cobbled lanes towards the back of the inn.

Once there, Fox stopped again and watched for twenty minutes or so and saw only pot boys and serving maids going in and out of a door to the rear of the building. He moved quickly then past the young men gathered round a pretty girl, through the door, past a surprised cook sharpening a knife on a stone, and emerged in a side passage.

He stepped into a small parlour which, apart from a man in a serge jacket and dark trousers, was empty. The man looked up, irritated by the interruption. He was working at some ledgers.

"I said I was not to be disturbed . . ." He stopped. "You expected, mister? If not, the other bar is more lively. I'm afraid I use this as my office and . . ."

"I am expected by Mr Rosemount," Fox said.

"What did you say your name was?" asked the portly man, standing up as he spoke.

"I didn't," said Fox.

The man, gesturing for him to sit by the fire, hurried puffing out of the room as if the very fiends of hell were after him. Fox walked over to table and flipped open the ledger. It was a mass of figures and spidery writing. This portly man was who he seemed to be.

Fox looked out of the window and across the square in front of the inn a young, long-haired man in a black and silver doublet, starched white shirt and plain sword hanging to his left, stood in deep conversation with a handsome girl with auburn hair and direct eyes.

The man had pale skin and a determined, even petulant mouth. His bottom lip seemed almost too heavy then suddenly he smiled and his face lit for a moment. The girl shook her head and walked away and then came back to the young man as if she had had second thoughts. Was she a whore doing business? A friend of the young man? Hard to tell.

"Sergeant. My, but I'm that glad to see you. It's been long enough." The old familiar North Country voice was warm in greeting.

Fox turned to find his old colonel standing in the doorway and behind him, the panting smiling face of the innkeeper who had the look of a retriever who'd delivered the game to his master.

"Six years, Mr Rosemount, give or take."

The older man walked into the room and held out his hand. The two men looked each other over as the portly man scooped up his papers.

"Will I send in drink . . . or food or . . . ?"

Fairfax glanced at him. "Nothing," he said, "Nothing."

"You'll not be disturbed sirs."

The fat man puffed his way out and closed the door behind him.

"Different people, different times, Sergeant Fox."

"Mister Fox now, John Fox, Colonel Fairfax. No sergeants. No titles. It's the way of it."

"Trader Fox would be more to the point from what I hear." Fairfax was almost mocking. "Is it true that you're really as stuck at home in Stretton as a church mouse in the wainscot? You're Sergeant Fox to me. Always will be."

The confident tone began to annoy Fox. What could Fairfax want after all this time?

Fox asked "That girl out there, Colonel? See her? One of yours, is she?"

Fox stood in the shadow of the shutters and pointed out across the courtyard. Fairfax looked out and his face darkened as he saw the girl. He shook his head and shrugged.

"Pretty enough for them as like that sort," he said.

"You don't know her then?"

Fairfax shook his head and sat in the great settle near the fire.

"I think you do, Colonel. She's followed me since I went to get my letters of introduction from my master's connection here this morning. And there are two sailors who make a good team and not so noticeable as might be."

"You knew!"

"I knew. You don't lose the old skills so easy. Yes, I knew."

Fairfax was angry now and turned back to his old sergeant.

"You knew and yet you came here, you led her here . . . You're losing your skills." Fairfax sounded disappointed.

"I came here, sir, by back alleys and lanes. She has no idea I'm here nor anyone else for the matter of that. But she knew to come here and so did the sailors. They are either your people or you have no cover sir . . . But my skills, such as they were, are still there. D'you know the man talking to her?"

Fairfax ignored the question and sat at the table.

"I came for curiosity, not to oblige you, sir," Fox went on.

"Ever blunt, Fox," Fairfax smiled, "It's not me you'd oblige."

"Nor do I want more soldiering. Saw enough and did enough in the Swedish Army. Lost a good friend . . . my damn fault. I promised then if I got to you, warned you of the ambush, then I'd take my release and go home and marry, even. And I kept my promise to myself."

Fox turned from the window to the quiet man sitting watching him. He was angry because he knew what Fairfax wanted. He was going to offer work, to offer what he most needed . . . freedom from that damned village and the mealy-mouthed man who ruled his life. And Fox was angry because he was going to refuse because he'd made a promise to a woman he truly loved.

"D'you know, I see Pat yet? Hanging on his own blade. I saw his eyes go out. The light, you know?" Fox pointed to his own eyes. It was a physical hurt with him still.

"Why d'you lie to me? You know the girl and for all I know you know the man she was with."

Fairfax sighed. "There is a man wants to see you."

"Why would I want to talk to him? I did what I swore I'd do. Married a girl no-one in her family wanted me to marry, settled down and even took work with her uncle. I am content enough."

"And now you lie too. You hate the work and the man you work for. I have eyes and ears too, Fox, and I know you are not content or why would you be here?" said Fairfax sharply. He looked at his hands and went on softly. He knew the man was nudging the hook, testing the bait.

"You go to Bordeaux for wine from time to time. Look after a warehouse from time to time, buy wool from time to time, farm a little . . . And there you will rot." Fairfax shot the word at him with contempt.

Fox shut his eyes.

"You are a man should be out in the world."

"I am a man vowed to stay home and love my wife as waited for me."

Fairfax nodded. He stirred the log in the fire. Fox was not an easy man and Fairfax knew he had to be as honest as he was able if he was to win Fox over.

"I am married as well, Sergeant, to as good a woman as dragged breath. And your wife is no doubt the same. Alison, isn't it?"

Fox said nothing. Fairfax went on quietly.

"I love my wife and my home in Yorkshire. It's fine country and we are both happy there. I could stay there, farm and be a happy man."

Fairfax laughed at himself.

"I'm lying of course for I'd not be happy. I'd be but half the man I want to be. Don't you miss the excitement . . . the adventure we had when

36

we were younger? It's not long since and we don't forget do we? Do we?"

Fairfax felt almost sorry for Fox for he was, he knew, weaving a net to trap him which would make him break his vows. He'd want him to leave the valley on the Marches and go and do what he did best in the world . . . to go gathering news, tit bits, information . . . spying. Fairfax looked up at him and Fox saw the friendship and respect of an old comrade.

"I know how it is to be torn between family and peace and then to remember spring mornings how it used to be as we waited for action, for the charge, the battle, the noise . . . as you remember, I'm sure."

"No, Colonel. I remember best being out between the armies or in an enemy town. The waiting. The watching. Peace and quiet as we stalked men like animals for what they could tell us . . . Watching a camp, a track in a forest . . . alone. I remember that. And the danger always nagging there. But I made a vow."

"Indeed you did and you have a family and Rebecca, a daughter who loves her father."

Fox shut his eyes and saw his child who was fifteen now and as lovely as her mother had been at that age. He counted his luck and shut his ears to temptation as Fairfax went on, "Your wife's uncle hates you. He was to marry Alison once, did you know that? Happen he or his son'll sniff around your daughter now she's of marrying age."

Fox shook his head in some confusion. What else did his old commander know, and how did he know?

"She's too young and I'd geld the man first."

"She's fifteen and old enough, is all I'll say. Oh, and did you know the uncle owns almost all your debts?"

Fox looked sharply at the man on the settle. Fairfax leaned forward.

"I have connections, John, and eyes everywhere. And I like to know where old comrades are, for one never knows. I can tell you so much . . . no more. I live on my Yorkshire lands, yes. But I spend more and more time in London trying to attend to the business of government. No interest of yours, no doubt."

Fox shrugged.

"But it's a business made the harder by a hag-ridden King and his bedamned and bejewelled favourite Buckingham who pretends to be a soldier and knows less than spit about the business."

Fairfax sounded bitter and angry. Fox yawned.

"Fox, this may bore you but there is an urgency about matters now. The business of Parliament is coming to a head. The King demands, the King orders, the King refuses to listen and the time is coming when . . .

when we may be forced to take matters of government entirely away from the monarch and into the hands of the people - our people."

There was a long silence in the room. A log crackled and rolled forward in the hearth.

Fox stared at his old Colonel as he spoke this treason. It was open, not hidden, not couched in general words. Black Tom Fairfax laughed as he saw the surprise on Fox's face.

"I trust you with this, which is to say I trust you with my life, John, for what I am saying reeks of treason. It's of little interest perhaps to a man like you but there are things to be done. Plans to be made, information to be gathered. There will need to be men about us who can be trusted beyond a peradventure. Men like you."

It reeked of danger and Fox could feel the blood quicken in his veins. Yet he'd made a vow. He shook his head.

"Not me. Not me. I'm done with all that. Leave me out of your plans. I won't say a word of what has passed here but no. I will not help you."

It was as if Fox had not said a word.

"There is a man wants to meet you. A young man, a coming man. See him. Speak with him. I know you, Sergeant. I told him you were a man who'd be right for the work."

"I cannot help you, nor him. I made a promise."

Fairfax sighed and stirred the logs in the fire again with his foot. Sparks flew in the dark chimney. He looked across at Fox and sighed. It was so easy to tempt a man.

"For old times sake will you do one thing for me, then?"

"For him, you mean?"

"Very well. Yes, for him. Take a message to a man in France?"

"Why not send someone he knows? Someone already in your hands?"

Fairfax shook his head gently.

"It can be no-one known to us or them. There are countless spies and agents willing to sell anyone for a copper coin. The man you'll see was in the ranks of Gustavus Adolphus . . . a reliable man. We . . . we are concerned. Two men have been lost already trying to make connection . . . I'll be honest. There is a risk."

Fox smiled a little. How cunning his old Colonel was . . . What a web he wove.

"A risk?"

Fairfax laughed and lifted his arms wide.

"John Fox, I know what tempts you most. I know you well."

"Too well, sir. Too damnably well. When wasn't there a risk . . . a danger?" Fox smiled. "Where is it to go to?"

Fairfax shrugged. "D'you know Niort in the Marais?"

Fox nodded.

"I know it. 'Tis like the Somerset Levels. Water and mist and islands and narrow cuts . . . punts and wild fowl and men with webbed feet and women with scales and mermaids tails. I love the Marais. I suppose your man knew that too."

"Thurloe? No. He didn't know that or if he did he didn't tell me. Will you take the letter?"

"Will you tell me what's in it?"

Fairfax shook his head, "At the end of the Spice Islands quay tonight. There's a chandler's shop with a candle lit in the window. Meet there."

"It's dangerous work to plot against the King."

"The King goes his own merry way to hell. We make plans to be sure the country doesn't pitch into chaos. Yes, it's dangerous. But you made a promise to a woman, Fox. So is it all milk and honey with you now, Fox? Is it so? Pat Shea would laugh."

Fox's eyes glittered in the half light of the room. "Don't use his name, Sir. He would never laugh. He was my friend. Don't try to use Pat Shea against me or you'll make yourself an enemy. That is the first time you ever misjudged me."

Fairfax lifted a hand in apology. Fox went on.

"I go on the tide. But you already know, don't you?"

"You'll take a different boat. On the night tide."

Nothing moved in the room.

"Will you do it?"

It was still for a moment and then Fox nodded and Fairfax offered his hand.

"Let it be understood that this one thing is all and will be done for old times' sake, Colonel. Don't ever ask me again. Please."

Fairfax heard the pleading in the voice and knew how much it cost Fox to dishonour his vow.

If ever a man was suited to the work it was Fox. He watched as the man walked briskly across the courtyard and away into the maze of streets and the tangle of yards and shops and markets and the mass of people who lived on and by the port of Bristol.

Fairfax sat, eyes closed as the door latch lifted and the young man from the courtyard slipped in.

"Well?" he asked.

"He'll take the message, for old times' sake. No more. I warned you, Master Thurloe. I did warn you he'd be a hard fish to land."

"But worth the taking, you said. The game is on, Tom."

7

The girl was bold. The girl was good. But the girl was not good enough. She had followed Fox for most of the day. He glimpsed her twice and made no more effort to avoid her. She would wait.

He had spent most of the day seeing merchants, arranging business, agreeing prices and gathering other letters of introduction to merchants and traders in Bordeaux. He'd gone back to talk with Steven Shea at the inn and made various plans. Then he'd gone to have a drink with Alison's uncle's factor to make some final arrangements.

Fox knew that the other merchants he'd talked to could see little purpose in his going to Bordeaux so early in the year. They reminded him that there would be thin pickings and were surprised that Martin would send anyone so early . . . What was the man thinking of?

Fox had mentioned it to the slug of a man in his ledger lined room. The man had not bothered to reply. He had papers ready and bills for some and orders for others. All Fox had to do was deliver them. His job was not to ask questions.

"You'll be taking the Rose of England on the morning tide?" Matthews asked for the third time just as they parted.

"You seem very anxious that I take that boat? Any reason?"

The pale slug shook his head and averted his eyes and said no more.

In the late afternoon Fox had waited in the alley opposite the inn in which he had taken a room. He had six hours before the tide would see him on his way. He had watched and waited in the early evening shadows.

Then the two sailors passed the door of the inn and walked on. An hour later, one came back alone.

Fox had learned patience in a hard school and knew the danger of moving too soon, of revealing yourself too early. He stood and watched and waited. It was his profession after all.

The girl was good alright and he'd have missed her if a dog hadn't barked to Fox's right. She was close to the wall in the shadow and dressed in a dark cloak from head to toe. As he watched she moved fast over the cobbles and into the passage down the side of the inn.

Fox waited five minutes and then another five. Then Steven Shea came out and left an old ale pot on a window sill and walked back into his inn. The sign Fox had waited for.

Fox had money enough to pay the passage and to see him on his way in France. The coin was in his room, hidden, though not well enough to have escaped the attention of the girl. She'd already stripped the bed, slit the mattress and there were feathers and ticking all over the room. On the table by the door stood his leather satchel.

She was pulling the drawers from a chest by the window from the bottom upwards. She was a professional. As she opened them she reached into each to ensure she missed nothing.

Fox's travelling bag was emptied over the floor, his business papers scattered, his clothes strewn about and as the girl finally reached the top drawer and opened it Fox walked in.

She whirled round, a thin blade in her hand.

Fox closed the door behind him and waited. He didn't take his eyes off her. If she used the knife as well as he feared she might she'd bear watching.

Her eyes were quite still on his. They were the colour of the sea or a mountain lake. Her hair was tied back from her pale oval face. Her mouth, full, her chin, if anything, a touch too strong. But it was her eyes that Fox watched.

Across a chair the dark green cloak lay discarded. She wore a low cut blouse and a short jacket. Her woollen skirt was full, simple and held in place by a belt of Italian design, if Fox wasn't mistaken.

For almost a minute they stood so and then she laughed a full-throated vibrant laugh. It entirely disarmed Fox who'd expected attack or flight. But she simply put the knife back into its hiding place under her jacket and laughed again.

"Did you want something?" he asked and provoked more laughter. It was infectious and he smiled at the foolishness of the question as he looked about the debris of feathers, clothes and papers.

"I want many things, mister," she said and he noted the Irish twang to her voice.

"I'd a good friend from Connemara, once," he said.

"I'm a Clare woman myself. Though it's years since I was home. Was he a loyal friend?"

"My best friend," he said.

"Is he about you, still?"

"He's dead," said Fox flatly and for a moment his eyes had the stillness of a shark's about them.

She said nothing and he liked her for that. Then she moved from the window, round the end of the bed toward him and waited, one hand on her hip as he stood unmoving in the doorway.

"I'm sorry about this. But a girl has to take the chances she gets, isn't that the truth? Are you handing me to the Watch then? If you do, you know what it means?"

She smiled again and he stepped a temptation closer to her.

"Hanging," he said.

He felt the heat of her and she knew it. She shut her eyes as if to close him out.

"I'll exchange something with you," he said.

She waited, her head tilted in the question.

"A name. Just a name," he said.

"Ah well, that might not be so easy as dancing the hemp, for names are hard come by."

"Yours?"

"That's hardest and easiest. I can give you a name and I might be lying. How will you know?"

Fox walked past her, shoved the mess of feathers and papers off the large chair and sat down. She turned to look at him. It was her turn to be surprised.

"I would, if you wanted, if it meant I'd be free to go, I would give you what men mostly want of me," she said quietly. For a moment he felt the heat rise. "I can't trade in names," she went on.

Fox nodded.

"I'm sorry John Fox. I have yours, you see. From the papers, here," she indicated the debris about the floor.

"Or did you get it from the young-pale faced man in the square this afternoon?" he said.

"You're a surprise, I own that. I'd expected a middling fat, bustling, puffing man of business. God knows I've seen enough of them from Dublin to Barcelona. And what are you . . . ?"

"A soldier. Once."

"Like your Connemara friend?" she asked. "What happened to him?"

And the cold came down on his face again and she was, for a moment, afraid.

"You won't call the Watch?"

"You know I won't."

"And you won't take me? You'll let me go?"

He nodded once.

"Why?"

"Maybe for my Connemara friend. Or because I know why you came because I know why you didn't come."

For a moment she thought about that and then smiled and picked up her cloak.

"You were too long in his company then. The Irishman. Tell me," she said.

"You didn't come for money for if you had there was enough and more in the satchel by the door. So it's not money. You assumed I had hidden things or you wouldn't have ripped open the mattress. So maybe you're wanting to know something more about me. For some reason."

She took from inside her cloak the small locket Alison had given him. She clicked it open to show the miniature inside.

"I might have taken this John Fox." she said, "Then why did I come?"

He moved faster than she'd believed any man could move. Her arm was crushed up her back, her hair pulled hard back to reveal her throat looking into his eyes she saw what others had seen. The cold black fury, the chilling darkness of death.

The scream was choked in her throat by his hand closing in under her chin close to her ears. He'd pinch her life out like a candle flame.

She began to choke, instantly stopped struggling and dropped the locket.

He let her go and picked up the silver jewel. She felt her bruised throat.

He closed the locket and pushed it deep into a pocket. Then she turned and moved to the door. Stopping there, she looked at the man who'd taken her to within an inch of dying.

"I'll give you a name for the sake of your Connemara friend. Maeve Ahern is a name." She lifted her hand to him and went quickly out of the room.

44

****

The evening mist still had a chill in it. Moisture dripped from masts and ropes, from sheets and anchor chains, from inn signs to chandlers' boards. The hint of a wind was rising and with it the evening mist was beginning to clear off the river.

Fox stepped carefully across chains and ropes, past warm inviting doorways and warm inviting women who'd all shipwrecked alongside Bristol Dock and who'd now shipwreck any who'd be sirened onto their shoals.

Fox carried what he had in one bag slung to his left, his sword arm free and ready.

Shea had had the girl followed but she was almost immediately lost.

Fox had expected no less. Shea wanted to take Fox to the ship on which he'd arranged a passage to France but Fox refused and left the inn alone.

The sudden shouts and laughter from the opened hatch of a ship split the air and stopped as whoever had come out slammed closed the hatch and trapped the music and life inside the cabin. Fox moved on his way.

Spice Island quay was a shadow to the right. There were no lights along it. Fox moved quickly over the cobbled and rutted road and towards a chandler's shop window in which a single green light glowed. Back in the dark mass of the city a church bell tolled the hour. Fairfax was late.

A slight, lone figure turned quickly along the quay and hesitated at the window. He took off his hat. It was the young man who'd been talking with the girl in the morning. He turned away and Fox had an arm round his throat and Pat's knife under his ear.

"Well, Mr. Thurloe, easy to see you're a desk man. Your girl was better in the business than you are. Don't struggle . . . don't. Answer me one thing. What's her name?"

He released the pressure on the young man's throat but kept his knife in place.

"Ahern, she says it is."

The young man was brave enough and showed no fear.

"Is she one of yours, that girl? You should know she searched my room. Of course you know . . . you set her on, Mr Thurloe. Yet you're not sure if she's yours."

"I don't know. She won't come to the point as far as that goes. I really don't know, Sergeant Fox. She could be a thief or a whore or both."

"Or one of yours."

"Maybe. Did you let her go?"

"What's that to you?" Fox asked. "You don't even know if she hunts with you or against you. Now, let's get the business done. I said I'd take a letter to a man for my old Colonel's sake. Then I am done with all this. So! Let me have the letter."

Thurloe took a package from inside his cloak.

"Do your business in Bordeaux. Go to Niort in the Marais. The Sign of the Ram. A man will ask you how Black Tom is. Give him the letter. He will read it there and then and answer yes or no. Come back with the single word."

"No!" Fox shook his head. "I said I'd take the letter. No messages, no words. I made a promise. I have no good reason to break it."

Thurloe nodded a little and shivered in the night air.

"I'll tell you then. The man has connections in the Court of France and with the family of our Queen. We need intelligence of their plans and hopes as a precaution, John Fox, against stupidity and chaos."

This, whispered urgently in the darkness. A dog barked. A fiddler played somewhere. Nothing moved on the quayside.

"You already know more than you should. You already carry enough to interest those who'd betray us. Our man there has no wish to lose his place in the heart of the French Court. Seen with an agent known to be with us and he is dead. This work is to stifle civil war my friend. To smother it at birth. Believe me. Please."

Fox looked at the hook of his nose and deep set eyes, the curl of the thin lips in a passionate face. Determined.

Fox took the package and stepped away from Thurloe who put out a hand to hold him back.

"Your boat for France is the Arethusa. From Spice Quay, on the tide."

Fox shook his arm free.

"My boat is neither the Arethusa nor the Rose of England. I go my own way, Thurloe." And he stepped into the dark.

Somewhere a woman screamed once and a dog yelped. Still nothing moved on Spice Quay save the green light in the chandler's window. It guttered out.

8

Three men, dressed head to toe in black, rode along the dried-up track. There was the promise of spring in the hedges. Cow parsley, pimpernel and thick old man's beard were flowering, a blackbird sang while, distantly, a cuckoo began its call.

The dark clad men rode remorselessly on, past a crumbling wattle and daub farm cottage and on, away from the yapping dogs that snapped at their heels until the leading man slashed viciously at them with his whip. The boldest dog retreated, whining from the cut.

They rode on without faltering, past a group of women coming from the nearby river with washing piled in rough baskets. They rode by them as if they were not there.

One of the group, a girl, raised her hand in greeting to the strangers. The leader looked across at the girl and her hand fell to her side as she caught his cold eyes. She looked away in sudden fear as the rider smiled like ice. The men rode by without another glance.

They had been long in the saddle but nothing slowed their journey. They had business to see to, questions to ask and answers to demand. The leader looked back as the two men riding behind him kept on coming. The leader didn't smile . . . didn't acknowledge the other two.

He turned back in his saddle and rode on towards the declining sun. They had God's work to do and the King's warrant to do it.

In London, the demands of that King from the House of Commons made the members restless . . . The apprentices and others in the streets were already coming out in discontented mobs. Marauding the streets from time to time, the monster of civil unrest was beginning to flex its muscles.

The men in the Commons, dull men from the country and the equally dull city lawyers and old soldiers, older men from even older families were tired of being made to pay revenues to the King for hopeless expeditions to France led by incompetent primping men like My Lord Buckingham.

More, those lawyers and merchants, those of good and ancient lines, those men who believed in a personal God and a personal faith were also sick of the demands from the King for more taxes and by the King's refusal to offer something in return.

No taxation without representation were words they whispered amongst themselves. The rumblings in the belly of the beast were becoming louder.

It was April and the ancient rituals of the land, the villages and the small towns went on, never changing. The further from the centre, the less the rumblings in London were heeded. So, in the steep valleys leading to Shropshire, life went on as it always had.

In sawyers' yards and farms, in inns and cottages, in tanners' pits and brew houses, in coopers' yards and amongst the ancient higgledy piggledy streets of village and market town, life and death moved inexorably. Patient as cows.

The three men rode large horses with a pack mule dragging behind, away from the lush countryside around Worcester and, following rumour and story and whispered information, on towards the Welsh borders, the hills and valleys leading up to the Devil's Armchair and the Long Mynd.

Matthew Hopkins, the leader, reined in his horse and stopped to look back along the wide river valley and on up into the inhospitable countryside ahead. Thirty two, pale faced and with the scrawny neck of a grebe, Hopkins carried in his saddle bag a Bible, a book of signs and portents and a pair of metal tongs.

His hands were long and pale and thin. Unused to manual work. More suited it would seem, to a cloister or a lawyer's office. Hands as narrow as his mind.

He had the cold blue eyes, the pale lips and the thin face of a fanatic. His hair was shorn to a pale halo on his scalp. He sat his horse in the black cloak and doublet, black hose and shoes with silver buckles and looked about him and saw nothing of the beauty around him. He cared nothing for the people he took and condemned. His work was God's work and he was well paid. As often as not he was paid by the Devil's victims to ensure a quick departure from the world and the pain he brought with him.

It was in Evesham he first heard a rumour that the cattle in a market town in the Welsh Marches had fallen sick. There had been seen huge flocks of crows . . . unusual in size and number.

Then at a fair in Stourbridge and another in Bewdley, Hopkins heard stories of sheep run mad. Then of a horse dying savaged by some huge clawed beast. The signs were there for sure and then, in Worcester, a young man had come to see him with some serious information. Hopkins smiled coldly at the memory of the terrified young man with the Bible name, Saul.

He clicked up his horse and rode on towards the purple haze that was the rocky moorland where his business would take him.

Hopkins was a wrestler for souls. Wherever the Devil had his way, Hopkins came and took him by the throat. Hopkins wrestled for the souls of those who sold themselves to Satan. To do that work he carried the King's Charter and was empowered to act as he saw right and proper in the pursuit of it.

For Hopkins and his companions were witchfinders who knew they had divine access to the souls of those who'd admit . . . those who'd confess.

Confession was the work of the two men riding behind him. Confession must be wrung from any accused of congress with the Devil, for their soul's sake.

Hopkins hunted down the Devil with fanatical fervour. Why would he notice the pale pink dog roses or the dew-spangled spiders' webs in the hedgerows?

He rode on towards the seat of the rumours he'd first heard five weeks before. An older man who looked uncommonly like a relative of the young man called Saul came into the inn where he was waiting to burn a woman who finally cheated them by dying at her own hand in a dark cell.

The man came with a tale of dead cows, dying sheep, flocks of crows, a plague of frogs, wells running dry that never ran dry.

Hopkins had promised never to reveal the man's name and equally, had promised to come about his business if he sent more information. There was a real need or the Devil would gain such a foothold as might take years to exterminate. A woman's name was mentioned when the young man with the bible name came to him.

49

So he rode through the spring morning while over his head larks sang and swallows darted as they came back to old nests under ancient eaves.

The men came quietly to the village, rode straight to the small inn and took lodgings for the night. No-one appeared to know who these strangers were.

Not yet.

9

Pierre Henri smiled at Fox over the rim of his goblet. "It's madness, my friend. Why would he send you out here at this time of the year when there's nothing to see, nothing ready to buy you don't already know about, nothing. We pruned the vines back early and now we wait. That's how it is."

He sipped at the rich red wine that glinted in the light from the fire.

Henri had been a good friend to Fox over the years. They had discovered early on that Fox had known Henri's son when he was a mercenary soldier. Fox had been with the young man when he died under the bloody saw of a field surgeon.

Fox stared at the fire and remembered the young French soldier with the leg half shot away. The surgeons had done their worst and butchered the leg completely off. Then they had moved on to the next with the same vile saws and knives. The boy died, of course. Fox shook his head to rid it of the image of eyes staring, teeth clamped onto the leather pad as the saw bit.

He had never told the boy's father the truth and always said he'd died of a gunshot wound to the head in a field in Austria. Or was it Prussia? There had been so many such fields. Fox had admired the boy for his courage.

Now they never talked about the coincidence but it brought them close and Fox had learned about the wine trade from a good teacher. What

Henri didn't know about wine was not worth knowing . . . from planting to pruning, from cooperage to racking, from blending to tasting.

"I am an expert, I admit it," he'd say without any modesty and then he would roar with laughter. "And I am a Gascon and we always know best."

The thin faced, sun-burned man poured another glass of the dark wine for himself. Pierre Henri patted Fox's hand and they sat for a moment in silence.

"Since you've been coming to discuss the vintage, to learn, at my unworthy hands something of the mystery of wine, I have been a happier man. To find an Englishman who can speak my language . . . it is always a pleasure when you arrive here. At this time it is also a surprise."

He sat back from the table on which the debris of a fine meal lay scattered. In the house behind the Relais du Pont de Pierre they had eaten very well and drunk even better. The local goose and a fine foie gras, early spring vegetables and a purée of beans from Tarbes, followed by peaches bottled in Armagnac. It was a fine meal.

The thin man smiled at Fox as he swirled his wine around the deep glass before sniffing it and then drinking.

"Why, my friend? You must ask yourself. Do you trust your uncle?"
Fox shrugged.
"You know me and my wife's uncle."
The thin man nodded.

"He is not . . . *sympathique*. Not *comme il faut*. The world goes round if we trust each other. I trust you my boy. The other . . . well . . ."
Fox nodded and drank. "I know . . . I know."

"Was there another reason? Something he's not sharing with you perhaps. Something he wanted to do behind your back?"

The Frenchman worried at the idea as the Pyrenean sheep dog worried at the bone under the wooden table.

"He asked you to discuss the tariffs for the freight which were already agreed with him last autumn. I have the papers. I remember we had an argument. He was shaving my profit to nothing and I told him so. But he came on purpose for that. So why now does he send you to do the same business over again? It makes no sense."

"God, but I am sick of him. I swear I have nearly gutted him a time or two . . . But for my gentle wife I would have, I promise you."

Pierre Henri grinned. "And few would mourn him," he said. "I don't understand this faith . . . this religion of your wife's that seems to turn blood to water."

Fox put his hand up to stop the Frenchman and failed.

52

"No, Jean. A man must fight sometimes . . . stand for himself, for what he believes in. If necessary, kill to protect his own. You were a soldier so how can you believe this milk and bread, wish-wash religion?"

Fox shrugged.

"I love my wife, Pierre, and maybe I saw too much killing. Maybe when I saw my friend spitted on his own knife. Maybe I needed her to tell me. I swore then that if I lived I would go back to her, to marry her. She already had my daughter. I swore I'd to try to belong to her faith. It's very hard."

The Frenchman laughed.

"It's not natural, my friend. You cannot forget soldiers' ways."

"Maybe. I do know I have this feeling . . . this itch. Something I haven't felt since I was in the army. My mother used to say. "Beware that itch. Be wary, my son," she'd say. I feel it now as I've felt in the field, even in battle."

Pierre said nothing. He looked away and then back at his young friend.

Fox stared and slowly put the glass down.

"You know something, Pierre?" he asked.

The Frenchman hesitated and then leaned across the table towards the man facing him.

"It is no secret that he does not love you as a man should love his family. You marry his niece . . . you are family. Yet I have noticed, others have noticed also," the Frenchman went on, "He talks about his dreams for his son and your daughter. It's true, Fox"

Fox stared at the man - unseeing.

"Here when he has had too much Armagnac and his tongue is loose, he talks about the land your wife has, which he claims is his. He says he will get it back one way or another. Sometimes he says too much. Is that why he'd want you out of the way, my friend?"

"I will see them both roast in hell first." Fox slammed his fist onto the table and the glasses danced . . .

"You must heed the warning. Your mother was right," said Pierre. "And you have other matters to attend to here, I think."

The sharp eyes fixed Fox's for a moment and then lifted away as lightly as a bird.

"I see it in your eyes. You want to go home fast and yet . . . Yet you're trapped. I see it."

It was true he was trapped here. He had to make contact with the agent and do Black Tom's work. When it was done he'd be free to go. First he had to step again into the killing fields and only then could he go home and take the killing fields with him if anything had happened to his daughter.

"I need something from you, my friend," Fox said. "A pistol and some bullets. I don't keep them in the house in England any longer. My wife abominates them. I think perhaps I might have need. I can't tell you why."

"Of course, my boy," said the Frenchman. "Wait."

He left the room, limping slightly from an arthritic hip. Distantly a church clock chimed. Fox stretched a little and stood. He had a short walk to get to his lodging. The French so rarely asked you to sleep in their houses.

It'd taken a year before they'd even eaten together in the kitchen of Pierre Henri's home. He was a firm friend, but despite that, Fox wouldn't mention the letter he had to deliver.

He looked about the warm panelled room where the firelight glinted on the polished walnut. Thurloe's contact had little time to meet him. Fox intended to begin the journey home tomorrow morning. He'd find out what Alison's damned uncle was doing.

The old man returned with a wooden box on his arm. The corners of the box were brass inlaid scrolls and an initial 'P' in the centre of the tortoiseshell lid.

Pierre put the box onto the table and flicked the catch. He revealed a pair of superbly crafted pistols. Their butts bulbous and scored to make a firm grip, the blued steel of the barrels glinting in the firelight were exquisitely chased and inlaid with silver scroll work. German, by the look of them.

In the lid a powder horn, a bullet mould, a compartment filled with lead balls and another with wads of paper to hold the balls in place. The whole lined with dark blue velvet.

Fox took the pistol offered by his friend and found that the balance was perfect, the trigger guard was fine . . . the weight ideal. He handed it back reluctantly.

"I can't take that. I can't. They're magnificent. Thank you all the same."

"They were for my son, John Fox. He'd want you to have them. They may save your life. Please give an old man some pleasure. Take them."

Fox hesitated only a moment; took the box, closed it and leaned down and embraced his friend.

"Thank you," he said and took his cloak from the chair by the window. "We're both tired and I start early tomorrow. I will take care of them I promise you."

54

"I hope you haven't forgotten how to use them. Since you've become a religious man? Milk and water, Fox."

For an instant the older man looked into Fox's cold eyes and held up his hands as if to ward off what he saw in them.

"I will be on the road tomorrow," Fox said.

"Where will you stay?"

"I'll find a place," Fox said quietly

They stepped out into the hall together and Fox opened the door to the yard . . . the Frenchman watched Fox move off into the dark, then closed the door and walked back to the Armagnac and memories. He shivered. Perhaps it was the cold lifting from the river, etched into old bones.

Fox walked along the Quais. To his right the vast Garonne swept by majestically. A few glittering lights moved. Barges looking for a berth late at night while others moored on the far bank.

Further down beyond the Bridge of St. Pierre the sea-going boats waited for cargoes. Distantly the sound of a fiddle and of a man singing. On his left, the high dark warehouses. Their double doors on the first floor opening onto the quayside, over each a gibbet on which to weigh up cargoes or to lower barrels of oil, salt fish, wine for the North European trade . . .

The smells of fish and oil and wine a gut-heaving, almost tactile, assault. Beyond the river the slopes of vines curving across the land which at this time of the year were gnarled fists with one or, at most, two short shoots already trained across the taut strings that held them year on year.

In the city beyond the warehouses a bell sounded. The clock in the tower of L'Eglise St. Michel sounding the hour.

Fox turned quickly up a dark street. Overhead the houses hung and dripped the sea mist damp down onto his head from balconies that, in summer, would be a mass of flowers . . .

He emerged into a square alongside which reared the walls of the city. Beyond them he could smell the salt and the brackish air of the marshes of the Landes. He turned to the East and knew that beyond the low slopes lay a land of sweet chestnuts, tiny villages and hamlets built of honey-warm stone with cobbled streets that petered out into the mud and puddles of winter and the dust bowls of summer.

Fox nagged at the thought that Alison's uncle had deliberately sent him out of the way; at the monstrous idea of Saul with Rebecca. He dared not believe it. Had her uncle sent the two men to make cat's meat of him? Or had it been just the work of some footpad?

Bordeaux slept.

10

Fox had come to the inn at eleven. The inn had stables across the yard and a dormitory for poorer guests and stable lads over the horses. For the lesser servants of guests there would be straw in a barn perhaps. It wasn't Fox's concern.

He'd walked into the inn past the main public room, which was roughly furnished with heavy tables, chairs and long benches against the walls, stuffed heads of wild boar and deer hanging and catching the light from the fire.

He'd seen no face he recognised as he sat in the darkest corner of the room and drank an Armagnac before slipping upstairs.

He'd taken the message from amongst his business papers and shoved it roughly into his saddle bag after burning its envelope. But first he'd carefully placed the unbroken seal in a small bone pill box wrapped for safety in silk.

Should anyone want to steal the official message they'd hardly look for a dog-eared paper stuck amongst business documents. It would be even more readily passed over if it looked a trifle dirty and misused. Anyone searching for the dispatches would expect a seal at least.

It was a raw night outside and in the room he'd allowed the fire to die down.

It was four in the morning when he woke to a steady drip of rain from the balcony outside his window. Then he was aware of something scratching at the door of his room. He had placed a chair under the handle of the door, left the windows wide open and remained in his clothes. It was no hardship for a man used to sleeping in the open for days on end.

The scratching stopped for a moment and then came back stronger. Fox slid off the bed, took the long dagger from beside the bed and one of the pistols he'd borrowed from his French friend. It was primed and ready when he laid it on the table near the door.

Nothing had happened since the attack in England but it was as well to have a care until he'd delivered the letter that others might want as badly as the agent he was supposed to give it to.

He'd read it, of course. It named names in roundabout ways, talked of 'our mistress' and clearly meant the Queen. It talked of cousins and favourite dogs and clearly meant particular people.

It was a letter that told as much as it asked of the agent into whose hands it was to go and would be a dangerous tool if the wrong eyes saw it.

He slid silently out of bed and lit a candle from the ashes of the fire and stood it on the mantle where it would cast enough light for him to see what he'd skewered if it came to it.

Silently he removed the chair that he'd propped under the latch. He stepped aside so that when the door opened he'd be standing with his back to the wall behind it.

Fox could feel the pulse at his forehead began to beat a little faster. He felt the steadiness of his hands and smiled as he waited. You don't lose all your skills, he thought. The door was gently pushed open.

A dark figure stepped, hesitantly, into the room. Fox closed the door behind the figure. As it swung heavily shut the figure turned to him with hands out and clearly empty.

"There was something I wanted," she said with the familiar hint of an Irish brogue.

Fox began to laugh. "It's on the bed," he said. "And if you came to take it, I'll have to kill you."

The girl threw back the shawl that covered her head. Fox closed and latched the door, walked to the armoire in the corner, opened it and took out a bottle of Armagnac and two thick glass goblets.

"And there is a man wants to see you," she said. "If you know Black Tom, that is." Contact was made at last.

"And no doubt you can take me to him down these dark streets. Would I trust you?" he asked her.

Her dark green eyes smiled thanks as he handed her a glass.

"No," she said. And lifted her drink and drank it in one. He did the same and waited.

"Have you any food?" she asked. "I've ridden a way today and had nothing."

He found her some bread and cheese which she wolfed down as she talked.

"Thurloe wanted me to warn the contact here that you were coming. The meeting will not be in Bordeaux. It's full of eyes and ears, the contact says. If he's seen talking to you he claims he'd be compromised and a rich source will wither on the bough. There is a place, a day's ride . . . A night and a day if we like . . . There will be a meeting there."

Fox looked at the girl as she ate.

He saw the light on her pale skin and the beauty of her eyes and her body a promise under the cloak she wore yet in the cold room. She seemed to travel alone, carried no baggage and was free as the wind.

What was she . . . whore, travelling player, gypsy . . . what? Whatever she was, she was lovely.

"D'you always sleep in the wind?" she asked, staring out of the window and pulling her cloak closer.

"Who the hell are you?" he asked. She shrugged, poured more Armagnac and sat down near the fire after laying her cloak aside.

Her throat arched up from the wide neck of a pale shirt under which her breasts were firm and high. Her dark auburn hair lay loose over her shoulders. She smiled at him cynically.

"I'm who I want to be. What would you tell me about yourself I didn't know from looking at you, sir?"

"So who am I?" he asked.

"A soldier once. A man . . . once, brave . . . once."

He said nothing. Waited. She looked into his face and he saw the intensity of her eyes and the buried passion lying there.

"And not now a soldier, and only half a man perhaps. Not doing what he wants to do. Not taking his freedom with both hands. For what? A woman's trap. I take my freedom, friend and God knows that is hard for any woman to do. So some say I'm whore, or thief, or vagabond, gypsy . . . or worse."

"Are they right?" he asked. She shrugged.

"Am I?" she asked.

"You have no reason for thinking me less a man because I try to follow Christ's way. Because my wife leads me in it. She has a right to what she wants. Are you a whore?"

"Well," she said, "You refused me the last time I was in your room. You want me now, sir?"

He nodded once. And the smile left her face. Snuffed out. Fox went on,

"I'd be a liar to say I didn't want you, though I don't trust you. Nor understand who you are or who you hunt with."

"You," she said. "For the moment."

She stood up and walked to him and stared down at him. His hands held her waist and she touched his face once with her right hand. In her left a blade appeared.

"Trust no-one, Fox," she said. "No-one"

There was a moment and then he began to smile and then to laugh and she laughed too and leaned down to him and stopped his laughter with a kiss and he threw her across the bed.

"You bitch," he said.

"Fox," she said, smiling, "You've been buried alive and lived too long away from life."

She stayed on her back on the bed as he looked down at her.

"You want me and only that milk and water wife prevents it."

"No," he said gently. "My word prevents it. I gave my word to try for her sake and our Lord's sake. I gave my word while she lives . . . "

He poured Armagnac for himself and drank it and she watched him and smiled.

"It seems a shame," she said. And reached for his glass. He gave it to her and she drank.

You know," he said, "You seem so sad. You push and push and push, Maeve Ahern . . . to prove what? That you're free? You pay a price. Now you have a message for me to meet him where?"

She stood in the pale light from the candle and began to unlace the front of her dress, never once taking her eyes off him. Her mouth a mocking half smile and her green eyes dancing in the light.

He stepped to her as she opened the top of her dress to reveal the firm breasts, the dark hard nipples, pointing . . . eager . . .

"No girl. No."

Fox put a hand on hers as it pulled a lace and stopped her. His hand was as gentle as any woman's hand.

"I've a woman as trusts me but I'm still a man," he said.

"You've a strange way of showing it, Fox" she said.

Bitterly he looked at her and shook his head.

"I had my fill of women like you when I was a soldier. You're a whore or a messenger, a slut of Thurloe's or of any riff raff from the riverside. I don't give a spit i'the wind. Go back to them and I'll tell Thurloe you did what you were paid for."

The girl pulled her dress about her and shook her head in wonder.

"Milk and water, they said, and it's true this wife has unmanned you."

"You say you're free," he said. "You pay a price for it." He spoke quietly now. "Trust is a powerful cage, Maeve, for a man like me," he added.

"She's trying to show me a way, a better way than the way soldiers go. To give, to give and to be faithful to the giver. It's a hard lesson that I may never learn and one you'll never know. I won't see you again. If I do I might end your whoring with a blade across your face."

She picked up her cloak and looked at him almost tenderly.

"No you won't, Fox. No you won't."

Fox smiled then and she smiled too.

"You have a message for me to meet a man. Where?" he asked.

"At the Sign of the Ram in Niort. It's a long ride. He'll see you there."

"And if it's not the right man? "

"It will be the right man. I know him. But if it were not you'd have to kill him I suppose. Could you do that?"

He smiled at her again.

"The soldier's not lost then . . . entirely?" The girl said mockingly and went quietly from the room.

He stood, regretting his promises. Knowing that behind her eyes was a desperation born of sadness. And this desire he felt was hardly a transitory thing which is what the men and women in the meeting house claimed. She was beautiful, this whore . . . and a mystery.

Below his window a muffled bell chimed the half and a barge with a dim lantern moved on the far bank of the river, a shadow under the fog.

11

Beyond the port of La Rochelle, inland over the pale earth, the sky was high, pale and cloudless. Narrow lanes and tracks cut across the countryside leading to tiny hamlets, occasional farms and small villages all built of dun coloured stone. Even the spring foliage in the trees was muted by the brightness of the early morning sunlight.

In the distance, a lone rider made his way along the coast road from La Rochelle heading north to a meeting with one Major Marian, deep in the Marais. The Major was Thurloe's agent amongst the English Royalists in France. The rider turned along a rutted track between the soft and pale fields. He seemed to be familiar with the road he was taking and seemed to be in no hurry to arrive.

At the same time, an auburn haired girl left the wagon of the market trader who'd given her a lift into La Rochelle. There were few people in the streets that led down to the fishing port.

In the narrow street beyond the Gate of St. Pierre, traders were already setting out fruit and vegetables . . . a butcher was preparing a freshly slaughtered sheep and blood ran over the cobbles and attracted thin dogs and cats.

The butcher kicked a dog aside, drew out the offal from the sheep and threw it onto a pile of steaming entrails in a barrel by the stall.

The girl slipped past him, under an arch, into an even narrower street. She stopped and stood for a time in the shadow of an ancient doorway, watching the entrance to the alley she had come through. No-one followed her, so she turned and walked to a wooden door, grey with age and lack of paint, the grain springing open in dark delicate lines. She hammered on it urgently.

"Mother of God, let him be in," she whispered. "He has to be at that meeting with the damned soldier in good time."

For a moment she smiled at the memory of the earnest man who'd refused her. She was amazed at the thought of what Major Marian might say if he knew she'd made the other man an offer, for he was a jealous lover and a dangerous enemy.

She turned back to hammer on the door again and realised it had been open. Glancing back down the alley, she slipped inside, turned the latch and walked softly across the dark hall.

The wooden panels were of another age, the stairs that curved up to the main apartments, lit by early morning light leaking in from windows set deep in the ancient stone walls.

She stood for a moment in the gloom and could hear her own breathing. She stepped onto the first tread of the stairs and shivered.

"'Tis the angel of death and his wing touching you," her mother used to say. The girl moved on up the stairs and stepped across the wooden landing in the silent house. A door opened and a cat ran past the girl and away down the stairs . . . silently.

For a moment her heart stopped then she moved on. She had work to do and Maeve Ahern was not afraid of work. It was paid for and it appealed to the wildness in her.

The door to the room from which the cat had come was ajar. It was her lover's bedroom. For the first time she had forebodings about what she might find.

In her right hand she carried the blade she always used. Sharp, small and deadly. Five inches of honed steel was enough to snuff out the largest attacker. Get close enough and it was easy done, she knew. She'd done it before and men made it easy for they were happy to get close . . .

She stepped quickly into the room and moved fast to the left as she pushed the door hard open to her right. It would give her a moment if anyone was waiting for her.

The curtains across the long windows were drawn which left the bed and the furniture beyond the door in dark shadow. She was tempted to open the curtains and only prevented herself by an act of huge willpower. She would have to deal with the dark. If she opened the curtains she signalled to any watcher that she was there.

She waited for her eyes to adjust and as she waited she looked about the room. Beside the window she knew there was a long mirror, beside the large bed a table holding a candle and usually a book. Marian was a great reader. They'd often laughed about it. She read little. He'd a taste for Shakespeare and that amused them both.

"Marlowe was all very well . . . But there's little subtlety in tragedy with bodies piled floor to ceiling," he'd say and she would take the book from his hand and make him notice her.

She moved then towards the bed and felt, for the first time, under her foot a slight stickiness. Then she caught the smell, blood and piss and . . .

She pulled aside the curtains round the bed and saw a huddled mass on the bed. As her eyes adjusted to the light she saw that the dark mass was not a pillow or cushions but a naked figure. Tied.

She moved the curtain a fraction and pale sunlight leaked into the room and she could see then how hard he'd died. The poker in the still warm ashes, the burns on his naked feet, his thighs, his stomach covered in weals and then . . . then . . . Sweet Jesus!

Whoever had been here had been merciless. Scattered about the bed were papers and envelopes, scattered about the floor torn books and more papers . . . There was nothing that had not been looked into. She prayed that he'd said nothing before he died but she doubted any man could stay silent through what they had done to him.

She found his coat thrust under the bed and quickly searched the pockets. Found a soft leather purse, opened it, saw gold, took it and dropped the coat back under the bed into the sticky pool of blood that now stained her hands. She wiped them on the sheet.

She'd learned when she was no more than a girl that it paid nothing but pain to care too much for any human being. She'd seen her mother and father burned out of their home. Her brothers talked about marrying her off to some English lordeen who lusted after her. And if not married, they'd've lent her to him for the price of a sack of potatoes. So she'd taken the coppers from the pot in the back of the hearth and a gold ring of her father's and left.

She'd gone from Renvyle and the wild waters of the Atlantic south to Cork and away, for the promise of her body for an hour's pleasuring, by boat for Roscoff. The man betrayed her and left her in Wales . . . and she none the wiser . . .

She'd learned never to trust any man and then a woman took her in, befriended her in London and stole her last coins . . . so she'd learned not to trust women either. Take what you can, give nothing and, if it looks like you're caring, run.

64

Now she looked once more at the scream frozen on the face of the man on the bed and could remember little of his eager thrusting body on hers, little of his hands touching her to a heat, nothing of his promises. Hadn't he abandoned them by dying?

And now that taciturn, strange man, Fox, was in danger. For the man in the bed was Major Marian the agent Fox was due to meet. Someone had no doubt taken his place and would collect the messages Fox carried and these would no doubt betray Thurloe's spy in the French Court.

Maeve gave not a spit for the politics but the man, Fox, was interesting enough and hurting in some way and she knew he was one of her sort.

She closed the door softly, slipped along the landing to the stair head, hesitated and then walked down the wooden staircase, eased out of the front door into the alley and quickly moved into the gathering crowd of shoppers at the market.

The butcher was hanging livers and lungs on the front of his barrow. She passed the steaming meat and vanished into the narrow cobbled streets. She'd need a horse for Fox was in grave danger.

She knew also that if she failed should Thurloe hear, she'd be a marked women. She feared that young, ice-cold man more than she feared death.

She had to get to Niort . . . near the abbey . . . at the Sign of the Ram, find Fox, and warn him before a man calling himself Major Marian made contact and gave the codes they had no doubt extracted from her lover.

They'd been merciful in their way for after they'd finished with him, he'd've wished to die.

12

They'd been in the village two days and said nothing to anyone. They'd ridden off the day after they arrived along the valley and then up onto the desolate land that led to the ancient rocks forming a huge armchair overlooking the purple space. The villagers called it The Devil's Armchair.

Two village boys followed them and reported to Michael, Alison's uncle, that the three men had stood by their horses for an hour and talked. Then they turned away from the stones and rode back down towards the valley.

They'd stopped at Old Mother Baugh's hovel and she screamed at them and they threw her aside and searched the hovel and the cave behind it. They'd ridden back with the terrified old woman who was crying and shaking and mumbling the way she did.

When the men rode back, many were shocked by what they saw. The old woman was tied by a halter to the saddle of a horse and crying with fear as they rode into the centre to the village. Michael was in Alison's kitchen when the boys came back and told him.

He had been warning Alison that men, once bitten by the need to run wild, never lose the desire. He never lost the opportunity to abuse her husband.

"He'll never settle to the life here. You'll see. You may think he's milk and honey since he came home. You may feel he'll stay for ever but mark me, he'll go. He'll leave you . . . Men like him always do in the end."

Alison laughed in his face.

"Maybe but for now he's stayed. And you wanted me to marry any one'd take me when I carried his child. Even your own, son."

"I offered him to save your shame. And you refused. Brazen it was. Brazen!"

"It was your shame you were concerned for but there was more than my shame. You wanted my land and my father's house. You'd rather I'd gone to Mother Baugh and let her finish the child for me? And die, like as not?"

"How can you say that, Alison? Didn't I take you in when your father died and . . ."

Alison turned then and interrupted him angrily.

". . . You took me in? You were only concerned to get your hands on this place. You were never concerned about my father, never stepped near us when he was sick, when I was carrying the farm. Just came sniffing round like a dog on heat. Rebecca was a child then. And your son can stay away from Rebecca too or John will geld him."

Her uncle turned away from her anger. He stared out of the window across the neat yard and over to the byre with the cows feeding and the stable where she kept three good strong horses for the plough. It was true that this was a good farm and a fine old house. He did want it and he would get it yet.

"What'll you do if he doesn't come back?"

"He will come back," she laughed in a sort of triumph. "He will come back."

Michael was aware, for the first time of how much her man meant to her. Well, by the time all this was over they'd have to find each other in another place.

"Don't worry Uncle. John will do the business you sent him on and be back in a month . . . less maybe. He promised Rebecca and me."

"And that's another thing . . . Rebecca."

Alison stopped chopping the carrots and looked at him sharply.

"I told you keep Saul away from her. Well?"

"She's getting talked of. Headstrong and rude and . . ."

"Rude? Who was she rude to?"

"Me!" he said. "Me! She refused me when I told her I wanted to see her looking a mite tidier about the village and to mind not to speak to them beneath her and she laughed in my face at that."

Alison smiled at the angry puffed up man.

"I seem to remember, Uncle, you said the same to me and I said the same to you when I was a girl of Rebecca's age."

"And that's another thing. She should be married or promised to someone. She's old enough."

"How d'you know she isn't promised already?" Alison asked and he turned to her in anger.

"I'll have something to say in that matter. It might be my son will think she'd suit him."

Alison stared at him open mouthed

"Have you heard me? I mean it. John will geld Saul if he so much as looks at her. You surely over reach yourself, Uncle. Saul's old before his time. Anyway Rebecca's not marrying anyone yet and when she does, it will be between her and me and her father. You'll have nothing to say in the matter."

Michael turned quickly away from the window as a man rode into the yard.

"Who is it . . . who is it?" Alison moved angrily to the door as Matthew Hopkins walked past the dogs and chickens and came into the house. He brushed past Alison with barely a glance.

She watched him as he put his hat on the table and as her uncle greeted him nervously. He pretended they didn't know each other but Alison saw that this was show. She watched the man as he looked about the room. He's afraid of women, she thought. He smiled thinly at Michael.

"My house, sir, were you asked into my house?" she stood at the head of the table and he then glanced at her and back at Michael.

"My niece. Alison, this is Mr. Hopkins. He has warrants direct from the King, so mind your tongue."

"Not warrants to walk into my house, he doesn't."

"To walk in anywhere I choose, mistress." He barely looked at her and turned to Michael. "There no doubt there is an infection in this place, sir. You did well to send for us to root it out," he said.

"What infection would that be, Uncle?" Alison asked.

Michael blustered, "I know there are bad things done in this village, Alison. Things you may not understand. Mr Hopkins will root it out and we will be safe from the Devil's evil."

"What Devil's evil? Who?" asked Alison, and she whirled across the room to confront the stranger who even now could not look her in the eyes. "Who?" she asked.

"The old woman up the valley is tainted with it and she will cry out names for us." He turned away from her and held out his gloved hand. "I need the keys to the market hall and the cellar. My men and I will work from there. You have the keys?"

"That old woman is harmless. Mother Baugh is old and harmless and would no more hurt a fly as harm anyone."

"We've brought her back with us."

"Whatever for? She's a little addled in the brain is all."

Hopkins stared at her now with pale grey eyes.

"Have a care, mistress. You don't know what you speak of."

He looked across at Michael.

"I want the keys. My warrant says any official must help me or incur the King's displeasure. So . . . keys!"

He left without another word to Alison. He had the keys in his hand.

Alison slammed the vegetable knife down onto the table as soon as he had left them.

"What the devil is he doing? I know the old woman. You know her as well as I do, Uncle. She's sick in the head maybe, but has medicines and simples for any who need them. Cures sickness in cattle . . . Men here will attest to that. There's no harm in her, Uncle. You know her. Who cured your chin cough? She did. Who bound up Saul's leg when he cut it so badly? She did. Tell him. Why has he taken her?"

Michael shook his head.

"It would be best to mind your own business, Alison. That man's here on God's business. I warn you . . . avoid him and his men, avoid them like the plague."

He left his niece and walked out into the yard and Alison watched him go.

Later, when the sun had gone down, Michael walked through the dark lanes past the Market Hall. A lantern burned in a window there. He walked on out of the silent village. A dog moaned in the distance. A fox yelped once and then again amongst the trees.

Hopkins waited at the end of the lane outside the village near the spring and the well the people used for drinking water.

Michael came to him through the dark and the two men walked quietly away into the deeper shadows beyond the hedges and the well.

"You were right about the old woman, friend. We'll make her confess black is white."

Hopkins' pale skin was stretched tight over his cheekbones; the pale moonlight glittered in his eyes.

"Where are the others?" Michael asked, and Matthew Hopkins took his arm in a grip of iron. "I was just wondering . . . that's all sir . . ." said Michael.

"They're with the old woman. Night's a good time. She might be flying with the devil of course . . . But if not, it's a good time. The child that died . . . the baby? Something was said about a dead child."

"Buried with its mother."

Hopkins was angry now.

"When we talked you swore the mother lived and would tell all . . . I wanted to make my case before rooting it out neck and crop."

"The old woman will talk to you. I know she will."

Hopkins smiled a little and nodded once.

"She'll talk. Yes, she will. She'll tell what we want to hear, my friend. Believe me, she will. But show her the instruments and she will vent it all, filth and truth and fear and vileness. The devil's own fundament will be as her mouth. Put her to the question . . . ask her who else has made a compact with the Devil in this place. She'll tell us what we want her to tell us."

****

Old Mother Baugh sat on a stool in the dark room and stared up at the barred window. The moon had waned already and the stars were going out. She'd been afraid until she confessed all.

She felt better now she'd told them what they wanted to hear. How she'd given suck to the devil, cursed cattle, and horses, compassed the death of Goody Marshall and had danced the night she died in such pain. And the baby of course. They asked her about that. Told her what she'd done.

How her Master knew how to help those who worshipped him. She'd admitted all . . . confessed all. It was time to reveal others for their sakes and for her own soul. Tomorrow she would find the name they wanted to hear and she might be allowed to live.

It poured from her . . . vented as Hopkins had said it would. All the foul air and bile, all the filth and the lies she could tell to save her soul and her life.

70

13

The land began to fall away in front of Fox and his horse. His wide-brimmed, tall hat shadowed his stern face in which only his eyes were forever moving. He shifted in his saddle and looked back along the track low across the French marshes.

Behind him nothing moved and the sun slanted cross from his right. He was riding along a ridge and where the land fell away to his left there were occasional glints of water. Beyond the trees a tower stood out against the late morning sky.

The Monastery he was looking for stood on dry land amongst the slow moving rivers, surrounded by a morass of rushes and stunted oaks, falling willows and dense beds of rushes.

He turned off the ridge, left the sun behind him and rode down towards the water and the marshy places he knew and loved so well. It might have been the Somerset Levels that the he rode down to without hurrying, savouring the peace and the knowledge that danger stalked him. He was going into no-man's land and he lived for that.

Poor Alison would never understand, though he believed Rebecca might. He dared not acknowledge it even to himself when he was back at home. He could only taste the knowledge of it now. For hadn't he told Black Tom Fairfax it was only this one journey he would make?

He came down to a wide slow river where two cottages stood at the side of the path alongside a narrow ditch that drained into the river. On the other side he watched a heron waiting . . . waiting with its long beak and poised neck . . . waiting.

He took the narrow wooden bridge over the ditch and, looking to his right, saw a tunnel of trees arching over the green water in the ditch and where the ditch curved out of sight, a man paddled a punt trailing lines for fish.

It was the first human he'd seen since he left Bordeaux and he was happy for that.

He rode on along the river bank, past a village, past a few deserted and lonely cottages, on towards the monastery where he would find the house called The Sign of the Ram. Where he would meet Thurloe's man, pass him the message and be free to ride for Caen, to take a boat for Bristol and then ride home to his dear wife, gentle Alison.

Over the tall trees standing isolated in a sea of dark rushes a heron flapped its drooping wings as it trailed long yellow legs . . . The bird bent its flight to the left and came softly to rest in a dull flutter. In an instant it took one tentative step into the reeds, ducked its head and the vicious dark beak stabbed into the river mud . . .

Fox rode by and considered why he'd been attacked, who the woman was, who might betray him and why he'd spent time before he set off from Bordeaux with a sheet of paper and the seal carefully lifted from the original letter.

It was the first time he'd felt alive for so long. Pat Shea used to say "You take too long, friend, look behind you too often, check too much, think too much . . . plan too much . . ."

It might be the truth. It might be that he did but, he reflected sadly, he was alive yet and Pat, poor man, was not.

So he planned and considered and made arrangements in his mind as he tipped the seal from the pill box and lit a taper. He creased and folded the paper on which a new letter was written.

First he pricked holes a number of times in the corner of the sheet. He'd used a pin to make five pin holes undetectable unless you were looking for them. The fifth letter of a series, just as the original, which lay amongst his business papers in his saddle bag, was marked five.

He'd written a new letter and sealed it carefully, using the original seal, and put it away. He rode on, the trees and the ditches and herons and lakes and man-made cuts amongst the reeds of the Marais close around him. For a moment he thought of the Irish girl and of the women of the Levels and web footed men and mermaid's tails. And the water and the land and the sky were pale green and shimmering in the afternoon light.

14

Michael woke early and was working with two of his men preparing bills of lading for the next consignment of wine he'd ordered from France. The clerks were slow and Michael was nervous.

Hopkins walked into the clerks' room and Michael told the men to get on as he took the pale man into his inner office.

"Master Hopkins, good morning sir." He offered his hand.

Hopkins didn't take the merchant's hand but closed the door, walked to the window and looked out into the yard.

"A little something?" Michael's hand hovered over the brandy bottle that stood by a half-filled glass on his desk.

Hopkins didn't turn to him as he spoke.

"You want that farm . . . that woman's house . . . All of it?"

"It's mine by right . . ."

Hopkins turned then and looked at the eager face of the merchant.

"It comes closer then. The old woman mentioned Alison . . . Alison Fox . . . your niece. Accused her and her husband . . ."

Michael sat down drumming his fingers on the rough plank of the desk. He felt a need to use the rush of energy that swept through him.

"You'll drink, sir?" he asked.

"No. I came to tell you your niece is taken. I will expect you at the Market Hall, protesting, grief stricken . . . It would be best. The old woman accused her. This is to the good for it is known your niece befriended the old woman and took her food and even beer or cider from time to time. She brought the old woman to the Devil, her master.

She herself accuses your niece of leading her to the Devil's fundament. She may have saved her own soul. Now we must save your niece's."

Michael looked up.

"You sound almost as if you believe . . ."

The young man's pale eyes bored into Michael's then and he backed away from what he saw there.

"I must come to see her," he said and went to bustle past Hopkins who put at arm out to stop him.

"Not yet. I have her safe. You can go to her house and you will search it to see if you can find anything to help us. I'm sure you'll find something. A doll, a cat . . . something."

Michael was afraid now.

"You believe the old woman. Isn't that enough?" he said.

"We'd best be certain, don't you think? She smells of witchery and I have smelled enough to know. There was a baby born that died. This baby was to be given to Satan. Alison demanded it, the old woman says."

Michael was appalled and even more afraid.

"No-one in the village will believe that Alison would kill a baby."

"Do I concern myself with what the village believes? What your Master orders, so you do. She must confess it to be absolved. She will confess."

"And if she doesn't?"

"We will show her the tools and she will confess and if she refuse then we shall know what to do and we will do it."

"I never thought to put her to that."

"This is no game, sir. This is the Devil's playground and we must show him who is Master. You help, sir, or you too may find a question or two put to you. She is your niece after all and these things go in families as often as not."

"You can't believe that, I'd . . . my son brought you here . . . told you."

Hopkins shrugged and walked from the room. Michael opened the bottle and refilled his glass.

It was much later in the evening that Michael left the room and walked out of the village towards Alison's farm house. An owl hooted and swept by on silent white wings. In a window of the farm a light burned. He tapped at the door and called out his name, unlatched the door and went in. He found Rebecca sitting in the shadows of the room - wide awake.

He found another candle and lit it at the smouldering fire and turned to look at the girl. She was lovely in the candle light. Young, beautiful and very strong. She looked at her Uncle and waited.

"She won't be back for a time, Rebecca."

The girl said nothing yet continued to stare at him and to wait.

"It is a serious matter. You know who those men are that have come to the village?"

"Hopkins is a witchfinder. Yes. They came here this morning and took my mother. Why? They said they knew her to be in a compact with the Devil. It's a lie. Why don't you do something for her? I know you've just drunk all day. Even my cousin is upset. Why, Uncle?"

Michael reached for the girl. She backed away from him. He moved a step closer. She inched back until she was trapped by the angle of the wall. He moved then to touch her, to feel her. Put a soft hand on her arm and another on her breast.

Then he felt the aching slash of a blade slicing along his forearm opening the flesh like old meat.

He slapped at her, shoved her away and confronted the girl who held the blade up and ready. Her father had taught her well as he would have taught a son.

Michael cursed and cradled his bleeding arm. He took up a cloth from the table and bound the wound to stop the blood.

"That's my mother's shawl," the girl snarled.

"Where she's going she'll have no need to keep out the cold," he said and walked to the door. "You'll beg me yet to take you in, you bitch," he said.

"And if I tell who was the father of the baby that died?" asked the girl. "I know, you see. You think Mother Baugh talked to no-one? She talked to me and to my mother. I'll tell them who the father was. You, Uncle. And you'd have me to your whore if you could, wouldn't you? When my father hears, he'll know what to do with you."

He stood swaying, panting from the pain and from drink. Rebecca spat at his feet.

"When I have this house as my own you'll be lucky to find shelter in the kennels," he said and walked quickly out into the dark night leaving the girl to lock and bar the door. She also barred the windows and sat alone, staring into the dark, nursing the knife. Afraid.

15

The man calling himself Major Marian sat ramrod straight dressed head to foot in green with silver lace and gold edgings to his collar and cuffs. His sword, Fox noticed, had a plain serviceable hilt but the scabbard was covered in tooled leather and gold.

He leaned across the table in the corner of the small room behind the dining room at the Sign of the Ram. There could be no mistaking his man, Fox thought, as he closed the door after the servant who'd brought in a plate of cold pigeon and a bottle of their best wine.

The Major lifted a nonchalant hand and took the bottle, sniffed delicately at the cork and seemed surprised at its quality. He poured his own glass and put the bottle on the table in front of him. He offered nothing to Fox and even seemed surprised when he sat down opposite him and poured his own wine.

Fox had seen him first when he had taken his horse into the stables on his arrival in the small village. From the shadows the Major emerged and stared at Fox as he rubbed down his horse and found water and oats for her.

"Damn me if I'd do that . . . stable boys' work. You a stable boy?"

"I'm a soldier sir. Look after your horse and your weapons and you'll not come to much harm, my master used to say."

"Did he, be God? Did it serve?"

"I'm alive," said Fox quietly. He turned from his horse as he stepped into the afternoon light spreading through the stable door.

The Major nodded.

"So it seems. Tell me, how is Black Tom? Well?"

"Well enough, sir. And Anna his wife is too."

The big man roared with laughter. Fox watched him in surprise.

"These damn fool codes and greetings and formulas . . . Amusing, what?" said the Major. "Your brother had a cold on Thursday. That's it isn't it? And you say . . ."

"Not a cold, a fever," said Fox. It seemed he was the right man but surely he'd know that Fairfax's wife was called Alice, not Anna.

They moved out of the stable and into the Sign of the Ram where the Major demanded a private room. They were shown the room behind the dining room that Fox had already arranged.

The Major had also demanded a cold bird and a bottle of wine.

"Damned foolery, all these formulas. I meet you, I ask for a message and you give it to me and go packing . . . You do have the message I assume?" the big man asked.

Fox drank the wine and poured another glass and filled the Major's.

"They call you something, I believe. I was warned. A dour man. A man of God or some such, they said . . . 'The Preacher', was it?"

Fox waited. Surprised it seemed that anyone should say anything of that to anyone. He looked into the big man's eyes and nodded once.

"My wife, sir, is a Christian. She follows a small sect of peaceful people. I try to follow that path."

"A soldier turned peacemaker," the Major laughed. He poured another glass of wine for himself. "Tell me about yourself."

"There's nothing to tell, Major. Nothing."

"Come sir, you'll be back with messages from old Tom or whoever is his master. I forget his name. Come, sir, here . . . have a glass of wine. Eat a little . . . "

Fox poured a little more wine.

"Your health, peacemaker," the Major said. Fox looked into his mocking eyes as they drank.

****

A sea mist had drifted across the Marais and with the onset of darkness the track between the deep narrow canals became treacherous even for the most sure-footed of horses. The Irish girl cursed and, sliding from the horse she had stolen, walked until she came to a fisherman's hut beside the canal. She had a warning to deliver but she was not going to risk falling into a bog in the fog.

Stooping inside she pulled the horse in after her, hobbled her and made herself as comfortable as she could. She'd slept in worse, she thought. At least this was dry.

****

In the small room at the back of The Sign of the Ram the two men talked and drank, and drank some more. Fox emptied his glass and took another.

"It's a long time since I met anyone who'd served with Black Tom. Where were you?" he asked the Major.

The Major shrugged and made a vague gesture with his hands.

"Oh, Germany, Northern Italy . . . for a short time," he said, vaguely. "Where were you?"

Fox looked across and smiled.

"I was made a sergeant in the field by Black Tom." Fox said proudly and the big man looked at him patronisingly. He poured the sergeant more wine and Fox drank it down immediately.

"Indeed? I was with the cavalry, of course."

"Did you do the advance on the flank of the Austrians when Colonel Fairfax in a deuced hurry to outflank them was assaulted from all sides in that high valley? I heard it said he was damn near wiped out there . . . I heard he didn't bother to send out scouts? Is that true?"

The Major nodded and poured Fox more wine.

"He should never have advanced, drink up."

Fox obliged.

"Didn't he always act hastily?" Fox excused his Colonel.

The Major agreed that he did and motioned for Fox to drink up so he could refill his wine glass.

Fox said, "I heard it was bloody carnage under the guns when the regiment was marching along the valley after crossing the bridge. That once the colour party was over they raked the regiment with fire . . . I thank God I was out of his regiment by then."

"Where were you, Sergeant?"

"Oh, long gone. Home, I think. I don't remember much. 'Nother drink Major?"

The Major poured another glass. It was brandy now. He pushed it across the table at the soldier opposite him.

"You too, Major . . . come on man . . . drink up."

Fox drank and shoved his glass forward for another.

78

"I like a drop now and again. The wife gets angry but who gives a hoot for that? Thanks Major. Good stuff this . . ." And he drank another glass and smiled vacantly at the sneering face opposite him.

"You're in a bit of danger you . . . Anyone of them lot in the King's wife's court see you with me . . . Your life not worth a spit . . . Eh . . . eh? Here. I was told the message I have for you is something special. Something of a surprise . . . Something . . . 'Nother drink . . . ?"

"When you give me the message, then you can have another drink - Preacher."

Slowly Fox shook his head.

"You'll have to wait, Major . . ."

The drunken sergeant wagged a finger and smiled as if through a haze.

"I thought it best to take care. I know you're in danger from the King's wife's supporters in the Frenchies' court if they suspect you're passing information to men like Black Tom. They'd hunt you down no doubt."

"They would of course and treat me damned uncivilly," the Major laughed. "Have another drink, Sergeant." He poured another glass.

****

It began to rain across the Marais, a soft soaking drizzle coming in from the sea and enveloping the land in a mist. It was impossible even with the moon up to tell land from marsh or marsh from water . . . The auburn haired girl slept soundly in the barn.

In the small room at the Sign of the Ram, Fox lay in a stupor over the table and surrounding his head were a number of empty bottles and glasses and the debris of a meal.

Standing looking down at him the large man shook his head. He'd already searched through Fox's coat and found the sealed letter. He stared down at the snoring man with his head in a pool of stale wine.

He checked the seal on the letter, grinned and pushed it into the pocket of his long coat. Threw some coins onto the table and walked out. His masters would be pleased with this week's work. A shame the real Major Marian died under the question, but he'd given them enough to gull this drunken fool lying here. Black Tom Fairfax must be going soft to employ such a sot for a message boy.

He left the room, closed the door carefully and stepped out into the drizzling night.

16

Maeve Ahern was hissing with anger as Fox stared out into the early morning. His head ached a little but he was none the worse apart from that as he sat in the room at the inn.

"What in the name of the Devil and his sister were you doing? Drunk were you . . . drunk was it?"

"No," he said. "Not drunk at all. Remember what I do . . . I buy and sell wine. I drink and always have. I have never been drunk. They used to say I had hollow legs in the Regiment. Men won bets on me . . . I'm not proud of it but it's a fact. I let him think I was drunk . . . I let him take the letter."

"My friend died for that letter. Damn you!" said the girl. "It was that important and you let it go."

"No," said Fox. "Died, did you say?"

She nodded.

"I'm sorry," he said

"Don't be," she said. "He worked for all sides, a treacherous man. It's a treacherous world you're in, friend. Believe me."

He smiled at that.

"Yes, isn't it though?" he said.

"And you let him take the letter from your master in London. You said you knew he was an imposter?"

"I wanted him to take it. He had to take it. I knew he wasn't a friend of Black Tom's, nor never had been."

She wiped a dripping nose on her sleeve as she looked out of his window across the square.

"How did you know?" she asked eventually. She seemed tired.

"I named Tom's wife, the wrong name. He said nothing. I talked about an ambush in a high valley in Austria. About carnage and he agreed it was. There was no ambush and no carnage."

"Oh?" she said. "How d'you know that?"

"I was the scout that discovered the ambush and warned Black Tom not to make the advance. It's why he trusts me and why I knew that major was not the right man. Now, I think we must go . . ."

"But the letter? You let him take the letter?"

"I wrote another. In it I mentioned that the information we had received from my lord Buckingham had been most useful and that the Parliament men in London were well pleased with his work."

Maeve began, at last, to smile.

"I sealed it with the seal from the other, the real letter, which is in my saddle bag amongst a mass of business papers."

And Fox began to laugh and she too began to laugh with him.

"It's time we went," he said.

The girl turned away from the window.

"Too late," she said and pointed into the courtyard as four men clattered into the yard below them. The Major was back and shouting at his men.

"I want him alive. We've some questions to ask him."

Fox glanced out of the window and saw that the Major was standing with a man who could have been his twin. Brothers, then.

Three of the men ran to the main door of the inn. Fox took up his saddle bag and dark cloak.

"Take my horse from the stable when they've gone. Get to the abbey over the bridge and wait there. They're only looking for me."

"But where will you hide?" she asked.

"I'm going where I know my ground. I'm going into the waterways and canals of the Marais," he told the girl. "I've been here eeling and wild fowling. I know it well enough to lose these men. So . . . go now."

The girl turned and walked slowly along the corridor. Fox watched her for a moment and admired the coolness with which she went towards the men who'd killed her lover. They were already pounding on the door.

He stepped down a narrow stair to the back of the house. Unchained the door and stepped out into the walled garden. As he ran, a dog began to bark and then another and another. He raced for the end of the garden.

He thanked God he'd spent time last night before he met the Major reconnoitering the area. Old skills, old habits.

He ducked down a short flight of steps and he found himself in a tunnel under the road. Almost as soon as he entered it he was out into a small orchard and running hard. At the end of the old trees there was dead ground and the narrow strip of water that would save him.

Behind him men were confronted by savage, snarling guard dogs. One yelped in pain as a blade cut him off.

Fox had vanished.

Two men ran under the road through the tunnel calling the others to join them. They came out quickly with swords at the ready and at the end of the orchard they found a rotting wooden jetty and beyond it a canopy of trees over the green weeds that covered the surface of a narrow canal.

The Major joined them. He stared at the water for a moment and then turned to the nearest of the men, the one who was so plainly his brother.

"Harry, look, see where the weeds have parted? It's as good as a trail for us. Get a punt, brother. He mustn't get far or we'll lose him in this maze. Hurry . . . Hurry damn you."

His brother stared at him and then at the water.

"Well . . . damn you, Harry, for a fool . . . get a punt . . . under the jetty. Look, there."

They found two punts and with one paddling and one steering in the rear they took to the water in the primitive boats.

They paddled under the green canopy and the dappled morning light along the narrow cut. At a junction, the Major looked at the thick floating weed. So they followed the trail of Fox's boat.

All was silence now as the men paddled through the mazy waterways. Occasionally a water bird would rise slowly, hang in the air until they'd moved on then settle back in the shallows . . . waiting.

Fox paddled hard. He'd chosen the abbey as a rendezvous because he knew that from time to time it became visible from the canals where trees had been cut away or the rushes cropped for use as thatch. If he could find the way to the main river he'd get to the girl and the horses.

He trusted her to be there.

A sudden squawking of geese rose up from the water ahead of him and, cursing his luck, he paddled harder. There was little point in trying to conceal himself now for they'd know what had alarmed the birds.

The wide, flat bottomed boat had a low platform built across the front and on it were two bolts. Attached to the bolts by shackles was a huge bell-ended tube. It was an ancient fowling piece. A primitive gun that he'd seen used in autumn duck shoots to take a hundred ducks at a time for salting.

The gun he'd cleaned so carefully and put into place the night before in case of need. Old habits. Fox smiled.

He'd found it in the green gloom of that late afternoon. The gun was dry and clean when he'd set it in place. Tied to it he'd found an eel skin bag. Inside it, a powder horn wrapped in more eel skin.

Alongside the bag, under the platform he'd found a box in which were small stones, bits of lead, small bolts. Enough to scatter and to kill a hundred ducks at one shot. Before mounting the gun on its shackles he'd loaded it and rammed home the projectiles with a wad of material torn from his cloak.

Behind him he heard the men calling softly to each other. He backed his punt up into an even narrower cut, little more than a ditch. Fox pulled the canopy of trees over the entrance and quietly checked the pan was dry. He poured powder from the horn into the pan. He aimed the prow of the punt directly for the entrance they had to come through. He waited.

The pursuing punts passed the opening of his ditch. He heard the Major cry out angrily, "For God's sake, Harry, are you blind? Get into that canal there . . . the trail goes under the willow."

Fox lay flat in the punt and waited behind the fresh young foliage of the willow. He already had a piece of rope smouldering, ready to touch the firing pan of the old punt gun.

The first boat pushed gently through the fringe of the willow, followed closely by the second. As they came through they saw an empty punt lying face on to them and a curious bell shaped tube pointing . . .

"Back! Get back . . . get back!"

The paddler in the first boat screamed and tried to escape. But the ditch was too narrow for any manoeuvring. As he back-paddled his punt rammed the one behind. There was a terrifying thunderous roar from Fox's punt and a lethal charge of stones, old metal, steel rod and debris lashed through the two leading pursuers and into the second punt.

Fox eased back into the main channel. Behind him a man screamed and clutched at what was left of his leg. Another lay, mercifully dead and the Major cradled his brother, Harry, in his arms as the young man bled to death.

The water closed behind Fox. Weed drifted across and hid his passage. On the mud banks by the abbey, two herons stood gravely with beaks like swords . . . waiting.

It was quiet again. The green weeds swayed a little after the passage of the boat, the green canopy of trees hid the carnage at the other end of the cut. The reeds grew high over the banks and old bull rushes released their cotton into the wind . . .

Fox looked across the flat land and saw, through the trees, the pale stone of the abbey tower. The leaping buttresses leaned against the high walls.

A heron stabbed its yellow beak into the green waters.

17

Alison had lost count of time. She had no way of counting time in the dark place in which she was kept. On the first day they took her from her cell upstairs which they showed her very carefully. A long table, three chairs and a fireplace in which a fire blazed.

The Witchfinder showed her the things that lay on the table and the iron glowing white in the heart of the fire. They showed her, in a corner of the room, a large pile of boulders and a wide plank. Just showed her. Told her to look and then took her back to her cell without a word. She was terrified of the moment when she'd be taken back to the room.

It was only ten days but she had no way of knowing that and dared not ask.

After the first visit from one of the elders of her faith, she asked him not to come again. The old man stood in the foul straw and she stood too. There were no chairs, no table, no bed . . . only straw. It was a place for a dog. It was where she lived now and prayed every day for John to come home. He'd do what had to be done.

"Please," she begged the old man. "You'll endanger yourself and the others. I am not guilty, whatever they may say . . . whatever I may say. Remember that," she said. Then she begged the old man, "Take care of Rebecca."

"She's gone," said the old man. "When they took you, your uncle took her in for he's a kindly man but she ran, she ran away. He says he took her in most kindly and at a risk to himself for she's touched because of you."

"Gone where?" asked Alison. "Where is she . . . ?"

Alison was crying now. She hadn't cried before. She refused to cry. Hopkins and his servants filled her with a sick fear and she knew if she cried before them she was done.

"Please, find her. Take her in for me," she begged and turned away to the wall and leaned on the cold stone. The old man touched her shoulder and she turned and he held her for a moment.

"Believe me?" she asked. "You do believe me?"

"Yes sister. I believe you. We pray for you."

"Get word to my husband. Tell him what's happening. Tell him, please tell him I asked for him . . . prayed for him. Please . . . if they . . . if anything . . . if I say anything it will be lies. If I confess anything it will be lies."

The old man stood away from her now and she stood head bowed, shoulders shaking under the thin dress. Her hair was matted and dirty and her face drawn and pale for lack of sunlight. The room stank of course.

The door opened and the old man walked out past one of the Witchfinder's men.

The Witchfinder stood in the doorway after the old man had stumbled up the steps away from the stinking room.

"You can come out now, Alison" whispered the Witchfinder.

She went up into the room she feared.

****

"No . . . No I will not . . . I cannot say such things. No. I will not. No! Please, no!"

Hopkins leaned closer to Alison. On the table was a Bible and beyond the Bible, hinged, spiked and clamped, the metal instruments. Pincers and scissors and needles.

One of the assistants leaned against the hearth watching her idly as she shook her head.

"But you will. It is the only way to peace. You will confess. I promise you will."

Alison looked into his empty eyes.

"Why . . . what do you serve here?" she whispered.

"God," he said, "As you serve the Devil. We have proof. Confess it."

"You can't have proof of what is a lie for I am not a witch."

86

"You have a dear friend?" Hopkins whispered. "An old friend. No-one in the village has a good word for her but you visited her, fed her sometimes, talked to her . . . An outcast from the village and a familiar of the Devil . . . She has confessed."

And Alison looked away from him and begged him not to hurt the old woman.

He came closer now. Whispered to her.

"The old woman names you. She confesses that you brought her to the Devil. She gave you that aborted child for you to sacrifice to your Master. The cattle with the sickness were caused by you. She saw you dance with the Devil. Saw you. Heard you compact with your Master. Saw you kiss him. In his arse."

She backed away from the man with loathing.

"It's not true. What did you do to her? She's not well . . . sick in the head but she never saw such things nor heard such things. She'd never say I was so."

"She says you were so."

"I don't believe you."

The old woman was brought then and pushed into the room. She was murmuring to herself and muttering as she often did. She saw Alison but did not recognize her. Alison managed to get up to go to her and to hold out her arms to hold her. Suddenly the old woman screamed and screamed and pointed and screamed. She backed against a wall.

"I see her Master. I see her . . . I see the Master watching her . . . smiling at her. The Devil's business . . . I repent . . . I confess . . . I repent!"

She fell to the ground in a fit of fear.

The old woman was taken away and Alison watched her leave. Hopkins turned her face to his.

"You're a pretty woman. A trap for men that lust for you. How many did you entice to the Devil for a share of your body? Women are filth and you the filthiest."

She could smell his breath and feel it on her face.

"All you have to do is confess."

"I cannot."

"You can. You can. It is so easy. I know your Master. How seductive he is but will he save you now from the torments of hell . . . here, now?"

He turned her to face the table and picked up a pair of pincers.

"From this . . . or these." He swept aside the twisted metal instruments. "You will confess. Everyone confesses finally and comes to the Lord. Finally. Or goes to hell."

Alison began to cry. Where was John now? Why would anyone mark her for such a man to take? No-one in the village. Why? Who hated her so much he'd send her to this?

"Tell me . . . tell me now. You can confess to me and it will be over. No pain . . . no pain. Just tell me when you made your compact. Did he suck that teat under your left arm? Did he mark your left haunch with that rose coloured mark? You see? You see? I know so much about you. I know you made a compact with the Devil; for that child."

"No . . . No . . . I . . . no!"

"Your daughter . . . shall I bring her here? Show her what I have shown you? Tell her what we know of you . . . She'll hear you confess."

"No. Not my daughter . . . You wouldn't harm my . . . she knows nothing. She's run away. Can't be found."

Hopkins smiled at her and shook his head. She screamed then.

"Dear God, you can't have her. No!"

"You know the Devil. You do. And his works for you fly with him. Don't deny it."

Alison shook her head. She looked up into Hopkin's face as he tormented her.

"Never! I will not confess. Never!"

Hopkins smiled then . . . His assistants walked into the room and stretched Alison on the table.

18

They came ashore from the fishing smack onto the dark quayside in the estuary of the Hamble. It had been a long crossing from the Normandy coast, and a hard one. Fox paid the captain and, taking up his single leather bag, he walked past the cottage and the yelping dog at the end of the jetty and up through the cobbled streets. Maeve followed him without a word.

Dawn was breaking over the forest that lay along the river valley and stretched east and west for fifty miles.

They both glittered in the early morning sunshine from the silver salt of the sea and the scales of herring from the nets they'd slept on, which coated their clothes, their skin and their hair.

Maeve and John Fox walked out of the still sleeping village and left no sign of their passage. For the moment they'd shaken off the pursuing Englishmen who'd vowed to kill Fox. He knew they would look for him in England.

The two walked on up the track, through the edge of the wood and onto the downs beyond. A mile along the springing turf they came to a well used drover's road.

"Well?" Fox asked. "Where d'you go now?"

"With you," she said and stopped to look about her. "I was never here before," she said.

Fox put the bag down by the track.

"This is the edge of the New Forest, the Hamble River lies below and here a road takes wagons and carriages so maybe we'll find someone to stop for us."

"No doubt it's a long walk to Bristol if they don't," she said.

****

It was evening two days later, that they walked through the Bristol city gate and into the port. Men and women of all sorts and shapes were bawling their wares, selling and buying food, clothes, drink, walking, shouting, laughing, crying, loving, living on and around the busy streets.

Fox and Maeve shouldered their way through the crowds. There were plenty looked as they went by. The man in his dark cloak and hat was tall enough to make them notice. With a stillness about his sunburned face and a look in his eyes to silence any man.

The man, however, was well able to blend into the shadows and to vanish in a crowd.

The girl still had crusts of silver salt in her long hair which she swept back from her face as she strode after Fox. She walked with the freedom of a man.

At a pie shop the tantalising smell of meat and pastry stopped her in her tracks. She stopped him and gestured at the selection of pies cooling on the windowsill but Fox shook his head, took her arm and moved her away.

"We'll eat at Shea's and then decide what to do with you. Maybe your man, Thurloe, will be there."

"Maybe - and he's not my man," she snapped.

She walked on along the cobbled street. He followed her around the corner and on down the hill towards the dock. She was eating a hot pie.

"How the devil . . ? I never saw . . . You'll get us whipped, girl. I'm a respectable man, remember?"

"But I'm not a respectable girl it seems. You want some?"

She offered the pie and laughed in his face as he refused it.

"Shea's it is then, friend, and you can decide what to do with me."

She walked away in a peal of mocking laughter. He followed her through the jostling crowds arguing and laughing together like children. They didn't notice the silent figure standing in the doorway of a chandler's as they passed.

She threw the pie crust into the dock. Before it hit the black water a dozen gulls screamed, mewed and snatched it from each other.

90

The man who'd followed them from the chandler's waited for a moment and then turned and walked out along the jetty through the tangle of ropes and bollards. He walked up the gangplank of the last of the boats moored ready for the next tide.

"He's back . . . and the girl. Together. Tell your master who seen 'em first." The man took the small bag of coin that was put into his hand and walked off the gangplank along the quayside and away into the shadows.

A little later another man would step ashore, walk briskly to a small house, pass a message to the old man waiting in the decrepit downstairs room. By evening the message was on its way to London where a pale young man waited over a watchmaker's shop.

"I've been waiting on you this past week," roared the vast Shea as Fox sat quietly in the empty back room where Shea held court from time to time. "I'd a message for you from a man we know as was most urgent," he said.

Fox was tired now. The dust of the summer having been settled with good ale he could feel his eyes begin to prick with weariness.

"Well?" he asked, "Tell me."

"The man left this for you, Fox," he said, and took a package from his apron pocket. It was greasy with handling and creased where it had rested in pockets, under pillows or wherever Shea would feel it safe.

"Which man?" asked Fox, "My old colonel or the other? For if it's Thurloe, he can whistle and be damned. I was nigh on killed for him and his damned messages and he gave us no warning of that sort of danger. So is it Black Tom?"

Shea nodded and pushed the package across the table to the angry man.

"Black Tom it was" he said.

Fox slit open the package with his knife. He took out the single sheet of paper, glanced at it and threw it aside.

Shea was startled. He said nothing.

"Read it," said Fox. "It tells me to give any report I want to make to Maeve Ahern who is at this minute asleep upstairs in her bed - I pray. She is to take anything we learned to Thurloe, I suppose. I have no friendship for that little man. And what news would I have . . . ?"

Shea grinned at Fox then and poured more wine.

"So he makes you angry and you do have news for him?"

"We do," said the girl from the doorway. "We have news will cause him to lose sleep."

She walked into the light from the fire, took up Fox's glass and drank.

Her tiredness seemed to have gone. A few minutes sleep and she seemed refreshed again. "We have news, that's certain."

Fox shrugged and drank.

"The question is, Ahern, will you pass it to Thurloe or Fairfax, or not? Or will you let him dangle in the wind?" asked Shea.

Maeve took up the bottle, filled her glass and sat apart from the men and stared at the fire as she nursed the red wine.

"You tell him, Shea. I'll tell you and you pass it on," said Fox quietly. "If you have the stomach for it. Or you, Maeve. I've done what I said I'd do."

Maeve considered for a moment the drink in her hand, then the fire and then looked across at the big Irishman waiting on her word.

"What is it to be bucko?" she asked. "Who pays for this . . . information?"

Shea shook his head then and stood up in a dark anger.

"Tell her, Fox, tell her to shut her poxy mouth or got to hell the hard way of it. I work only for my old colonel. No-one else."

And he looked at her in astonishment as she began to laugh in his face and to nod and to choke on the wine as she tried to drink it and then to wave her hand in the air asking for a moment as she choked again.

Shea watched as Fox thumped her back and she regained her breath. There were tears in her eyes as she explained

"I don't know you from Adam do I, Shea? Our friend here knew your brother and good luck to him. But what do I know save that you talk with Black Tom Fairfax and with that little wasp of a man, Thurloe, and have what is it . . . an 'arrangement' with them? Here's a cosy thing, Fox. Think on it. This city will side with the King if the time comes when it has to decide. And it will. For Bristol is too important for the King to let lie.

So the other side have a man here . . . an Irishman with a good eye and a way of business and who the devil knows what that business may be? Grand for our man Fairfax, good Black Tom and the others of his persuasion for getting gobbets of information should they need it . . ."

"Should it come to civil war . . . to fighting . . ? Will it?"

Maeve looked at Fox and smiled at him in real amusement.

"I look in the flames and I can see things . . . I look in your hand and see things . . . here, Shea, show me your hand. Show me!"

He pulled away from her and crossed himself and she laughed again and the flames from the fire glittered in her eyes. She snapped her fingers in his face and turned back to Fox who watched this by-play intently.

Maeve drank up her wine.

"I have the skills, I have the sight. My mother had it and my grandmother and now I do. I will tell you, Shea, that the man was supposed to meet Fox was a man I knew well, very well, though Major Marian was not a kind man nor a gentle one. Anyway we speak no evil of the dead and he is dead. Tell Fairfax that."

She drank deep and stared into the flames as she spoke.

"Tell him there is someone taking up his messages and betraying them to other interested parties. Like the King's court in France. We were followed as far as Caen . . . No doubt we will be picked up here and followed again. Me? I might go home. Tell the little man, whey-faced Thurloe, that."

Fox watched the girl amazed at her confidence. She'd made up her mind and there would be no use arguing with her it seemed.

Shea nodded. "You'd better know something more then," he said. "We'd a man on the quayside asking for you, Fox . . . some five days back. And another asking for you, Ahern. Just asking. If you were wise you'd move on. The man had money to burn, blood money no doubt."

The big man sat close with them at the table and spoke quietly. Outside a dull bell chimed the hour, a squawk of music that stopped as soon as it was heard, a yell and a silence. Dogs barked and stopped barking.

"The King is raising an army. There's talk of Civil War soon. Dangerous times indeed. Between the King and the Parliament is a wall building, it seems."

"Not my business," said Fox

"It is. You carried a message for Thurloe which makes it your business. Those looking for you will make it your business. It's the way of the world, Fox."

"Makes no difference to him," mocked Maeve. "He turns the other cheek and brings peace to the world. You should've seen what he did with a fowling gun and the havoc he wrought. Men died from it and he made an enemy for sure."

Maeve threw back her head in laughter. Fox leant close to Shea.

"You want us to go now?" he asked, "Do we endanger you, my friend?"

"You stay of course and leave early, secretly. I'll show you. Seriously Fox, these are dangerous times. Thurloe wants to see you, both of you. He said to tell you he is mindful of your refusal to work for him more than to deliver a message but he'd be grateful for one more meeting. For Black Tom's sake, he said."

"Where?" asked Fox. Maeve began to whistle a silly tune and then to mock him.

"You'll see him. And you swore not to. All he has to do is ask in the name of your beloved colonel and you eat from his hand like a poxy lap dog. His party is infiltrated by the enemy and leaking like a sieve and a danger to be close to what with double agents and the like and you go yap yap yap! Lap dog!"

"I'll see him the once to warn him. Where?"

Shea hesitated and then spoke. "You go for home tomorrow. He'll find you at the first crossroad on the river road. There's a copse."

"I know it," said Fox. "We'll need strong horses, Shea, and sleep."

The logs in the fire tumbled, sparked and the flames danced one last time before it died.

19

Under the dappled shadows cast by the trees, flies played across the rump of the grey horse. The slow switch of the tail cleared them for a moment and then allowed them back to continue their soft torment. The girl rode from the track into the shade of the hazel and beech trees. There was no-one with the horse which was tethered to a low branch.

She began to turn to leave when the young man she was expecting stepped across the track and lifted a hand in greeting.

"Where is he? Where is Fox?"

"Here!" said a voice from the other side of the clearing. Fox waited for young man to turn and see the pistol he had levelled and primed. Thurloe was not amused.

"You alone?" asked Fox.

"I said I'd be alone. I'd rather people didn't know my business. 'Tis safest for me and safest for you also." He seemed to have no fear of the pistol pointed at his head.

He moved away from the shade and down the bank of the river to a place concealed from the track. Two old fallen trees made convenient seats. Thurloe helped Maeve down to the first of them and waited while she arranged her skirts and sat.

Fox took his time putting his pistol into the saddle bag and, seeing nothing to concern him, he dismounted and stepped into the shadow of the last of the trees.

"Well, sir?" asked Thurloe.

"Ask her first. She knew your man there. Ask her."

"He's dead. He was burned about the feet and other places. He can be glad he didn't live."

The girl didn't look at either of them but she spoke quietly and with no hint of feeling. As if what she had seen was no more than a picture on a wall or at the back of her mind. As if she was already forgetting that she had shared the man's bed which both Fox and Thurloe knew was likely. It was as if nothing of that touched her.

"He would have told them all they needed to know. He once confessed to me he was afraid of pain but anyone would have told them anything. I saw what they did to him."

Idly she threw a pebble into the stream and stared away over the water across to the trees on the other side and the hint of blue where the hills began to rise and the Welsh Marches began.

Thurloe left the silence hanging and Fox watched him. Here was a still man, with the patience Fox admired and knew so well in himself when he'd waited in the dead ground between enemy troopers. When to make a sound, to cough, was death.

The girl would not look around from the dark swirling water.

"So your man is dead and yet we met a man said he was one of yours." said Fox abruptly, "He seemed to want to kill me too."

Thurloe turned to look at him then and Fox was astonished to see the sadness on his face.

"You gave him the letter?"

Fox shrugged, "It was what I was told to do. I was a messenger boy, remember?"

Thurloe stood up and walked along the river bank a pace or two,. turned and came back to Fox.

"You've betrayed five men to the other camp."

Fox shook his head and took from inside his jacket a dirty, folded piece of paper.

"I think not," he said. "This is your letter. They had something else from me and whatever they tortured out of your man. Your little network is gutted, Thurloe, so you'll need to begin to build that team again."

Thurloe took the letter, unfolded it and glanced at it. Fox waited. Thurloe looked up at him.

"Who gave you permission to break the seal, to take out the letter and read it no doubt . . . who gave you permission?"

Fox smiled at him and shook his head.

Thurloe snarled in anger then. "This is a matter of State."

"No sir, 'tis a matter of my life, sir, and of treason against the King just now, sir. Not a matter of State to encourage dissent amongst the King's people? To offer payment for information from those who'd sell their King? 'Tis as well I'm not a political man sir so don't talk about matters of State to me. I did what any sensible man would do. I prepared another letter in case I was dealt a bad hand."

"Another letter . . . saying what?" Thurloe almost danced with anger as he asked Fox.

"Saying that my Lord Buckingham had come to the side of the Parliament, privily and looked to find a way to remove the King from power. That there should be no taxation without representation, as John Hampton said. In short that he was not a favourite of the King but very much his enemy."

Fox could almost hear Thurloe's brain working on that information.

"Will they believe it?" he asked eventually.

"It will sow doubts for some. That's better than allowing your people to die solitary deaths in the Marais, or the Garonne, or the Seine, for nothing. It was all I could think to do. And then the substitute major clearly felt I had to be killed. I suppose he believed that I knew your man in Bordeaux or La Rochelle was already dead. And the longer no-one in England knew, Mr Thurloe, the more people you'd lead to their deaths. It's a dog's world, the world you live in, Thurloe, without loyalty and where nothing is ever what it seems."

"Our world, Fox, it's our world."

"Not my world any more."

"You're made for it, Fox."

"I am made to go home to my wife and to forget I was ever in Niort and to forget I killed that major's brother in the canals there, to forget they will no doubt follow us here. The major will want to avenge his brother on me. Well, let him find a retired soldier in a tiny village up by the Long Mynd and should I have sufficient warning, he'll not take me nor touch me. So I'm going home now to my wife."

"I want you working for me, Fox. I want you with me."

The girl walked to Fox and looked up at him. "He's right you know, Fox, you're born for the work, as I am," she said quietly.

"I'm born to go to my wife, Alison, and my daughter and to live as I promised them I would. In peace and amity and no more of this business."

Maeve knew what it cost Fox to say that. Thurloe stepped into his path and then stood aside as Fox strode for his horse.

"Fox," he said, "Thank you for the letter. For what you did. Many thanks."

Fox leaned down and adjusted the saddle of his horse, mounted, turned and rode away from the water up the track alongside the river and headed north towards home.

The road he took along the river narrows sharply where the huge bluff of Ross rears over the English lowlands. Beech trees and elms tower over the crags and cliffs that have been gouged by river and wind.

Here the river runs fast and furious, with shallows where the salmon fishermen net and spear the returning fish or, paddling clumsy wicker and tar coracles, lay traps across the river for eels and crayfish.

For the first time in two months Fox was alone in the countryside. On the one hand he wanted to go home to see his wife and daughter and on the other he luxuriated in the feeling of being alone.

The only sounds he could hear were the chatter of blackbirds and thrushes, the sudden screech of a heron as it approached its nest high up the cliffs and the river lapping and tumbling over the dark green rocks in sudden runs and flashes. Fox smiled, leaned forward and scratched his horse between the ears and relaxed. Going home.

The meeting with Thurloe had been much as he expected but he felt a sense of relief to be free from him. There was something chill about that young man, something remorseless. Fox knew he'd turned aside from a dangerous path and he felt regret stir.

Had he truly abandoned the life he loved, being out on the edge, waiting for a hint, a nod, a whisper that would give him the information he searched for?

He reined in the horse, dismounted then stepped out leading the horse just to feel the ground under his feet, to sense the land, to absorb what it told him. To read it as he had done since he was a child.

A man had gone this way not more than twelve hours before him, a deer had crossed the path only minutes before Fox and his horse came to the crossing. There was a small cottage hidden in the trees to his right, a fisherman had passed across the track down to the river on his left . . . He'd taken some trout if the scales left on a tree stump at the side of the track were anything to trust . . .

Softly Fox stepped along the track and savoured those old skills so lately used in France.

He took the long knife from the saddlebag and slung it and the scabbard across his back. The weight felt right where it lay easy for either hand. One of the pair of pistols he'd been given in Bordeaux lay in the deep pocket he had in the fold of his cloak but he trusted the knife more than any pistol.

There was no chance of a misfire, no chance of wet powder, a broken flint, a faulty ball . . . The knife was immediate and final.

He stepped on through the thrusting bushes and followed the path round and over the bluff and stopped at the top to look back. Far below him the river wound away through a carpet of trees and thick scrub.

In the distance, to the east, lay hills and the blue beyond them was the English plain. To the west lay Wales and the Marcher castles. South lay the muddy estuary and Bristol through the gorge and beyond that the sea.

Fox sat on an outcrop of rock and looked down the track and thought of what he was giving up and of what he was returning to. He'd made a promise and had kept it as well as he was able. If he broke, it was because he was forced to. But he'd remained faithful to his wife and God knows Maeve Ahern was a temptation for a saint.

Sure he'd killed but had he not, he would have been killed and dear Alison would have nothing to do but mourn.

He sat and whittled at a length of wood and knew he should have been the happiest man in the world. Yet . . . yet Thurloe had opened a window on a world he knew was his world and he had slammed it shut for the sake of Alison's smile and a kiss from his daughter. Maybe he was right. Maybe. Anyway it was all done with now. Finished.

He was going back to being a merchant and a farmer. He'd decided.

20

Michael sat in the large dining room and looked about it as his son sat in the settle by the fire and supped his ale. In the kitchen a serving girl cooked supper and Matthew Hopkins looked out through the window into the grey evening light.

"She has been put the question. She has refused us. I need her daughter. Find her."

"Who the devil d'you think you are, ordering us?" Michael asked angrily.

Hopkins looked at him pityingly.

"I warned you before that I often find in these investigations that when one member of a family has sucked the devil's fundament then others have also."

He left the idea hanging in the air a moment.

"You understand me?"

Hopkins looked about the room at the dresser with its pewter plates and the good table.

"All this is yours if she confesses. You tell me her husband is already accounted for."

Michael looked at him craftily, took him by the arm and walked him into the garden at the back of the house. They talked there for a time as they walked amongst the herbs and roses and smelt the fresh smell of evening.

Later Michael and his son, Saul, found Rebecca in the hovel up the valley where the old woman had lived. With the help of Hopkins' men they brought the girl back to the village and into her own house where she was locked in her room.

"Tomorrow, Rebecca, you'll see your mother. Until then be still and be glad we allow you back into the family home."

The next morning she was taken her mother. Hopkins and his men had been there before her.

Alison lay stretched on the floor. A wide plank lay over her breasts and covered from there to her groin. Piled on the plank were a dozen boulders each of which took two men to lift. Alison could hardly breathe. It was painful because her ribs were cracking. A small trickle of blood oozed from the corner of her mouth.

Rebecca was taken in by Hopkins as his men lowered another boulder into place.

She said nothing for a moment and then broke free and knelt beside her mother and kissed her, pushing the hair from her mother's sweating face.

"Rebecca," her mother whispered. "Whatever they tell you . . . I am good and have never had connection with the Devil . . . whatever I may say . . . whatever . . ."

The girl was pulled away by the two men and taken out of the room. Hopkins continued his threats.

"Now, we can stretch you and burn you, we can press you and go on putting you to the question. All I want is for you to confess. Or we shall press you more and yet more. You will die."

"I will die anyway."

"I'd bring you to the Lord before you die. It's my duty."

Hopkins seemed to believe what he said. Alison shook her head.

"Then I shall be forced to consider your daughter."

"No!"

"She shall be made to watch you being pressed and then . . . before you die she too shall be put to the question. Will it be the pincers . . . the pliers . . . the needles from the fire . . . ?"

"But she's a child. Innocent!"

"And her mother is in the Devil's hands. Would he leave a beautiful girl aside? You will watch her confess and admit her mother led her to the Devil. She will. She most certainly will."

Hopkins looked down at Alison's face as she coughed and more blood appeared at the corner of her mouth. He waited and she whispered . . .

"I made the cattle sick . . . we killed the horses . . ."

"The child . . . the dead child . . . ?
"No!"
"I will bring your daughter here . . ."
Alison moaned in agony.
"Please don't ask me to confess to that."
"Say it!"
"The child was a gift to . . . to . . ."
"Your master. Say it. Confess it!"
"I . . . I confess it. A gift to the Devil . . . I confess it . . ."

21

Outside the village, at the foot of the rocky climb to the moorland, is a small meadow. In the field a fresh cut post was planted and beyond it a pile of brushwood and gorse.

In her cell Alison lay on the straw and waited. She looked up as the door opened.

Her uncle walked in, afraid of what he might see.

"Alison . . . Alison . . ."

His face screwed up as the stench of the place hit him. He held a hand over his mouth as he walked to her. She struggled to sit up but her ribs hurt her too much. She lay, sweat, piss and blood-soaked and looked up at him.

Michael stared at the pale sweat-streaked face. Her bruised arms and broken nails and bloody hands were evidence, if he needed it, of how she had already suffered.

"I had to say . . . I had to confess, Uncle. He said he'd put Rebecca to the test . . . he said . . . Confess and she'll go free. Did he lie?"

He shook his head.

"She . . . Rebecca ran away. I had her with us at home. She's gone stark wild. I locked her in a room and she climbed out and ran. I have no idea where. I will find her. I will look for her."

Alison coughed a little and blood flecked the corner of her mouth as she dragged in a breath.

"So long as she's out of his hands. I confessed to vile things."

"Everyone has been told what you confessed to. People are surprised. Angry even. They believe him, Alison. Why did you do it Alison?

Alison stared up at him.

"You know why I confessed. You can't believe your own niece?"

Michael walked away from the wretched broken figure on the floor in the corner of the cell.

"He told them about a birth mark on your back. About a teat under your left arm . . . he told them about the mark on your buttock"

"How did he know? He never saw me naked. Someone told him. He had no need to rape me to make me confess. He loathes women. Just a pressing and a threat to bring my daughter to it. Have you seen my hands?"

She showed him the tattered remains of her fingers where the nails had been.

"How did he know about the birth mark? John has seen it and only John . . . No other man . . . save you. When I was a baby. You saw it."

She stared at him now and coughed more blood and watched him.

"It was you," she whispered, "It was you."

He stared at her and said nothing.

"And I'm to die. He said I'd not be hanged but burned for the dead child. You knew . . . you told him . . . lies. I'll not burn in hell, you shall . . . you shall. Why? Why did you accuse me? Why?"

She lay back panting with the effort of her accusation.

"The house Alison . . . the land. I'll have the land and the house."

"John will have it."

"No. He's accused also. He'll get nothing. If he's alive."

She looked at him then from dark eyes brimming with tears.

"You sold me to this, Uncle. John will come back and he will know who and then the wrath of God will be nothing to what you will face."

"He won't come back, Alison. I sent him away. Not business . . . not for that. For a knife in the back . . . a cutpurse in an alley . . . paid for. He won't be back."

Her uncle smiled and turning his back, walked away from her.

They carried her out on a hurdle as far as the field. The villagers were there around the post and the pile of furze. Hopkins, with the Bible to hand and his two helpers, stood a little aside.

No-one said anything as she came on the hurdle and was placed by the stake. When they saw her face as she was lifted from the hurdle there were some started forward while others crossed themselves and others began to pray.

104

"See her," shouted Hopkins, "Confessed and so saved for her Lord. She shall burn for her crimes but know she will go to the Lord if she truly repents."

The men on the edges of the crowd began to murmur.

"Prepare her . . ." said Hopkins, and his two men lifted Alison to the stake and began to tie her with chords about her breast and waist. Her arms were trapped under the chords. It was soon done.

A cuckoo sounded distantly as one of the men lifted a cup of water to her mouth. She drank a little and looked about her hardly understanding anymore what was happening.

An old woman came forward and showed her a crucifix. Alison smiled at her through her broken mouth. Behind her one of the assistants was sparking tinder to make a flame.

From beyond the hedge they heard a girl's voice singing. It was a nursery song sung so sweetly. Into the field came a figure draped in flowers. Her hair hanging long and pale and golden to her waist, her dress torn, her face streaked in tears as she sang . . .

There were forget-me-nots and ghillie flowers, honeysuckle and violets strung in bunches about her body and in her hands a crown of wild dog roses pale and pink . . . No-one dared move.

Rebecca walked to the pyre, past Hopkins. She walked over the furze about her mother's naked feet. She stood close to her mother and stopped singing. There was a silence about the field as the village looked at a woman they had loved and respected and at her daughter.

Rebecca leaned closer to her mother and kissed her. Then quietly placed the crown of roses on her head and a bunch of forget-me-nots in her tied hands. She wound the chain of a cross about them.

Alison smiled at her daughter and stared at her for a moment and then closed her eyes. Men and women in the crowd began to murmur and to protest.

"Light it!" rasped Hopkins, clothed in black clutching the Holy Bible.

And the flames roared through the dry furze and gorse about the woman's feet.

Rebecca walked away through the silent villagers and away up into the shadows beyond the valley. In the distance a cuckoo cried its plaintive cry . . . In the distance, too, the girl began to sing her nursery song again.

And the fire burned.

22

In Bristol, two men sat in the snug of the dockside ale house and waited until two crimpers by the bar had supped their ale and gone looking for victims. One of the men, thin and whey-faced, called for another jug of beer. The other, a taller man with a scar across his right cheek, got up as Shea came over with a pewter jug.

"We want a word with you . . . business word. Gold, in fact."

Shea put the jug of ale on the table and straightened up and said nothing.

The whey-faced man went on, "There's a man we'd like to see. We think you know him."

Shea looked and waited.

"He's an old soldier. Killed a friend of ours. We'd like to see him for some unfinished business."

Shea turned and walked back to the bar and smiled over his shoulder at the man.

"Money? Gold you said?"

"Gold!" said the seated man.

Shea walked back to the two men and poured ale into the standing man's pewter mug.

"Who wants to know?" he asked.

"Just tell us when he comes here. And tell us where he's going. It doesn't matter who asked. The gold is gold whoever asked. He's an old sergeant."

Shea nodded slightly and asked

"Black hair, dark eyes, dark clothes. Him?"

"Fox," said the standing man and came closer. Shea pushed his drink towards him.

"Gold, you said?"

"Didn't I tell you, you could always buy the Irish." grinned the standing man.

The other gestured impatiently and the standing man came to the table beside his partner and drew out a purse from which he poured coin onto the table.

The two men watched as the coins lay glittering on the wooden table. Shea reached across the table and took them both by their hair and pushed down with all his strength. The two men's faces hit the table and scattered the gold coins . . . Their noses split, their mouths too were slashed by their own teeth and ground by the coin.

Shea still held them as he straightened up and slammed his hands shut in a great clap and their heads between.

"Here's one Irish you don't buy. If I ever see you again, you will be fish bait."

Saying which, he took them from the ale house, walked across the quayside and, without another word dropped both moaning, bleeding men into the black water of the dock.

Shea strode back to the inn, told one of the porters to clean up the room and began to think how he might warn Fox, his brother's friend, that people were already asking for him.

It's a dark world Fox has stepped back into, Shea thought, as he tapped another barrel and tried the ale.

****

Fox was going home. As he rode, he knew he was being followed. It was nothing he had seen, nothing he had heard, nothing but instinct. He rode on along the track. High overhead a kestrel mewed as it spiralled and turned and flowed on the air. The horse plodded slowly on up the valley.

Fox waited at the side of the track hidden by the bole of a scrub oak. He had the pistol in one hand and before him, stuck in the ground, the long-bladed knife, ready to hand. Whoever was following was careless of the noise they made. The horse was being pushed hard enough to risk losing a shoe on the hard stones under the leaf loam that covered the track.

The horseman went past Fox, around a bend in the track and stopped by a riderless horse.

"Dismount!" ordered Fox from behind, "And keep your hands where I can see them."

Slowly the cloaked figure slid off the horse and waited. Fox stepped closer and his pursuer turned and she was laughing up into his face and only stopped when she saw how cold the man she was laughing at was. Fox waited. Maeve tried to read his eyes but saw only that cold flame flickering there and death a spit away.

"Did Thurloe send you?"

"No! No, John Fox . . . no. He didn't send me. I promise you he didn't send me."

"Promises . . . from you?" He didn't smile. The contempt was clear in his face. "You and he are carrion on the corpse," he said, "Doing what you do in dark places for darker reasons."

He stepped a pace nearer her.

"Your lover dead in La Rochelle and you show not a sliver of sorrow. Thurloe just thinks about putting another man in his place without concern or sorrow. The man had a wife maybe . . . children maybe . . . No care."

"She has taught you well, your soft wife," Maeve snarled. "Wasted a man, is my belief. Thurloe says you're no use to him as you are and maybe no use to me."

"Use? I'll be no use to you, Maeve Ahern," Fox snapped. "I told you as much the first time we met. And as for him, what does he offer but danger or death?"

"One other thing, the thing you and I want more than anything in the world, Fox. Excitement. Feeling your heart pitch faster, your guts churn and your brain race. He was not my lover, that man. We laid together for comfort's sake but he was not my lover and . . . Alison has addled your brain and your feelings and your needs."

"Why have you come after me if not for some purpose of Thurloe's?"

"I've come because I too want to go home, maybe. I can cross from Holyhead and I had thought a woman alone might have a cold journey."

"I thought you craved danger?" he said.

She smiled then, turned and walked back to her horse.

"Will you refuse me your protection?" She already knew the answer.

Fox stared at her as she looked back over her shoulder at him. Her eyes were dancing and her hair the colour of beech leaves in autumn.

"Will you? Who brought the horses to the abbey in Niort? Who rode alongside you? Who was your companion?"

"I stay in the country . . . no towns, no villages. I am losing myself. I want no-one to follow me or know where I have gone until I am home."

Maeve put a foot in the stirrup and waited. Fox walked to her and offered her a hand and lifted her into the saddle.

"You'd've killed me had I been a stranger. Yes?"

"I might," said Fox and walked to his horse, mounted and rode on without a backward glance. He would have killed. He knew.

****

The fire sparkled in the dark under the trees while beyond the small clearing the river ran endlessly by. Fox leaned back against the bole of a tree and licked his fingers clean.

Maeve sat opposite him and picked the last of the meat from the small brown trout he'd guddled from the river with his fingers. Wrapped in the leaves of wild garlic, coated with thick clay then left to cook in the embers of the fire, the fish were good. He'd made flat dough cakes from flour and salt he carried in a saddle bag. He'd cooked them on a heated slab of rock alongside the fire.

In the light from the fire a pale shape glided by silently, hunting. Fox watched the owl as it vanished amongst the trees.

The two sat in silence for a time then Maeve stood up then and wiped her hands on the moss growing across the bark of a rotten tree. Fox watched her across the flames of the fire as she turned.

"What is it? You watch me, look at me all the time. What is it?

"Maybe I find you good to look at?" Fox said and picked up a fish head and sucked it clean of meat. He threw the head onto the fire and a spiral of sparks flew up with the heat into the night air.

Maeve shook her head.

"Don't lie to me. You've only got eyes for your wife. Not to say I'm not willing and very able if you wanted to try changes wi' me."

She saw that the cold flame in his eyes was no longer there. She walked to him and looked down into his face by the light of the fire.

"What is it, John? So near home . . . so close and I tempt you now?"

"You'll find this hard Maeve. But I have never shared the loneliness of being out in enemy places with anyone but Pat Shea, and he is dead. You and I understand that loneliness - and you are what you are and I regret that. I do regret that for your sake. It's a hard road we tread, you and me."

He sighed. She crouched down facing him and began to talk. He watched the light and the spark in her eyes and the flickering shadows over her face as she talked.

"From Connemara, with its rock and lichen and plovers and soil in the cracks of the bare stones and my Daddy planting those cracks and pulling

109

sea weed ashore for making more places to grow. The stink of that on a bright summer afternoon sticks in my nose still.

"Six children who lived and God alone knows how many who died at birth or soon after and me, the youngest, and my life laid out already for me. For the last daughter had to look after their Mammy and Daddy. So that was me."

"There was a priest saw I'd the bare bones of a brain and showed me how to read a little and write a little and had me marked down as a Bride of Christ. But I'd as soon jump off the Clare cliffs as enter a nunnery."

She looked at him briefly and laughed. Fox listened and said nothing.

"There was hard times for us all the time. It was nothing new to have no more than potato and point to eat day in day out . . ."

"Point?" he asked and she marvelled at his ignorance.

"Sure, you sit with a potato on the wooden plate before you and salt from the sea and overhead the end of the ham that has lasted from the winter before when the pig was killed and salted and dried, hanging on the beam. You'd point and that was as close as you got to a square meal."

Fox sniffed the wood smoke and pushed a log closer into the centre of the fire and a shower of sparks rose up again and died in a thin column.

"I had four brothers and me sister went for a nun anyway so that was a mouth less to feed and prayers to God from her daily for our salvation. Bad luck to her. She died before she'd finished her novitiate. And two of my brothers gone as well and then one married and Mammy and Daddy died one after the other like snuffed out candles and me left with a brother and his wife under the same roof."

Maeve stared into the glowing core of the fire.

"She hated me. I hated her to tell the truth of it. I had no place to go but I'd never endure to stay in that cottage on the rocks by the cliffs and the wild sea crashing into them from across the ocean. So I went to see the priest and he made me an offer and I took it for a while.

Then told him I'd tell the world and he gave me a few pennies from the collection and I left the next day."

"And lived . . . ? How?"

She shook her head in wonder at his question.

"I've lived this past eight year on my wits, my body and sometimes, but rarely, on the generosity of men and women. I've whored and played and danced and spied my way from Clare to Constantinople, sure. No-one notices a woman slipping through the shadows, no-one asks questions. Who cares about women anyway? It's a great protection to be a woman. But a danger also, for men are what they are."

110

"But better this than slave to that woman my brother's wife, or whore to the priest for that matter. Or worse, a nun with the sisters in their naked cells loving nothing at all but the cold iron ring on the marriage finger."

She clutched her knees to her as she sat on the ground staring into the fire.

"At least I'm free. I live as I want. How I want . . . You could be again, John Fox. Why be a merchant's dog when you could be free?"

"I have a wife and a daughter," he said quietly. "And perhaps I am a little afraid to taste freedom again. It's no time for regret, Maeve, much as you tempt me."

"Your promise? You regret that too? No-one would know. No-one would be told. You're a strange man, Fox. A cold man, hard and soft at the same time. Distant? Yes."

She put a hand to her mouth and stopped speaking. Removed her hand as he leaned across her. Fox kissed her very quietly on her mouth and she didn't move.

He pulled away from her and she stared into his eyes and saw only the flames from the dying fire.

"Give me your hand," she said and took his right hand in hers and opened the fingers and looked closely at the whorls and lines in the palm.

Fox looked uneasily into the dark shadows beyond the firelight.

Maeve glanced up at him. "Don't be afraid. I'm no witch. 'Tis not a dark art but something my mother had and her mother and for all I know her mother before her. But never the dark art, I promise you."

"But there are some would say . . ."

"There are some would say Fox was afraid of a woman's game. Maybe that is all it is. Now . . . will I look or will you wonder for ever what I might have said?"

"Look," he said.

She stared at the hand and began to trace the lines with her finger as she spoke.

"Resourceful, strong . . . will live a time yet. Might have another child, no, *will* have, though maybe you won't know it. I see snow and pain and a good woman, and a child is certain."

"How the devil can I . . . ?"

"Hold your tongue now. I can't answer questions, only tell you what I see."

She leaned closer to his hand and held it into the light from the embers of the fire.

He watched her bowed head as she peered and traced the lines and suddenly she let his hand go and leaned back on her heels away from him.

She stood then and crossed herself and stared at him.

"What is it? What is it Maeve?"

"Nothing," she said. "Nothing but women's tattle." She stood up, shook out her skirt and looked away into the darker shadows beyond the firelight.

"Don't lie to me. What did you see?"

Maeve shook her head, pushed the mass of hair from her face and stared down into the embers of the fire.

Fox stood now and touched her arm and she shook her head and moved away.

"What is it?"

"I told you, nothing. A woman's game. Nothing but that and tales for fools and hen wives." She turned to him then and put her hand on his face gently and looked up into his eyes.

"Go home to your wife and your child. I'll be gone in the morning."

"No, girl. You'll come with me, stay, rest. I owe you that and my wife will feel she owes you more for your helping me, so come home with me?"

"I can't. You told me once of some stones . . . the Devil's Armchair. I might find them before I leave. But not with you."

"Tell me what you saw." Fox took her hand and pulled her closer. She did not resist.

"You would be sorry, John Fox, to take me now and I'd be sorry if you did."

After a moment he bent to pick up her cloak and gave it to her. Fox wrapped himself in his cloak and lay on the horse blanket with his head on the saddle and prepared to sleep.

Maeve lay on the other side of the fire and watched the dying embers.

"John," she said, softly. "Another time in another place. Maybe."

She turned her head away from him then. How she pitied him.

And the girl who Thurloe had sent closed her eyes and Fox lay and watched and listened to the night. There was no-one out there. No-one following. The last glowing ember of the fire slid into darkness.

23

The sun began to cut a line on the horizon as Fox watched Maeve slip away leading her horse quietly away from his. He smiled regretfully, lay with his hands under his head and listened to the surge of the early morning chorus. She thought he slept.

It'd been more years than he cared to remember since he'd slept out where no-one could find him. He knew that if he vanished from the face of the earth it would make no ripples except for Alison and Rebecca.

At the thought of them Fox got up, went to the river and splashed his face and hands, then watched as the sun blazed a pale gold light into the sky. There were no clouds. It promised to be a hot and a hazy day.

He rode beyond Hay-on-Wye, past the castle and the dull village at its foot. He heard the troopers before they clattered over the bridge and doubled back along the river in the direction of Worcester. There were fifty mounted men in lobster helmets and padded shirts and jerkins. The soldiers were sweating in their serge jackets and trousers and many seemed to have no idea of keeping step.

They carried a banner such as he had never seen before. In the corners, crosses, on the centre ground, a lamb surrounded by colour sergeants' axes and all surrounded by black and purple ribbons.

Fox held his ground and rode directly towards the troopers. They halted when Fox drew level with the sergeant-in-charge who rode to him in a fury.

"Get off the road. You want to be ridden down?"

Fox grinned at the sergeant and shook his head.

"Nothing changes, Sergeant. You've got some lads there green and wet behind the ears from the look of them."

The sergeant looked at him more closely now.

"It takes one to know one, Sergeant. I was with Gustavus Adolphus in Germany and other places in my time. You?"

"Not with him, sir, but I was with others in other places. To tell the truth I'd given up soldiering and come home. You get restless . . . I got restless. You understand me?" Fox nodded as the ragtag soldiers walked on along the track. The two old soldiers talked.

"We all do, Sergeant. It takes a good woman maybe to hold us down after a life with the colours."

The sergeant grinned.

"Yourself?"

Fox shrugged. "I'd not know where to sign on for a mercenary after all this time, even if I wanted to," he said.

"The Exchange at Seven Dials is run by an old sergeant. One of your mob if I remember right. You'll find news there of wars in need of old sweats."

Fox smiled, "I'll remember that . . ."

The troop of soldiers had been halted by a drill sergeant and allowed to fall out along the bank of the stream.

"Maybe you found the good woman, sir, and so have no need."

"Sergeant. Not sir. Sergeant."

"I was with Black Tom Fairfax only one time, Sergeant. You were with him?"

"I was. And this rabble? Whose banner is that?"

"They are Parliament men. For parliament and the people and against the King, I suppose," the soldier spat across the path.

Fox looked along the lines of the men. They looked what they were . . . militia gathered from the highways and byways.

"You have my sympathy, Sergeant. They'll need some whipping in from the looks of them."

The sergeant smiled grimly

"I'll see to it, with the help of the Lord."

"Ah, yes. Indeed. And a strong right arm, I'd think. Your name?"

"Adenham . . . Sergeant Adenham. Sergeant . . . ?"

"Not a sergeant now. Now a merchant and a farmer. "

Fox saw the contempt flicker for a moment on the old soldier's face.

"Where are you going, Sergeant? If I can ask."

"Silver catching. There's plate being taken to the King's men from all over the West . . . Bristol, Cornwall . . . Worcester. Plate and silver to pay for his rabble. We'll head for the road from Shrewsbury to Worcester and see what we can flush out for our own cause."

"Who leads them?" Fox asked.

"Prince Rupert, they say, who has some devilish good horsemen. He's a savage when he takes a village or a town, they tell us."

"Then be careful, friend, for he was trained in a hard school. Work on your lads' drills or they'll die else. The only way to take on his cavalry is to shoot low, take out the horses and you've a chance then."

"I'll remember it. My orders are to stop the commerce in silver and gold plate. To tell the truth, not me alone. There are two officers we're expecting to join us, Lieutenant Browne and Captain Fiennes, who will be as experienced, no doubt, as these lads."

"A sergeant's lot. To carry the officers on his back and the troopers under his arm. I wish you joy of it. Good day, Sergeant."

Fox smiled at his rueful face and lifted a hand in half mocking salute. The sergeant returned it and Fox spurred his horse, rode off the track and past the troopers.

One of the men began to sing a hymn as Fox went his way up towards the rising land on the Welsh borders.

The sun was already high and hot over the land . . .

Fox rode between high hawthorn hedges and spiked sloe bushes purple with bitter fruit. He was nearly home.

The stream was full and ran past the mill outside the village. The wheel was still as Fox rode by and flies drowsed across the faces of cows in the buttercup-strewn fields. A small boy was first to see him and to know he brought trouble.

The boy ran through the centre of the village, through Tanner's Alley and out into the open land beyond the village, turned down Kenelm Lane past a stout stone wall and into the yard of the large farmhouse under the arched entrance. Ignoring the dogs that snarled and snapped at his feet the boy hammered on the door.

Alison's uncle Michael opened the door and the boy tumbled out the unbelievable news.

"Master Fox is back!"

Fox rode past the small white Meeting House at the edge of the village. The door was closed and the windows shuttered. Inside, he knew, the simple benches and desk would be catching motes as they danced in the beams that eased through the cracks in the shutters and the door.

The Book would be in its place and the smell of good beeswax polish would hang in the air.

He smiled as he thought of Alison sitting at the side of the Meeting House in her simple grey dress and white shawl. The gentle face looking down into her lap with her hands crossed on the folds of her dress. And himself beside her trying to take in the gentle belief they all had.

The elders would be watching for a sign and then someone standing and making a prayer as the spirit moved them or talking quietly about something that troubled them. And Fox hoped that the feeling of God in the place would touch him as it touched his dear Alison.

It hadn't yet, he thought regretfully, as he walked his horse past the market hall and saw a neighbour.

He lifted his hat. She saw him, hesitated and then turned away into the cool shadows of the market cross. Then a man walked quickly along the street and ducked into an alley out of his sight.

Why would two people he knew well avoid him?

He walked on past the black-beamed cottages on the edge of the village and down the lane, passing a small boy as he rode by. The boy looked up at him and ran.

Fox rode on towards the farm, past the high dry-stone wall and under the archway into the yard. Two of the dogs came to him and welcomed him with soft mouths and wagging tails. Nothing much moved. Chickens scuttled across the yard and a goose came hissing at him and then backed away.

He led his horse to the trough. The horse drank gratefully as Fox took the saddle from its back and the bit and reins from his mouth. He took up his leather bag and looked about the yard.

Alison must be in the fields and maybe Rebecca was on some wild escapade. He'd been able to warn no-one when he'd arrive. They'd be surprised when they came back and found a strange horse in the stable.

What a joy it would be to see their smiles and hear their laughter and their insistence that he give them their presents immediately and teasing them that he'd forgotten. He never forgot.

As he walked up the steps past the staddle stones to the oak front door it opened and Alison's Uncle Michael stood there.

John Fox felt his heart constrict as he walked past the sweating man into the house. Michael watched him as if he could not believe his eyes. Fox walked through the cool hall and into the long back room where they lived much of the time. He slung his bag onto the shining table and whirled round on Michael who stood nervously in the doorway.

"Where is she?" Fox demanded. "What the Devil are you doing here?"

"John Fox, things have happened here. Such things. Terrible things."

"Where is my wife?" Fox demanded.

116

"I don't know . . . I don't know," said the sweating man, "I don't know what happened."

Fox stared at his pasty face and whispered, "Where is Alison? Rebecca? Where are they, damn your eyes?"

Fox took him by the throat, leaned over the glistening face of the terrified man and asked again. And he felt the grip of terror take him. What had Maeve seen when she refused to go on looking into his hand? Was it this? And what *was* this?

"Where is my wife? Your niece, my wife . . . Alison. Where is she? What d'you see in my eyes, tell me?"

Michael saw death and knew it.

"She . . . men came . . . Men came from Worcester . . . from Oxford . . . London. I don't know . . . Men came."

"Who came?"

Fox flung the man aside and took water and dashed it over his own head. He looked up, dripping water, at the frightened man cowering in a settle by the fireplace. Fox picked up a cloth and wiped his face and hands.

"Where is she?"

"The men took old Mother Baugh from up the mountain. She confessed . . ."

"Confessed . . . confessed what?" Fox could feel his heart tightening in him.

"Tell me what the old woman confessed. Dear God, she's half crazed and would confess black was white if asked . . ."

"She confessed to knowing witches . . . a witch . . . someone who'd tried to bring her to the Devil."

Fox shook his head to clear it. His damp hair glistened in the light through the old mullioned window.

"She confessed. Please don't hurt me. I swear I knew nothing about it."

Fox stared at him as he felt his head explode in fear.

"She . . . ? You mean Alison . . . Alison confessed to . . . to . . ."

"To having congress with the Devil himself. Yes."

Fox looked at him and laughed. The cowering, sweating man was truly afraid then. Fox laughed again, turned to the table and pulled his bag to him. He took from it the scabbard with the knife and the box of pistols.

"What're you doing?"

"I'm going to fetch my wife. Who has her? Where is she?"

Michael shook his head a little and groaned in fear.

"You told them they were damned fools? Listening to a mad woman. You sent Alison away? You told them it was all lies? Your niece . . . ? You protected her? You did, didn't you?"

Michael sniffed and wiped his sleeve across his nose.

"They were witchfinders, John. Licensed by the King himself to sniff out witchery. There was nothing we could do and then she admitted to it. She had the signs. The witchfinder, Hopkins, knew her for what she was."

Fox hit him then. Smashed him across the face with his open hand and back again with his knuckles splitting the screaming man's mouth open.

"Alison is no witch. Where is she?"

Michael looked away. Fox hauled him to his feet and slapped his face again. And again across his broken nose. The man screamed as Fox asked and asked again, "Where is she . . . your niece? Where is she?"

He threw the slobbering man from him and stormed out of the room calling her name as he went up the wide stairs to the landing and their bedroom. Already knowing what he suspected was true he opened their bedroom door. The room was being used by someone. By Michael.

He slammed the door and walked along the landing past the table on which an old arrangement of flowers still drooped in an old jug. No-one had bothered to change them. It was this that confirmed what he suspected already. Neither Alison nor Rebecca would have left them as they were.

He flung open the door of Rebecca's room and stood in the doorway shattered by what he saw. All round the walls were scrawled obscenities. They'd been chalked on the walls with the charcoal end of burnt sticks.

And in it all the name, "Matthew Hopkins", being damned to hell!

Rebecca had left a sign for him.

He thundered down the stairs as Michael edged his way to the front door.

"Stop there!" Fox snapped. Michael stopped and turned to face the anger of the man. He wiped the blood from his mouth and tried to speak.

"You touch me once more and you'll be arrested. I'll see you locked away. People listen to me and they'll lock you away for a mad-man. They said you'd be infected if you came back. We have only to tell the witchfinder and he will come back and take you."

He tried to go on but stopped as Fox stepped closer to him and he saw death again.

"You'll do two things, uncle. You will tell me where my wife is and you'll tell me where I may find my daughter. You're flesh and blood after all."

"I don't know. I don't know, Fox. I don't know anything. I was afraid. We were all afraid. They came and said they had information that a witch was here. They questioned Mother Baugh and she told them . . . she told them . . ."

"Alison?" Fox asked again.

"She confessed. She confessed, John Fox. I'm sorry. I am sorry but she confessed . . . They burned her . . . They . . ."

Fox howled in grief. He ran from the cowering man and threw a jar of long dead ghillie flowers against the wall. He came back to the man with his knife in his hand and madness in his eyes.

"Where . . . where is she? You will tell me or I'll geld you slowly. Where is she? In the churchyard . . . where?"

"Not in the churchyard . . . Nor in the plot neither. No-one was allowed to have her. No-one wanted her. She was buried where she was burned, what was left. In the field where she was burned. No mark. Nothing . . . but the wind on her . . ."

Fox stood quite still until the man went on.

"The men insisted. The King's warrant they had gave them the power. Where are you going . . . Fox . . . where are you going?"

"You too. You'll show me. What did you do while she burned? Did you watch her? Did you? You hated her enough . . . hated me enough. Did you watch her burn?"

The fat man was weeping in self pity and the tears mixed with the blood on his face.

"We were ordered to be there . . . an example, they said. I swear I begged them not to . . . not to . . ."

"And Rebecca. Did they force her too?"

The fat man said nothing. Fox lifted his knife the man nodded once.

"She was there. Singing. She gave her mother . . . she gave her mother roses from the hedges and sang and they lit the fire and Rebecca went away and we heard her singing . . . singing . . . Dear God, John Fox, I may have . . . I may . . . I'd never have wished such an end on any one."

"We'll go and see her now. Alison. And find one of the elders. Find one and bring him to me. Where was it?"

"Ten Acre field. There!" the fat man whispered.

"Bring the vicar and two men with spades and a coffin. Tell them. Tell them if they don't come I'll burn their homes about their ears. If you don't, I'll butcher you. Tell them."

He strode away across the yard, under the arch and up the lane, away from the village. Michael watched him go and wiped his hand over his bloody face.

Fox walked as far as the stone-walled fields and came at last to that known as Ten Acre. On the far side he saw against the pale stone walls a small figure moving. He strode over the field towards the intruder. He stopped at a small patch of burned earth. He looked then at Maeve who stared at him in horror.

Then he knelt on the ground beside the new green shoots of grass growing in a circle around the ash covered earth. Maeve watched as the man reached with stiff fingers into the ashes and scraped up the earth and lifted the ashes and poured them over his own head. The pale ashes filtered down over his hair as if he'd bathe in her remains.

Maeve waited and said nothing.

"You know what happened? You knew?" he said eventually.

She nodded.

"I saw it . . . some of it. And this I saw and it is terrible to carry, my friend. I found something here. I dare not touch it, it is too powerful. Too strong for me to touch. I'm blinded by the . . ."

And she broke off and began to murmur in a broken whisper.

"Sweet Jesus help me . . . Sweet Jesus let me carry her roses too. Let me have the roses and . . . Roses. I see roses."

Maeve stopped and crouched down and showed him a burnt and twisted piece of metal. A small cross, bent and burned and cold now half hidden in the grass.

"Take it," she said. "It was hers. Given to her. I know it was. I can't touch it. Please, John Fox, take it."

Fox leaned across the ashes and picked up the silver grey cross and stayed kneeling there with his head bent.

A boy limped across the field towards them. He stopped at a distance.

"Master Fox" he said. "Master Michael sent me. The elders won't come. No-one will come. No-one will come here to this place. Master Fox . . . I'm sorry sir. Mistress Alison was good to me and to my mother and I do not believe what they say."

The boy jerked and twisted around in a small spasm.

"I can do nothing for her but to pray, sir, so I pray for her and know she's with the angels. I'm sorry, Master Fox."

And Fox, still kneeling in the ashes, began to weep.

24

Fox and the Irish girl had come home from the field together, Michael had already left with little sign of his having been there.

"What was he doing living in your house?" Maeve had asked, "Unless he was certain you were not coming back."

She picked her nails with a knife and looked across the table at the exhausted man.

Maeve seemed astonished at the size of the farm house. She first befriended the yard dogs and it was as if they'd known her all her life. Then she looked into the long barn where two shire horses stood. She'd watered them and found them fresh straw. Fox had done nothing. He was numb, unable to think.

Maeve came into the house as the dark settled down over the yard. Fox had lit a small candle and set it in the deep window recess. She walked into the hall and kicked off her straw and dung covered shoes. She walked, he noticed, with her feet splayed slightly and on the balls of her feet. It was the walk of a courtesan. Upright, proud and probably unaware of the way it made her move.

She took up a candle and without a word, lit it from the one in the window and walked out of the room and up the wide staircase to look over the house for herself. After a time, he stepped after her and found her standing looking at herself in the long mirror on the wall of his bedroom.

She turned as he stood in the doorway and walked to the table on the other side of the room. Propped against the wall was a picture. She held it up and stared at it in the light of her candle.

"It's not as fine as the miniature you have. She is lovely."

Fox turned away from the doorway and she let him go and then walked out of the room along the landing, past the oak coffer polished to a deep dark sheen. She found him in the end room. His daughter's room.

She raised her candle and saw the graffiti on the wall.

A dress lay on the bed and another on the floor where it had been flung in haste. A chest was open and things had tumbled out, abandoned, thrown aside.

"Rebecca?" she asked. He looked at her then as he picked up the dress on the floor. He buried his head in its folds and smelled in it the body of his daughter.

"Yes," he said. "I was looking for a shawl I gave her. It's gone. So she has gone too. It was something she would never leave behind. Soft, soft wool from France. She loved it." he said and let the dress fall to the floorboards again and walked out of the room past her.

Maeve picked up the dress and laid it on a chest in the corner and walked along the landing, down the stairs to the room where she found he'd lit all the candles he could find.

He was sitting at the long table which his father had made as a wedding present for them. He didn't look up as she took a horn mug from a dresser and poured wine for herself and refilled his glass.

"I thought maybe if she was outside, if she was hiding . . . if she saw the candles she might come home," he said.

Maeve sipped her wine.

"Maeve, could you find her if she's run away? You have the gift. Your mother and her mother and her mother's mother. You have the gift. You told me."

Maeve put down her wine and leaned across the table to the desperate man.

"It's not something to turn on and off like a spigot in a barrel. Sometimes I see things . . . then maybe I can help . . . but not yet. Not now. I'm sorry Fox, but should anyone hear you say I have the gift of sight what would happen to me? Another witch . . . another burning?"

Fox flinched at her words and she knew he'd be hurt by them. He was too tired to think anymore. He stared at her and then drank more wine. What was her uncle doing in the farm? Why had he seemed surprised to see him back? Why hadn't he lifted a finger to save Alison?

He looked, unseeing, across the table at Maeve's face dancing in the flickering lights as his head reeled and merciful sleep took him.

He heard Maeve moving about downstairs. It was early and he lay staring at the ceiling. Deep in his gut a knot of anger hardened. He had no purpose now but to find the man who'd burned his wife. And then to find his daughter.

How he came to be in his bed he had no idea. Who'd undressed him, rolled him in a sheet he could only guess. No-one had seen him naked save his wife for more years than he cared to think about.

Downstairs a door opened and he heard Maeve calling the fowl to eat as she spread scraps about the yard for them. A dog barked once and then was silenced. He stepped out of bed onto the broad polished boards, pulled on a shirt and trousers and went downstairs, through the hall and into the kitchen where he could smell bread baking.

Maeve walked in through the door and for a moment the morning light gave her auburn hair a bright halo as she hesitated there. He walked past her without a word, into the yard where he stripped off his shirt and washed at the trough.

It was as bright a summer morning as a man could wish for yet all he felt was a dark anger.

He looked around and Maeve was standing watching him as he dried himself and pulled on his shirt.

"How did you get that scar under your right arm and the one on your thigh . . . knives, or a fall?" she asked.

He walked by her into the kitchen.

"Bread?" she asked, "And fresh eggs and ham."

He shook his head. "I'm not eating."

"Then more fool you for you've as hard a day as any man had ahead of you. Eat while you have the chance."

The girl put fresh baked bread on the table and two eggs and ham on a platter. After a moment, he sat at the table and wolfed down the food.

As he sat back she offered him a jug of fresh milk and he drank.

"Now," she said, "What?"

"They let her die. They let that man take her and burn her. Why did she confess? Why?"

Maeve grimaced a little. "You know why, John, you know why."

He looked at her and stared as her meaning became clear.

"I'll kill them. I will *kill* them. They forced her . . . I *will kill* them."

"What happened to the peaceful John Fox?" Maeve asked quietly as she cleared away.

"My daughter is gone . . . She was . . . she *is* only fifteen . . ."

"I was less when I left my home for the wicked world," she reminded him.

"Would I want her to end like you?" he asked. She stopped for a moment and he cursed for the words but they were out now and hanging between them.

"It depends how I end, I suppose," she said quietly. "So John Fox is dead?"

"Maybe," he said, "Maybe not."

He stood up then and looked round for his jacket and for his leather bag which he'd thrown aside the previous night.

Maeve handed him the bag which he opened and took out the box with the pistols. He looked up, challenging her but wisely she said nothing as he took the first of the pistols and told her how he'd come by them. He checked each of them, cleaned each, looked over the box of lead balls and the primers as well as the powder to be sure it was still dry.

"Always check, every morning and every night. Check weapons, check safety, check doors and windows . . . That way you live." He slung the long knife openly across his back. It had become again his weapon of choice.

Maeve smiled then.

"Now I believe Fox is dead," she said. "Shall we go or will I wait here for you?"

"Wait here," he said. He left the box of pistols on the table. At the door he turned back to her.

"Take what we need, we will not be here long. There are clothes which might fit you and a bag like this in the store room over here. A clean blanket each and food and drink . . . Take what we'll need."

She stared at him then and shook her head in disbelief.

"Am I coming with you when you go? Is that what you want?" she asked. And then she laughed.

"I'll be ready," she said.

Fox walked out of the house, strode down the track into the village, crossed the square, through the weekly market, past people who looked up and then hurriedly looked away and whispered in shocked tones as they saw him. One man only stood in his way.

The clergyman, Reverend Blagg, stood bareheaded under the market cross and barred Fox's way. A tall, thin-necked man whose clothes hung on him like a rook's feathers. His eyebrows bushy but under them warm and kindly eyes.

Fox stopped and waited and Reverend Blagg cleared his throat and the villagers watched.

"You have heard what happened?" he said.

Fox waited, staring into the eyes of the man who went bravely on.

"They say that a man come to a woman by witchcraft is tainted himself. You are not welcome here, John Fox. 'Twere best to sell up and to leave. It would be best."

Fox looked around the square and men began to edge closer to him. Some took up staves and others closed their fists. He continued to look around and then turned his back on them and stepped a pace closer. When he spoke it was very quietly.

"You knew my wife?" The clergyman nodded. "Did she or did she not do much good about the village and beyond it? People knew her for a kind soul, a good soul. Did they not?"

He turned and pointed at the closest man to him who held a large stave in his hand.

"When your mother was sick, Peter Owen, who came to her with soups and jellies, who helped her get well? Answer me!" But the man turned his back.

Fox turned to a woman at a stall selling cabbages

"When your child was dying, who came to her with physic and saved her life? Alison. My wife. Work of the devil, was it? Is that your daughter there?"

The woman looked away.

He pointed to a tall handsome girl of seventeen.

"Spare her shame. Did any of you say this to the man as condemned her? Killed her. Any one of you? You, Alan, who as good a lost your wife from sadness and sickness. Did my wife visit and care for her or not? Was she a good decent woman and kindly to all, old and young ? Did a single one of you stand up for her?"

He turned then to the clergyman and his anger was clear in his eyes.

"You knew her for a good friend. A Christian. Not of your church, maybe, but a good-living woman, modest, clean-living like all of her sort and gentle as doves. What did you do? Light the fire?"

He stared long and hard into the sad face of Reverend Blagg until the man stood aside, head bowed.

"We had to obey the King's warrant. This man, these men came with a warrant and she confessed, John, remember she confessed. What were we to think but that she was guilty? It's why she burned."

Fox turned on him.

"She burned because not one of you dared stand up for her and tell the truth. You were afraid. I'm leaving soon but I warn you I am coming back and when I come back I will know who delivered Alison to those men and they will wish they had never lived."

He spat at the feet of the clergyman and moved on, fast, away from the market place and down the hill towards the meeting house. No-one followed him.

There was a fly humming about the room. With the shutters down, light flooded over the wooden walls and benches. The elders sat in their grey and black clothes together in silence. The women in simple dark dresses and aprons . . . Everyone in their place and everyone focused on their inner thoughts. Waiting for God to speak through them.

When the door opened, no-one moved and as Fox closed the door no-one moved. As he walked quietly to the centre of the room, men and women began to look up and to acknowledge that he was there.

He looked around. Two of the elders saw the long blade slung on his back and neither said a word. For a long time the silence held as he stared at them and when he spoke it was softly, almost sadly.

"Is no-one moved to speak?" he asked. "No-one moved by the Spirit to give us their word . . . ?"

He walked across to the elders and stared down at them.

"You, Alan? You, Master Simon? You, Samuel? Not moved? God not speaking today?"

"Don't blaspheme, John Fox." An old white-haired man sitting aside from the others spoke to him quietly, "You may be angered but we are in God's house here."

"And one not here. One is missing? Not like my wife to miss a meeting is it? Is it?"

Fox turned and paced to the old man.

"I respected you above all of them and you were silent."

The old man was about to retort and then nodded once.

"To my shame."

"To her death."

He looked around at the men and women sitting there and one after another they bowed their heads in their shame.

"Who stood up for her in her hour of need? No-one! Like the Lord Jesus Christ? He was denied three times and you all did the same to Alison who was one of yours and you know she was not a witch. You know what she was. She had wanted me to join this Christian society. Decent honest friends, she said. Friends?"

They shifted uncomfortably on their benches.

"She burned in that field and no-one here was willing to say nay to the Witchfinder. No-one dared to bring him to the word of God."

The old man stood then.

126

"I have to speak. I have to say we are all shamed by it. We are all lessened by what we allowed to happen. I'd only beg you, John Fox, to forgive as our Lord forgave. I want you to consider what our dear sister Alison would have wanted for you had she lived. She dreamed of your joining with us in abandoning violence and anger and finding the Lord."

Fox stared at the gentle old man and the words dried in his throat as he saw the violence in Fox's eyes.

"Too late. The Lord is dead for me. I only look for vengeance. And I tell you now if I find that any man or woman here was responsible for bringing that witchfinder here, I will kill them as mercilessly as you helped kill my wife. See if your Lord can save you from that."

And he walked quietly out into the sunlight.

The fly hummed and then settled and around the room, the men and women sat locked in their own thoughts.

The room was silent again.

25

The woman, Mistress Allen, had come in the early morning across the fields, her dress sodden with dew. She'd crossed the yard past the dogs who hardly bothered to get to their feet, for they knew her well.

Maeve watched from the window as the woman came the door. She was thirty or so, her face was already lined with sun, hard work and poverty but she was clean and held herself well. Her hands proclaimed a peasant but her piercing eyes gave no sense that she felt herself the less for that.

Mistress Allen walked to the door, opened it and stepped into the hall. She was familiar with what she saw and surprised to find something strange when she closed the door behind her and turned into the room.

Maeve stood with her back to the window and the woman looked her up and down. She took in the simple dress and the long auburn hair, the dark eyes and the set of the mouth in a defiant line as Maeve prepared to explain herself, as far as she was willing, to this stranger.

Mistress Allen looked Maeve over slowly and took in her bare feet. Maeve was tall, but this one was taller by an inch. She nodded briefly once and stepped into the room past the mess of dishes and old flowers and strewn clothes about the place. Maeve had a cloth in her hand and had clearly begun to tidy it.

"That damned uncle of hers. Lives like a pig," said the woman. "He came as soon as she was burned. Him and his son lording it over us. He threw most of the house servants out. He said he was bringing in his own."

Maeve poured water into a mug and handed it to her, she drank it and handed the mug back. The Irish girl had welcomed her as well as she was able.

"You're as my son said you were," she said. "My boy came to you last night in the field. He has a dropping illness which shakes him sometimes and he's like to die of it. God have mercy on him. Which I doubt. Alison was kind to him. I was nurse for a time to Rebecca. Is Master John here?"

The tall woman picked nervously at the strewn debris of flowers across the table and Maeve saw that she was suddenly near to weeping. Maeve gestured to a chair and sat herself at one end of the table.

"He's out. He'll be leaving soon, I think."

"I knew him when he was a roaring boy," said the older woman and a smile hovered for a moment. My name is Allen, Mary Allen." The Irish girl nodded.

"He set all the hearts in this place racing but had eyes only for . . . for my mistress. He'll be looking for those who did this thing no doubt."

Maeve shrugged a touch.

"He was never the one to make a quiet man, a religious man. I told Alison as much but she believed she could change him. Her sect makes such demands. 'Tis a particular hard faith for a man."

Her eyes fluttered a look around the room as if she hoped to see Alison or Rebecca in the doorway. It was Fox who stood there . . . silent.

The tall woman rose then and Fox walked to her and took her into his arms and embraced her and then she wept against his shoulder. Maeve watched them for a moment and then walked to the door.

"I've a bag to pack. Food and drink. Saddle bags to see to. When do we leave?"

"Soon," said Fox and gently put Mary Allen from him and helped her to sit down. Maeve nodded and softly closed the door.

****

"They say you knew all the time what Alison confessed to," said the woman, "There are people in the village who are afraid, angry and wanting vengeance. They say you were in league with the Devil and led her . . ."

Fox stared as she told him.

"They will come soon and demand you go. They even say you brought her as a bride to Satan."

Fox laughed then and stood up from the table and walked to the window where the sun poured into the room. He turned then and stared at the woman sitting at the table with her head bowed.

"And you?" he asked. She hesitated a moment and then lifted her head.

"No!" she said. "Not me, nor them really. They don't really think it, but they are afraid and angry and guilty because they let it happen. She was loved, Master John. But they will come here and they will demand you go. They are saying it behind their hands now but soon, soon they will come here and . . ."

She shrugged and laid her large hands on the table. Quietly she said

"She admitted. She confessed. That's the truth."

"Why?" Fox whispered. "Why confess to a lie? Why confess to something that will end in such a death? Why?"

He came to the table, leaned down and took her hands and she looked up and he saw the pain in her face.

"They took Rebecca to see her, the Witchfinder and his men. They took her into the room where they questioned Alison. After that they let the child go and Alison confessed."

It had been as simple and as cruel as that.

The woman stopped and wiped the tears from her eyes with the corner of her shawl. He pressed her now.

"What did they do? Why did she confess?"

"She was told that if she didn't confess Rebecca would be put to the question. Would be pressed as they pressed her."

The woman began to weep again

Fox stepped back from her as if he'd been hit. He turned away but the woman saw his mouth open to scream in his anguish yet no sound came from him.

He spun around and swept the bottles and glasses and plates from the dresser in a crescendo of noise. He shattered the bowls and pots and tore the drapes from behind the door. He turned, wild-eyed and lunged across the table for the box of pistols but Maeve had come back when she heard the noise and had taken the box from the bench and hugged it to her.

"I'll kill them all . . . I will *kill* them *all* . . ." he hissed and reached for the box.

"You'll wait. You'll wait, Fox. You'll kill yourself if you go down into that village now. You'll wait and think and plan. You're a soldier, not a bloody peasant. God sakes and bones . . . You will wait!"

The older woman watched as Maeve stood toe to toe, eyeball to eyeball with the desperate man. For the first time since she had known him, Fox backed down. He walked to the jug of water in the basin and

130

poured it over his head. Then he turned, dripping wet, back to the Irish woman who still stared at him. He held out his hand for the box and pistols and she shook her head.

"Not yet, not yet." she said.

A moment and he sighed, took a deep breath and then sat down.

"Tell me, Mary," he ordered. The frightened woman had not moved.

"I can't tell you, Master John, for you'll go mad with it."

"No," he said. "No. I won't go mad. Tell me."

"They pressed the old lady, Mother Baugh or threatened her with it or worse. She'd've told them anything. Anything. She told them what they wanted to hear. Some say, John Fox, some say there were people hate you, want you gone from here. Some say there was a whisper that she, Alison, had the marks of Satan on her. A third tit under her arm. Bites and nips about her body from the Lord Satan. There were cows fell sick. Your uncle had two. My husband lost one. Others too . . ."

She went on.

"There was a murrain on the sheep which died in droves. A horse was flayed alive and left in a field. A cat was found spitted with a pitch fork to a tree. All signs . . . all signs, the Witchfinder said. She was blamed for that too and for a baby that died at birth. That too."

Fox sat silent with his head down staring at the floor as the woman told him what she knew.

Maeve walked out of the room with the pistols and while the village woman talked she came back and forth packing her bags and finding flour and cheeses for the saddle bags. A knife for herself she took from the dresser. As they talked, Maeve prepared for a long journey.

"If you stay, Master John, you will be harried by those who believe the lies they've been told by the Witchfinder. My husband believes. He forbade me to come by here. I come because she was kind to me and because I am afeard for your daughter who I nursed and who I love. Driven stark mad by what she saw. She sang. Did you know? She sang as she gave her mother flowers from the hedges and then watched as they lit the fire and then walked away singing. Not seen since but clear stark mad. Some say she went with the Witchfinder. Others that one of his men took her."

Fox stared at her then and she put her hand on his and he wept.

Mistress Allen made ready to leave. Pulling her shawl about her, she leaned down and gently laid her hand on the broken man's head.

"If Rebecca comes back here she will have a home with me as long as she wants it. If you stay there are those here who'd kill you for fear you might find the whisperer who talked to the Witchfinder. Matthew

Hopkins is the man to find and ask. Make him tell you who it was lied to him. Who led him to dear Alison. But remember not to hurt any man. Not in her name for Alison would have hated that."

Fox shook his head.

"I can't promise. I am not her. I can't abandon my nature to suit whoever was responsible. Whoever whispered her name will regret his loose and lying tongue. I will find whoever whispered that filth and I will cut out his tongue before I kill him. Killing is my trade."

He sat then staring at the wall. Maeve went on packing bags as the woman stepped past her into the yard, past the dogs and away into the afternoon sunshine.

The shadows had lengthened. By the time they were ready to leave. Fox was calmer. The prospect of action settled him down and focused his mind. It grew dark outside.

"We'll wait for the morning," said Maeve, and Fox agreed. Maeve offered him wine, but he refused it. It was then that they heard a scratching at the door.

Maeve looked across the room at Fox. He gestured her to wait and, sliding the long blade from its sheath, he stepped to the door. Maeve waited in the shadows.

Fox stepped to the door, opened it as the scratching continued and found a bareheaded young girl standing on the step looking pale and very frightened.

"You remember me, Master Fox? Barbara, from over Wooten End way, Rebecca's good friend."

Fox remembered her. The girl looked up fearfully. Fox stood aside and after a moment, the girl stepped into the room. She looked round and stopped when she saw Maeve in the shadows.

"Sit down, girl, sit down, nothing to fear here for any friend of my daughter."

"I own I am afraid," the girl looked at Maeve with her large dark eyes glowing in the candlelight. Maeve poured ale from a jug and handed it to the girl. She drank a little and looked about the room.

"She's not come back?"

"As you see, Barbara. What happened to her?"

"It's what didn't happen matters," said the girl. "After her mother was taken . . . before they . . . before she . . ." The girl looked at Fox and there was pleading in her face.

"We know what happened, child," said Maeve softly, "Tell us what else you have to tell."

The girl began again . . .

132

"She came to me one day. Most of the time she stayed here alone. Waiting she said, for her mother to come home. She saw no-one and said nothing to anyone. Her uncle came to her here. Talked to her. He said she went for him like a wildcat. Tore his arm open with a knife she'd concealed on her . . ."

"Why?" asked Fox

"Think!" said Maeve. "Think why a girl would cut a man . . ."

"Her own uncle . . . ?"

"It's been known."

The girl went on.

"No! No he came to tell her his son would protect her. All she had to do was marry his son. As the only child she would have the farm as a dowry. He was angry when she laughed in his face . . . she said."

"Where is the son?" hissed Fox.

"Gone for a soldier with the King's men. A month back there was shouting and an argument between the father and son. I came by the house from time to time to see if she'd come home . . ."

The girl was weeping.

"The son was telling his father he'd go for a soldier. It was his duty and his father told him not to. Ordered him not to but he left anyway. By the next morning he had gone. Rebecca's uncle stayed. To look after the farm, he said."

"Where would she go?" Fox asked.

The girl shook her head, hesitated a moment and then said, "Maybe old Mother Baugh knows. Rebecca knew her. Was not afraid of her. They let her go back to her home after it was done. She went back up the mountain. Madder than ever. Screaming and crying and wailing and . . . they let her go."

Fox sat silent now. The girl stood up and pulled her shawl about her.

"I want to say I'm sorry I didn't speak out. I am sorry. I was afeard. We all were. And now there's soldiers coming and going over the countryside and us all afraid again."

She stepped past Fox and Maeve picked up a dress that had been Rebecca's, which lay on a bench near the door. She handed it to the girl who took it, nodded her thanks, opened the door and walked out into the dark of the night.

26

Thurloe cursed. In his room, looking down towards the Thames and the quayside where the fishing boats came on the morning tide, Thurloe cursed again.

Two candles lit the table that was strewn with papers. The rest of the room lay in dark shadow save beside the fire where Tom Fairfax sat staring into the flames. His shadow danced on the panelled walls.

Outside there was no moon and the City of London lay quiet except for the barking of dogs and the occasional scream of a cockerel pretending morning had come.

"Vanished!" said Thurloe, "Off that damn boat, agrees to see us for a moment in secret and then gone! I never believed he meant it. And the damned girl as well."

Fairfax smiled and shook his head.

"You never believe anyone has a will except yourself, do you?"

"At this time we need men like Fox. And the damn girl has gone on some wild goose chase of her own. She's good, is Maeve Ahern, or whatever her real name might be, very good."

Fairfax kicked a smouldering log back into the hearth and stood up. He was restless, anxious to be out of the stuffy room. Why on earth any man needed fires in the summer was beyond him. But then Thurloe had never spent nights on the ground in cold tents on colder battlefields.

Fairfax grunted and opened the window to breathe in the fresh air. It carried only the hint of fish and night soil. Thurloe looked across, irritated.

"The King pushes, Tom. He seems not to understand the mood of Parliament or to care little for it if he does."

Fairfax said nothing. He continued to stare into the dark street.

"Makes demands on Parliament, which he knows, his advisors know, his wife knows . . . even that damned cockscomb Buckingham knows . . . Parliament will not grant him. More taxes, more money, more stupid expeditions by that idiot Buckingham pretending to be a soldier."

Fairfax spat into the fire. Buckingham played at being a general and then blamed his commanders in the field for his failures. Thurloe knew he flicked Black Tom Fairfax on the raw when he so much as mentioned his name.

"We need information about the sources of revenue for the King and his armies, we need to target them, close down the supplies of plate and silver and gold that steals its way to the King's cause. We need men and women like Fox and Ahern to track it down. To give us verse and number so we may throttle the King's cause at its conception."

Thurloe threw down his pen and leaned back in his chair. He watched Fairfax to see if he was reacting. Fairfax looked round at him. His sharp eyes dark under his craggy forehead. He gave away very little as he listened to this treason . . .

"Will he be defeated?" asked the old general.

"The King has gone to the Midlands. I know that much for he's made enough to do about it. He's raised an army and will no doubt raise his standard there and men will rally to him, no doubt of that either. Men and women of good blood will stand under his standard and think they fight for England. Close that damned window, man, I'm getting a cold."

"You won't get Fox to your cause by rattling the King at him. He's a regular soldier and gives not a hoot for kings or princes. Cares only for the battle or, in Fox's case, for being in the dead land between armies . . . in enemy cities . . . Well no matter. How you get him to our side I'm no longer sure."

Thurloe sniffed and wiped his nose on the lawn kerchief at his sleeve.

"We won't get him. He's said as much and it seems to me he means it. And the girl seems to have taken some sort of fancy to him and gone her own way. I need them as will obey orders . . . ."

"Do as you tell them?"

Thurloe looked up in surprise at Fairfax's mocking tone.

"Certainly," he said.

136

"So get puppets, get dogs, get parrots, get panders and pimps who'll do your bidding, no more, no less. You'll get little intelligence of interest for your coin."

Thurloe poured a measure of brandy and pushed the goblet to Fairfax as he sat once more at a distance from the fire. The light glinted on the edge of the goblet as Fairfax drank. For a moment or two neither man said a word.

A watchman called the hour and walked below the window.

"There are others where those two come from," muttered Thurloe.

"The girl is unique in my opinion," Fairfax said. "He might be. He *might* have been," he corrected himself, "If he hadn't married a wife and worse, loved her enough to make promises to her that take him out of your hands . . ."

Thurloe sat by the fire and sipped his drink. He stared over the rim of the glass into the shadows where his friend sat.

"If the King raises the country against Parliament . . . and we both know he will . . . then this country will be in chaos. If he dares to bring in the Scots in the name of his father and in the name of bringing peace to England, then we may look for a blood bath. There are men in Parliament who have everything to lose, should he decide to go to war with them . . ."

Fairfax looked at the young man as a question hung, unsaid, between them.

"We are wiser men, Tom, than to fall truly on either side," John Thurloe smiled for the first time and shook his head gently. "It's a matter of balances, Tom. You've seen it in the battlefield, I'm sure. This is no more no less than that. The King rides away to Nottingham . . . a feint . . . a test of the Parliament's resolve. Will they dare go the next step of the road to chaos and civil war?"

"'*They*', you said?" Fairfax leaned into the light from the candle on the table.

Thurloe nodded. Fairfax sat back.

"Not '*we*'?" he sighed.

Thurloe shrugged.

"*We*, my friend, *we* need to take time. We need to understand which way the game is being played. We need to keep mouths shut and wage our war in secret. And the way we may do that is through gathering information, through acting only on certainties. You taught me that, sir."

Thurloe smiled again and Fairfax sniffed through his long nose and lifted his head. He got up from the heavily carved chair.

"I believe I need to go north, my friend. Tonight. Quietly. To see my wife and to prepare my ground."

Thurloe looked up, not surprised by this decision.

"You have men to go with you?" he asked.

Fairfax stared at the pale face and shook his head.

"Alone, no fuss. Just a lone man riding north. You're tired, John," he said, "If the girl comes back, Fox will come too. But reel him in gently is my advice. Very gently. Fox will be a catch worth waiting for."

Fairfax smiled at the very idea.

"Did I ever tell you the time he was six days in a hole in the ground watching . . . waiting and watching the movement of some horses in the Duchy of . . .? No matter. He is a catch worth taking."

The two men clasped hands.

"Have a care, my friend. Such times are an excuse for every lawless fool to take arms and take what he can gain for himself."

"Unlike us, John? We have such principles?" Fairfax smiled a little.

"You do, Thomas Fairfax, I believe. For me? Well . . . we shall see."

The door closed on the old soldier. Thurloe sighed and walked back to his table and stared for a moment out of the window. Two horses clopped briskly away into the dark and headed north for Yorkshire.

Thurloe began to read another report from one of his pairs of eyes and then he pulled the ink well to him and began to write.

A log slipped and bright sparks flickered up the chimney.

****

Fox woke at dawn and it wasn't the rising of the sun that woke him so much as the sound of dogs barking in the yard. He was out of bed, dressed and armed as he moved fast down the landing. Maeve was already on the stairs.

Silently he handed her a pistol. She took it and moved on down the wide stairs to the back of the house. He checked the bars on the doors and the shutters at the windows.

He noticed that she had placed the bags and stores for the saddle bags close to the door. She'd made enough quick exits to know what needed to be done.

Fox felt the rush of excitement as he heard the murmur of a crowd of men coming closer.

Maeve stepped into the doorway of the dark kitchen and waited for him to join her.

138

"There are men coming. Not soldiers but ordinary neighbours. As that woman said they would."

Maeve nodded and began to prime the pistol.

"No need. They want us to go and we're going anyway. No need to kill anyone unless they make us. These are my neighbours and were good friends, once."

She looked at him. Her eyes quite dead in her face.

"Once," she said, "Not now. They say your wife was a witch. They will say you are and then it will be me, and I have no wish to burn as they burned her. By saying nothing, they burned her. You have no friends here."

Maeve poured in the charge, packed the lead ball and the wadding right into the pistol and stared at him as she did it.

"I will kill the first man to come into this house," she said. "Friend of yours or not. And then I will go and find the man whispered against your wife and I will slit his throat because you will be dead anyway."

Fox half shook his head, half smiled and turned as silence fell outside in the yard then someone was hammering on the door.

"Shall we see what they have to say?" he asked the girl. She shrugged.

Fox pulled out the bars, lifted the huge latch and swung the door open.

In the yard twenty or thirty men stood facing him. They carried pitchforks and two carried flaming torches. As the door opened and he stood there, they fell silent. The same villagers who'd been his friends, the same he'd made harvest with, drunk ale with at Christmas, laughed with, seen married, helped . . .

They stood there before him in the early morning light and they were angry. Pale faced, tight lipped and angry. Three or four had the courage to step forward but the others hesitated, seeing the pale glittering face in the doorway.

In the dancing light of the flares, he looked for the man he knew might be there. He saw Michael standing in the shadow of the barn, out of harms way. Michael was a part of them, but not a part.

Fox waited and then spoke quietly.

"Come to burn us out have you? All of you against one man and a girl. I suppose we might expect that from men allowed a woman to die as you allowed my dear wife to die. Afraid to speak out for her. Afraid of the truth."

One of the younger men stepped forward then. A broad built man with the arms and shoulders of a strong worker on the land. He'd the brashness of the young and the belief that it only took brute strength and belligerence to beat any man.

"Not afraid of you though, Fox, not afraid of you. Yes, we come to burn the place to rid ourselves of witches. They warned us you'd be infected. You come back with that red-haired girl and she lives with you. You have her, do you? So much you cared for your wife who confessed she'd given suck to the devil . . . kissed his fundament . . . confessed to it."

Fox stepped to the younger man. The man backed away, tripped and fell.

Fox moved fast to him, drew back his booted foot and kicked him viciously in the mouth. The young man lay gagging on broken teeth and an eruption of blood.

The crowd surged forward in anger and were only stopped when they saw the girl on the steps with the pistol steady in her hands.

"Do it," she said, "And you are dead."

The crowd of men murmured amongst themselves but stepped back from Fox and the young man whimpering on the ground. Fox looked across at Michael.

"You have something to say? I work for you, travel the land for you. Now you come here with these men . . . to fight me . . . to kill me? What?"

Michael stepped through the villagers but did not come close to Fox. His eyes took in the moaning figure on the ground. He licked his lips, screwed up his piggy eyes and looked around for support. He felt he'd found it and spoke though he was wheezing with fear.

"There is no need for her to threaten us. None!" he said. "The feeling is high, John Fox. You'd be best to go. Just go. Maybe in time feelings will change. But my niece did confess to witchery. She confessed it. They did warn us you were tainted too. They did. And we are afraid that is also true. They want to burn the farmhouse down. I say no. They want to burn the barns. I say, no! Think of your own interests, John. They want to kill the cattle for fear they'll bring ours to sickness. I say, no! But if you stay, it will happen for one day you will sleep and they will burn it all down about your ears. I can look after it. I would even give you a fair price for it. If you stay it will burn. Such a waste. Such a foolish waste."

The fat, pig-eyed man stared at Fox who said nothing. The heavy jowled man stood sweating.

"Your wife, my niece, said she believed in the peace of Christ's way. Maybe she did. If she did and if you honour her, let's have no more violence. No more anger. Just leave us. Take what you need and go."

Fox stared at the pale-faced man. Then he looked at the silent mob and round at Maeve who still stood in the doorway with the pistol at the ready.

He stepped to Michael who shuffled a step back for fear of being hit.

"For her sake," he said softly. "Never let me hear you speak of Christ again. You shame yourself and Him. Now get this rabble off my land."

Then he turned to them all. "I warn you. If we see hide or hair of any one of you when we leave, I'll kill him. And if my land and house are touched I will return and find who did it and kill him too. You understand . . . Uncle?"

Sweat beaded the man's forehead and Fox could smell that feral stink of fear.

"And you," Fox whispered, "Will take care of this house and the land, but in trust for my return."

He put his hand on the fat man's cheek.

"Or for my daughter, for if she has come to harm, I'll hold you to blame. She was flesh and blood to both of us. And if she comes and she be harmed, I'll cut your eyes out first and then your tongue. I'll make the Turk look like a butterfly. Now go!"

He stood and waited then as Michael turned and walked unsteadily through the crowd of men. Two bent and picked up the bleeding young man and trailed after the others as they left the yard. The dogs walked snarling at their heels and Fox watched until the last of them was off his land.

27

As they rode up into the high ground beyond the valley and the village, Fox stared about him with a kind of hunger. It was as if he was leaving the place of his birth for the last time.

The fields and meagre stone walls, the poor crops in the strips that had been cultivated for thousands of years lay in rows along the contours of the hills until they became too steep even for the local cottagers to bother with.

There the small, nimble-footed sheep foraged. Their thick, oily wool would find its way north to be spun or to France where it was traded for wine and oil.

He pulled his wide brimmed hat lower to shade his face from the glare of the sun as a blackbird chattered a warning to its mate from the deep hedge.

When they'd ridden through the village, not a soul moved and doors were firmly closed . . . it was as if the place itself was dead.

They had passed the last of the cottages when Maeve saw something move in the shadow of the trees by the pond. At first she thought it was a horse flicking flies with its tail but then a girl stepped boldly into their path.

Fox reined in his bay horse and waited. He never once looked at the girl after she stepped from the shadows. He watched the shadows behind her, the ditch to his left and the line of the old grey stoned wall on his right.

All places a man could hide, where an ambush could be prepared. A killing ground. Old habits die hard, the difference between life and death. Nothing showed itself. Still he watched.

The brown-faced girl was little more than a child of fourteen or fifteen. Rebecca's age.

Maeve reined in her horse and waited at the edge of the pond. The girl wore an old apron over the shift that was slightly too small for her newly maturing body. Her wrists poked awkwardly through the sleeves and she had the slightly fragile look of a young doe as she stood high on her feet and ready to run if needs be.

Over her long hair she wore a simple scarf against the heat of the day. Barefoot, she stood quietly by the horse's head and waited for Fox to look at her.

"Well?" he asked eventually.

The girl looked at the packed saddlebags and the roll of blankets at the back of their saddles. She stared at Maeve who sat astride her saddle, like the wild woman she was. Maeve's face betrayed no sign of welcome.

"You're going?" the girl asked. "They said you would," She answered herself.

Fox's horse shifted uneasily and she waited until he settled her.

"I promised I'd come back. You can remind them. Now, tell me who you are and why you stopped me."

"You don't remember me? I'm Mary, Rebecca was my best friend. I've been in your house many a time. Maybe you were too busy to notice me."

Already she had the coquettish look of a young woman and Fox smiled gently at her.

"Of course I noticed you. Just your name I forgot," he lied.

"I was only a child then," she said and looked up at Fox as he took off the hat that hid his eyes. She saw only pain.

Maeve's horse stepped a few paces to the left and stopped. Maeve chewed a stalk of grass as she sat and waited.

"She told me what she saw . . . Rebecca did. Before she went away. I begged her to stay. To get well . . ."

"To get well?"

"She was crazed, sir. In her mind she was unwell and afraid of so many things . . . She saw what they did to Mistress Fox who was so good to us all. She was afraid then. But her mother confessed and saved her from pressing and being put to the question. She told me that."

What mother would not to save a daughter being racked and stretched and pressed, torn and pierced with needles? Any mother worth a spit would confess to congress with the Devil himself to stop that.

Fox put his dark hat on his head.

"She would not stay. She said something about her cousin Saul. She said he wanted her to wife but she hated him."

The child looked up then into Fox's face and was struck silent by what she saw under the dark brim of his hat. Eyes dead as coal.

"His father, she said, came to her when she was alone in the house waiting for her mother to come home . . . he came to her and . . . I didn't understand what she told me then. I was afraid for her then. But I do know Saul and his father had a falling out and Saul went to the King's army . . ."

"And Rebecca?"

Both Fox and the girl were surprised at the sharpness of Maeve's voice. Neither of them answered.

"Gone up into the high valley?" asked Maeve. "To find an old woman . . . a woman who frightens you?"

The child stared at Maeve who reached down to touch her head. She shied away like a scared animal. Maeve shrugged and sat firm as her horse switched the flies from her shining rump.

"She said she'd go to Mother Baugh in the high valley and ask her what made her point at her mother as a witch. For it's true the men brought in the old woman and only after that did they take Mistress Fox."

There were tears in the child's eyes as she lifted her face to look at Fox.

"She was my friend . . . Rebecca. When you find her, tell her I miss her. Tell her my mother and father say I must marry soon. Tell her I want to run away too but dare not."

Fox looked quietly down at the child.

"Resist them," murmured Maeve gently. "If you are firm, if you make them see you mean what you say maybe they won't force you till you find a man you like. But do not go easy into the state of marriage for it's a harsh state to live by. Be brave and think of your friend."

Maeve tightened the reins and heeled her horse to make her move on.

She nodded at Fox and rode on up the track.

High overhead in the pale blue sky a hawk soared into a warm current of air and banked higher in its never-ending search for food.

Maeve sat her horse easily as the animal stepped delicately amongst the stones and rocks in the rough track which soon narrowed between ancient high stone walls . . .

144

Below, at the edge of the village, the child wiped her dirt-encrusted hand across her eyes.

Fox took a coin from his purse and held it out to her. Mary shook her head when he offered it, though it was gold.

"Rebecca is my friend," she said. "I want you to find her and to tell her I send my love. I need no coin for that"

The gold glittered in the sun. It was worth as much as a man could earn in six months on the land. Fox spun it into the air and the sun sparkled off it as it fell into his hand again.

"'Tis not for that," he said, "It is to give you strength to fight. When I was a child and lived here much as you do, no doubt, I had a place . . . up by the Devil's Armchair . . . high up there on the Stiperstones. I had a place near the chair . . . a stone I knew that I lifted out from time to time. I'd money there. Hidden. It lies there still. Find yourself a place. Hide this against a time you may have need and for my sake and for your friend's sake, pray for her."

He leaned down from the saddle and put the gold coin into the girl's hand. She put her hand on his face for a moment and then turned and walked back into the shadows by the dark green waters of the pond.

Fox rode slowly after Maeve who had already vanished through the scrub oaks and hawthorn thickets that shielded the track rising away from the village towards the high valley, the Long Mynd and the Devil's Armchair.

The hawk hovered on whirring wings, dipped and fell out of the sky.

The bundle of rags, hanging from the tree outside the wattle hurdles and turves that leaned crazily against the rock face concealing the old woman's' cave dwelling, swung in the breeze.

A crow sat on top of the bundle and pecked jerkily at the black cloth that covered it. As Fox stopped his horse near Maeve's, the bundle twisted and revealed that the crow was pecking at the space where the eyes had been. The bundle of pathetic rags was what was left of the old woman.

Fox dismounted, tethered his horse and walked over to the slowly turning body. He took his hat from his head and looked up at the old face.

"Not dead long," he said to Maeve as she stood by his side.

"No," she agreed.

She reached and touched the narrow yellow feet hanging below the black rags.

Maeve looked away down the valley and then up into the pale sky where the hawk waited to feed on the human carrion.

Maeve pointed at the turf and wattle structure.

"Rebecca was here," she said.

"How d'you know?" Fox asked and moved quickly into the dark and stinking hovel, kicking away two lengths of wattle fencing to let in some light.

They looked about them and saw only a narrow bed in a recess covered in sheepskin and rough wool blankets, a fireplace against the rock face on which stood two pots and beside which was a jug of water.

Fox lifted it, sniffed it and nodded. He put his hand to the ashes and was surprised to find them still warm.

Maeve nodded as he looked at her.

"Two hours, three at the most," said Maeve. "Maybe the old woman had something to tell us. Maybe someone stopped her mouth."

Fox stared at her and sniffed the air.

"You smell it too. It's here. On the sheepskin. The water your daughter used. Rosemary and oil and . . . Here, smell it. Smell her."

Maeve dragged the sheepskin from the bed and handed it to Fox who had caught the scent already. He sniffed and then buried his head in the sheepskin and smelled his daughter.

Maeve waited, then as he looked up she handed him a locket.

"Hers, I think . . . the double of the one you have."

Fox took the silver locket on its chain and flicked it open. His likeness and Alison's likeness facing each other across the two halves.

"It was here, behind the shelves and the pots. She felt safe here, I think. Or she came to discover something. Whatever the old woman knew. And then she ran again and left nothing but this and her scent."

"The old woman may have killed herself," suggested Fox.

Maeve shook her head.

"Go and look at her again," she said.

Fox walked back out of the gloomy dwelling and looked again at the body twisting on the rope. He looked again and then came back to Maeve who was peering into a drawer in a small chest at the back of the cave.

Maeve turned and waited for Fox to speak.

"She was killed and hanged after. There's no way she could have put herself on the rope without something to stand on . . ."

"And she hasn't shit herself or the ground under her. So she was killed first and then hanged up to make believe she'd done it herself."

Fox nodded, put the sheepskin on one of the wattle fences he'd kicked aside and walked to the body. The crow cocked his head, then lifted off from the black-shrouded figure and flapped hazily away.

"We'll take her down," Fox said, "And cover her as best we can."

Maeve stared at him and shook her head and crossed herself.

146

Fox took his knife, mounted his horse and inched her close to the body. The horse was nervous . . . flouncing and inching sideways away from the old dead woman as she turned on the knotted rope.

Fox cut the rope that held her and the body flopped to the ground like a disjointed doll.

A lark rose on a pillar of song higher into the sky away from the purple heather and these intruders.

As they wrapped the body in the rough blanket off the bed, Maeve sniffed at the dead woman's mouth.

"She was poisoned. See here . . ."

At the corner of the mouth a slight trickle of brown liquid stained the skin.

"The smell of violets about her mouth . . . It's essence of turpentine killed her."

Fox stared at Maeve as she looked round at him and touched his hand.

"I'm no witch, my friend. I know these recipes from time spent with gypsies in the Carmargue in southern France. Common simples for sickness can turn too easily to death in the right quantities. See in the box. See?"

She pulled the box from the cave and into the daylight beside the body.

Maeve opened the box and took out three leather bound books.

"See them. This old woman was well read in Latin and in English too. See?"

Fox opened the first of the books and then the second. The third was a Bible from the look of it, also in Latin.

"What are these?" he asked, holding out one of the ancient books.

"Simple remedies for sickness. She read them, made them up . . . See here in the box . . . powders and potions prepared."

And it was true. In the box were bottles of powders, small bone pots of salves for wounds and bites and the itch . . .

The wrinkled old woman, regarded as mad by most and indeed often crazed by the moon, had once had great skills. No-one knew her history, her parents or her past. She'd lived up here as long as John Fox could remember. And she and Alison often talked together.

Maeve helped him wrap the old woman in the blanket and she strewed amongst the folds the dried herbs from the box and sweet smelling rosemary and bay leaf hanging in the roof of the cave. She put the book of recipes, wrapped in leather, into her saddle bag.

They rode away from the ruins of the hovel leaving the severed rope hanging from the tree and, beyond it, piled over with stones, the broken body of the mysterious old woman.

Carrion crows hopped and pecked about the hard ground and, giving up, raised themselves on night-black wings and floated down towards the dark mass of the Devil's Armchair which loomed over the land.

And the dark clad figure on the brown horse rode silently away from the village where his wife had been burned and from where his daughter had been driven away. He rode with a remorseless pace across the wide flat land that looked over to Wales and in the other direction down across the Midlands to where the King's men had already raised their banners.

Fox rode on with the sole purpose of finding the Parliament troopers who'd stopped him on his way home. If anyone might know where the King's troops could be found, it should be the Parliament men. And when he found those men, he'd find Saul, son of Michael and cousin to his dead wife.

If anyone knew about what had happened it would be Saul and he would tell. One way or another he would tell and when Fox discovered the truth, vengeance would be his.

Behind him, Maeve rode at her own pace. Never quite letting him get out of sight but not wanting to ride alongside him or even close to him. He'd his own fate to see to and his clock was ticking to a different time and a different tune to hers just now. She watched him as he rode purposefully after the vengeance he sought.

He urged his horse on down towards the Midlands and soldiers and the fighting he understood.

And in his heart was fire.

28

Fox and Maeve had ridden east, away from the borders and towards Worcester where there was word that a troop of Royalists were billeted. It was the start of a war that would set father against son, brother against brother, friend against friend, for the cruellest of wars is civil war. The King had thrown down the gauntlet or picked it up, depending on who you believed.

Fox and Maeve Ahern rode through the land, ignoring what they saw.

Apart from the set piece battles yet to come, this was a war of skirmishes, of forced recruiting and an excuse to settle old scores.

They came upon the work of soldiers only a week after they'd left the village and come down towards Stratford and into a small village on the borders of Gloucestershire.

Todenham was a village public house, a church and a row of labourers' cottages along the wall of a large estate and under the shade of a vast yew tree growing near the green.

It was a quiet place and, when Fox and Maeve rode up the hill into the village, it seemed ordinary enough.

At the edge of the village lay a pile of charcoal and behind it a dark shed that was a forge. Fox slowed as they came to the forge. He looked over the fence surrounding the yard and saw that the fire was not lit.

Maeve saw the smith first. He'd been pitchforked through his chest to the bole of the yew tree and allowed to bleed to death. Flies hummed and gorged on the drying wound. Three old men stood and looked on as Fox and the girl rode towards them.

They said nothing as the two riders dismounted and led their horses to the small and drying-up pool near the green.

The riders drank from their water bottles and watched the houses for a sign of movement. No-one stirred.

Fox walked over as the old men looked listlessly at him.

"Where is everyone?" he asked.

The three men shook their heads as one man.

"Where is everyone?" Fox asked again. "Who did that?"

He gestured with his thumb at the man pinned to the bole of the tree.

One of the old men stirred then and looked about as if to see that no-one could hear him.

"Troopers come through the village three days since," he whispered.

"Most of the village ran to the fields then. Afeard. 'Twas soldiers see, and we have heard things; such things. Women and children killed . . . worse. Men taken for soldiers or killed an' all. So they ran to the fields."

"He didn't run far, did he?" sneered Maeve. And she spat in the general direction of the man pinned to the tree.

"Peter was a good smith, like his father afore him."

One of the old men stood up straighter and looked at Fox in his dark cloak and large-brimmed hat.

"We're too old for going for a soldier. They left us bide but Peter refused to shoe their horses or to mend their swords. He could read a bit could Peter and he had heard tell these were King's soldiers and he'd have none of them, he said."

The old man walked quietly down to the dead man and stared at him. Fox followed. Across the face and naked chest of the dead man blood and charcoal had mixed in sticky streams.

The old man stooped close to the pitchfork handle that stuck from the man's chest and tried to pull it free and failed.

"He's been trying to take it out the past two days since the troopers left us. He's too weak. It's his son d'you see," said one of the other men.

The old man by the tree turned from the dead man and opened his arms and then let them fall helpless to his side.

"I'd bury him if I could but take him down."

Maeve and Fox slept that night in the abandoned ale house. They barricaded the doors against the return of the troopers, cleared as much of the debris of glass and spilled wine and ale as they needed to and found feathers from bolsters scattered in the rooms over the bar room below.

Fox washed the soil of the grave he'd dug from his hands and arms while Maeve had silently routed out a meal for them from what was left in the alehouse. She neither knew nor cared what the old men did after they'd buried the dead smith.

Fox was more silent than he'd ever been since she'd known him. It was as if a rat was gnawing at his guts.

They ate together at a table by the empty fireplace and drank a bottle that had not been smashed and Fox said nothing. They'd drunk a little more and she tried to make him talk about the way they'd go tomorrow and he said nothing and stared at the table and ate and drank only to refuel himself.

He was honed only to two tasks, to find Rebecca and to wreak vengeance for his wife.

"King's men?" she asked, and gnawed at the rind of an old cheese.

One of the old men had told them the men were led by officers in plumes and feathers, in silk and gold braid and with fine swords.

The villagers had no idea who the soldiers were but they were certainly cruel and vicious men and they'd boasted of killing a whole village back in Gloucestershire and they were headed for Oxford, the old men had heard.

"If it's Prince Rupert's men, he learned the trade in a hard school. He knows the value of a dead man like that dead man. It's worth a dozen victories to terrify the people."

Fox stared at the girl and didn't see her. The search was taking its toll on him and also on her. She wanted to go, to leave him and yet she felt tied.

She'd made a promise to that strange young man, Thurloe, to bring this man to his table, ready and willing to work in the clandestine world she'd moved in this past six years.

She half smiled for she knew that John Thurloe had no notion if she was truly on his side or not. Maeve looked around the shattered room, drank the last of her wine and stood up. Fox didn't even look up.

Maeve knew that he had to break down or go stark mad with the grief that had burned him since he'd clawed up the ashes of his wife in that cold field under the Long Mynd.

****

She lay in the blankets they'd discovered in a press on the top landing. They were reasonably clean. She listened for Fox to walk up the stairs and along the corridor to the room he'd chosen.

She heard him walk up the stairs and heard the heavy steps along the landing and then they stopped at her door. Maeve released a sigh as he opened the door and stepped into her room.

They lay in the bed together and listened to the soft creaking of the inn sign in the wind that stole up through the night. She turned to him again and felt his body harden as her hand found him.

They'd slept deep after the first love making. It was no act of love for Fox but a release of the tension pent up in him. Maeve had been battered by the frenzy of his need. She knew well enough it was not her he was feeling beneath him but a lost memory. She knew also that he needed to release his need either in this bed or later in terrible and violent anger.

For her, who'd not made love for longer than she cared to think of, it was a release also. They were two wild animals in a sack as they felt and pushed, squeezed and bit, hit and pulled and demanded from each other. When it was done they lay in their own sweat and there was nothing of love in it. Nothing.

Fox slept instantly. When he woke it was to feel her body close to his. Her firm breasts and the promise of her thighs against him and her hand already moving on his body. He turned over with his face down on the pillow and wept.

She tried to soothe him tried to gentle him as she'd gentle an angry animal. It was a gift her mother had that she could calm the angriest of animals, yet Fox was not to be soothed or calmed. He lay and wept on his back, open, naked and the tears ran down his face and he stared at her as if she were a hated thing as she lay beside him.

Indeed she was for the moment, which she had been prepared for. Yet she had not been prepared for how she would feel and was surprised to find she was desolated by his rejection even though she'd expected it.

She wanted him to take her again, this time to be gentle, and yet she saw in his eyes the naked anger, the deadliness of a man bent on one thing and she knew that it was better for her to go.

"I'm sorry," she said and getting up from the bed, she stood naked by the window and watched the sun just begin to rim the edges of the land and the trees beyond the village behind the black elm.

She turned then to see him staring at her, folded her arms across her breasts and shook her head so that her tumbled hair fell about her face and neck.

"I'm going now, John Fox. I'll not stay with you when all I sense about you is death."

She dressed then and waited for him to say something, but he was silent. She took up her leather bag and opened the door. He was silent. She walked out of the room and left the door wide open.

He lay and stared at the ceiling and was silent.

He rode out of the village two hours after she'd gone. The old men were standing in the street watching as he mounted up. He rode towards them and stopped.

"She's gone north," said the father of the dead smith.

Fox nodded and the old man came closer.

"There was a name I heard," whispered the old man. "Major Andrews was the leader of the troop. He told them to kill my son. He laughed when they held him against the tree. He laughed when they leaned on the pitchfork and he laughed when they rode away."

Fox stayed the horse then and leaned down to the old man standing by his stirrup.

"This man . . . Major Andrews . . . what did he look like? Tall, dark, short, fat, what?"

"Tall . . . not fat . . . white face and long hair. One of his eyes had a slight cast. A terrible man. Sir, I'd thank you for what you done for my son. I have no money. Nothing but this which you are welcome to. Should you find this man show him no mercy. Should you find them, sir. For I see anger in your eyes and no mercy. Show him none."

The old man took from under his old coat a sword with a broad blade almost like a naval cutlass. Not long but beautifully balanced and good for close work. Around the cupped guard, silver was embossed in a spiral of oak leaves and tendrils.

"My son made it," said the old man.

Fox hesitated and then took the sword and felt the balance of it and nodded, unsmiling, at the grieving man and hung it and its leather scabbard from his saddle.

"No mercy." Fox said and he clicked up his horse and rode on as if the old men were no longer there. He rode past the yew tree and headed south. He'd a soldier to find and vengeance to take.

The earth on the new grave had already sunk a little. A bunch of wild flowers lay on the loose red earth, with the dew of the morning still on them. Maeve had gone her way.

153

29

He'd ridden away alone from the silent village and the new grave. Past the elms at the end of the track he turned beneath the fold in the rolling hills hiding Great Chew and other, even smaller villages.

Down through the soft hills that took him towards Oxford he rode, unthinking through the lush countryside, his mind shut and unwilling to accept what had happened.

He hardly noticed the way people looked at him as he passed through their villages. He didn't see how they whispered when he'd passed them nor feel the chill they felt on his passing.

He'd had but a few friends before he went for a soldier. Now, after these years, most were either dead or still in arms abroad. The thought stirred that with the troubles coming, the grapevine would be letting soldiers as far afield as Ghent or Genoa, Sweden or Austria know that there was work to be had in England.

In London at the Exchange in Seven Dials, also known as The Sign of the White Swan, mercenaries would be drinking, planning. Men would be riding to join whichever army would take them, the King's or Parliament's. Fox knew many would not care a spit but only count the pay and the chances for plunder.

It would be a dangerous time for those without arms in this lush country. Fox didn't care; he cared for nothing save the fire in his gut and vengeance. Above all he had to find his beautiful Rebecca before she was lost in the chaos that was about to sweep the land.

He knew war and he knew the danger for such a girl at such a time and his blood turned to ice as he remembered towns in Austria or Germany after soldiers had been through.

And then he remembered one particular old comrade.

Mark Pearson had been a sergeant with Black Tom, and he and Fox had been good friends who drank together, roistered together and only rarely whored together. Mark had a girl he was determined to marry back home near Oxford. He and Fox had dreamed of seeing each other when they left the army, of having sons, of the life they'd lead.

Mark had been his only true friend apart from Pat Shea. He had saved Fox's back twice by standing up and telling the truth and be damned to the consequences. The young officers disliked the three of them and they didn't give a spit.

When Fox left the service, he'd lost track of Mark and more or less forgotten him until now. But he was the one companion in arms he'd talked about to Alison and to Rebecca. They'd laughed about marrying Rebecca off to one of his sons; of going to find his farm in the village called Bourton. Maybe Rebecca had remembered her father's trusted friend. Maybe.

Fox found the farm in the late afternoon of a September day.

He rode along the overgrown, rutted lane towards the farmhouse then stopped and waited for a time to see if Mark might appear. There was smoke from the chimney and washing drying on the line and once he saw a bright-haired girl come out and throw scraps for chickens and go back and slam the oak door.

The yard was dirty and seemed to be choked with rank grass and weed. The open-fronted shed was in need of tiles to keep out the rain and, with winter not so far away, it needed doing soon.

He sat patiently under a huge oak and watched and waited. No-one came out and there was no more sign of life. Yet he was sure this was the place his friend had said. This was where he intended to come when he left the army. He'd urged John Fox to come and visit.

Fox edged his horse out of the shade of the tree and across the yard. He sat then staring at the house, a gaunt figure in the afternoon sunlight. A minute, two, then he noticed at the corner of his eye the flicker of a face at a window.

He felt exposed and naked sitting in the middle of the yard in this way. He made up his mind, dismounted and walked to the door, which opened as he reached it.

He'd expected the tall figure of his old friend, not the tiny girl who stood on the step and looked up at him so gravely. Behind her stood her mother, a tall, scrawny woman with large work-torn hands and an air of tired defiance as she stepped forward into the light to greet the stranger.

He saw the disappointment in her face as he took off his hat and revealed his face.

"I'm Fox," he said, "A comrade of your husband's."

"I'd thought, happen it'd be my man come home," she said. She ran a hand through her greying straggling hair. Once she had been a pretty woman, but was no longer. "Mark promised to turn up like a bad penny wi'out a word of warning and God knows we've waited long enough."

Fox stared at her and at the little girl.

"We saw you under the tree . . . waiting, but couldn't see your face," she said. "Marky saw you first."

"Marky? Where's he?" Fox asked.

"Here." said a young voice behind him and Fox turned and saw a boy of fifteen or so standing with a bell-ended arquebus pointing directly at his back. Fox lifted his hands to show they were empty. The muzzle of the ancient gun didn't move.

"I knew your father," he said, "He'd be proud to know you'd out-foxed Fox and had me covered so secure."

"Fox?" asked the gaunt wife now, "Fox as was going to marry his sweetheart and settle down and live on the land . . . Mark told such tales. Are you John Fox?"

"I am John Fox. Yes." He said quietly without taking his eyes off the boy with the gun.

"Marky, it's all right, he's a friend," said his mother and the boy slowly lowered the ancient fowling piece. "You'd best come in, Fox," she said, "Though we've little enough to offer you."

It was true enough. There was little food and little comfort. Mark had got the farm into shape, had bad debts, had to sign up for the army for the money and left his wife to try to make the farm pay.

They sat at the table while the youngsters got on with their chores.

"I met your daughter," said Mark's wife slowly and Fox stared at her.

"She was here. She said you'd talked about Mark and me, and she remembered. She was afraid she said . . . afraid of people searching for her. Afraid of her uncle."

Fox said nothing. Rebecca had been here. It was something.

"She was nervous. I truly think her mind had been damaged by what she had seen. She said little enough but she hurt to tell what she did tell." said Mark's wife. She stood up and ladled more stew into his bowl.

Fox shook his head in disbelief.

"When did she leave?"

156

"Three weeks ago . . . She was afraid to stay too long in one place she said. I begged her to stay but she said she came because my man was such a friend of yours . . . She talked about you and her mother laughing about meeting up again. Then one morning she was gone. To tell the truth, I do miss her."

The worn woman sat and pushed her lank hair out of her face.

"So close," he said, "Did she hint where she might go?"

"To crowds, she said . . . where she could be lost. A city, she said. She said she might come back if it didn't suit her. Or for the winter, maybe."

Fox stayed two weeks and did his best to put right what he could. He showed the boy what had to be done and how to do what he could till he grew into a man.

They worked well together and the boy tried to please the taciturn man as if he'd a father to please. Sometimes he tried to talk about Rebecca but the man said nothing.

Then Fox left them as silently as he had come. He'd owed the sergeant and he'd paid his debts.

"Tell him when he comes home, if he wants to find me to ask for Black Tom. He will know where I am," he told the woman and her son on the evening before he left.

"You going home to your wife, Mister Fox?" asked the little girl and was hushed by her mother.

Fox smiled gently at the little girl and conjured a coin out of her ear. He gave it to her despite her mother's protests. The boy watched but said nothing. Then Fox did the same for him but the boy didn't smile.

Fox looked across at the frightened little girl who stood in the crook of her mother's arm. The room was lit only by the guttering light of a tallow candle and the dying glow of a fire.

They'd killed and begun to cure a pig that day. They'd singed and cleaned it with water warmed on the fire. Taken the intestines and washed them clean in basin after basin of water and congealed the blood with barley. They'd made blood pudding as well as beginning to salt cure the sides and hocks as well as hanging hams for smoking in the wide chimney.

They'd eaten well and he was provisioned for the next few days. They now had enough food for a long hard winter. He'd picked them up and made them see they had to make the best they could against the time her man came home.

The barn no longer needed wooden tiles, the yard was cleared of rank grass and the fields had been tended. He'd mended the cart and he and the boy had taken and sawn fallen timber from the nearby copse against the winter cold. The logs were neatly stacked in the open barn.

Fox had not thought of anything through the two weeks save how to make life possible for this troubled, lonely woman and her two children as they waited for the sergeant to return. And to wonder if Rebecca might come back.

He knew the chances were that Mark had a woman in a baggage train or had settled in a kinder place where the farming was easy with some French or Italian woman who'd be softer than what he'd left behind him. It was the way of things for soldiers. She knew it as well as Fox but lied to herself and to her children

And if Rebecca was hiding in a city from her uncle, he asked why she was so afraid of him? What did she know that made her so edgy? And where was she? Where?

He'd ridden away in the early morning. It'd been a simple parting. Mark's wife sat at the long scrubbed table and cut bread for him and cheese and he ate and took water from the earthenware jug by the window.

"Tell him if he wants to leave word for me that The Exchange at Seven Dials will find me. He'd've called it the Sign of the White Cross. There."

He'd picked up his leather bag and his sword and the young lad carried his long dagger for him and his hat to where he'd been currying the horse for the man who, for a few days, had been a father to him.

He put a purse with coins in it on the pillow of his bed. It would be no use offering the money to the woman, he knew that.

Fox left the woman sitting at the table. She had smiled wanly at him as he left. She was afraid to be alone and he understood that. He walked across the boarded room and out into the bright October sunshine. It shone gold and yellow and pale across the canopy of the oak tree.

There was no sign of the little girl. Fox mounted, took his hat from young Mark.

"Thank you, boy," Fox said. "Your father will be proud of you. Tell him Fox said he'd be proud to have a son like you. Look after your sister and your mother and remember I told you always have a satchel packed with food and spare clothes and hidden by the oak in the big field. In case you need to run. Never trust a soldier. Never. And if Rebecca comes by, tell her to find Colonel Fairfax at the Parliament House. Remember it."

And the boy nodded and repeated the name and said nothing more for fear he'd cry. Fox held out his hand and the boy clasped it, as a man would have done. Fox rode out of the yard, past the house cow and the pigpens and the chickens scattering the earth about his horse's hooves.

158

He didn't look back. If he had he'd have seen the boy leaning against the gate with his fists clenched in his eyes.

At the end of the lane, the little girl stepped out of the hedgerow and held something up to him. He stopped, leaned down and took what she offered and, leaning closer kissed her cheek.

"Thank you," he said. "Your mother will need you. Do what you can for her."

"Stay," said the little girl not looking up into his sad face.

"I can't. I'm sorry but I have things I have to do. Someone I have to find. If your father comes . . . *when* your father comes, tell him I needed to see him. Tell him I owe him another debt for letting me meet you, child. Tell him you remind me of someone else," he said.

He looked down at the bundle she had given him where it lay on his saddle . . . Dog roses, glinting with dew.

Alison held dog roses when she burned. Maeve had seen them.

Fox rode blindly through the lanes. To Oxford.

****

And through the rest of the land men rode and marched, walked and took coaches,. Wagons, carts, were enlisted, dispatched, ordered or volunteered, were dragged into one army or another by the King or by my Lord Essex, by Prince Rupert or Tom Fairfax and some went singing psalms to the glory of the Lord and others sang the praises of the King.

Slowly, much of the country began to take on the appearance of a garrison. In the depths of the countryside, whole populations were untouched yet by the madness that was slowly crawling over the land.

Madness in which brother would fight brother, father would fight son, wife would betray husband in the name of the Lord God of the Levellers and the Puritans, or in the name of the King who believed the same Lord God appointed him ruler over all England. In the name of God and the King, men and women were going to die.

Fox rode down the country towards the spires and churches, cloisters and chapels of Oxford where the King was favoured.

He'd a mind to see the King in whose name a farrier blade-maker had been butchered. He wanted to see the man by whose agent his wife had been burned to the ashes he carried.

And with him he carried also dark anger and ice for a heart.

30

Fox took a room in The Mitre, stabled his horse and began to quarter the city as he quartered any place where he might stay for a time. It was a habit taught him by an old soldier who'd known more than most about survival in the no man's land every spy inhabits.

The routines were the same in the wildest of countryside and in the most benign of cities. Check routes in and escape routes out, find food and water and a place that was dry and warm if possible. Keep money and weapons about you and leave as little of yourself in passing as possible.

Then learn to move through the new territory in daylight and in the dark. Oxford was easy enough in the hours of daylight but at night the city was patrolled by army and by civilian watchmen whose movements had to be learned.

Fox began by observing the routes of their patrols then checked the gates of the city for the times the guards changed. He made notes, learned and then burned them. At the end of a week he felt he'd done what was needed and could begin to feel safe in the city.

He walked through the pale stone cloisters and into the vastly ornate chapels attached to the colleges. He watched processions of clerics and of learned bodies going about their business as if the army of the King was not in and about the city. It was as if they ignored the threat of war hanging in the air.

One morning he passed through a market and into a chapel. Here the rich gold ornaments and hangings didn't move him but the peace of it was something he valued. It was also a useful place to make a meeting, to pass information, to pick up a letter, if the time came.

Every city he had ever been in he'd made it his business to find such a place. And at the front of the chapel, half hidden by a stone buttress, he saw Rebecca. She was kneeling with her head half covered by a shawl but it was her.

"Rebecca," he called out and ran down the aisle to the kneeling figure. She turned her head then. It was an old woman disfigured by some wasting disease. She covered her face and went back to her prayers as Fox stumbled out of the chapel and leaned against the wall in the sunlight and vomited into the lane like a cat.

Through the alleyways and closes, along cobbled lanes and street markets Fox walked, watched and listened. He noted everything in detail so that if anything changed, a pattern shifted, he would know. He saw the water flooding under the bridges and along the water meadows still green with the last of the autumn lushness.

Oxford was becoming a throbbing caravanserai. He watched and counted their numbers as men and animals and even women rushed about in a common feverish activity. He never consciously searched for Rebecca here. She would go to London if she searched for crowds and anonymity.

Soldiers were for ever coming and going, riders meeting in ale houses, men and women of every sort and condition floating about the public houses and rooming houses where the junior officers of the King's army were quartered from time to time.

Senior officers would take over civilians' houses, tell protesting owners that they would be well paid for their trouble and then turf them out into the street. Once in place the plate and linen the food and stores, the wine cellars and all that spoke of creature comfort was requisitioned in the King's name and used for the comfort of his officers.

There'd be precious little recompense paid when King's officers moved on. Parliament men were said to be less arrogant in their use of the people they billeted them themselves upon.

Fox watched as a city dignitary stood in the street before his own front door and demanded entry to his own house. He saw the officers leaning out of the windows of the house laughing at the red faced, angry man. Saw the young whores who'd come to see to the creature comforts of the officers shouting abuse at the fat old man straining his silk jerkin and shaking with anger. They screamed at his wife and young daughter until

162

they were forced to turn tail and leave their own home. The old man stood his ground with considerable dignity.

Fox cried out a warning too late as two young officers leaned out with full chamber pots and emptied them over the old man.

He had seen it often enough abroad and indeed been part of that locust hoard, an occupying army. When an army moves into a city it does not wait politely sitting on its thumbs . . . it takes what it wants and be damned to them as would say enough is enough.

Fox watched it all, and then he saw the King.

The King was riding out into the meadows to review a troop of well-mounted men. He had brought to his colours the sons of the gentry. Young men who'd been in the saddle since infancy and who'd money enough to provide a mount for each of their servants. They each brought with them men they'd volunteered off their estates to fight for the glorious Stuarts.

Fox spat in the dust as he watched the manoeuvres and the formal drills of the soldiers. What did they know of war?

As he looked over the meadows outside the city walls he became aware that he was being watched. It was the same man he'd seen in the ale house as he ate his chop last night. The same man he'd seen reflected in the window glass of a baker's shop, the same man who'd been at the back of the choir stalls in St. John's Chapel. Fox leaned against a tree watching the King reviewing his soldiers.

King Charles was a small man, dwarfed by the colonels who rode alongside him. He was wearing dark burnished armour, gilded across the breastplate and down the arms with acanthus leaves and leopards. The best of Italian work.

He had a fine dark red cloak lying back from his shoulders and about the haunches of as good a horse as Fox had ever seen.

The sharp-featured monarch stared about him and seemed not to be at ease with the horse, the colonels or the world at large. His stiff face stared from slightly bulging eyes along the lines of men whom he'd expect to die for him. His well cropped beard a 'V' under his chin. On his hand the Ring of State, about his neck more jewels and in his plumed hat yet more.

He lifted a languid hand to salute his soldiers and turned impatiently to the colonels and whispered something. The three men rode quickly off the parade ground and leaving the soldiers disappointed for they had wanted to see their King. Their lives were his to spend as he might, and spend them he would.

Fox could feel the eyes of the man watching him on his back, but he went on with his work. He was counting the files of soldiers on a pile of pebbles in his right pocket. Then he counted the ranks on a pile of pebbles into his left so he'd keep a tally of exactly how many men the King had here.

He had already noted the number of horses and the baggage trains on another foray into the outskirts of the town where the camps had been set up.

He'd sat in ale houses and listened to the gossip and from it had gleaned some idea of the condition and the morale of the men. It was meat and drink to him. It was his work and he knew his business well. When he met Thurloe he'd have a great deal to trade with.

Fox felt nothing for that bearded, bejewelled, over-dressed little man. For the moment, he felt little for anyone or anything.

He walked up into the city thoughtfully after the King had left the field. He walked away from the bustling streets and the market down into the backs where the water flowed dark brown through the city. And as he idled into the quiet back lanes he drew his watcher after him.

The man who had followed him so carefully turned a narrow corner and found the cobbled street ahead of him empty. Worse it was a dead end.

Worse yet he felt an arm around his throat and steel under his ear. Fox dragged the man into a deeply recessed doorway before he let his throat go.

"Shout and I'll cut your throat," he whispered in the man's ear.

He was astonished to feel the man shaking with laughter. The man turned to him.

"Fox!" he said, and Fox looked into a familiar face from the days with Tom Fairfax. A fortunate meeting.

The man had been wounded and left for dead on some battlefield. Fox, Mark and Pat Shea had dragged him away from the scavenging women searching out the dead and dying to rob and seen to it that he lived.

"Davy Parker! I'll be damned."

The two men sat until late, first in a chop house and later in the rooms Davy Parker had over the college gate where he was guardian and gate keeper. The upper rooms looked out over the college green and were little used.

They'd laughed a great deal and talked of old times and old long dead comrades. Here, for Fox, was the perfect plant. A man he could use if and when the time came. A man who owed him. A man who wanted to repay the debt. It was as good as knowing the man was cheating on his wife. It was a lever.

Fox told him nothing of his immediate past and little of his plans. Here was a man to put into storage to be plucked out when the time came. He mentioned the chapel and the man knew it. No more was said of it.

Davy, it seemed, was a man whose only concern was to keep out of the coming fighting and to keep his head down.

Fox sympathised and plied him with drink. He praised the old, limping soldier and became a sycophant, an eager ear. Davy Parker relived past glories, boasted, exaggerated and lied about his skills while Fox listened and marvelled and plied him with more drink.

He would use the man and his vanity when the time came but he would never trust him an inch, for Davy Parker was a loose tongue and a time server. Pat Shea had had no time for him but for the moment Fox needed a man to use and Davy presented himself.

The King's troopers rode out of the city the next morning. The King followed in his carriage. It was more a progress than a General going to war. For a moment, Fox thought of the hardships he and his friends had faced in the battlefields of Europe when he'd been little more than a boy. It had been a hard growing up.

And yet . . . yet he felt some nostalgia as he watched the horses clip by and the foot soldiers marching out under the eyes of the people and their women followed in the baggage train as they do all armies.

Fox counted the baggage trains and assessed the condition of the arms and of the men. It gave him more information to trade with Thurloe when he met him in London.

He walked away from the noise and the bustle and the weeping women and the youngsters who follow any army like dark clouds and sat beside the river staring long at the brown water of the Cherwell as it flowed under the bridge to his right.

He'd heard rumours that the colleges were going to do as some colleges in Cambridge had done and give their valuable silver to the King's cause to be melted down to pay his armies. Cromwell, a country Member of Parliament, had stopped that nonsense, Davy had told him, when he'd taken troopers to stop the heads of colleges supplying the King's war chest.

Cromwell, had now turned himself into a soldier. Fox had laughed aloud at the idea of some farmer and member of parliament trying to lead soldiers when he had no experience. Davy had laughed too, but assured him it was a fact.

Here in Oxford, who was to stop the royalists doing as they wished? Fox had decided then to take a real gift to Thurloe in London. If he wanted something from him he knew he'd have to offer something in return. He'd learned from Davy that old soldiers were often appointed to oversee the security of the colleges of the University. Fit men to sit in porter's lodges and to ensure no brawling students caused breaches of the peace, to keep undesirables out of college grounds and to see to the safety of the men who studied and taught there. Davy Parker did nothing for nothing nor ever had. He had been a terrible man in the field. He'd been unaccountably afraid of the dark and of the silence of the countryside. Fox had remembered his weakness for drink.

They met two or three times after that first contact in Oxford. They'd taken a drink or two together for old time's sake. Fox knew that for all his pretence at friendship, Davy was afraid of him. Now Fox called in his debt. He wanted to know which colleges gave plate and valuables, how much they gave and how it left the city.

Davy had protested at first but when Fox mentioned Black Tom Fairfax as someone who'd be grateful for the intelligence and when he'd suggested there might be money in the business, Davy had agreed to do what he could. It would take time, need tact and care and maybe even a bribe or two.

Fox gave him enough for the purpose and knew it would line Davy's pocket, but if anyone could find out what he wanted, Davy could. On his home ground he was infallible, it was only the silence of the countryside and the strangeness of foreign places that unnerved the man. The very things Fox relished . . .

Fox had started to weave his net. It was a beginning. It was a Thursday in the second week of October. Autumn was showing now and the trees around the city were a blaze of gold and rust. Soldiers were in billets about the city and were beginning to take up quarters for the winter. The campaign season was over and it was time to plan for the next.

Fox knew he had little time. He was whipping himself to action each and every day but knowing in his heart he was searching for a needle in a haystack. He knew Rebecca was not in Oxford and he was eager now to begin his campaign to put Thurloe in his debt. And if he was to find the man responsible for the death of his wife, he had to find the King's witchfinder and question him. Nothing is given for nothing and if he wanted Thurloe to help search out the witchfinder, he knew he had to take some juicy information with him.

The ivy, already beginning to turn colour, grew thick across the front of the inn under the mullion windows of the first floor where the bedrooms were as Fox walked towards the courtyard of The Mitre. He hesitated and stopped in the shadow of an overhanging house and watched the yard and the street in front of the inn. Instinct? Fear? Concern? An itch?

Below street level, through metal bars, he could see the fire in the kitchen glowing as the cooks began to work themselves to a frenzy of baking and roasting.

The officers might not pay but they did demand food and got it.

"The King will pay," they'd say and laugh and order more wine.

"The Mayor will pay . . . Parliament will pay . . ."

In a pig's ear!

Fox leaned against the wall under the overhanging upper window and waited.

"Aren't soldiers the same the world over?" he thought.

He'd seen it in Germany and Spain, in Austria and France and he had little fear of the chaos he knew was coming. He was a soldier again and it was like slipping on a favourite boot . . . or an old coat. He felt easy within himself.

Black Tom had been right to try to snare him for the work for Black Tom knew that for men like Fox the blood runs quicker with a spice of danger.

As he watched the inn, a carriage raced to the yard and stopped before the arched entrance. Two men got out and stepped quickly onto the creeper-covered terrace which blazed gold and red in the late sunshine behind them. The two were talking animatedly.

The shorter of the two was a colonel of a cavalry regiment. His broad brimmed blue felt hat was trimmed with a peacock's feather and fur around the crown. The brim curved down over the forehead to keep the sun out of his eyes.

The plain white collar of his sea green jerkin stood over a lace jabot that lay across his shoulders. A single row of silk covered buttons ran down the front of the doublet. There were buttons also at the cuffs of the slightly puffed sleeves.

Fox smiled a little as he saw how highly polished the thigh boots where. These had never been in a mêlée of horses, harrying foot soldiers across thorn hedges and ditches. They were new and soft and unscuffed. Breeches of dark green canvas were tucked into the wide Tops of the boots.

He took in the cup-hilted rapier the man carried slung in a tooled leather belt under the folds of a peacock blue silk lined cloak. A sword made for show and not for the thrust, hack and parry of a mounted trooper's charge. The hilt was made of intricate gold wires. A sword for single combat, where the genteel rules of the duel were more important than killing or maiming the opponent.

Fox preferred the Pappenheimer sword he'd been given so recently or the Walloon sword with its stiff blade and wide guard. Weapons perfect for the slash and parry of a cavalryman.

The taller man turned to his companion and Fox saw him full face for the first time.

The pale, long face, the curled hair, and a fresh wound across the forehead part covered by his hair. The man's sardonic smile was hardly what Fox expected to see.

It was in the spring that he'd killed this man's brother in the Marais. This was Major Andrews who smiled at his companion, put an arm around his shoulder and drew him into the door of the inn.

Fox waited patiently. A clock struck the half. He waited yet. The sun had gone now and there was a chill in the air to remind soldiers that autumn was already here. The season for war was certainly nearly over.

Fox huddled against the wall and was rewarded when Major Andrews and his companion walked laughing, out of the inn. The Major was driven away.

What was Major Andrew doing with the Royalist Colonel of Horse if he was supposed to be with Prince Rupert in the field? Was he working as liaison for the Royalist armies? Would he be worth snatching and talking to in the quiet of a secluded room? Thurloe might be interested and he should certainly be told.

Fox waited until the colonel had stepped back inside the inn before he crossed the road and walked into the warm entrance of the building.

There was no-one, apart from the landlord in the hall. In a room to the right men sat at benches and ate chicken and rabbit pies, washed down with ale and wine. Served by women who'd seen better days and better men, Fox thought. He watched them slap away the exploring hands of eager soldiers left behind after the first troops had gone north.

The rearguard of cleaners and sweepers tidying up stores, paying debts. They made something on the side, placating households if they felt like it and, as often as not, denying responsibility for any damage the soldiers may have caused.

These women had been used, misused and abused, no doubt, and had been miserably paid for what they traded. Soldiers were a rough and ready lot. The women who served their needs were rougher and readier. Fox shuddered at the memory of some he'd known.

He stepped past the doorway into the dining hall and walked on up the wide and curved stairs to the room he'd taken.

At the top of the stairs he looked out of the newly installed window that looked across the spires and domes and walls of the colleges and their chapels and churches. The stone dun-coloured under the last light of the setting sun. Out there, Davy would be asking questions, making notes and tomorrow would leave a report in the recess by the confessional.

A distant bell began to chime and then others began seconds after. Soon the city was reverberating with the noise of bells. Tenors, basses, trebles, rings and double rings, chimes and peals rang out across the city and the sound for some reason suddenly brought home to Fox how alone he was in the world and how desperate he was to see his daughter, to hold her . . . his flesh, his blood. Rebecca.

Quite suddenly and for the first time, he admitted to himself that he knew his wife was dead and that he would never again touch her. Never again hear the gentle admonishing voice, never feel her strong brown hands, never see her amused eyes laughing as he tried to curb his temper or his tongue.

Never touch and soothe and be soothed by a caressing hand or the soft swelling of her breasts. Never feel her tongue in his mouth nor her thighs about him. Nor the urgent thundering of blood in his ears as they rode to pleasure together.

For a moment he remembered the roaring abandon of the Irish girl. He stared about him and put Maeve out of his mind.

He stood on the landing, staring across the belling city and knew at last that he would never again hear her sighs in his ear, never feel her hair . . . never . . . never . . .

He knew that all he could expect was a cold journeying. There was only one end of the journeying for a soldier. He was no longer in thrall to the woman he'd loved so well. A soldier wants direction and he knew he had none. Not yet.

Hadn't Maeve, the wild auburn-haired girl, said vengeance was a cold feast? She was right. Yet, with vengeance might come the chance to find his daughter and there, on that stair, hearing the jangle and thunder and ripple of the bells he knew he'd confirmed a real purpose beyond vengeance.

And he knew that to make it happen, to find the direction he needed, he'd a man to meet, a man to make a compact with. He would be sure to have a price, a price that Fox would have to pay, John Thurloe would see to that.

31

Fox watched from the high hill overlooking the sloping heath land that ran down to London. He stood beside his horse and stared down into the haze that lay over the city and the river as the sun showed through the broken cloud of an early morning.

Below him on the open slopes were cleared plots and broken brown strips of cultivated land as well as clumps of coppiced woodland.

Smoke rose in straight grey columns from cottage chimneys dotted about the slope. Distantly, a dog barked.

Even at a time when the London apprentices marched shouting of their power in the city, as men of real power manipulated the hopes of the masses who lived in the slums and rookeries, as the promise of war came closer, the beauty of the city took his breath away.

Furthest, to his left, St. Paul's stood half hidden amongst the buildings huddled around. Beside it and between a blur of buildings could be glimpsed the sheen of the River Thames as the sun burned off the mist, silver in the morning light.

Fox remembered other cities he'd passed through. Paris, Venice, Hamburg, Celle, Stockholm, Amsterdam, Madrid, The Hague and knew that none of them had the magnificent boldness, self-confidence, cruelty and cupidity of London.

Below him ranged the riverside houses from Temple Steps to King's Bridge. Merchants, bankers, great men and women were living in magnificence alongside the abject and the beggarly.

Their gardens of sweet-smelling herbs, continental fruit trees, formal hedges and flower beds were hidden from the vulgar by high red brick walls.

No-one wanted to be seen by the one hundred and twenty thousand who worked there, those men and women who pushed and hustled and shoved and grasped livings. No rich man wanted the poor to intrude into their gardens which had water-gates opening direct onto the Thames.

Folding back from the main artery of the city lay alley after alley, plague-infested streets and open sewers running down into ditches that flowed eventually into the river which would throw back the filth as often as not when the tides forced the water over the low walls set to contain it.

Squares and hidden oases of green meadowland were surrounded by yet more houses, paved courtyards and cobbled lanes and through it all roved the people of the city. Lively, lazy, arrogant, demure, rich and hideously poor, well and crippled, leprous and beautiful, people in a hurry, people at ease with themselves, businessmen, lawyers, butchers, bakers and the flotsam and jetsam of any port-side city.

London!

Wealth and abject poverty lay cheek by jowl. West Cheap with Goldsmiths Row and a glittering tower and the fountain playing continuously. Holborn, a lung in the city with gardens and fresh air untainted by vapours from the river or the stews to the East or the fumes from the sea coal fires burning in the older houses.

In Cornhill merchants and lawyers walked the streets, talked and made contracts and money from other people's labour. Some men and women in the fashion and others, more reserved, in sober clothes.

Beyond stood the stolid mass of the Tower, its armoury and massive walls looming over the river. On a small square of green within those walls, Anne Boleyn had been beheaded less than a hundred years before.

Black crows and grey-headed jackdaws hopped and pecked about the green, strutted and fluttered over the walls and across the river from time to time into the cherry orchards and woods beyond.

Fox sniffed the clear air on the high hill. He'd ride down soon into that thronging city and find his man there and begin another life

Through the narrow foetid alleys, past hurdy gurdy men and prancing bears on poles, past women selling oranges and themselves, past the smell of meat cooking on spits and the stench of cat piss and rats on each and every corner. Walking by beggars with stumps for arms and holes for eyes and noses, Fox would search out his man and through him, find the man on whom he'd vowed to take his vengeance. At whatever cost, even if the cost was to work for such as Thurloe again. Even so.

Down through cobbled streets too narrow for carriages and too filthy for decent people to stain their silk shoes or tooled leather high-heeled pumps he would walk.

He watched the haze lift off the river and knew that beyond the houses lying at its edge were warehouses shaded by masts and sails as dense as a forest of trees. They were the measure of the wealth of the country and of its power.

Here the merchants stood and counted sacks of spices, bales of cloth, tuns of wine and pipes of port. Here they fingered silks and jewels and packages of aromatic tobacco as it came from the holds of the ships lying alongside. From the Spice Islands to the Americas, from West Africa for slaves to the East Indies for cinnamon. These merchant ships lay berthed and waited for the next six-month journey across half-charted waters.

Fox knew he'd walk down there and smell the smells and hear the sounds he loved, of foreign places and people. He'd melt, as he could, into invisibility and people would talk and tell secrets and ignore this faceless man. To be disregarded was Fox's greatest skill.

So the ships brought in fortunes to the merchant traders who walked dogs, rode horses, talked to fellow merchants, laid laughing orange girls across sacks of nutmeg and pepper . . . and took the pox as a gift from the girls to their doting wives.

Even before Fox began to ride slowly down into the waking city, he could smell the place where people traded anything from pepper to people.

Down there in the hugger-mugger streets was Thurloe. Thurloe would know where to find the witchfinder if anyone did, and Fox had something to trade that Thurloe would want . . . information.

****

Thurloe walked through the stinking, rain-sodden streets. He ignored the filth about his feet, the piles of refuse rotting against open drains. He ignored the dogs fighting over rotten offal. He ignored the men and women of the night who still sat in doorways, under rags, against the piles of the bridges and wharves along the river or stood huddled in small groups, looking for shelter from the incessant rain and the cold of the night.

Thurloe cursed the girl for insisting they met away from his office and the warmth of the fire burning there day and night, month in and month out. He could hardly help having been born with sensitivity to the cold.

172

She sent a message by a wharf rat who'd demanded coin before he handed over the folded note. He'd paid the child and told him to get out. The child stank of riverside refuse and mud.

Thurloe remembered that he had met Maeve Ahern for the first time near the shops along London Bridge. One side of the bridge was lit with flares and candlelight from the shops that had not been destroyed by the recent fire. The light was enough for the traders and customers who took care as they walked along the wooden beams across the river. The burned shops were boarded up, blind and shadowed. It was an eerie place at night. Thurloe looked along the bridge and watched the people pushing and jostling in and out of the shadows.

The shops which had not been burned were open for trade. They were lit with flares and candlelight which gave enough light for traders and customers alike. Thurloe stood at one end and looked along the crowded passage over the river.

After a moment he stepped into the crowd and inched his way through the first crush into a clear space where he could stop and wait to be seen.

He shivered as the rain increased in strength for a moment and then as suddenly, died away and stopped. Men and women cried their wares at the various stalls for food and drink, clothes, horse tackle, herbs and brooms.

To his right a man danced a bear on a pole and, further along the bridge, a young black woman was being sold off as a house servant. By all accounts the woman had been brought into England recently and her master was tired of her and proposed going on another slaving voyage. He was not only selling the girl but also shares in the next venture overseas.

There were some who would be fool enough to invest, Thurloe had no doubt, and walked past the shivering girl who was little more than a child. Her lips were purple with the cold and the whites of her eyes huge as she watched the handsome young man in black hose and doublet by.

She was used to being used by her master and knew well enough how to please him. No doubt she would delight the young man in black should he buy her. He walked on. Clearly searching for someone else.

Thurloe wondered for a moment how Maeve would be if he bedded her. No doubt she'd be willing enough. A coming man like John Thurloe was no bad catch for a girl like her. Not that she'd catch him.

He sniffed, leaning on the flimsy railing to look over into the water. The reflected lights from the bridge sparkled as the tide raced out making white water against the piles that held the bridge.

She joined him where he stood with his back to the charred wooden buildings on the other side of the walkway. She leaned alongside him.

"Well?" he asked the rain sodden girl. "Where is he?"

"On his way, I'd think. What was it Thomas Fairfax said? You could reel him in now if you want him still."

"Should I want him?" Thurloe turned to look at Maeve and she turned and stared up into his pale face. The rain lay across her face and she appeared not to notice it, her hair was darker where it had soaked it. She shook her head.

"I don't know. He's dangerous. Empty. Cold as ice and very dangerous, I'd say. Pointed at the right man, he would snuff him without a blink. Do you need a man like that?"

Maeve turned away. He had no interest in her as a woman and she had little in him as a man for that matter. He was too bound to his own dark plans and plots. She pitied his wife and children for they'd rarely see him.

"He lost his wife." Thurloe surprised her. How had he known that?

He smiled a thin smile and began to walk into the crowds teeming along the bridge and in and out of the shops. Thurloe hardly glanced at her, he expected her to follow his lead and to hang on his words.

"I can find a use for his skills. Yes."

"And mine?" she asked

"Perhaps."

"He and I work well together."

"Does he think that?"

"I know it," Maeve said. He stopped then and looked at her.

"You're wet through," he said as if he'd only just noticed. "I think you might work well together. Find him. Bring him to me and I'll make him a proposition. And you."

"Tell him where to find Witchfinder Hopkins and you could have his soul, I think," said the girl quietly.

Thurloe pulled her into a corner between two burned-out shops on the Surrey side of the bridge.

"I don't want his soul. I want his attention and his loyalty. That's all."

Maeve smiled a little at that.

"Witchfinder Hopkins? Why?"

"He was the man who burned his wife. Didn't you know that?" she mocked him.

"He doesn't want to kill him so much as find the name of the man who whispered the name of his wife and led him to charge her with witchery. There was someone, there was certainly someone known to an old woman who died and not by her own hand. Hanged . . . by someone who planted a name with her. Someone Fox would know . . . someone the woman knew and feared . . ." Maeve stared up at the pale face as she stopped speaking.

"And Fox wants him?" said Thurloe, amused.

"Give him that man or woman and he will be your man. Well?"

"Find him and bring him to me, I'll find the witchfinder for him, tell him that."

Thurloe took a small purse from his pocket and handed it to the girl.

"For your trouble," he said, "'Tis better than whoring, I suppose!"

"What would you know about whoring, Master Thurloe? Maybe working for you is kin to it anyway. Sweet Jesus, Mary and Joseph, but it's a soft evening, is it not?" she said as another flurry of rain swept down the length of the bridge snuffing out flares and candles.

Taking the purse from his hand, she turned and vanished into the crowd on the bridge.

Thurloe walked back to the room over the watchmaker's shop and considered where he stood. Fairfax had been right about Fox.

Fairfax was due to go north that evening after a last afternoon in the Parliament house down by the river. Thurloe needed to see Tom Fairfax before he went back to join his soldiers.

Thurloe lengthened his stride and ignored for a moment the man he always had shadowing his back. You never knew when you might need protection and Thurloe was not a man to take chances.

He moved slowly and surely and safely which was always his way and he'd no reason to change it. It would have been dangerous to change in times like these when loyalty was always for sale.

****

It was noon when Fox began to search the city. He'd stabled his horse at a discreet house at the end of the Fleet where he stayed whenever he'd come to London in the past.

Walking towards the Sign of the White Cross he'd passed the usual array of jugglers, clowns, puppet masters, fire-eaters and side shows. Colourful and noisy streets alive with pickpockets, hustlers and hucksters of all sorts and conditions. They kept their distance from this man who seemed so sure of himself, so at home.

Fox moved fast after leaving his horse, seeing his room and leaving his bag and the farrier's sword. His only weapons the broad bladed Phapeimer and Shea's blade slung and hidden along the small of his back. He could reach it with either hand and fight with either, too.

175

Down Cheapside and along the river, back up through Needless Alley and up to Ludgate Circus, then past Seven Dials, Fox threaded his way towards the Sign of the White Horse.

Outside, a milling crowd spilled along the filthy pavements. He stopped on a corner directly opposite the huge ale house. Then he pushed through the crowd and walked quickly across the crowded room and into the yard at the back and down into a cellar area where the cockpit was.

"Get the birds in, Whippy," the sweating man cried across the sea of intent faces perched around the wooden walls of the ring.

"Let's see the colour of their blood, eh?"

The handler looked across at the gap-toothed man and laughed. Then he took from his pocket tiny clinking slivers of metal and beckoned to the two men standing on opposite sides of the ring.

The faces of the men and women were reddened by the hard liquor they'd been drinking. They stank no better than the foetid straw at their feet. A mixture of sweat, piss and old drink. The women were no better. They screamed for blood and showed the broken stumps of black teeth in slack mouths.

"Get them in, Whippy," roared the crowded cockpit as bets were made. Money changed hands as the punters at the front greedily clutched at any chance to gain a penny or a silver sixpence from the richer merchants and clerks who stood about at the back of the room.

Fox watched impassively as the two handlers finished strapping the small but vicious spurs to the legs of the fighting birds. The light of flares and greasy tallow candles glinted on the razor-fine blades and revealed the sheen of the feathers and the red of the cropped wattles and combs of the two cockerels.

"Here's even money on the Bilston Cock." A swarthy man moved closer to Fox with a tankard of ale in one hand and the other arm ending in a stump covered in a stained leather stock.

Smoke swirled over the pit, as the two birds were beasted by their handlers. Being pushed beak to beak but firmly held and then suddenly released into the pit in a flurry of wings and feathers and high stepping and slashing spurs. Around the pit men and women screamed for blood.

Fox looked about the room searching for soldiers. He knew from his soldiering days that if you wanted to find a soldier with his guard down then a tavern was as good a place to start as any. But find a tavern with a bearpit or a cockpit and you'd find women and where you found women you'd a better than even chance of finding soldiers on a spree and he needed men with loose tongues to give him what he wanted.

He stared from face to face about the screaming room.

176

The birds were flying across the pit with legs extended for the kill, wings thrashing the air and razor spurs slashing at each other. The Bilston Cock had blood welling from deep gashes on its breast and oozing through the dark green feathers. Yet it launched a ferocious attack on its opponent.

Feathers and blood spattered the faces of those leaning across the wall as both birds clattered in their frenzy against the sloping wooden walls . . .

Fox took a last look around and then shoved his way out of the cellar and up into the yard at the back of the inn.

He walked back to the door from the yard and into the main room. It was filled with smoke and noise and the stink of stale wine and beer.

He looked about in the gloom for a face he might know. The White Horse was an exchange where soldiers of fortune congregated from time to time. Here they drank together, spent their hard-earned pay, whored, gambled and ate; here they learned of other armies who needed a pike, a trooper, a cavalry sergeant or a plain infantryman.

Fox caught sight of himself in a mirror hung behind the counter. He looked his thirty eight years. Not a man in the place was more than twenty five.

As Fox walked between the tables past groups of men they fell silent and waited until he'd gone by before they spoke again.

He felt their hostility. When he sat it was at a table against the wall where he could face the room and waited for a girl to bring him wine.

Eventually she brought the wine jug and set it down. He paid her and poured the sour wine and drank some for form's sake. The owner of the inn watched him and waited, as Fox did, for trouble to start.

Three men lurched over to his table. One sat down, another took the wine jug and the third sat to Fox's left. The young man with the jug poured the wine into a glass he carried and drank it off. He poured another and gave it to the man on Fox's left and the seated man in front of Fox watched their mark.

Someone in the room giggled while Fox stared across at the three young men and said nothing.

"You . . . old man. This is a man's ale house, not for old has-beens."

One of them sneered at Fox who sipped his wine.

The man to his left jogged his arm and the wine spilled from the glass.

By now some of the men in the room had come closer. The owner of the inn began to wish the young man had not begun this for he'd seen the eyes of the older man and knew enough to know what they had taken on. But he was not prepared for the speed of what happened next.

As the man who stood in front of Fox leaned forward to say something to him, Fox stood up, slamming backwards with his left elbow into the face of the man seated on his left. At the same time he pushed the table into the man seated in front of him and taking great care, slammed the empty wine glass into the face of the standing man and twisted it.

Even as the blood started from the cuts it made, Fox had reached over his shoulder and taken out the long, wide-bladed knife and waited quietly for the men to respond.

He let the blade dance across the arc in front of him and waited. Around the room, men let out their breath and wondered at what they had seen. It was less than a second and here was this older man quietly waiting and now they too saw his eyes as he leaned over the man pinned under the table. The point of the blade pricked the young man's throat.

"I have only to lean on the blade and you are spitted dead as a frog," Fox said. And the young man, looking up saw death in his eyes. His hands scrabbled sideways for a purchase on the floor and Fox hardly moved six inches to the right to stamp on the clutching hand with his heeled boot.

The young man squealed like a dying hare as his hand was shattered.

"Now . . . anyone else?" Fox asked and his eyes flickered around the room. No-one met his eye and men began to drift back to their drinks. The inn-keeper came across with a new jug of better wine, two glasses and a smile.

He flicked his head at the two men beside Fox and they backed away, nursing their faces. They helped their companion to his feet who went out holding his shattered hand.

"They're only boys," said the inn-keeper. "I don't know you mister, but I know a soldier when I see one. You were slow to take the man on your right and risked a lot. He'd a knife in his sleeve. They prey on drunken soldiers and sailors down on their luck. They're the scum of the earth, or were. So . . . ?"

He lifted his mug and drank and Fox smelt the wine and then sipped it, savoured it and drank deep.

"Bordeaux, near Langon . . . on the slopes over the Garonne . . ." he said and the ale house keeper nodded. Astonished.

"I used to buy it for a merchant."

"Used to?" Asked the alehouse keeper.

"Now . . . now I'm looking for a man. Two men."

"And a girl is looking for you," said the ale house keeper.

Fox stared at him and then nodded briefly

"Is the girl your wife, mistress . . . ? She wanted to find a man who she said was dangerous. Pale faced, tall . . . and cold. You?"

"She Irish, with dark red hair?"

"She said you were searching for a woman also."

"She said a lot. I'm looking for two men to take me to a girl. My daughter."

He took the locket from his pocket and opened it. He showed the portrait of his daughter. The man studied it for a moment or two and nodded and gave Fox back the locket.

"Not seen her," he said. "And I'd remember, but if I do, you shall know. Where was it you were soldiering?"

"I was with Black Tom Fairfax in the Swedish Army," Fox said and the ale housekeeper broke into a broad smile.

"I was too. A cavalryman, till I broke my thigh or some damn half broken German nag broke it for me. Rolled on me and saved my life, to tell the truth, for the rest of the troop were wiped out in the charge . . . So here I am. Running an exchange for soldiers looking for a war."

Fox nodded and drank.

"Two men you said?"

"You might help with one. 'Twas my reason for coming here to the exchange . . . I want to see Black Tom. I need to see him. You know where he might stay if he's in London?"

The old soldier nodded.

"I can help you with that, . You'll find him if you're lucky down near the Parliament house where he sits and doles out law like he doled out orders. But he's a straight man nonetheless. You can ask the sergeant-at-arms and tell him you're an old comrade and to be sure he'll see you."

Fox drank the last of his wine, stood up and put a coin on the table.

"No," said the alehouse owner. "Not from one of Black Tom's men. And as for the girl, your daughter, what's her name?"

"Fox. Rebecca Fox," said John, and walked easily out of the dim room into the bright sunshine and the crowded streets.

32

Thurloe was eating his chop and reading through a pile of reports he had massed on his desk. It was six in the evening and was surprised when Colonel Tom Fairfax came thundering up the stairs with Fox walking more slowly behind.

Fairfax left after delivering Fox. He wanted to be in Yorkshire by the end of the week and was being driven up in his carriage for the first part of the journey. He hated being driven and ached to ride but it was too far now for a man of his age to do in the time he felt was available.

So, he'd left this awkward, prickly and largely silent Fox to make his own business with Thurloe. It had been like pulling teeth to get anything from him for Fox did not give up information easily. But eventually he began to talk of the plan to take silver and other valuables from the Oxford colleges in the King's coach to pay for the King's armies and Thurloe's ears pricked up.

He leaned forward across the desk while Fox sat in a chair with its back to the wall and facing the door.

"And if the colleges are sending all their plate, what is that worth? And are they all going to do it?" he asked Fox. Fox shrugged.

"It hasn't moved yet. I've no-one I trust in the city to do any more than watch and to let me know when they plan to move it. My contact puts himself in some danger but is more afraid of me than the danger he faces. So."

Fox stated the fact coldly. "But we could be too late."

"We?" asked Thurloe and standing, spun a globe on a table near the fire which was never unlit. Fox and others could sweat, Thurloe would have his fire. He turned back to Fox.

"We?" He repeated.

Fox shook his head. "I have something I need too, Mister Thurloe. Something you can deliver for me. I want a man found. I want a witchfinder of the King's located. I want him for my own reasons which are no concern of yours."

"To avenge your wife?" Thurloe asked quietly.

Fox stared down at his hand and Thurloe saw that the knuckles were white with tension. Thurloe knew he had the advantage now and could hook and gaff his man now and at little cost.

Thurloe went on softly, "I was sorry to hear what happened. The Irish girl came by and she told me something of it."

"She had no right to tell you anything." Fox was angry.

Thurloe shook his head. "Maybe not. But she's a woman and her tongue wags . . . this time she was right. I will scratch your back . . . you will scratch mine? Yes?"

Fox hesitated. He knew what he was doing and after a moment he nodded. Thurloe had struck, gaffed and landed his fish. Fox was taken.

****

It took Fox a time to understand that he'd be taking Maeve Ahern with him to Oxford and, when he did, he refused.

"You take her with you, Fox, and use her, for she can go to places you can't. Wheedle things from men you'd never discover. Her arts are her own. A whore, maybe, but a natural intriguer she most surely is. So use her as you will. She comes with you."

Fox had to make do with Thurloe's promise to discover the whereabouts of Witchfinder Hopkins and to send him news as soon as he had delivered the Oxford plate to the Parliament forces.

"The Irish girl will be waiting on the Oxford road," Thurloe told him. "In the morning."

Maeve laughed in his face when she discovered what he'd agreed to.

"You trust that pale faced dog?" she said and laughed again.

"He's all I have. I can spend a lifetime looking for the man and for my daughter. Thurloe has agents, friends, and contacts all over the land. He'll find anyone he wants. He'll tell me."

"When he's used you, when he's milked you dry. I know men like him, Fox, and better than him. Italian men who'd eat him for dinner. He thinks he is ruthless, cold, an iron man. I tell you, my friend, he's making a fool of you. He tells you to use me? Yes?"

She laughed again as she saw that she'd hit the mark.

"He tells you that I will do as I am told. Am useful . . .?"

Fox nodded and the girl rode on ahead of him laughing still. Fox let her go on.

This strange girl was so sure of herself, so confident. Afraid of no man, it seemed, and free as the wind. Fox began to feel a nag of envy.

They came to the city of Oxford and parted just before the gates.

"I need to find out when the plate is coming from the colleges and where it may be going and how. I need to know how many will accompany it and how it will be taken. If indeed that is what they intend to do." Fox told her.

"The Master of your friend's college is a noted cocksmith." Maeve said. "Maybe he can be persuaded to tell me a thing or two."

Fox shook his head. "Maeve, I'll not ask you to do . . . to . . ." the words stuck in his throat.

"You know, Master Fox, you have a good nature. It won't give me any pleasure, my friend, but needs must. I'm no maiden, Fox, and I will take care he doesn't get me with the pox. I'll get what I want from him."

Fox looked away and she smiled and rode alongside him and put her hand on his where it held the rein of his horse. He looked across at her and she saw in his eyes the pain he felt, not only for her.

"Fox . . . John," she said quietly, "We are bound to Master Thurloe and he expects us to give him what he wants. We fail him and he can be as ruthless as any other spymaster, I have no doubt. He's young and has not learned how frail we all can be."

"Meet me in the Abbey Cockpit at ten of the night. Three days from now."

She let his hand go and spurred on her horse. Stopped and looked back at him. "Thank you, Fox." And she rode on through the market day crowds into the city of pale stones.

He followed her slowly.

Fox sat in the upper room over the gatehouse, where Davy had put him.

"They're gathering it all together," said the excited little man. "I know that and I know where and I'm doing no more for you."

He was afraid, as well he might be.

"You'll put me where I can see what they are gathering. And if word gets out about our meetings, Davy, I will make sure to come back and cut your tongue out. And you know I would."

That evening Davy stayed in the porter's room, watching the entrance to the college while Fox was secure in the room over the gateway from which he could watch the movement to and from the college green.

182

The room was dusty with lack of use. Boxes of lumber, old cases, tools, bags of books and broken chairs, lengths of brass rod and huge folds of curtains in which mice and probably rats had made their nests from the scratching and scrabbling he heard as he lay looking out over the courtyard and the green garden in its centre.

Around the secluded yard, a cloister and within the cloister flares lit up the arches and the fine pillars. Fox shifted uneasily. This might be a wild goose chase and yet Davy was no fool and knew well enough what Fox wanted of him.

A bat flitted into the light from one of the sconces and out again. Another and another swooped and fluttered as fast as the eye could follow. Hunting. Distantly an owl called once, twice and then at the same distance a scream as a rabbit was hit by a flurry of wings, talons and a curved beak.

Fox smiled. It was just this that had terrified young Davy. Not knowing what the sounds he heard were, he'd made them bogeys for himself. A bell struck and from clock towers all over the colleges the bells struck and rung and sounded . . .

As they did so, Fox became aware that a darker shadow stood in the corner of the garden directly opposite the doorway from the college into the street.

A flare leapt alive and lit three men waiting together. Then there was the soft thud of the wicket gate as it opened and let in a number of men.

"Wait here!" someone said, "I'll tell the porter he's not needed tonight. We'll guard the gate."

Two men muffled laughter and two of the figures under the flare stepped across to the middle of the court and waited.

Fox counted ten men, each carrying heavy satchels on their backs.

Another, carrying nothing, followed them. This man wore the long gown of an academic, faced with silk and ermine and bearing a staff in his hand.

He stopped in front of the men waiting in the middle of the cloister garden as the other ten men put down their satchels.

"I think you'll be happy with what we have here," he said quietly to the waiting men. One of them took out a tally stick and began to count.

"Show us, if you please," said the taller of the men. "The King will want to know how much to thank us for no doubt."

The newcomer snapped his fingers and the ten men stooped and opened their satchels. One of the men carrying a flaring torch stepped closer and Fox could see from where he crouched at the deep set Tudor window, the glitter of fire on silver plate.

The newcomer bent down to take things from the bags at random and showed them proudly. Plates and servers of silver, goblets chased with fantastical designs, candle holders decorated with ivy leaves in gilt, knives and spoons with rat's tail handles and silver inlaid with gold, salts and wine jugs.

One after another, from each of the bags, the robed man took plate and laid it beside the leather bags.

The flames danced across the silver and the gold and left dark liquid pools between the plates and salvers.

Fox went on counting as another party of silent men walked in and replaced those already there. They, too, brought bags and laid out the treasures on the dark grass and they, too, shone and glittered and shimmered under the flaring torches.

The small group from the cloister watched and said little or nothing. The clerk laid aside his tally stick and began to list what lay on the grass in the torchlight. The shadows of guards moved in the cloister.

As each group came in to add their treasures to the growing heap on the grass the clerk crossed off a name, the names of the colleges who'd chosen to offer the King their college riches.

Oxford bled gold and silver, bled treasures by great masters in precious metals and stones to be reduced in the end to cold lead and dead men and women. It was a sorry sight that Fox watched. These men had bought their protection dear, but no army would come through the city while the King's men could protect it. Blood money lay scattered about the green grass, bleeding in the light of the torches that burned in the cloister.

Fox gave up counting but knew there was enough here to arm and feed an army for many a day. The King would keep his troops happy for a time at least. Fox grunted to himself. It wasn't money in the long run that kept armies together but victories which kept men believing they'd chosen the right side. And plunder.

Thurloe might be concerned about the amount of plate leaking out of the city and from Worcester and the Welsh borders but in the end it would be the generals leading their men to victory who'd secure the prize whatever it might be. Black Tom knew that. Maybe this man Cromwell knew it too.

Fox lay on his back and stared at the plaster ceiling of the room as dawn began to come up over the city. There was no sign of the plate left on the grass square below. The stink of dead flares was all that was left to remind him of the night.

****

Thurloe had been right about one thing. Maeve could get to places Fox could not. He'd admit that.

When the mysterious Irish girl had first understood how the plate was to be removed from Oxford and taken to the King she had been flat on her back on a bed slept in by the chancellor of one of the Oxford colleges. Dr. James was an old man much given to boasting and very proud of his sexual athletics.

Maeve hauled the blankets back over her bruised thighs and lay looking up at the man who'd just enjoyed her. She took no pleasure in the old fool but when she mentioned the King and money he'd not been able to keep himself from boasting of the arrangements that had been made for the plate to go north in the King's coach.

The scrawny, wrinkled old fool left no detail out while he feasted his pale eyes on her exposed breasts. Maeve Ahern shut her eyes as his hands began to move on her body again. This one was priapic.

Fox had been busy too. Davy had been paid for his silence and for his help.

Fox had already sent a message to The White Cross in London with the promise of a little plunder and a great deal of excitement for ten carefully chosen men who had experience of working in the field. He wanted no dumb infantrymen, no cloddish dragoons. He wanted men who could think for themselves, ten men, in short, not unlike himself.

The owner of the alehouse came with ten men. They slipped into Oxford discreetly one by one. And met in the snug bar of the Swan. A ragbag of men but all with the slight swagger and the dead eyes of those who have gone for a soldier.

Fox watched them come into the room. There were jugs of ale on the tables. They'd been promised a regular supply of ale and meat and a promise that no-one would interrupt this reunion of men from the old army of Gustavus Adolphus. They were celebrating a victory at Dettingen, the publican was told, and would be drinking for ten men and all their dead mates.

Fox had warned his contact at the White Cross that this was to be a quick skirmish. Each man would be paid the same money. Fifty English pounds, no more, no less. Any dead man's money to be shared amongst the survivors.

The men were all to be supporters of the Apprentice Boys of London and not supporters of the King and his favourite, Buckingham.

As Buckingham had been responsible for more bungled military excursions than any of them cared to remember and, through this, for the deaths of many of their comrades, this had not been hard to predict.

The soldiers drank up and waited for Fox to brief them. He felt his blood racing again to be amongst these men, for they were his kind. Someone lit a pipe and then another joined him, and room began to fill with the sweet smell of tobacco.

Fox stood up and began to speak. Their aim to take the plate from the King's coach. It was to be a straightforward ambush. The coach would be driven off away from the inevitable skirmish and lost deep in the English countryside. It relied on split second timing and impeccable planning at the point where the hit was to be made.

All they were to do was to affect the ambush and draw off the troops guarding the coach.

The men began to smile. This was their sort of work, as Fox had known it would be.

****

The King's Coach was thundering along the rutted track that served as a road between Oxford and the north. Two outriders before and two behind to guard the carriage as it bounced on wooden springs, hauled by four black horses.

Beside the coachman sat an assistant and, standing behind and hanging on for grim death, a servant of the King.

Inside the coach, the King was conspicuous by his absence. There were a dozen wooden strongboxes covered with lengths of old sailcloth, furniture and effects for His Majesty to be delivered to Charles at his headquarters near Ludlow.

The route lay perilously close to the Puritan army commanded by Lord Essex, which was billeted in and around Stratford. It was the only route that would ensure the 'effects' reached the King safely and in good time.

Riding out of sight and always keeping close to the route of the carriage, a troop of cavalrymen rode behind their grim faced colonel.

Nothing was to be left to chance for there were thousands of pounds worth of silver in the carriage and whilst they did not want to draw attention to the carriage, they needed to be sure it was adequately protected.

The horsemen jogged silently across heathland and through woods always keeping in touch with the carriage as it took the road through the midlands.

186

Three grim-faced men sat guard on the boxes inside the carriage. They leaned back against the tooled leather and swore as the carriage jolted and threw them from side to side.

Two of them were young officers of the Guards. Their horses were being ridden by the outriders who flanked the carriage. Every effort had been made to ensure that the carriage was not conspicuous. The gilding was painted over, the wheels with their bright red and green paint, had been deliberately covered with grime. The outriders were apparently armed only with swords.

The three men inside the carriage checked their pistols as they bucketed along. They had an arsenal of weapons ranged on the seat and boxes before them. They had no reason to expect anyone would want to stop the carriage. The journey had been arranged secretly and the coach set out at first light having been loaded through the night by men sworn to secrecy.

The cavalry jogging below the skyline were there as security and back up. Major Andrews leaned across his companion and looked out through the drawn leather curtain. They were heading along a beech-lined track towards Woodstock.

The horses would be changed here for fresh animals and the carriage would go down the steep hill and then make the long haul on the other side.

The outriders were bunching closer to the carriage. Their orders had been to keep well spread to give ample warning should there be any trouble.

Beyond them, the cavalry waited silently on a rise amongst a stand of trees and watched as the carriage came into sight below them. The bright morning was well advanced but the sun was still low in the sky as autumn was creeping across the land.

Harvest had already been taken in but there was enough cover in the copse to conceal the horsemen waiting there.

Major Andrews sniffed and leaned back against the tooled and padded leather seats. His pale face was disdainful of the young men with him. The air in the carriage was becoming stifling and soon they'd have to raise the leather blinds despite the dust it'd let in.

Beyond Woodstock, they'd pass by Shipston, they were not going to stop there either for horses or for food, then the haul along the road towards Todenham and the run down into Morton.

The road at the Todenham turning fell away and narrowed across the small bridge over the stream that ran into the lake on their right. Elms towered near the bridge.

The track led over the bridge and into a hard left-hand bend that also rose a little. The coachman slowed the horses as it was not wise for a carriage to approach at full gallop

****

The young Todenham farrier whom Fox had buried had been well liked and when the villagers returned there was a genuine anger and a feeling that they wanted their revenge on the Royalist troopers who'd killed him. A natural feeling and yet there was nothing simple country people could do . . . until Fox showed them a way.

He'd returned to the village, talked to the farrier's father and to some of the young men. The money he had offered was refused for they only wanted revenge.

Fox understood that.

****

The carriage slowed for the bridge and the bend and then, and only then, did the coachman see the two tree trunks that blocked the road. As the carriage stopped, the first of the outriders was dragged from his horse by two villagers taking him bodily from both sides. They dragged him away and left him for dead on the ground and turned back into the fray.

The coachman reached into the box beneath his feet and took out an old fowling gun. He was shot before he could aim it.

The servant had already jumped to the ground and thrown open the right hand door of the carriage as a blast of fire erupted from both its windows. The servant was killed by his own people.

The cavaliers on the hilltop moved too soon for they began their move almost before the carriage had halted. As they swept down the hillside, nine battle hardened horsemen came on hard into the flank of the cavalier troopers and scattered them on their first thrust. Fox, for he was leading, kept control, turned his men as soon as they had turned the flank and came back into their rear. It was a classic attack and Black Tom would have been astonished to see his favourite intelligence gatherer leading troopers into the second phase of battle.

The three men who'd been riding inside erupted from the carriage. Major Andrews took careful aim and shot one of the attackers. Then took a horse from one of his outriders, mounted and joined the Cavaliers in their desperate skirmish. They were steadily being led away from the coach.

188

Fox had briefed his men well. As the skirmish spread along the field and across the road beyond the bridge, the villagers pulled the tree trunks aside and two wagon drivers took the reins of the carriage and drove it up the track to Todenham, through the village and along a farm track and through an open gate.

By the time the skirmish had settled into hand-to-hand fighting, the carriage had vanished. It had been driven straight into a barn, the horses taken out of the traces and led away. Bales of straw were piled over the carriage and the boxes removed and carried to old wagons carrying piles of dung. The boxes were buried there. By nightfall the dung and all it contained would be on its way to London and the Parliament coffers.

Back on the main road, the skirmish was almost over. Fox and his men broke off the engagement and turned away, their work done. As they broke off, Fox rode close enough to the enemy to see their leader level a pistol at him.

The tall, pale-faced man with the sabre scar across his high forehead squeezed the trigger. The Major had recognised Fox as the man who had killed his brother in the marshes surrounding Niort. As the Cavalier troop regrouped and began their charge, Fox was hit in the shoulder. Fox knew he could do no more than ride pell-mell from the ambush and hope to draw off some of the Cavaliers. Major Andrews pushed his way through the mêlée and rode after the wounded Fox.

Swaying in the saddle Fox rode for his life as the soldiers he'd brought with him scattered and rode for theirs. Their work was done. They'd earned their money, three were dead and their money would be divided between the survivors as they'd all agreed. Fox could take his chances on his own.

He rode hard across the country looking for a way to shake off his pursuer. They rode at full stretch across the undulating countryside. Both men pushing their horses to their limits.

It was a hunt to the death across open land with stands of trees and coppiced land where thick undergrowth grew densely. To evade the Major he needed luck and Fox, for once, was charmed.

A hare got up under the feet of the Major's horse, the horse shied to the right and broke its leg with a crack like a pistol shot as it went down still at the gallop . . .

The major was trapped under the body of the horse. Fox was too tired and too hurt to go back and finish him. Nor had he any wish to.

As he rode away over the desolate landscape he nursed his left shoulder where the Major's bullet still lodged and thanked God for it, for it stopped him losing too much blood.

He rode on over the autumn stubble; it was hard going and cold. It would soon be winter. Once Fox saw a hawk quartering the pale sky and shook his fist at the carrion eater. He'd make no carrion for any bloody bird. The sky was grey and heavy with the promise of snow and still Fox rode on.

He reeled in the saddle and leaned forward to ease the pain. He knew if he once dismounted he'd never mount again and he knew he had to get to hiding to be safe from Major Andrews and his cavalry. He'd left a trail that was easy for them to follow.

He looked up once and saw, massing across the land, huge grey sheets of cloud against a deep yellow sky. Snow would bring the end of the season of war. It would also hide the signs of his escape.

He swayed as the wind came and chilled him and then across the dark land the darkness moved harder and faster towards him. He was enveloped in rain that turned soon to a whirling, freezing snow.

33

Fox rode on into winter. Light began to filter down across the hillside from below the dark line of cloud that covered the rest of the winter sky. Along the crest of the hill it shaded into silver and then sulphurous yellow where the clouds reflected the low sun.

The falling snow slanted across the land, over the black moorland pools, drifting into clumps of grass and tussocks of sedge that clung to the east side of the grey stone outcrops, sifted under gorse bushes and into the bark of the few trees already bent under a load of snow.

Snow had fallen here for days. Across the long valley nothing seemed to move except the slanting lines and sudden whirls of falling snow. The rounded hills led up from the sienna brown line of the narrow river that in warmer times chased down the dale and joined the main valley five miles away.

Below the lip of the rounded hills, outcrops of naked rock stood eerily bare of snow because of the winds that had blown for three days.

A wind that polished the ice and the compacted snow into a treacherous surface. It was a wind that made razors of every particle of frozen rain to cut and slice, a wind that made water trapped in crevices and cracks in rock and trees to freeze and expand and shatter like pistol shots. Unheard by anything save the exhausted voles and foxes trying to lie still and to conserve their body heat. Uselessly.

Branches sheared by expanding frost, rocks would be shattered into scree that tumbled from the higher points around the upper end of the dale and left grey rivers of stone lancing down through the snow and ice that covered the dead land.

Winter in the Dales is a cruel time; an unremitting, unforgiving time. Snow slithered down the side of the valley and lay in another drift along the ancient drovers' track that curved along the bank of the river. In summer it was an easy path to the next valley and up over the crest into the more hidden long hanging valley that sheltered a large stand of ancient trees.

A single jackdaw fluttered down over the slope to a patch of bare earth. It might be soft enough to yield a worm or grub.

The bird settled, hopped two steps and stopped, grey-capped head cocked to one side, unblinking. There was meat here, not yet carrion for it seemed to be alive.

The bird hopped closer. The snow began to fall in flurries. It sifted down and covered the leather strap that hung over the belly of the animal that lay shrouded and almost dead under the snow. Fox's horse.

The bird cocked its head again, looked about and moved closer to peck once into the cooling hide of the dying animal. The jackdaw was desperate for food, any food and some lay here for the taking.

The sudden explosive crack of ice and rock fluttered the bird away.

Winter was tightening its hold, soon men and animals would not be able to move across the land.

Along the length of the valley and from dale to dale there were occasional tiny pockets where the snow had shrunk below the natural surface of the drifts. In each pocket screened by a thin sheet of ice, curled as if a furred foetus, lay the body of a field mouse, a rat, a stoat, a rabbit or even a fox. Each had searched for food, been frozen to the bone by the cold winds and become tired, disoriented and lain down to sleep and died.

The heat of the dying animal melted the snow beneath it and allowed it to sink and the snow melted as it drifted down over its body and for an hour, or less, the warm-blooded animal lay in a sheen of water that froze to make an iced coffin. If they once stopped moving they'd be encased in ice until the spring came and they became carrion as the horse lying back along the valley would.

As would Fox who lay against a rock, waiting for his heart to freeze over and his eyes to become ice . . .

He remembered riding away from the Major who'd shot him. The Major lay trapped under his horse, screaming with what Fox assumed was a broken thigh.

He remembered riding north away from the coach and the village and up across the spine of England through valleys and spurs and re-entrants up into the Dales in the vague attempt to reach his old master Black Tom Fairfax who lived in the north. But he could not ride for ever nor his horse survive the terrible conditions.

He half dreamed, half remembered that terrible journey as he lay slowly freezing to death.

He had ridden on and knew his wound was not healing but all he could do was pray it didn't become foul. The ball had lodged against the bone and grated with every movement of his horse. Yet Fox rode on, hardly able to control his horse as they moved down over the soft boggy land at the foot of a steep hillside.

Snow was again filling the air. Rocks jutted out over the brown scrub and heather. A lone curlew mewed and swirled higher into the grey mists.

Fox dreamed of home and Rebecca and Alison, smiling up at him as he walked into the kitchen after a long journey. The welcome he remembered and he'd wake from this dream with tears on his face and a deep sorrow.

There seemed little point in having lived. And yet Rebecca lived . . . Maeve might find her yet. She had what she called 'the sight'. Maybe he'd meet her again. Ask her . . . and the cold seeped into his bones.

He remembered riding up into the high ground and down into remote hamlets and villages asking for news of the Witchfinder and he had heard nothing, received nothing, but hard stares and no invitation. He'd learned to live off the land when he'd been a soldier. He had forgotten none of the skills but his arm handicapped him.

God, it seemed, had abandoned him as he had abandoned England.

Fox woke screaming in the night. He lay close to his horse which had fallen into a snow-covered hole and broken a foreleg. Fox lay taking shuddering breaths in the dark. He knew it was over now but even so he huddled close to the horse and took what warmth he could from the dying animal.

He remembered a burned village and two naked women lying inside what was left of a barn. They were alive and he'd covered them and given them a rabbit he'd just killed. Soldiers had been through and the young village men had run to the nearby woods to evade being enlisted, the older men had waited and watched helpless as the soldiers did what soldiers do.

He seemed to dream of that village. The soldiers had burned it when they discovered that the church had an alter screen and images on the walls. They'd smashed the images and the screen and disrobed the preacher and taken the holy cups and platters and ridden away laughing. Leaving the women to their shame.

Fox dreamed of those naked, bleeding women and a young girl cowering in the ruins of the church where they'd been raped across the altar.

He leaned against the neck of his broken horse and wept for his daughter and for girls like her . . .

Nothing moved down the valley where he had been looking. Nothing moved on the path he had been following. He'd long ago abandoned the idea of living and now the only mercy was that the pain in his arm and shoulder had vanished, anaesthetised by the bone-cracking cold that seared his whole body. He tried to stay awake for he knew sleep would kill him.

Far away a dog barked and once, through the mist that enveloped his head, he thought he heard the yipping whistle of a shepherd calling in his dogs so far away that it might have been imagination.

The snow still sifted along this valley and into every crevice of his clothes, perversely feathering up into the scarf he wore about his face and forming solid ice as it melted and then refroze against his skin.

The snow scoured along the rock in whining eddies of wind and down his back, under the jerkin and the cloak and through the tops of his boots down into the woollen stockings where it melted and refroze until he could no longer feel his feet.

It seeped up over the contours of his body, into the sleeves of his doublet through the buttonholes and down along his chest and stomach.

He knew if he failed to move, he'd die here alone in the high valley. He would never find his daughter nor see the Witchfinder nor learn who'd betrayed his wife. The snow sifted gently over his face and froze inside his nostrils to make breathing an agony of daggers in his chest.

Winter is a savage, relentless time in the Dales and crags and kills without pity, without mercy, anything that waits for it. Death and winter walked hand in hand . . . worked hand in hand . . . And still the snow slithered and slid over the dying man.

Once more he thought he heard a shrill broken whistle of command and then he'd fallen back again into the dark.

High on the rim of the valley, dark against the silver light that shone like pewter above the land, a figure moved carefully. He stopped and raised a hand to his face to wipe away the snow and whistled through his fingers.

Far below him a dog ran in a curving, loping run over the impacted snow searching out trapped sheep that the shepherd knew would be here.

194

He'd already released five that morning and sent them into shelter along the higher valley. Again the dog yelped far down on the edge of the frozen stream where the path ran down towards the main route across the country to the north. The Parliament Army had marched here weeks since and marched away again.

Not that the shepherd cared for them or the others. He'd stayed well hidden in the higher valley and watched them marching up and fewer straggling back

No-one was taking him for a soldier.

Insisting, the dog barked again and waited legs spread, head up. Not digging as he would if he'd found another sheep. Carefully the shepherd eased his way down the face of the valley. One slip might mean a broken leg and here that was a death sentence.

The sun lipped the rim of the valley and almost instantly began to sink for it was late. The shepherd put his fingers to his mouth and whistled again and the dog yelped once and refused to obey.

The land began to freeze again. It was a grey and silent landscape in which nothing moved save the careful shepherd and, hidden, the fluttering heart of the man . . .

Winter was a cruel month for all men and Fox not least.

****

The first sound he heard was the crackling and hissing of wet logs on a large fire. Then he felt a terrible pain in his shoulder that clubbed him mercifully into unconsciousness.

It was a smell that mystified him. It was something that reminded him of a place . . . a person . . . his mother. It was the smell of fresh linen that has been stored with lavender spikes and camphor against the moth . . . For a moment he tried to open his eyes and failed and fell back again.

He knew it was night because all the light in the room was from the dying embers of a fire in a huge grate. And he felt a hand on his forehead and the coolness of a damp cloth wrung out and pressed across his temple, then darkness again.

He was sitting up and his head hurt him so much he dared not open his eyes for fear that the pain in his head might explode through his skull. He could smell something . . . beef . . . and he felt a hard thing close to his lips and he opened his mouth and felt the oily warmth of the liquid running over his lips and into his throat. He seemed to have forgotten how to swallow and he went back into the darkness again.

He heard a woman's voice, measured, quiet, soothing, and he could feel a cool hand on his.

"You're safe now. It's safe here." He heard her dress rustle as she turned away. She smelt of rosemary . . .

"We must keep him warm. Bring more logs and ask Mary to make more broth."

"Yes, Ma'am," came a girl's voice close by and a door closed quietly.

She was looking down at him when Fox opened his eyes and looked up into her face. She looked almost as if she was looking at a child who'd hurt itself. She smiled and put her finger on his mouth as he tried to speak.

He could smell the linen sheets and feel them on his back. He was naked and for a moment he wondered who had undressed him. He couldn't see the woman beside him clearly because the window behind her let in a blinding white light, the sun reflecting off the snow that covered everything outside.

If he tried to move his head, he felt the sudden stab of pain through his right shoulder and down his arm. He closed his eyes and when he opened them again she had gone. When she returned, she was holding a steaming bowl of broth and a horn spoon.

"Try to eat a little, but you are not to speak. You are to eat and sleep and eat and sleep more and grow in strength."

She was closer now and he could see the soft-spoken woman's face more clearly. She went on talking as he looked at her and drank in her face as he sipped the broth in the spoon.

She had long, curling dark hair held back under a simple cap and yet always, it seemed, escaping for she was forever pushing it back into place out of her face. He tried to remember her face so that when he woke in the night as he had each night he'd been there, he would have something to remember. Something to tell him he had not frozen to death in that terrible bleak place.

Her face was a wonder to him. He sipped the broth again and again to keep her close by him while he stared at her. He'd been so sure he'd never see a face again he owed it to himself to sate himself on her smile.

But it was her hand he noticed most. A hand used to no more hard work than plying a needle or a crochet hook. A hand that had never scoured pans with sand, nor cut timber, nor planted, nor shovelled manure about a farmyard, nor curried a horse nor anything that proclaimed its owner other than a gentlewoman.

Despite her face being unlined there was a wistful caste to the eyes and stillness about the mouth that told him she'd not been without a care.

196

As for her face, truly it was not open as Alison's had been. Nor beautiful as the Irish Girl was. Behind the gentle grey eyes there was a serenity that showed from time to time. The skin was bloomed by weather and not fashionably pale. It relied on no artifice and was the better for it in Fox's eyes. A full mouth and a firm chin. A strong face.

"What happened to me?" Fox asked as he pushed aside the hovering spoonful of broth. He could eat no more. He felt as weak as a kitten.

"Later," she said. "Sleep now."

He dreamed again and heard a scream and knew it was himself screaming as he saw his wife standing on flames holding dog roses in her hands and then she was shaking her head, and he woke up sweating.

****

He lay still. He said nothing to whoever came into the room. Even to gentle Lady Elizabeth Morton he'd been able to say nothing. Would he find his child? Would this chaos through which he'd ridden ever stop.

"God has left me," he said when Elizabeth came into the room again. And she put her cool hands on his and shook her head. He was still confused.

"You may think so," she said. He slept again.

He remembered watching a hawk stoop for a kill and flutter across to a rock near where he lay so still in the snow. The hawk held a small rabbit in its talons, pressed the living animal down on the flat stone and smashed its skull with a blow of its curved beak and then began to tear at the fur and into the soft gut of the still convulsing animal.

One fluttering scream of pain and the rabbit was still. The hawk tore open the flesh and fed as the snow about the stone turned red. Fox watched the relentless tearing and swallowing.

The snow fell and the dark grey curtain moved along the valley and filled his vision.

"John," she murmured and he opened his eyes. He was no longer hurting. He looked about him without feeling that at any moment he might fade away into a mist. He saw Elizabeth Morton watching him.

His shoulder no longer hurt. He lay on the soft mattress and pillows and closed his eyes for a second and opened them again and she smiled at him.

"Well, John, you slept without dreaming for the first time since you came."

"How long ago?" he asked. His voice, so little used, felt strange to him.

"Three weeks . . . more."

"I must go on. I have to go. Someone to find."

Elizabeth's grave eyes looked down at the grey-faced man staring up from the pillow then she turned away from him and took a mirror from a dressing table nearby. Silently, she held it so that he could see himself. She had no need to say more.

The gaunt face staring back from the mirror was evidence enough. The dark lines of pain, the grey shadows, under deep sunk eyes, the sunken cheeks and the mouth tight as a skull's showed a man who'd been to the edge of hell and back.

She put the mirror aside.

"But you shall wash and shave and eat and rest, John Fox. And maybe thank the God you don't believe in for being found by one of my shepherds before you died, which was a close run thing."

Fox could not argue. He had no strength for it. And for a week Elizabeth and one or other of the maids continued to feed him like a baby.

One of the men came in to wash him when he refused to allow the women.

"And who do you think undressed you when you came first, who dressed you in my husband's night clothes . . . ?" Her grey eyes lit with laughter as she saw the shock on his face.

"No women ever saw me . . . No decent woman save my wife, ever."

"Alison?" said Elizabeth, "You spoke of her, and wept and I wondered why."

He struggled to sit up and to tell her but she restrained him and shook her head.

"There's no need to tell me anything, John. You talked in your sleep and in your pain and . . . there's no need to tell me anything."

He watched her as she ordered more logs for the fire, more hot bricks for the bed, more food or wine and water . . .

Slowly, slowly he began to mend. He saw how her serving maids loved her. She was no beauty, but was gentle and very still from time to time. She'd sit in the room by the fire with a book or a sampler or mending and work on in silence while he dozed. It calmed him to see her there.

Sometimes she read to him but he fell asleep whenever she did. He loved the softness of her voice. He asked her about her husband, she had said nothing but changed the subject.

He later asked one of the maids. She shrugged and looked about to see that no-one listened.

"My lord, Sir Harry, is with the King. Or some say he's overseas raising money for the King's cause, or that he's dead. Who knows?"

The girl seemed indifferent to the fate of her master.

"He's an old man and they say he has more interest in young men than in his wife. So now you know as much as I do, John Fox, which is not much. But I tell you for nowt . . . his wife's worth ten of him and no-one here would say 'owt else. And he'll not bother us 'til the snow goes now. He's no way to cross the Dales to my lady's house. None. If he lives."

They were isolated by the snow, besieged by it and trapped or protected, depending on where one lay. Fox knew he had to regain his strength.

"What happened to my shoulder?" he asked. "Who took out the ball?"

"I did," Elizabeth said. "I've always doctored my horses. I took out the ball and cauterised the wound with fire. I thought you'd die a second time. But it had to be done for it was infected."

Fox stared up at this woman who could speak so matter-of-factly about doing such a thing.

To dare to probe the wound, to cut away infected flesh, to pull out the ball and all the cloth it had taken into the wound. For it was the cloth which caused the infection. Then to take a blade and heat it and to place it in the wound. How did this gentlewoman bring herself to do that?

"You'd've died else," she said and smiled. "Women have more uses than one, my friend." And it was the first time she had called him that.

She sat by the fire in the evening and listened as Fox told her something of his life. Of going for a soldier as a boy, of the village, of the work he did for Alison's uncle. Once she asked him who Rebecca was and he lay silent, unable or unwilling to speak.

He was still too weak perhaps to compass the idea of Rebecca living. He stared past Elizabeth in his distress and she took his hand.

"I'm sorry," she said. "I didn't mean to hurt you."

He tried to smile up into her eyes and he felt the compassion she had for him and her pity and didn't want that.

They got him up the next day. He felt as weak as a bird, his legs hardly supported him. Elizabeth and the maid laughed at him as he clung to the bed and cursed his fumbling steps. They held him, one on each side, as he walked to the window and looked out for the first time.

Fox stood for a moment holding the stone pillar of the wide window and stared down over the yard and the stables. Everywhere he looked was stark white or etched in black where the snow had been rubbed off the trees, the edges of roofs, the tops of gates and distantly off the larger outcrops of stone. The land was a soft undulating sheet of white as far as he could see.

His legs began to shake so he sat in the leather armchair the women had placed within his reach.

Each day now he would be taken from his bed and would sit in the window looking down the snow-filled valley. The house lay at the end of a dale and beyond lay further rising land, down which anyone approaching the house would be seen a long time before they arrived.

The house of Derbyshire stone stood foursquare at the end of the valley. Its windows and chimneys built in Tudor times. These were built onto an older house that had itself been built alongside the site of a monastery.

Henry the Eighth had made the additions possible. Stone had been pillaged from the older building and the outbuildings showed some of the lines of the abandoned monastic buildings.

Below the house the land sloped down to a series of ponds, now frozen. A long row of stone pillars was all that was left of the ancient cloister and to the right, the ruins of a vast arch showed where the main chapel had once stood.

Fox sat in the chair from the early morning through to late afternoon as the sun went down blood-red across the sheets of white snow.

On some days a fresh fall would add to their defences. Elizabeth would sit and play backgammon with her guest as he slowly recovered his strength. Each day she delighted in the recovery he was making but it was too slow for Fox. He fretted at the inactivity for he had work to finish and he was still helpless.

In the house there were but a few servants. A cook and kitchen maid and a boy to do the heavy work. Outside in the yard a stable hand and a shepherd. There were two other maids about the house and three men for the animals and the fields who lived in cottages on the land.

"Don't you feel afraid . . . a woman alone here?" He asked her one day and she laughed aloud.

"Why on earth would I feel afraid? Do people hate me? Am I a hard mistress? I think not John. I believe not."

It was evening and they had a candle lantern on the table and were playing yet another game of backgammon. Fox lost again.

"You're mind was elsewhere. Maybe you're bored, John."

"No," he said. "Anxious, maybe."

"Why?"

"I come into your life a stranger . . . you too, a stranger to me. I have no notion who you really are. Nor what you are or why you took me in

200

and saved my life and didn't leave me to one of the stable boys to look after.

"No more do I," she said and placed the last of the ivory pieces in the box. She closed it. "I'm lying," she said and put aside the box. He was suddenly aware of the silence in the house. Only the soft hiss of burning green logs and the distant creak of floorboards on a landing.

The fire flared for a moment and lit her face as she leaned closer to him. He saw the warmth in her eyes and the full lips and determined mouth and chin. Elizabeth looked at him then and he saw the tension at the edges of her eyes. She leaned back and sighed.

"Yes," he said, quietly. And she nodded.

"The girl?" she said suddenly. "Not your child . . . nor your wife . . .a girl. You spoke of her as if, almost as if you were afraid of her. Temptation, you said."

"Did I?" said Fox. He sipped the glass of wine that she'd poured for him from the Bristol glass decanter.

"You did," said Elizabeth and smiled. "I'd almost think you guilty, if I believed any man felt guilty about his women."

"She's not my woman, Elizabeth. I . . . once . . . one time . . . Oh, it doesn't matter now."

"No. It doesn't matter now, John Fox." She murmured, and sipped her wine.

The firelight lit her profile as she sat beside him and breathed such life into the room, into the space she lived in. Why was this warm-blooded, blooming woman on her own in the snow-locked countryside?

Outside the snow froze hard again and locked the land in its grip and closed the roads and the tracks and the paths.

Fox was no longer impatient to go. He knew he'd need all his strength and he'd experience enough from his days as a soldier to know that a wound such as he had suffered takes more than time to heal physically, to be better.

The flesh was knitting well and would leave no more than a puckered scar. She'd burned the poison out of it.

Left alone as he was for much of each day, he had time to brood on Alison's death and how he would find his daughter. He dreamed about her each night and about the ashes he'd gathered up in the field below the Long Mynd. He'd wake to find himself sweating and shaking and then he'd lie staring out of the window waiting for the dawn.

And at dawn he'd watch as the sun came roaring up over the rim of the hills, a huge, angry, red ball hanging in a slate-silver sky.

Each day there was a soft knock at the door and Elizabeth or Mary, one of her house servants, would come in with milk and bread and cheese from the dairy. He'd eat because he knew he had to build up his strength and because he liked to make Mary smile.

She was a round-faced, short-haired girl with a quiet manner and merry eyes. And without an inch of disloyalty to her mistress in her. It took a time for Fox to gain her confidence but when he had gained it she was a quiet source of information about her mistress. Whom she loved.

"Her husband's got no time for anyone save himself and that's the truth," she burst out suddenly when he asked again about the master of the house.

"He married her for the land and the house and the dowry she brought him and much of it gone already on gewgaws and boys. He'd sell the lands if he could but they're entailed to my lady and not to be sold at the risk of losing all income. But she's nothing to him nor never has been."

"So why did she marry him?"

"Why does any free woman marry any man?" She spat the words, banging a tray onto the table. "'Cause she is forced to it by her father or by circumstance. And her father never forced her for he loved her as she loved him."

"So why?" Fox demanded. "Why?"

"Debt!" said the girl. "My lady's father owed money and her husband bought up all the debts and demanded my lady in marriage and the land and house as dowry. It was all her father had left to give. He had been bled dry. She married the master to save her father's reputation."

Mary looked round as she heard someone in the corridor outside the door.

"You'll not tell my lady I told you . . ."

Fox smiled and shook his head.

"You like her?" he asked.

"We all like her. More. She loves us and cares for us and will not turn us out, as he demanded when he first came here. He's a cruel man and bad to her. She never complains though nor tells us half of what she suffers I believe. I heard he might be dead. We all pray he is."

In the evenings they sat and read or played cards together but mostly they talked. He of soldiering and his work as a merchant and she would laugh then.

"It's the very idea of you being a merchant grubbing about with clerks and men of business when you so clearly are not suited to it."

"Alison made me promise not to go for a soldier any longer. I lost a friend, butchered, and vowed then to stop, came home, married and . . ."

202

He broke off and stared out into the dark night beyond the window and she was wise enough to say nothing.

Slowly his strength came back and he began to walk through the house holding her arm. At first only the few steps along the panelled dark floored landing. Leaning on carved oak presses and linen chests that ran the length of the long gallery off which the bedrooms lay.

Then he navigated the stairs and stood panting but triumphant on shaking legs at the foot of the stairs facing Elizabeth whose open smile made him laugh for the first time in so very long.

He took her arm and they walked slowly into the main hall and to the fire burning at the far end of the room. Two portraits hung over the fireplace. One of an old man in the finery of another age and the other of a beautiful woman.

"My mother," said Elizabeth. "She was very happy here except she had only one child who lived and that a daughter. She never loved me as much as she might've loved a son."

Fox stared at the portrait for a moment and then turned away and saw Elizabeth staring at him. She looked away guiltily.

"What is it?" he asked, but she shook her head and made excuses and left him for the rest of the day to find his way about the house. She found him, eventually, sitting in the kitchen with the cook and Mary and the kitchen boy eating pie and amazing them with stories of his soldiering with Black Tom Fairfax.

Christmas was a quiet feasting. No visitors could cross the moors to the house, no mummers come as they often had in the past to amuse the guests in the house.

Elizabeth asked John Fox to read the gospel in the family chapel and he did so. Then she read aloud from Corinthians about love and smiled about the chapel where the servants were gathered as they had, by tradition, gathered every year since the house was built.

Elizabeth gave small gifts to the children of the house and then something to each of those who worked for her. Fox marvelled to see the pleasure it gave her to do this and to see the love they all had for this gentle, lonely woman. The servants left them then to eat alone together.

At last they'd eaten enough and Fox looked at her across the rim of his wineglass and she smiled at him.

"So serious?" she said. "Why?"

"I was thinking . . . what would your husband say should he come home and find me here. Or what would he say if the servants told him I'd stayed so long . . . ?" Fox said.

"Would it matter to you?" she asked him.

He stared at her for a moment and then shook his head gravely.

"No," he said. "But it might matter to him."

"He won't come, John Fox."

"You sound so certain."

"He went to the King's standard. There was a battle," she said, "Between the King's men and the Parliament's men."

Fox stared at her.

"So . . . it's come. Fighting. Just as Thurloe said it would. God help us all," said Fox.

"Amen to that," she said and crossed herself.

In the glimmering light from the tallow candles he saw how beautiful she was. Her eyes down cast for a moment in prayer and then looking so fiercely across the shining table at this strange and difficult man. This man about whom she knew so much for he'd wandered in his illness from sieges in Austria to the death of his friend in a lonely valley, to homecoming and a Royalist soldier whose brother he had killed . . . A girl called Maeve and the hideous death of his wife. She knew so much and yet she knew there was nothing in what she knew, nothing of the man himself.

"He went to fight then, on the King's side."

"I've a King's man to see soon. A debt to pay, a revenge to have."

Fox poured more wine then sliced more meat from the joint on the table, took it in his fingers and ate, wiped his fingers on the cloth at his side and stared blindly for a moment into the candlelight.

"Your husband? What happened?"

She shrugged.

"My husband?" For a moment her eyes brimmed with tears. "My husband died in the first charge. Bravely, I was told." She sighed. "I cannot bring myself to mourn. There was no marriage to mourn, no love to mourn. Only sadness." She leaned towards him across the table and gave him a small package. "Happy Christmas, John," she said and walked quickly out of the room.

Fox sat by the dying embers of the fire with the Christmas package in his hand.

He was sorry for Elizabeth and afraid for her, alone here. Yet she was surrounded by people who'd love and protect her to their dying breath. There was something in that sort of love Fox knew was worth more than friendship.

He opened the package and stared at it for a very long time. It was a book, in French which he'd learned to read long ago in another place. Poems by a Roman poet . . . Ovid's Poems of Love.

204

****

Elizabeth found him in the stables one morning looking at the horses and mending what they'd found of his harness on the dead horse up the valley.

"John," she said. He looked up as she stepped out of the glare of the light in the doorway into the warm shadow of the stables. A horse snickered and Elizabeth walked to the horse with the white blaze down its face. The horse knew his mistress and let her scratch his ears.

She didn't look round at Fox though she knew he was watching her. They'd been together now in the house for two months and more. He'd learned so much about her from watching as much as from talking to her.

He sensed her moods and understood her as he'd only ever understood one other woman in his life. He felt rooms were empty when she left them, he looked forward to hearing her read or listened to her play the lute she'd been given by her father when she was married.

He looked at her now and put the harness aside. As he stood she still didn't turn. In the sweet smelling warmth of the stable he walked across her and then she looked at him.

"No, John Fox," she said and he saw the sadness in her eyes.

"Elizabeth, I . . . "

She put her hand to his mouth and stopped him speaking the words she knew he would not mean.

"You're waiting to go. Aren't you?" she said.

"I can't go, I . . . can't go," he said.

The horse with the white blaze skittered on the straw-covered floor of his stall and nuzzled under the arm of his mistress.

"You can't go yet. No. You'd die out there if you went now. But you're impatient. I know. I understand John. I do understand. I wish . . . I wish so many things . . . I wish." She said and looked up at him.

He reached then and touched her face under the hood of her cloak and she put her hand on his and stared into his face.

"It doesn't matter, John. I know you're afraid of the guilt you feel. Losing your wife so. And she was so lucky . . ."

He started away from her at that.

". . . Let me finish, John. She was lucky to have known a man. A man who lived . . . breathed life and pleasure and . . ."

She broke off for a moment and put her hand to her breast. John Fox moved her. He knew she was moved and knew he wanted her. To bury himself in her. To smell her body, feel the soft blooming curves of her close to him. To be smothered by her. A warm woman.

Fox longed to lie with her but he could not pretend to love.

She walked across the stable into the shadows where he could hardly see her. Nor she him. Which was what she wanted.

"My husband," she said quietly, "My husband was no man of action. He plotted and planned. Nothing he did was for love or even friendship. Even marrying me." The note of bitterness hardened her voice.

"I paid a debt for my father by marrying him, knowing him to be uninterested in women."

Fox said nothing.

"I am not asking you to love me, John Fox. I'm not asking you to stay after you are well enough to go. I'm not asking you for anything. I am telling you how it is with me."

She turned them smiling and eyes bright with a new found confidence.

"I will tell you because, before you, I am shameless. But I will tell you," she said softly, "That I have never said such things to any man before. Nor will I ever again."

She stepped into the white light from the stable door and smiled a sad smile as she come towards him and stood close to him.

"I want you to be well and I want you to be free. I want everything you want John," and she took his hand and put it inside her cloak over her breast.

Outside in the yard a chill wind began to whine about the stone buildings. Snow began to drive into deeper and deeper drifts and in the sweet-smelling warmth of the stable, in the loose piles of clover and hay, very gently, they made love.

34

The end of winter. Water was beginning to free itself from the ice on the barn roof. The pale yellow sun was rising higher each day over the top end of the dale. In the stable yard was a scatter of thin foot prints where mice had scrabbled for grain left on the wet cobbles. The silence of the snow remained.

Inside the house the blast of cold in each corridor was relieved only a little by the heat coming from the fires piled and roaring in each room.

High in the Dales, the wind no longer whined so keenly in the night. The paths below the valley would soon be open, the streams flooding with brown melt water and the first show of grass, crushed pale yellow under the snow cover, would begin to shoot green tips.

It was that magical time when the harsh grip of winter is released and yet spring is not yet quite able to free the land.

Fox felt a dreadful lassitude. He had believed he would never lose the fire and the anger in his gut, yet over the last weeks the pain of it had died a little. As he lay in Elizabeth's bed and heard the sounds of the house waking he marvelled at his good fortune. If he wanted he could stay here and begin a new life with Elizabeth, who loved him.

Yet he knew he could not stay. Elizabeth understood that he had been tied before to life on the land, with a woman he truly loved, and it had been a living prison for him. She understood better than Alison had, that to try to hold him would condemn him to daily purgatory.

Through the long ticking days of winter they had lived in the cocoon of the house, served by loving and kindly servants. They adored their mistress and knew Fox for a considerate and a decent man. Their dislike of their master and their delight at being free of him made for a house full of gentle laughter and quiet warmth.

Fox lay, stared at the ceiling, and heard the gentle breathing of the woman at his side. He knew he had to wake up from this long hibernation and go about his business. He had a duty to himself and to his dead wife. Find the man who'd burned her; find the man betrayed her to him and then find the daughter who had been abandoned to the world and was yet wandering in it.

"I feel so helpless," he'd said to Elizabeth only the night before.

They were standing at the stable door with Peter, the shepherd, having fed the horses.

Elizabeth took his arm as they walked away. Across the yard the snow still covered the wall and the gate from which they could look down the dale, sparkling under the rising moon which lay on its back like a silver scythe.

Peter watched them for a moment and rubbed his palm across his nose and stared up into the sky and sniffed. He knew that soon the drifts would begin to leak water and slowly lose their shape and finally vanish into the swollen becks and streams that fed the river Dove so far below them.

By the gate the two figures merged as Fox draped his cloak around Elizabeth and held her close.

"Tell me about Alison," Elizabeth said gently. "Tell me, please."

"I can't, I'm sorry, but I can't."

"I don't want you to feel guilty about our time together, John."

"You talk as if it's ended," he said.

She almost smiled then at his self-deception.

"My dear man," was all she said.

Behind them, Peter watched. Overhead the stars and the moon hung sharp in the blackness. And below in the valleys and forests, in the towns and the cities men began to stir and armies began to think of moving from their winter quarters.

****

Thurloe sat at his desk reading interminable reports from agents around the country, from Jewish bankers in Amsterdam, from traders in Padua and Venice, from merchants in Riga and factors in Versailles and even from a wild-eyed Irish girl who'd wintered in the bed of a certain influential royalist aristocrat.

He had cursed Maeve for a whore when she told him that she intended to move with the coming of spring. She said she had an appointment with that fool Fox. Not written, not arranged, but she knew where to find him when the time came and she intended to be there.

If Thurloe wanted Fox reeled in again he'd better be glad she was willing to forgo a warm bed and a fistful of gold and the official position as his lordship's mistress to reel the strange man in.

Thurloe was no longer sure he needed Fox. He had expected him to come back to London rather than to vanish into the countryside and the harsh winter.

Within two weeks Maeve had left London and vanished from Thurloe's sight.

She had enough of the young, talkative and vain Royalist.

****

Fox and Elizabeth lay in the vast bed together and he took her as she liked to be taken. He knelt between her legs and looked at her breasts as they thrust upwards under the white linen of her nightdress. She slowly pulled the material away and offered her breasts to him. They were still firm for lack of children sucking there. Fox leaned forward, kissed her hard nipples and entered her. He felt her soft inner thighs lock around him and draw him deeper and deeper into her.

The firelight danced on the moulded ceiling and across the walls of the room.

He woke later to hear the sound of her weeping beside him.

"John," she whispered.

"Yes?" he said.

"When will you go?"

It was said now. It was in the open. Sharply like a knife or a hot blade to cauterise a wound. To cleanse something. To release him.

"No," he said. "I'll stay."

Elizabeth pretended to believe him. But they knew now it was done. She had cut the cord that bound him to her.

Their days they spent marking the unlocking of the land. The sight of a flock of birds, a mewing hawk crossing the Tops and searching desperately for carrion or a small animal crawling out of hibernation unwisely early.

The slow drip of water in the mid-morning sunshine was replaced by an iron frost in the evening that made the land treacherous and warned of the grip winter yet had.

Fox knew their time was nearly finished. His lot was not to be a farmer in the Dales, nor a lover for this sweet Elizabeth who lay each night by his side and who loved him.

She was the sort of woman who only gave herself for love. Now with her husband dead in some foolish fighting between a foolish King and a ruthless Parliament she was condemned to a life without hope. She cried quietly each morning in the darkness and he heard her and lay silent and still.

Fox had begun to walk across the snow where it had packed down into narrow tracks used by sheep and man alike. From time to time he went out with Peter searching for lost sheep. He was regaining strength each day.

Mornings found him working with the short sword and the long bladed dagger that he had taken from Pat Shea. Elizabeth watched him as he thrust and parried, thrust and parried and thrust and parried again and again and laughed with him when he stopped and looked around for her and kissed her and she could smell the sweat on him.

They woke one morning to the sound of water running off the house eaves, cascading across the yard, trickling over the windows and fence posts, running into the ditches still hidden under the drifts of snow. Water overflowing buckets and water troughs, water tumbling and snow sliding in great swoops from barn roofs and leaving piles of soft slush at the foot of the walls . . . they woke to the end of winter.

She was standing at the window looking out as Fox woke. He didn't move and she was unconscious that he was awake.

Her long hair hung in great waves down her back, her figure moulded by the nightdress she wore. She half turned to look back at him and he could see the swell of her breasts, the long firm column of her neck and the firmness of her chin. She came back to their bed.

He did not want to stay until the time when bitterness and anger might set in and destroy what would be a warm and generous memory.

She turned to him and pushed her hair back from her face and smiled.

"It's nearly time, my friend," she said. "I can feel spring coming. You must be ready and don't you dare to lie, John Fox. We're not children playing games of kiss and make up. I know what I do and you do too. It's time to go and do what you have to do. No pretence, John."

Fox had never seen Elizabeth so angry. Nor had he admired her as much as he did now.

"I will not be made a fool of by any man again," she said. "We've done what we have done. I have always known you'd leave me and the time is close now. I know you, John Fox, better than you think."

She wiped her hand across her face and he saw the tears start afresh in her dark shining eyes.

"Damn you for making me cry!" she said and he laughed then and she laughed too, she in his arms and both of them laughing.

Afterwards she lay with her head on his shoulder and he smelt her hair and her body and they lay close like two cats. He'd had his share of women as any soldier has, but she was braver than most. With a man's bravery, he thought. Willing to stare into the face of the future and to accept it for what it brought. He said as much and she looked up into his face then and grinned at him.

"You're something of a fool, John," she said, and ran her finger along his jaw and into his hair and pulled his head down to her and kissed him. He felt that flutter in his heart he'd felt only with one other woman and her tongue in his mouth.

"You shall have a horse, John, and harness and food and even money when the time comes. And don't refuse me, my lover," she said.

"I don't want to go," he said.

"You must, John. My dear good friend, you must go. Soldiers take their pleasures lightly as you told me once, I remember."

He denied ever saying it and she laughed in his face again and evading his arms stepped out of their bed and back to the window.

"Look," she said, and pointed into the garden below.

"Before the first primroses show in the hedge you will have to go. There's vengeance in you needs letting out."

Fox knew Alison would not want vengeance but he was a soldier and a soldier did what he had to do.

"No sadness John, please."

She left him then and went to the small chapel on the other side of the hall. For Elizabeth had committed more sins in the months John Fox had been with her than she had in the whole of her previous life.

There was no Catholic priest to admonish her, nor to offer any absolution and she didn't ask for any. For she felt no guilt however many sins she had committed.

She lit six candles by the small, carved altar and knelt on the cold stone floor and prayed. Prayed, not for herself but for her lover and for his safety, for his soul and for that of his dead wife and for the security of his daughter, Rebecca.

Elizabeth prayed then for the life within her, for she was late and she was never late.

The candles lit the hanging figure on the cross over the altar and on the cross she had at her throat. She went through the rosary and then again through it and again and, kneeling still looked up at the sharp slight slanting through the window of the chapel onto the silver chalice on the marble slab of the altar.

Elizabeth had found her own way to peace. She crossed herself as she stood in front of the altar, and walked out into the day.

Fox walked through the slushy yard past the two guard dogs in their barrel kennels. They no longer barked at him.

That morning he stood in the stable looking over the horses stabled there. They were all becoming restless at being trapped in stalls through the winter. They needed exercise and to run off their fat and their bad temper.

"'Tis over then," said Peter, walking in with a pail of water. "Winter's broke up and gone, more or less," he said. "'Twill be for the best." Fox nodded, grim faced. The sooner it was done the better.

"Go with ease, Master Fox, for we do love her, truly. So have a care."

Fox nodded. "If her husband had not been killed in some battle or other, would it have gone as it has, Peter?"

Peter shrugged.

"I don't know much as to that, Master Fox. Nor even if he be truly dead. I can hope it," he went on, "We all know you've wrought a great change in her life. And we are glad for it. And the women in the kitchen talk of you staying somehow and keeping her happy. But that's idle women talking. It won't be so, will it?"

Fox was astonished to find the shepherd smiling at him.

"You're not made for it, Sergeant Fox. And you have things on your mind. Remember I was the one picked you up first and kept you for the first nights in my shelter up on the Tops. You talked a lot, said a lot . . .

"A man looking for you called Major Andrews who'd lost a brother and vowed to kill you . . . you talked of witchcraft and burning and a wife as was dead and a daughter gone no-one knew where. I've said nothing of it to anyone in the house, for a man's business is a man's business. But I can tell you will not stay and I tell you sommat else . . . 'twere best not, maybe. Mistress Elizabeth will be well looked after, protected. She is well loved and is no fool. She has asked me to see to a horse for you for it to be ready when the time comes. I tell you, John Fox . . . My mistress does love you enough to let you go about your business. That's a rare sort of love."

Fox looked at the tall, spare man wrapped in shirt and jacket and layers of hose. He wore old trousers and a sheepskin belted with a leather thong and huge leather boots blackened with goose fat.

"I have to find a man," he said. "I made a promise and I keep promises, Peter."

212

"Hopkins . . . Witchfinder Hopkins," said Peter. "You talked of finding him while you were in a fever,"

"Yes," said Fox. "You know of him?"

"I heard he'd gone north to Lancashire."

"How? We've been snowed in this last eight weeks. How did you hear?"

Peter smiled then.

"I asked," he said.

"Who?"

"On the Tops of the Dales we meet. Other shepherds meet from time to time. When we go searching for lost sheep . . . They come from the next valley and bring news from over there. Sheep spread far and wide here. When you first came I asked those I met to discover what they could. I'd not have my mistress harmed by any man."

"Go on," said Fox.

"Hopkins went north and then doubled back towards the town of Liverpool and then south to Ludlow they say. They say he stayed a time there in the Castle. An unwelcome guest but, as he carries the King's writ, what could anyone do but take him and his in?"

"Him and his?" asked Fox. "Who, man . . . who was with him?"

"Some said two men, another said two men and a woman. A young woman. One other said one man and a young woman . . ."

Fox stood in the doorway of the stable and drew in great breaths of the icy air.

"A young woman?"

Peter stared at the man and was sorry for him.

"You hear many things . . . some are true . . . it changes, Master Fox. It may be he is with your daughter out of pity. It may be it is not your daughter. I can't tell. No-one that I asked knew. No-one will talk. They're afraid of the Witchfinder. No-one here will talk of it. On my word."

"I believe you, my friend."

Peter's breath hung in the freezing air.

"You should know there are two men down the valley asked after you from time to time. Or for a man uncommonly like you. Hunters, my friends say. Hunters. Waiting."

The spikes of primroses were already showing lower down the valley where the hunters waited to earn their bounty money. The crippled Major had promised he would pay well as vengeance for his dead brother.

35

The two men had been waiting down in the valley through the long snows. Only going away when they knew the weather would hold the whole of the upper Dales in its grip, when no man dared to ride out.

They had asked for Fox by name and for a long time no-one would confirm or deny there was a stranger up the valley. All the people of the Dales respected Elizabeth and if she chose to shelter a man from the winter then that was very much her business and certainly nothing to do with these two strangers.

It was a woman who told, eventually, for money. She'd heard from a friend who'd heard from another friend, that before the land was locked away by the snow and ice, a man had been found high up on the moors, wounded and like to die. That he had lived was as much due to the skill of the shepherd who brought him to the big house as to the ministrations of the mistress.

After the woman had described the man they knew he was their quarry. As the snow receded they rode higher up the valley, closer to the house.

The tracks were still a mixture of mud and ice-hard earth under a horse's hooves.

To the south a cloaked figure rode steadily up from the Midlands avoiding towns and even villages as much as possible. Heading towards the Dales and the high moorland.

The only sound the rider heard was the sound of water dripping into water, ice turning from pale glass to earth brown as it caved in, skittered away and squelched under the slow horse's hooves.

A high collar and fur hood covered the face of the rider and a scarf wound about the mouth, left only the dark green eyes of the Irish girl as she rode out to find the man where she had "seen" him six weeks ago.

Thurloe had not believed she'd find him and anyway he had other targets for her particular skills. The noble son of a noble man and a Royalist to his boots never knew she was going. He woke one morning to find the other side of his bed cold and his purse empty.

She'd taken what information she could from him and passed it to Thurloe before she left. He too had paid her so, doubly rewarded, she rode towards the melting snows.

Maeve had heard that Major Andrews, who was recovering slowly from a shattered hip, boasted of setting hunters to find and kill the man who'd led the raid on the King's coach, a sweet revenge for his dead brother.

****

In the Sign of the White Cross she'd found three of the men Fox had recruited for the ambush. She had talked to them. They'd been reluctant until the owner of the ale house gave word she could be talked to.

She knew that the coach had been spirited away as Fox had ordered them for Thurloe told her as much. It was unfortunate that Fox had had to decoy the Major and his troopers and if he'd died - well he'd been a brave man, they told her. Then they ignored the cold-eyed girl who stood biting her knuckles near the door.

They'd turned briefly to tell her she could sit with them if she liked but by then she had gone into the wet winter streets about Holborn and to the watchmaker's shop and the room over it where she told Thurloe what she had gleaned.

She also told him she did not believe Fox was dead. There had been an ambush, of that she was sure and there had been more Royalist outriders than had been expected. It seemed they'd been betrayed . . . or careless.

She stared into the ice-black eyes and watched the tightening of the flesh around his nose and mouth into a thin white line. Thurloe was furious that their plan might have been put at risk by a counterspy amongst them.

216

Maeve told him again and again that they had done all that had to be done. They had made no contact with my Lord Essex and his army camped at Alcester.

They had no time to do anything but make their attempt on the treasure in the coach.

"No man amongst us was a traitor or had a slack tongue. Fox chose his men carefully. Each had been well paid and it would have been more than any man's life was worth to do otherwise than to keep his mouth shut."

"And Fox is not dead, or why would the Major set killers to ambush him?" she insisted, and asked for something Fox had touched recently.

Thurloe laughed at her certainty. It was then that he gave her the paper Fox had brought back from France.

"If you have 'the sight', use it on this," he said, mocking her.

She had taken the paper and stared at it and sweat beaded her forehead. Thurloe sat impassively at the end of the wooden table and watched as the girl began to shake.

Suddenly she threw back her head and Thurloe stared at the white stretched throat and heard her moaning. Even he began to feel afraid as she talked of Elizabeth and a bed and ice on the window panes and a shepherd and pain in the shoulder and more pain. Then she began desperately to pluck at her own shoulder in agony.

Then the pain was gone and she smiled and said as much. Then it was over.

Maeve lay slumped over the thorn wood table panting and sweat running across her face.

Thurloe left her alone then. When she woke her head ached and she could hardly stand she was so weak.

"He is alive at the house of Elizabeth . . . I see her name in a book . . . in the fly of the book . . . Her name and a coat of arms and . . . he's there. Living. She loves him and he beds her."

Thurloe laughed then.

"And he?" he asked "You'll tell me next he loves her."

Maeve stared at him then and pulled her cloak about her, stood unsteadily and walked to the door.

"Where the devil are you going?" Thurloe asked the girl and she turned and looked at him under the mane of hair.

"He's in danger. I'm going to warn him. There are two men waiting. Bounty hunters. Sent by the Major from the Marais. They're going to kill him for sure when the snow melts and the roads are open. So who has betrayed who?"

He watched her step out of the watchmaker's doorway below his window and pull up her hood against the rain. She didn't look round, stepped across the flowing drain down the middle of the street and into the dark alleyway opposite. It led down to the river and the small congregation of ships unloading fish from the other side.

Ignoring Thurloe's anger, she rode out of London.

Thurloe turned back to the papers open his desk. He picked up the letter she had been holding when she 'saw' Sergeant John Fox. He shrugged and filed it.

Maeve began her journey.

****

As Fox rode across the wet cobbles of the yard he didn't look to right or left. Three of the servant girls watched him go and waved shyly at the silent man who had made their mistress so happy. He rode through the yard and across the front of the house.

Peter the shepherd was nowhere to be seen but Fox knew he would see him before he left the land surrounding the house. He felt the weight of the long blade lying across his back and took one of the French soldier's pistols from the leather scabbard he'd fashioned for it on the saddle. Its twin was in the roll of bedding tucked deep in leather bag behind his saddle.

He was prepared for whatever the waiting men were going to offer.

He didn't look back at the mullioned windows that reflected the morning sun, sparkling in the clean cold air. Nor did he look across the higher terrace beyond the curving steps that led down to this terrace and the path to the main gates beyond the fish pond.

The pond was still iced over. Elizabeth had talked so often about skating but somehow they have never seemed to have the time. Now that the ice was crumbling and thin it was too late.

Fox didn't see her standing in the centre bay watching him ride away into the early spring morning. Elizabeth knew nothing of the two waiting men for that was between her shepherd and Fox.

She'd tried to make their parting easier by choosing to argue with him last night over dinner. But he'd laughed at her anger and she knew he knew what she was trying to do, and she began to cry which she had promised not to do.

They sat for much of that evening watching the sun go down, blood red, over what was left of the snow and the ice. They'd watched the moon crest a bank of dark cloud and hang so pale in the blue night sky. They'd said little to each other that they had not said before.

He'd begin to make promises that he would come back and she had stopped his mouth with hers for she knew he would not, however much he meant it as he spoke.

They'd made love together and again in the morning and he'd broken his fast and she had not.

They sat at the table together in silence. The servants busied themselves elsewhere.

"John," she said eventually, "I have been thinking about Rebecca."

Fox flinched at the name and she put her hand on his much as Alison used to do. He looked then into her calm face and saw the half smile on her lips.

"When you find her she will need care and help. You will never be able to give it . . . not for the moment, at least. Would you go back to your old home and the farm? Would you want to live amongst those people again?"

He nodded for her to go on. She held his hand and there was pleading in her voice now.

"When you find her, send her to me, here. I will take care of her for you. As if she were my own. Until you're settled, at least."

"And your people?" he asked. "What will they say?"

And Elizabeth snapped her fingers for that and they both laughed for the first time that morning.

"Is it agreed?" she asked.

"It is agreed," he said and leaned to her and kissed her.

She got up from the table then and left him to finish packing his old leather bag.

He found her, when he was done, in the richly ornate chapel, kneeling on the stone floor in front of a crucifix. She had reached for his hand as he stood behind her. Elizabeth remained on her knees and prayed for his safety and then she prayed silently for forgiveness for the sins she had committed.

Then she stood and kissed him on the mouth and walked quickly out of the chapel to the hall where servants had already begun to pack the leather satchels she insisted he take . . .

Food and drink, a change of clothes . . . a kerchief of hers that he had asked for as a keepsake. She took a gold chain and locket from around her neck, and opening the locket showed him a miniature of herself.

"Only take it if you want it . . . to remember," she said. He took it from her, kissed it and put it inside his jacket.

In front of the servants then she reached up, kissed him and turned and walked up the stairs to their apartment. He walked quickly out of the house and away. As they had agreed.

Fox rode on down the carriage drive into the brightness of the morning. She did not regret the lie she had told John Fox about the death of her husband. No more did she tell him about the child she carried. She wondered, for a moment, how she would explain that child to her husband when he came back.

Elizabeth watched the last of the dark shadow riding away. Turning she scolded a maid who'd come into the room unbidden.

"How dare you?" she began, and the maid, unused to her anger, turned to leave as Elizabeth hurried to her and stopped her.

"I'm sorry. I had no need to scold you, child. Well . . . he's gone."

"Who has gone ma'am?" asked the girl. "We have seen no-one ma'am, heard no-one ma'am. We are all agreed . . . cook and house servants and all of us ma'am . . . we have seen no-one arrive or go away."

The child ran from the room and already she felt so lonely.

Around the house the waters ran off the hillside down ancient water courses, trickled over smooth rocks and hurried under peat-stained logs, burrowed round rock falls and fell in torrents beside the path and the noise of water rang out loud in the silent bright morning.

Peter waited on the hillside, as Fox knew he would. He offered to come with Fox to protect him from the waiting men.

"No, my friend," he said. "This is my affair. Go home and protect your mistress and let me go."

Peter shook Fox's hand and looked long into the man's face.

"'Tis dangerous to hate so much. You see nothing clear for what it is, Sergeant Fox. A soldier does not hate. He merely has work he must do. Cold, chill work. Even in the excitement of the charge, the soldier who survives is the man who goes about his business exactly, precisely and without anger to cloud his mind."

Fox stared at the tall man and smiled then.

"When were you a soldier . . . where and why didn't you tell me, Peter?"

"A time ago. I'd rather forget it. I saw too many friends . . . as you have. When I nursed you, you cried out for Pat Shea and for Michael and for some French boy about to be butchered by a field surgeon. We've both seen enough my friend. I'm sorry you can't find it in you to stay."

"I made a promise, Peter, to my wife who died. But no doubt you know of that as well, and of my daughter."

He saw from the pain in the shepherd's eyes he'd talked of that as well.

Did she hear me too?" he asked.

Peter shrugged . . . "Who would that be, Sergeant? No-one saw you, no-one heard you, no-one remembers so much as the colour of your eyes, save my mistress, and she will say nothing and you will do nothing but ride on."

Fox stared at him.

"Her husband may come home to her as merry as a tattered crow, as full of life as a rotten fence post and she will remember then. I know she says he died in a skirmish but who knows the truth? But we have never met you. And her husband will go away again. Remember she still holds this place and this land as her own. So, go carefully, friend, and watch, for the hunters have taken to riding up into the valley. Searching for a place to take you, no doubt. There is high ground at the end of this valley and dead ground beyond that where a man might hide an army.

"It will be a cold wait, Fox. Remember what I said about anger. It's a good lesson. As well to learn it."

Fox smiled then. This was his world, this was what he understood. The enemy in the field ahead of him . . . waiting. Devil take the weakest of them.

They two men nodded in mutual understanding; Peter turned his hill pony away and Fox rode down the valley towards a lonely clump of hawthorn and scrub oak. He rode into the copse.

Peter waited and watched and smiled as no-one appeared to come out of the other side.

****

Fox came on them in the middle of the afternoon, more as a result of their own foolishness than from his patience. He'd spent the best part of the forenoon waiting high on the rock-strewn slopes.

He'd climbed fast up a gully which was still in shadow over the spongy moss of the cold wet land where a spring stream ran. Moss orchids and the fine green shoots of rank grasses had begun to show from the dark brown clumps of turf strewn amongst the brackish, brown-stained water.

He'd moved as fast as he was able, across this to the steeper slopes, where there were still patches of snow where the weak spring sun never reached.

On two of these stretches of snow fox tracks led to small scattered piles of old bones and fresh feathers. On one, the kill had been made only minutes before for the blood still stained the snow.

Fox never saw the vixen who made the kill. No doubt she had gone to ground and was watching him as he moved upwards towards the ridge which Peter had assured him gave a view over the next valley and the killing ground below.

Once out of the shadow in the valley he'd moved amongst old boulders ground small a thousand thousand years ago by ice and then shattered by winter frosts expanding and cracking open limestone spurs.

Long grey piles of damp shards lay down the faces of the higher slopes. Dangerous to move across unless one ran with the tide of sliding stones and prayed to keep upright, for to fall was to risk a shattered leg or a broken back as the stones became large rocks and it all tumbled in a chaos of debris towards the lower slopes and marsh land below.

Fox skirted these stone fields and found himself amongst the rocks and small cliff faces that ran the length of the Tops. Below this ridge he was out of sight of anyone waiting in the next valley. He was too much a creature of habit to risk showing himself more than necessary.

He moved slowly, thinking about each traverse of a small face, each stride across an open ledge, each glide over the tussocks of high heather and grass left behind by the melting snows.

Far below him he could see the copse where he'd hidden his horse loosely hobbled. The sun lay behind him and anyone looking up would be blinded by the yellow glare.

Gently he eased himself up behind a group of wind carved-rocks on the rim of the valley and looked down into the next and saw no sign. He waited there, through midday, without moving.

Once he heard a faint scream and far below to his right a sudden flurry took his eye. The clatter of wings and the baby scream told him a hawk had made a kill and an early born hare was dead. The screaming went on and on through the silence and then stopped abruptly leaving behind it a deeper silence.

It was then he found the two men.

The hawk rose with the hare in its talons and a hunter looked up and turned his pale face to the light to watch the bird and the disc of his pale face showed clear to Fox. Nearby, Fox made out the figure of another man.

They lay looking along the track he would have to come down from Elizabeth's house towards the small town.

The shadows were lengthening and sweeping up the hill towards Fox as the sun fell lower in the sky. In an hour the ridge would be darkened and he could move freely.

It was a full hour before he moved. The killers were a hundred and fifty yards apart. One lay behind a large rock and the other was close to a tangle of heather and ferns. Fox moved down through the rocks and re-entrants, over stone and heather and beside snow patches and sheep tracks under low-growing broken heather.

The two men moved uneasily and felt the cold more keenly because they had been still for so long. Fox reached carefully for the long blade before he made his move. He was only yards from his target.

The first of the men he killed knew only the coldness of the blade at his throat and nothing more as Fox leaned into him with all his strength. The man flopped once and stopped almost immediately. Dead on the instant.

Fox lay quite still beside the dead man in the shadow of the long afternoon.

Away down the valley a dog barked once and high over them a flurry of birds clattered away in alarm away to the right beyond the second man.

Fox then ran, concealing nothing, and was on the second man before he could aim the crossbow he'd brought to bear on the track where Fox should have ridden.

Fox took him off his balance and rolled over him, gripping and kicking and writhing in a bundle like mad dogs. His opponent was hampered by the long cloak he'd worn against the cold. Fox had abandoned his when he'd taken the first of the hunters.

They slammed into the base of a rock buttress. The second man lay where Fox let him fall. His head lolled across his shoulder where his broken neck left it; his pale blue eyes stared into what was left of the afternoon sun and stilled.

Quietly Fox began then the work he was trained for. To strip off information in layers from his targets . . . their ages and their ranks, their weapons, their papers, their letters of introduction if any, their connections, with whom and when and where . . . These two men travelled light.

The first lay as Fox had left him. He had money in his purse but not over much, he had a small dagger and, like his companion, he'd a crossbow. Fox knew them then to be trained killers. The crossbow for close accurate work was a common weapon of choice for a German or an Italian assassin. Silent, easy to hide and deadly.

The second man carried a paper inside his doublet which gave Fox pause. Folded carefully inside a small volume of poems by someone called Dante, the paper slipped onto the frozen ground.

It was only three inches square and had been cut from a frame for it was a picture. A portrait. An image of Fox. The last time he'd seen this picture it had been in his daughter's bedroom at the farm on the Long Mynd.

How did it come here with these carrion?

He took the paper and the book of poems, took the coins he found in their purses, the usual mixture of groats and florins, German thalers and silver pieces from Padua . . . a soldier's purse just like his own. Whoever had sent them had not prepared them for action against another soldier. It was a chance they took.

How had they come by the portrait? Who might have given it to them? Where had they stolen it? Had it come from Rebecca?

Fox took a crossbow and a leather case of bolts and, in the gathering dark, walked back to the copse. Changed from his now filthy clothes into clean jacket and hose, rolled the rest into the saddle bag where he put the crossbow and rode into the last of the afternoon sun, down the valley and to the bridge and the clutter of houses that lay at the head of the lower valley.

The two men lay as they'd died, where the wind and the rodents would find them, where the carrion eaters would come soon enough and maybe before any man came, would have stripped them bare to their blue bones.

A hawk came first to the two men. Then, as night fell, the vixen, already pregnant and hungry . . .

36

Fox reined in the mare as the girl trotted from the track between two stunted rows of hawthorn which were black under the evening light.

"I was waiting for you," she said. "There was talk of two men asking for you."

"Dead," he said, and indicated the hills with a jerk of his head.

"Good," she said, adding after a pause, "I'm damnably hungry."

Fox reached into the saddle bag on his left and pulled out a loaf. He threw it to the girl who caught it and instantly began to eat. She looked at him over the loaf and her eyes sparked with laughter.

"It's been a strange winter, John Fox."

Fox shrugged then and held out a canteen of water which she took. Her fingers were ice cold.

"Thurloe wanted me to stay in London or to go to Oxford with Major Andrews or to bed some small lordeen who is close to our dear Queen. Well, to be truthful, your Queen, for she is not mine. He was a child but lusty, eager and I had every scrap of information from him in two days, and then he was dreary and I was ready to leave. Thurloe wanted me to see who he met, who he talked to, when and where and who *they* met, and when and where . . . work for any trollop, not for Maeve Ahern."

"Who is no trollop?" he mocked.

The slash of her cold hand on his cold face surprised him and he stopped smiling.

"Talk of trollops, then ask about Mistress Elizabeth up at the house in the Dale. Her and a mysterious man come in the dead of winter, wounded near to death and saved and soon warm in her bed."

Maeve threw back the bread and drank greedily from the canteen.

"She was no trollop either," Fox said quietly. "A healer more like, for she cured my anger," he said.

"Then you'll need to be uncured, for the men sent for you were willing to kill."

"Tell me about Thurloe."

"Nothing to say about Thurloe. He prepares for war, I suppose. I knew you were in danger and needed help and London was dull."

Fox smiled then at the girl who threw back the canteen and turned her horse to ride alongside him away from the Dales, the corpses on the hillside and Elizabeth.

****

They came down into the Midlands, away from the north and to the flatter, softer, forested lands that lead down to Oxford in the South, to the flat coastlands of the east, to the Welsh Marches to the West.

They rode at ease and let the road take care of itself as they worked their way towards the beginning and the end of their journey.

The first night they had lodged in a smoky-roomed inn at the edge of drovers' country. No-one was staying and the keeper was proud of his ale and indifferent to his lodgers who had the only decent bed in the place and talked long and companionably into the night.

It was on the next day they saw again what war brought to the country.

The smoke was first and then the smell, the stomach wrenching stink of burning flesh.

Fox reined in his mare and Maeve stopped alongside him. He looked about the land to right and left and saw no sign nor heard anything. No birds scrambling out of hedges, no dogs yelping, though smoke drifted towards them over the barren fields.

The first of the women had been taken as she ran from the field and lay half naked, with her throat cut, where the soldiers had left her.

The next, hardly more than a child, lay moaning and bloody, in a ditch staring out of mindless eyes. They rode down where the fires still burned over the ruins of the village.

Maeve stopped by the church and walked inside while Fox stared about him, careful, guarded, his pistols primed and ready. The Irish girl came out of the church and vomited behind a tombstone, a cat retching.

226

"Animals," she said eventually and Fox nodded.

Something moved in the gateway under the elm tree.

"Wait," said Fox quietly and nudged his horse towards the huge old tree.

A man was propped against the tree. He was naked save for a crucifix on a chain about his neck. Fox stared down at him.

"If you're a merciful man, kill me" said the naked man. "I see such things . . . kill me please."

Fox dismounted and knelt beside the naked man.

"Who are you?" he asked the man gently.

"Hugh Martindale, priest to this village. They came roaring into the village, took what they wanted. I begged them to leave the women, but they took them into the church and . . . and . . . I have tried to pray. I find I cannot. The words have gone. Please . . . please kill me. For my sake."

Fox shook his head gently.

"Who were they? Whose soldiers?"

"Does it matter? The officers wore green favours in their hats and gold lace and . . . the men were like other men. I was warned they were coming. I told the villagers they were King's men and could be trusted. They believed me. The soldiers stripped me naked and showed me to the women they took away with them. They said we were infected with witchery."

"Witchery was it? Does the name Hopkins mean anything to you?" Fox asked the naked man.

For a moment he lay still against the bole of the elm tree and shrugged.

"He came in the winter. How did you know? He came with two men and they stayed the night with me and rode on the next day. He was a troubled man, I thought, for he saw evil in all women. He was on his way to . . . I forget where . . . Brummagem maybe . . . No, Worcester again. He'd heard of witchcraft there, he said . . . Why?"

"There was a girl with him. Long dark gold hair, fine features with a mark here on her cheek. And on her neck, under her left ear a small mark, also aged fifteen or so?"

"Not with him. After him. How did you know? She asked for him a day, two days, after he had left us. She seemed angry . . . She had a knife she took from her sleeve from time to time. She had the look of . . ." The naked priest stopped.

He looked up then into Fox's ice-cold eyes and knew he'd find little mercy here. "Of you." he said softly. "Who is she?"

"His daughter." Maeve looked down at the two men and didn't turn her eyes from the nakedness of the one. She went on.

"She is looking for vengeance. John Thurloe told me that the soldiers go to Worcester. I learned from one of those slack-tongued Royalists that Rupert was in the Midlands. It is Prince Rupert's way to sow terror," Maeve said. "And Lord Essex is in Alcester with a force of Parliament men. There are Royalist soldiers under a man called Sir John Byron sitting in Worcester. Thurloe didn't tell me they were savages even against their own countrymen. I've seen what they are, Fox. What now?"

They rode away from the stench of the village and the carnage of war and the naked man under the elm. By the late evening they were making a fire in a barn, cooking a rabbit the girl had snared and drinking the last of Elizabeth's brandy.

In the still smoking village, on the black branches of the elm tree, a naked man swung a little and below him dogs waited and then turned back to easier meat.

The little girl watched and giggled, her eyes quite empty.

War!

****

In the barn off the main track, Maeve and Fox huddled over a small fire, wrapped in cloaks against the cold. Fox was drawing something on a sheet of paper he'd torn from a book of Italian poems. He used a piece of charcoal from the fire.

Maeve chewed on the leg of the rabbit she'd cooked with field herbs the way gypsies do. She glanced across at Fox as he sat back from the drawing and showed it to her.

"What is it?" she asked.

"Map" said Fox. "See here we are, north of Brummagem. Over here is Alcester where Lord Essex sits with his army. Here is Worcester where your man, Sir John Byron, sits guarding yet more plate for the King. The walls of Worcester offer no protection. Any child could walk through in any number of places."

Fox went on

"Three days forced march for My Lord of Essex to Worcester . . . Maybe another day to take the city and the plate. It's too long. Rupert will be ahead of him and will take on any advancing army. It was certainly Rupert who came through here creating terror. Now he'll move fast towards Brummagem and from there to cut off the line of any advance for Essex. And Essex will be forced to fight at Prince Rupert's convenience."

228

He drew the lines of march and the projected lines of advance by Essex on the city of Worcester.

Maeve moved closer to see the map in the glimmer from the fire.

"And your man is in Worcester, we hear, to find a witch."

"Or more like he'll go through Alcester and spy the route for the King's army. What safer cover for any man than to be Witchfinder? No-one will dare question a man like that."

Maeve crossed herself and spat over her fingers into the fire as Fox thought aloud.

"If I was Essex, I'd detach a troop of horses and send them ahead of my main army to engage any cavalry marching to the protection of Worcester and John Byron. Essex can afford to detach a regiment. They could force march to delay any Royalist re-enforcements for the garrison in Worcester. How many men did Thurloe say Lord Essex had?"

"Twenty thousand, I think."

Fox whistled. He stared at the map and drew another line.

"The river Severn. Hold the crossing places and you hold the key to Worcester and the Welsh borders."

"And your daughter follows the Witchfinder with a knife into the eye of a battle. What would you do, John Fox? "

She reached out a hand and touched his throat.

"Give me the cross," she said. "Give me the burned cross you wear there. Give it to me, John Fox."

Her green eyes stared into his and he hesitated and then took from under his shirt the burned and twisted shard of metal that had been his wife's and took it from his neck.

"Why?" he asked her gently. "You were afraid to touch it when it was found in her ashes. You were afraid . . ."

"I am still afraid, John Fox, but I know I must. I will lead you to this man, Hopkins and maybe your daughter and get her away from the battle ground. Then we can go about other business, Thurloe's business. Give me the cross . . ."

He put the grey metal into her hand and she closed her strong fingers over it. He watched her and was not prepared for the astonishing thing that happened as she took the burned metal.

Suddenly he heard a keening from her that set the hairs on his neck on end.

And tears running down her face and her mouth open and keening still and her staring into the fire before them and she spoke. But she spoke with the cracked voice of an old woman and she spoke in the ancient language of Ireland.

Before him she became that old seer . . . that old woman.

And she was in deep pain at what she saw. Her eyes closed and she breathed harshly as she spoke and then her head dropped, her hands stopped clutching at the burned and twisted metal.

Then she held out her hand and he took the cross from her. She lay shivering under the cloak. Her eyes rolled back in her head, as if she had died for a moment, and later her breath came again, shuddering through her body.

She told him then what had been told her, and Fox, for the first time in his life, was afraid of a woman.

"She is close to him. But not close enough. God, but I saw such things . . . flames and roses and three men watching and one holding a black book and faces . . . faces and long hair catching fire!"

Fox sobbed at the words and yet she went on, unheeding.

"There's a bridge and a house called The Chequers and a field called Wickfield. Rebecca is near there. There are soldiers and two men in black with them. There is a bridge and I see blood and blood in the river below the bridge and men screaming and horses . . . Powick Bridge."

"I know Powick Bridge. I know it," said Fox, as she went on.

"I see, I see . . . .murder done there, and Essex not there, and a tall man and a young man and another who's a broken reed . . . and men smashed about the face, and danger, and the girl and fire and . . . fire . . ."

And Maeve began keen again and then to sing a nursery song and then she stopped and slept like the dead.

Fox stared at her and wondered what sort of fate tied them so fast together.

He laid his own cloak over the girl and he was cold, but she slept. He knew the river and he knew the road to Powick Bridge where it narrowed. If ever any soldiers were fool enough to ride down that route without putting outriders up first, they were fools indeed.

Ahead of Lord Essex's men, Rupert's men would lie in wait and if My Lord Essex went by Powick Bridge, he would be leading his men into the prefect killing ground. The troopers of the King's Men under Rupert were as ruthless a killing machine as any Fox had found in the wars in Europe.

Maeve lay quiet now and he moved the curtain of hair that covered her face. He saw the peaceful face of a woman who was as dangerous a web maker as any man he'd known.

Now first there was a matter of hunting down the Witchfinder and plucking his daughter from the killing field for he had no doubt Maeve had "seen" her and that his child was alive and still in danger.

230

37

They woke early and started cross-country away from what they believed would be the line of march of Prince Rupert's troopers. They had to find Rebecca before she came too close to Hopkins and endangered herself.

And they had to warn Lord Essex and the Parliament army of the danger on the road between Alcester and Worcester. Fox was sure Prince Rupert would have detached troops to get to Worcester first.

It was late in the afternoon as they headed down the red sandstone slopes towards the river and the road alongside it. They'd outflanked Prince Rupert but there was evidence of a hurried advance by a troop of cavalry.

The hedges were broken, a mêlée at a small ford showed many hoof prints. Fox studied them for ten minutes or more; Maeve watched impatiently.

"Two hundred . . . more, and in a hurry. See, here and here, a horse has stopped to drink. The marks are deeper where the horse has stood but most have been driven straight on and through the ford without stopping. The Parliament troop's an hour ahead. We'll be on them before dark."

They rode through the first line of pickets before they were forced to a stop by a soldier. They were brought into the light of torches held high.

"Bloody woman here," a man yelled. "Pretty woman an' all," said another, closer to her.

He reached to pull her down from her horse and screamed in agony as his face opened and gushed blood where she had slashed him with the small blade she carried.

"The next will get his throat cut," she said.

"Or be shot," said Fox leaning with the French pistol on the pommel of his saddle. "We have information for your commanding officer which he'll want to hear."

"Who the hell are you to tell us what Colonel Nathaniel Fiennes wants to hear?" A granite-faced man stood before them. He wore chevrons of a sergeant on his arm and Fox nodded at them.

"You want to stay a sergeant . . . Take us to him. I'm John Fox, one time reconnaissance patrol sergeant to Black Tom Fairfax. Now do we get to your colonel or will you be broken to the ranks?"

"The girl stays here."

Fox smiled at that and there was ice in his eyes.

"No! Touch her, so much as by accident and if she doesn't make good her promise, I swear I will. She goes with me."

"Your woman?" asked the sergeant.

"No man's woman," Maeve said and kicked her horse alongside Fox.

"We waste our time . . . Let them rot. Bad luck to all soldiers." Maeve spat.

"Wait," said the sergeant, "Black Tom Fairfax, you said?"

" Yes."

The two men stared at each other in the light of the flares. The sergeant led them to a bivouac and went inside for a moment and came out with an officer.

Fox slid off his horse.

"Well? What d'you have for us that's so important?"

"Who am I talking to?" Fox asked.

"Captain Brown. Advisor to the colonel."

"Well, Captain, what's your advice now? Prince Rupert has got ahead of you and will straddle the road tomorrow. You'll be cut off from Worcester where, I suppose, you're bound. And you'll be cut of from My Lord Essex and his soldiers, who are behind you, no doubt. Prince Rupert may have fewer men but they're better mounted and better soldiers for sure. He'll stop you in your tracks . . ."

Captain Brown stared at the man in disbelief.

"Who the devil are you to dare to question . . . ?"

Fox ignored the blustering officer and went on, "You go on and, from the look of these soldiers, he'll slaughter the lot of you. They've been pressed hard and without proper rest. They will be dog meat. I've seen what his troopers do . . . Believe me, Captain."

"Well Brown . . . what is it?"

A younger and even more impatient man stood in the doorway of the bivouac and stared across at his advisor.

"Some old sergeant, thinks he knows better than his betters how to conduct an attack, Colonel Fiennes."

Brown turned away from Fox and walked to his colonel.

"Press him to the colours. If he's an old soldier he can show what he's worth," he said to the sergeant.

Fox stared at the young man and shrugged. He'd leave when it suited him and he had no fears that Maeve would do the same but he tried one more time.

"You have a weak position to take in Worcester, Colonel. The city has walls like a sieve, and whoever holds it holds a leaking vessel. But put a line of real soldiers across your route and you will be done for. You have no defensive ground between here and Worcester. Captain Brown, I know the city, I know the river and I know the lands beyond it and it's a fool's idea to go helter skelter into the arms of Prince Rupert's men."

He looked about him and went on, "You've got what . . . two hundred tired foot soldiers? And a hundred cavalry on piss-poor mounts. He'll split his men between defending the city and taking your troopers on. It's how he fights. Fast, furious and deadly efficient."

"The sergeant will see to you, soldier. And as for your advice, the Devil with it." Captain Brown turned away again.

Colonel Fiennes walked into the bivouac and clapped his arm around Brown's shoulders. The two men were laughing.

Fox looked round for Maeve.

"She slid away, friend," said the sergeant. "I'll not have a woman in the line of troopers. She did me a favour when she sliced the one as tried his luck. I'll tell thee sommat for nowt . . . yon colonel's a prick and his advisor worse."

Fox walked leading his horse alongside the sergeant to a circle of men around a small fire.

"She'll find a place with the women at the rear no doubt. She your whore or any man's?"

The sergeant crouched by the fire and took a pannikin of soup and handed it to Fox.

"You heard her. She is no man's. And God help the man who tries his luck on her. Your man was lucky," Fox said.

234

He sniffed the soup, drank a little and took in the old army smells that came flooding back after so many years away.

Sweat and dirt and horses, bad stew and leather, fear and shit and the acrid smell of smoke from the fires dotted about the area. Fox took the leather bag and his pistols from the horse and slept on them, wrapped in his cloak.

At four they were mounted up and waited for the order to march.

The Colonel sat his mount with all the arrogance of ignorance.

"We go to take Worcester from the Royalist scum who've dared try to defy the Parliament. It lies an easy three hour march and the defences are as nothing. We'll be there in time to enjoy the fruits of our work. You shall have three hours freedom of the city . . . unless they buy us off."

The men raised a ragged cheer and Fox shuddered at the very idea. For three hours the men would be let loose to bring murder, rape and theft to the good and innocent citizens of Worcester. In lieu of payment no doubt.

And so they marched towards the killing field known as Wickfield.

As they rode past a lonely ale house called The Chequers, Fox edged closer to the grim faced sergeant.

"Sergeant, do we have scouts out or not?"

"None," the sergeant shrugged. "Captain Brown seems to think there's no need."

Fox took off his cloak as they rode on in the cool of the morning. He rolled it and stuffed it into his satchel, eased the long blade across his back and took the short boarding sword he used on horseback in and out of the scabbard a few times.

The sergeant watched him, amused.

"You seem nervous for an old sweat."

"This old sweat is alive. After this ale house we come to a narrow bridge and, after the bridge, to a large field called Wickfield and in that field will be Prince Rupert's men, I will lay money on it," said Fox. "And on the bridge will be a blood-letting such as you have never seen nor will want ever to see again. I know because I've been told, Sergeant. Listen to me, do not ride back across the bridge but go straight through the King's men and ride on hard or you'll die alongside the others."

The sergeant stared at the strange man beside him, shrugged and rode on. The soldiers marched in broad order to the stone bridge. As it narrowed there was room only for two horses abreast. It was the only way over the fast flowing river. The banks on either side were very steep.

The two hundred men rode on round the bend in the lane, past the open gate to the field called Wickfield. It was just as Maeve had said it would be.

As Fox looked to his right he saw them. Royalist troopers sat and lay about the field utterly unprepared. They had no guards posted and the first ranks of Colonel Fiennes' company rode past the gate before anyone realised what they were seeing. By then it was too late.

As the Parliament men were pushed forward by the marching ranks behind them, a man burst from a group of Royalist officers under an oak tree in the middle of the field.

He ran to the horse lines, mounted up and at the same time cried, "Cha-a-a-arge!"

In an act of reckless courage such as Fox had never seen this lone soldier flung himself into the passing files of Parliament men and as he did so the other Royalist troopers mounted up, spurred their horses and crashed into the lines.

It was an act of brutal commitment by some of the hardest soldiers in the field at the time, but Fox had little time to admire it. They came on hacking and hewing and kicking their way into the lane. Even as they did so, they turned left and forced Fiennes and his command back to the narrow stone bridge where men were still marching forward.

Fox looked across at the sergeant whose sword was out.

"How the devil did you know?" the sergeant screamed, and then turned and spurred into the smashing mêlée after the men who had already passed.

Then Fox saw three men in black on horses under the oak tree in the field who were taking no part in the battle. The tall, gaunt man in the centre wheeled his horse away from the fight as Fox rode towards him. Fox was snatched up into the mêlée and prevented from reaching the Witchfinder and his men who were riding away.

Already the troopers were enveloping him. With his heavy navy sword out he hacked to right and left across the front of his horse.

His sword connected with the skull of a soldier who was bearing down on him. He heard the hiss of steel and the scream of a horse as he slashed at the neck and reins of a trooper riding hard alongside him with sword raised.

He rode on blindly against the roar of the battle, slashing and cutting and driving ever closer to the oak tree and, suddenly coming free of the cavalry, found neither sight nor sound of the three men in black.

They'd used the chaos to escape.

Fox turned then and looked back at the battle that was quickly becoming a rout. The Parliament men were pushed back into their own advancing troopers. Rupert's men were cutting and slashing freely as they forced the troopers back to the bridge.

236

The Parliament men were hit by a second wave of Rupert's men. Soon the ground about the bridge was a screaming milling mass of terrified soldiers stampeding to get back and out of the way of the relentless swinging swords of the King's men.

Skulls split, horses screaming, the river began to run red as bodies where hurled out of the way and as wounded men jumped into the water only to be shot down by gunfire from Rupert's troopers.

The Parliament men rode over each other in their panic. Control of horse or foot soldiers was impossible and then, like a cork from a bottle, the rearguard turned and ran.

The impasse on the bridge gave way as the Royalist troopers stormed down the lane after the remnants of the young colonel's pride and joy.

Some were trodden under foot, other were sliced and cut, some begged for mercy and were slashed by cavalry swords. The stampede went on through the small hamlet of Powick, along the Upton road.

There Rupert stopped pursuit and left the enemy to retreat in chaos into the arms of My Lord of Essex as he advanced, too late, along the road.

Prince Rupert had secured his advance to Worcester.

Fox waited in the shadow of some trees beyond the bridge after the troopers moved on towards Worcester. They took few of their dead or dying with them for it was Rupert's way not to be encumbered. Every man took his chance.

Fox knew that Saul, his dead wife's nephew, was with Prince Rupert's men. Maybe he was one of the dead or dying who lay on the bank of the stream by the bridge . . . If he was to look for Saul amongst the bodies, Fox had to move quickly before the women from the baggage trains came looking for coin or jewels on the bodies of the dead and wounded. . .

When the scavengers came they came with skinning knives, the easier to persuade the men to give up what they had. It made little difference to those women for they'd slice the throats of the dying for a copper farthing.

Fox waited until the last of the troopers had trotted away. He could hear the groans and sudden screams of the men left to bleed to death or to die of shock . . .

He dismounted and walked slowly past the bloody bridge and the corpses already blocking the road and the river.

It would be a gruesome business picking through this butchery searching for Saul amongst the offal. And if he found him, what could Saul tell him? Would he know anything about the dead old woman, or about the Witchfinder or who had brought Alison to his attention?

Why had he left the village in such a hurry? What had he been arguing with his father about? If he found the fat young man, Fox would have answers one way or another.

A man screamed high, like a woman. The scavengers were already at their work.

The evening light was fading when Fox found Alison's cousin. Saul lay in a ditch half-filled with water and the scavengers were coming closer. Many of them were old women from the baggage train, a few were youngsters from the nearest villages. Some had lanterns whose glimmers of light dipped and steadied whenever the women found a body to strip.

Fox knew that those to fear were the older women for they'd come on a wounded man and dispatch him to his maker soon as spit after they'd robbed him of all he owned of any value.

Fox found Saul just as one of these women found him. She was short and squat and lacked most of her teeth. Under her shawl her thin grey hair hung lank. She carried a bloodied blade.

She began to call her friends for help when Fox appeared and claimed the body . . . She cursed him, saw the chill in his eyes and moved away into the lengthening shadows. There were dead and dying enough for all in this ditch. This one was his for the moment.

Fox stared down at the terrified young man. He'd been badly wounded in the mêlée on the bridge. His right arm had been slashed open where he'd tried to parry a cavalry sword and the bone was exposed near the elbow. It would be infected without a doubt and he'd lose the arm even if he lived but he'd also taken a pike in his gut. The muscle and fat had opened into a great mouth under the rent in his leather jerkin.

Fax knelt beside him, pulled aside the cloth and saw the extent of the wound. He saw enough to know Saul would die.

It was only when Fox leaned close to him that the dying man recognised who had found him. He tried to back away but could not move.

"Fox," he whispered. "Take me away from here, John. For Alison's sake. Help me."

Fox spoke quietly to him. "You know Rebecca is near. Did you see her?"

Fox watched Saul's eyes dart right and left as he tried to work out if a lie would help him. Then the pain hit him again.

Fox wiped his bloodied hands on the grass. He stared into the dying man's eyes.

"Please, for Alison's sake . . . Take me away, I hurt," Saul gasped as pain hit him in the gut.

238

Fox put his hand on the man's wrist and wrenched his wounded arm. Saul screamed.

"Never ask anything for my wife's sake or it will be worse," Fox promised him. "Now, answer my question."

The young man's face was beaded in sweat as around them scavengers went about their work. Some were calling to friends if they had a difficult mark to kill. Some of them were armed only with mattocks and spades. It was rarely an easy death these women offered.

"Please," he said. "Please don't let them get to me. Please, John."

"Tell me about Rebecca. Tell me what happened. Tell me who set Hopkins on . . . who told him Alison was guilty? Who?"

Saul shook his head once. "Not me. You must ask Hopkins. Ask him. I saw Rebecca once. In Oxford. Hopkins was there. I would have tried to talk to her. I was afraid. I'm sorry."

"Tell me about Hopkins."

"He rides with Prince Rupert from time to time and brings in titbits of information. No-one dares to stand up to him. He hates women."

Somewhere in the dark a man screamed. Closer a woman laughed.

The fat young man tried to reach for Fox's arm.

"Please, cousin, don't leave me to those women. Please."

Fox shoved him aside. Saul began to weep. His tears cut through the filth on his face. He stared up at Fox begging him not to leave him lying in the ditch.

"You cared for Rebecca did you? Protected her did you?"

Saul sobbed. "How could I? How could I? Please believe me . . . She is cunning, vanished if she saw me, always I seemed to see her if Hopkins was near. She was following him."

Fox stared down at him then. "Does he know? Did you tell him?"

Saul wept and nodded through his tears. "I tried to tell him. He laughed in my face."

"You'd've sold her to him, as you did in the village? You abandoned her there. Your own blood."

Saul panted, "It was my father . . . He let her go . . . abandoned her if you like. He promised . . . If you didn't come back, I was to have her to break in. He said that. He told me I could have her. Promised. Then he found her in the house and she sliced his arm with a knife and I knew what he was trying to do. I know him. It's why we argued . . . why I left."

Saul reached up with his good arm.

"Take me with you now. I'll tell you how my father wanted to take Alison's land. How much he hated you. How he planned and planned to be rid of you. I'll tell you everything. Just take me away from here. You were supposed to die on that journey to France. It was then . . . Help me, please."

Fox looked down at the desperate man.

"I'll help you as much as you helped Alison, my wife."

About him he could hear the sighs and screams as men tried to deal with their pain and fear. A sudden scuffle and thrashing of feet and a man died nearby. Fox turned in the dark and heard a scavenging woman. He called out then.

"There's one here with a gold ring hid someplace. Anyone want him?"

"No!" screamed Saul, and half lifted himself from the slippery grass. "Help me . . . Fox . . . Help me."

"Go to hell," said Fox and turned away. A lantern bobbed closer and then stopped and the fat old woman stood in the pale light from her lantern and smiled a black-toothed smile.

"Well, my lover. Got gold have we? Or silver . . . ?"

She moved closer. She bent over him as a mother bends over a hurting child.

"We'll have the gold off you . . . cut it off if I have to. Slice it out . . ."

Then her blade glinted in the yellow light. Fox heard nothing for a moment. Then a high whimpering scream from the fat man and the bubbling frothing sound as the woman cut Saul's throat from ear to ear.

Fox stepped carefully back up to the road and away into the shadows and the night.

38

On the road, Prince Rupert's cavalry officers rode at ease. They were the sons of aristocrats and rode superb mounts. Their silk-faced jackets, feathered hats and gold-hilted swords proclaimed them to be what they were. But the Prince's sergeants and corporals were hard-faced men in worn leather jackets. Some padded, most torn. Men with scars on their hands and faces where they'd come close to death. Some of them had seen service throughout Europe. These were the experts of war.

They set up a new camp off the road to Worcester. Small fires glittered as they cooked what rations they had. The officers sat at their ease near the colours and not far from their horses. They drank and laughed and ate camp rations prepared by the women down the lines.

Sometimes a man would slip away from the firelight to find a woman from the baggage train or merely to relieve himself in the nearby coppice of pollard oaks.

Fox waited in the dark and stared down at the camp amongst the trees. Somewhere in there should be Witchfinder Hopkins. He waited patiently until early morning when he saw what he was looking for as he looked from the cover of the bushes half up the hill overlooking the temporary camp. Fox's horse was tethered half a mile away below the ridge.

Maeve Ahern was in the horse lines talking to a sergeant, they were laughing familiarly together. Fox decided it was time. He took off his cloak and sword and rolled them with his gauntlets and hid them in the bushes with the crossbow that the assassin had left behind in the Dales. He slung Shea's long knife across his back then limped down into the camp as the sun came over the edge of the trees.

He was almost at the horse lines when a corporal stopped him.

"Oi, you! Who the devil are you? Who are you?"

"Soldier," he said. "An old soldier looking for work."

He showed the corporal the long blade and the corporal laughed in his face.

"Old soldier? Look at you. Walking bloody wounded, you."

"It was got at Flers. In a cavalry charge. I was in the lines."

A young officer swaggered over to the two men.

"Corporal, my horse, if you please." He stopped as he saw Fox. "Who the deuce are you?" he asked.

"Says he's a soldier, Sir. Infantry," said the corporal. The officer laughed.

"Go away soldier. You're no use to Prince Rupert unless you ride well."

Fox shrugged. "I never rode, Sir. Always promised myself I'd learn. Never did, infantryman me, Sir."

"Go away," said the bored young officer. "Here," he flung a coin, "Get yourself a plate of soup from the women. Tell them Captain Frith sent you. For old time's sake."

"Thank you, sir," said Fox. He turned from them and limped slowly away. He appeared to be very disappointed as he limped steadily down the horse lines past Maeve. She was still talking to the sergeant of horse. She watched Fox head down to the baggage train and the women. She followed him.

"Hopkins is here, not the girl. Look for a tall man in black with another shorter man also in black. Hopkins has a streak of white in his hair at the front. He never smiles." Maeve muttered as he waited for a pannikin of thin soup given grudgingly by an old whore. "One of his men was drunk last night and boasting of what he did under orders from Hopkins. I heard him and even the soldiers he was with seemed uneasy at what he told them."

"I saw cousin Saul last night," said Fox. "Before he went his way. You watch for Hopkins and be ready to move when he does. I'll be waiting for him."

Maeve stood up suddenly, "And don't you come round here again, you lying, thieving bastard." She screamed at him and beat him about the ears.

Two officers walking by watched as she harried Fox out of the lines. Fox broke away as fast as he could limp up into the coppice. Maeve came back to the lines brushing her hands as she passed the officers.

"Can he have a free one? Bloody old man," she said. And the officers laughed again.

Hopkins rode out of the camp at noon. He had one follower who trailed a mule behind him with their baggage. He took the path through the woods as Fox had thought he might.

The track Hopkins took led him through the wood and along the ridge that led to the scarp overlooking the river. The two men moved in single file. Fox let the little procession pass.

The follower continued to lag behind because of the mule. He became an easy target for the crossbow Fox had taken from the assassin. The bolt was totally silent and took the man in his throat. By the time he hit the ground the man was dead. Like most soldiers, Fox hated torturers and particularly those men who delighted in hurting women.

Fox moved fast through the trees to cut out onto the trail ahead of Hopkins, who rode on unawares.

Hopkins was not pleased when a young woman appeared on the other side of a clearing. "Out of my way, woman," he said, and Maeve moved her horse directly in his path. Behind him a horse could be heard cantering along the track.

"Out of my way, damn you," said the man as the sound of the horse behind him slowed and stopped. The girl smiled then and Hopkins turned to see what was the matter with his companion. Instead he saw Fox sitting astride his horse with a crossbow armed and aimed.

"Who the devil are you?" demanded Hopkins. "I have no money. Nothing worth a spit."

"Just get off your horse . . . do it! Or you'll die as your man died. Off!"

Slowly Hopkins dismounted and stepped away from the horse.

"I have nothing you would want. You could regret this. I have the Royal warrant and you could hang," hissed the thin-faced and angry man.

"We're going to try some changes with you, Witchfinder. You'll come with us," Fox said. "Kneel down . . . kneel down, damn you eyes or she'll kill you before I do."

Hopkins looked back at the smiling Maeve as she held a pistol steady at his head.

"It would be a pleasure. Run, please, run so I can blow you to hell. Or kneel down as you were told."

Hopkins knelt and Fox dismounted, took rope from his saddle and walked to the bewildered man kneeling beside his horse.

"Who are you? There's a mistake. What do you want? Gold? I have gold . . . Anything . . . Who are you?"

As he asked the questions, Fox tied his ankles and his wrists and ran a rope around his neck to the saddle of the Witchfinder's horse.

"Now you can ride or you can be dragged . . . As you wish."

"Where are we going?"

You'll discover that, Hopkins, when you get there."

Fox picked the man up, slung him face down over the saddle of the horse, tied him there, covered him with an old blanket and gave the bridle to Maeve.

"One word . . . one single word and you will die. Believe me, you will die."

They rode then away from the road to Worcester, across country by forest tracks.

It was slow and hard going but by the evening of the third day they passed the village mill hidden behind the trees. They passed the Meeting House and rode through the empty village. People were eating their soup. It was almost dark as they rode under the wooden archway into the yard of Alison's farm.

Fox leaned down to the dogs who smelt their master and whined in pleasure and backed away.

Maeve dismounted and, taking the loaded pistol from her saddle bag, stepped quickly to the door and rapped on it. She called out.

"Master Michael . . . Michael . . . I have news of Saul. There has been a victory at Worcester and Saul did well . . ."

Fox grinned at her lies as he too dismounted and stood in the shadows. The door opened an inch and Maeve shoved it hard and was facing the fat man with her pistol in his face. Alison's uncle was alone.

****

Michael sat in the huge heavily carved oak chair near the table. Facing him sat Witchfinder Hopkins also in an immovable oak chair. Both men were secured in their chairs with strong ropes.

Maeve worked the bellows to make the fire roar. She sat back on her heels and nodded at Fox who took from a drawer a long boning knife, a sack maker's curved needle and from the kitchen he brought a pair of pincers. He gave them all to Maeve and she put the needle into the heart of the fire.

Fox took strong gauntlets and put them on a small table near the two men.

They were both sweating in fear now.

"Please . . . John, this is foolish." Fox looked at the fat man and shook his head.

"It's only what you and he did to my wife, your niece. You showed her the tools, didn't you, Master Hopkins?"

"It was what we had to do. To save her soul."

"She was a gentle woman with a quiet faith and no witch. You know that as well as I and her uncle do. Who brought you to our village? Who guided you, Master Hopkins?"

Hopkins stared at him as intently and said nothing.

"You will tell me. You will tell me. When I show you what I will do to you, you will tell me. You will beg to tell me who brought you here."

"John, no, in the name of . . . of . . . Alison would not want this. She was a peaceful woman." The fat man tried to push himself away and could not for the chair was firmly tied to the huge legs of the wooden table.

"She had the signs," Hopkins spoke suddenly, "There was a sort of growth under her arm . . . a teat for the devil. There was a strawberry mark on her thigh. It was there, as we knew it would be."

"How . . . how did you know it would be? You were told what to look for. You were told. Who told you?"

Hopkins stared across the room at the fat sweating man in the other chair.

"God." he said.

"Then I hope God looks after you when you see what you will face. Needles, broken nails, smashed teeth, torn ears, burned out eyes. In the name of a soul . . . in the name of Jesus . . . I'll show you . . ."

Maeve stood and moved from the fire.

"John . . . John, let's do what has to be done and leave here. No more cat and mouse with them. Be done with it, John. I've no pity for them. But concern for you. Torture them more and you become as they are."

Fox shook his head, "In a moment, Maeve, in a moment."

He turned to Alison's uncle.

"I have a message from your son. He told me you lusted after my daughter. A child. Innocent."

"He lied . . . he lies in his teeth. It was him."

"You both tell the same lies then. She cut you, didn't she?"

And suddenly Fox slit Michael's sleeve from wrist to shoulder and saw the livid scar. "Lying was he?" whispered Fox.

"Lies . . . You never saw my son. He went for a soldier. You lie, damn you." Michael sobbed in fear.

"I saw your son over Powick way with Prince Rupert's men. You can find what's left of him in a ditch. Mind, after the scavenging women and the animals have been at them, there's something merciful about death."

"You spoke to him . . . and left him to that . . . dear God." The fat man sobbed, "I love my son. I love him."

"Don't call on God now. Between you, you sold my wife to that offal there."

Fox walked to the fire, pulled on a gauntlet and took up the curved sack-maker's needle in the pincers. The needle was glowing white with heat. Fox walked to the Witchfinder.

"Tongue," said Fox, quietly.

The Witchfinder shook his head.

"Which eye will it be then?" he asked. Slowly the Witchfinder pushed his tongue between his lips. Then he spoke contemptuously.

"You won't do it. You need to have a soul to save to do this work."

And the Witchfinder laughed in Fox's face.

Fox hesitated and then flung the red hot needle and the pincers across the room. The Witchfinder went on mocking.

"I pressed your wife. I broke her ribs, I showed your daughter what I did and told her mother the girl would be put to the question, and Alison confessed all I wanted her to confess. Kill me now? I knew the signs to search for because her uncle knew and he told me. He paid me gold. Kill me now?"

Fox turned from the cruel face smiling at him to her uncle.

"He's lying . . . He lies . . . Saul told him. Not me. Not me."

Fox leaned closer to the sweating, stinking man and saw the dribble of water under the chair where Alison's uncle had pissed himself.

"Not just Alison but that mad old woman. You poisoned her to close her mouth. Didn't you? The one person who knew the truth . . . Who knew it was you betrayed Alison to Hopkins. Shall we press you . . . ? Burn you with needles?"

Michael slobbered in fear then and cried and implored and sobbed until he was exhausted.

"Mercy, forgiveness, sorrow, did you listen to Alison? Did you offer anything but pain and fear . . . and even then you tried to violate my daughter."

Fox took up the metal, throbbing with heat from the fire, and moved back to Alison's uncle.

"John. Let's be done here," Maeve touched his arm. "They're not worth spit."

246

"You can't do this . . . You can't. There's a home here for you and for Rebecca . . . There is . . . there is . . . Please don't . . . Please . . ."

Michael pulled and strained at the ropes as he begged. The Witchfinder was quite still. He knew there was nothing more to be said. Fox looked across at Maeve. She stared for a moment out of the window and saw the pale pink of dawn showing. She looked back at him and nodded.

"Come," she said.

She walked out of the room. The two men strained again against the ropes. Fox joined Maeve in the yard. She held his horse for him. He mounted up and together they rode away under the wooden arch.

In the withy basket in the corner of the room that held furze and cones for fire-lighting, where Fox had flung the red hot needle, spirals of smoke curled up into the room. The furze had begun to smoulder. A spark, and then another, and then a blaze began in the basket.

In a moment the corner of the room was well ablaze. The wooden floorboards full of beeswax polish and dry as tinder took fire fast and choking smoke began to fill the room.

The men wrenched, screaming now, at their ropes. It was already too late.

The floor on the other side of the table was alive with flame and whorls of smoke. It required only a draft of air to fan the flames . . .

For a minute, two, three, nothing showed in the yard and then the heat of the fire shattered the glass in a window and tongues of fire roared into the morning.

****

The two riders went over the top way, the old way towards the high clean air of the Long Mynd. Maeve insisted that they ride past the field where Alison had burned.

They came to the place where they had buried Mother Baugh. On the mound of rocks was a posy of flowers. Sleeping in the back of the ruined hovel they found the girl. As she slept, Fox knelt beside her. He reached out to touch her but Maeve stopped him. Rebecca woke and when she did she could not speak. She curled herself away from her father and stared, wild-eyed at him. Maeve held out her arms and took the frightened girl and held her gently.

"It will take time, John Fox. How can she trust any man? Even her father? It will take time. It will hurt you, John, but she will heal."

She rocked the girl in her arms. Maeve tried to make her understand that there was no need to look for vengeance any more. That it was done. Rebecca said nothing.

"You'll leave her with me. I'll do what I can."

Fox shook his head. "We'll go together," he said. "You can do what you can, Maeve. We'll take her to Elizabeth in the Dales where she can be looked after."

He mounted his horse. Maeve mounted, leaned down and held out her hand. Rebecca looked from one to the other and then walked to Fox and took his hand and mounted behind him. She leaned and nuzzled against him and sniffed his scent as she used to when she was a child.

Fox looked across at Maeve who smiled, turned and rode away.

The wind began to blow and a grey drizzle oozed over the rocks as they rode high against the steel grey sky, across the heather and along the wild ridge of the Long Mynd.

Maeve rode ahead of the others and thought of the grief of that young woman when she began to understand what had happened to her. Maeve felt sad for her.

Fox felt the warmth of Rebecca against his back as his horse picked its way over the rocky track. She needed care and love and he knew he could not provide it, nor could the wild Irish girl.

Rebecca would find that with Elizabeth.

He looked down across the land across the purple haze of the distance where men and women were already taking up arms, where a king would go into battle against his own people.

They rode on. There would be time enough, after they had taken Rebecca to Elizabeth in the house in the Dales, for Fox and Maeve to go back to London and the overheated room over the watchmaker's shop where Thurloe spun his web. He'd have work for them. In the village, the black ruins of the farmhouse still smouldered and smoked. In the field where the stake had stood, where the grass grew greenest, another posy, a crown of flowers . . . pink dog roses and old man's beard twined together.